A FAERIE'S
REVENGE

Also by Rachel Morgan

A FAERIE'S REVENGE

CREEPY HOLLOW, BOOK FIVE

RACHEL MORGAN

ISBN 978-0-9946679-9-1

RACHEL
MORGAN

PART I

CHAPTER ONE

THE SHIP ROLLS FROM SIDE TO SIDE AS IT RISES AND FALLS on the swell of heaving waves. Purple-black clouds darken the sky, spitting out beads of icy rain that sting my bare arms. Lightning zigzags across the horizon. It's the perfect storm. The perfect distraction.

From *him*.

Across the slippery deck, my opponent raises her wooden staff. "Ready for another ass-kicking?" Saskia shouts, her voice barely reaching me before it's snatched away by the wind. My only response is a grim smile. I'd like to tell her it's *her* backside that will be meeting this deck, but I'd probably be lying. I'm not particularly skilled with the staff, and she knows it. She punches the air with her fist and lets out a war cry. She takes her staff in both hands and, with enviable ease, begins spinning it in front of her—hand over hand over hand—until it becomes a blur.

Then she lunges forward and strikes. I raise my staff to block the blow, and a crack rends the air as our two weapons meet. Ignoring the sting in my hands, I twist on one leg and kick with the other. Saskia pivots out of the way and swoops her staff around. She jabs at me with the end of it, but I jump back. As I swing the wooden weapon from side to side, she slides one leg forward and slams hers down onto the deck, narrowly missing my foot. I dance out of the way and use the staff to help vault me up onto the ship's railing. I wobble and almost tumble into the water, but I regain my balance quickly.

For a moment I see everything—the ship and the waves and the storm tossing the entire scene about—and I remember the glass bottle on Chase's desk. The glass bottle with the tiny ship sailing on an enchanted stormy sea. What was I thinking? A perfect storm isn't a distraction. Draven was the *master* of storms. How can I think of *anything* but him?

Saskia's staff slams against the back of my legs, knocking me completely off balance. I fall forward onto the deck. The scene vanishes, and when I roll over, I find myself staring up at the wispy white surface of the Fish Bowl.

Footsteps sound nearby before Saskia's face appears above mine. She gives me a smug smile and mutters, "Loser," before striding away.

I let my eyelids slide shut as I catch my breath—

And I see Chase. Stepping away from me. Fading into the snow. *I've never lied to you, I swear. This is who I am.* My hands squeeze into fists at my sides because, once again, it hasn't worked. Once again, focusing all my attention on a training exercise has done nothing to distract me from the memory of him. Every time I close my eyes, I see the same thing: that moment in the forest with flurries of snowflakes swirling around me, wind tearing at my hair, and Chase vanishing into the whiteness. Then a frozen calm settles over everything and Vi says his name, and the weight of that one whispered word is heavier than a stone slab lowered onto my shoulders.

A chill races down my arms, both in my memory and here in the training center where I'm lying sweaty and breathless on the Fish Bowl floor, watching the forest scene play out across my closed eyelids yet again:

"Draven?" I repeat. "What are you talking about?"

"It was him." Vi's face is almost as pale as her dress.

Ryn steps into my line of vision then. "What's wrong?" he asks immediately. He knows something is amiss without us having to tell him. He could probably feel our tumult of emotions from the other side of the clearing.

Vi turns to face him. "Draven. Nate. He was here."

"What?" Ryn clasps Vi's hand.

"I swear it was him."

"That was *not* Draven," I blurt out. What a ridiculous notion. How could the tattoo artist by day, vigilante by night that I've slowly been falling for be the evil overlord who brought about The Destruction?

"He didn't look exactly the same," Vi says to Ryn, "but it was him. I have no doubt."

"The necklace," Ryn says without pause.

Vi nods. "We always wondered."

"Wondered *what*?" I demand. "What necklace?"

Vi presses her hands against her forehead and groans. "I knew it. I knew it, I knew it. Why else would his body vanish? Surely it should have remained there if he'd truly died."

"We couldn't say anything without knowing for sure," Ryn says. "You know that. And the winter ended, and you couldn't sense anything when you tried to find him. The logical conclusion was that he was well and truly gone."

Vi drops her hands and finally looks at me. "Eternity necklace," she says. "That's what we're talking about. It was made for the Unseelie Queen centuries ago. It was supposed to keep her from ever dying. Draven was wearing it right at the end when I … when I *thought* I killed him."

I blink. I open my mouth, but no sound comes out.

"Well, I didn't know for *certain* that he was wearing it," Vi adds, "but he had some sort of chain around his neck, and I always suspected it was the eternity necklace. It seems I was right."

I try to reconcile the image of Chase—the Chase who helps people in secret; the Chase who lives in an unassuming Underground home that looks like his grandmother decorated it; the Chase who saved my life—with the image I've always pictured of the powerful and destructive halfling prince who wiped out so many fae. My mind won't accept it. I slowly shake my head. "It isn't possible. He's just a guy! There's no way he's *Lord Draven*."

"Then why isn't he here to tell you that himself?"

"Because ... because ... "

"What was he doing here with you in the first place?" Ryn asks with a frown.

But I don't answer him because my mind is far away now, remembering things I don't want to remember. Scraps of information that fit together like pieces of a puzzle I don't want to see. *No amount of remorse can change the past.* The past. His past. His secrets. *Whatever it is,* he said, *it can't be as terrible as the things I've done.* What things has he done? Who is he? *You wouldn't like me nearly as much if you knew.*

I almost hear the click in my brain the moment I accept the truth. The whoosh of air as it's sucked from my world. The groan of my heart as it's crushed beneath the weight of betrayal.

"Calla?" Ryn reaches out and touches my shoulder. I shrug away from him, turn around, and run.

I've been running ever since.

"Calla?"

My eyelids spring apart and I find Gemma looking down at me. "Yes?" I croak.

"You're okay." She smiles in relief. "I thought Saskia might have knocked you out properly." Gemma is one of the few people at the Guild who likes me enough to come over and find out whether I'm unconscious or not. Almost everyone else, including my oh-so-friendly mentor, would probably use this failure as another opportunity to point out that I don't belong here.

"Don't worry," I say, pushing myself to my feet. "Saskia isn't that good."

Gemma chuckles as we head for the edge of the Fish Bowl and push through the swirling misty layer. "Don't let her hear you say that."

We walk toward the collection of training bags floating against the wall. I glance at her with a half-smile. "How about if I shout it instead so that *everyone* can hear?"

Gemma rolls her eyes. "Do you really want to poke the dragon like that?"

"Which dragon are we poking?" Perry asks, swinging a sweaty arm around Gemma's shoulders as he joins us.

"Saskia," I tell him.

"Perfect. I'll get a stick."

"Don't you dare," Gemma says, smacking at his hand until he removes his arm from her shoulders. "Why don't we go to my place and do that history assignment instead?"

"Gemma." Perry shakes his head with great seriousness as he looks down at her. "That is one of the worst suggestions you've ever made."

"I can't, I'm sorry," I say before she can ask me. "Olive has another assignment for me. She told me to report to her directly after the last session."

"Now? But you just finished training. You need a break."

"It's fine. I don't mind."

Gemma narrows her eyes. "You don't mind, or you don't have a choice?"

I consider her words. "Both."

She shakes her head. "You know Olive is going to keep

piling more and more on top of you until you either refuse or crack beneath the weight."

"Yes, I'm aware of that. I don't plan for either of those things to happen, though." And the added work is a welcome distraction from the thoughts that are never far from my mind.

Thoughts of Chase.

Stop it.

"Anyway, I'll see you tomorrow." I pull my training bag out of the air and swing it over my shoulder.

"Okay. And don't forget about the history assignment," Gemma calls after me. "I know you haven't started it yet."

"Yeah, yeah," I call back to her. I haven't opened a single history textbook in the past ten days. They all make reference to Draven at some point or other, and he's the last person I want to read about right now.

I stride along the corridor toward the main foyer. I'm almost there when a figure steps out of a nearby lesson room and stops in front of me. My stomach plummets at the sight of Violet. She and Ryn have been gone since the day of the wedding—the day I discovered the truth about Chase—which has made it easy to avoid talking to either of them. I thought they were away until tomorrow. I thought I had at least another twelve hours before they ambushed me. "Uh, how was the honeymoon?" I ask.

"Hmm, let's see." Vi places her hands on her hips. "We had a wonderfully relaxing time and didn't once think about you or Draven."

I raise an eyebrow. "Judging from the number of mirror

calls I missed from you and Ryn in the past ten days, I'm going to take a wild guess and say that was complete sarcasm."

"Missed? It felt a whole lot more like you were intentionally ignoring us."

"I was," I admit, "which you should be thanking me for. It was your honeymoon. You were supposed to forget about the real world."

"And forget that the guy who almost *destroyed* the real world is actually alive instead of dead?" Her expression is incredulous. "Were *you* able to forget about that in the past ten days?"

I let out a loud bark of a laugh and fix a grim stare on the floor as my mind skims over the days since the wedding.

Day one: I slept in as long as possible, ran laps around Carnelian Valley until my legs could barely hold me, refused to let myself cry, contemplated burning Chase's coat, and ended up stuffing it into the back of my closet instead.

Day two: I relished the distraction of lessons, poured every ounce of energy into training, splashed my feelings onto an angry painting—which I *did* end up burning—and successfully saved a businessman from being eaten by an ogre on his way home from a late night meeting.

Day three: I woke up early and found myself missing Chase more than anything. I got up, got dressed, and took two steps along an Underground tunnel before coming to my senses and realizing what a foolish idiot I was. I visited Mom instead, still trapped in her enchanted sleep in the Guild's healing wing.

Day four: Olive discovered I'd never fought with a staff before. My entire afternoon was spent practicing the basics, and I welcomed the distracting pain of every blister.

Day five: I cried. Then I pushed down the hurt and confusion and focused on the anger instead. My evening assignment went well.

Day six: More staff practice. More blisters. More training, training, training.

Day seven: *Don't think of him. Keep training.*

Days eight to ten: *Keep training, keep training, keep training.*

I fold my arms over my chest and look at Vi. "Yes, of course, I was able to *completely* forget about him."

She purses her lips before saying, "I don't need a wild guess to know that was also sarcasm."

"Well done."

"This is serious, Calla. Ryn and I need to know everything you know before we go to the Council with this."

Go to the Council ... The thought makes me sick. Everything about this situation makes me sick. "Well, you're going to have to wait a bit longer." I step past her. "I have an assignment right now."

"This is more important than any assignment," Vi says, catching my arm.

"Have you met my mentor? *Nothing* is more important than her schedule." I pull my arm out of Vi's grasp and keep walking.

"Calla!" she shouts after me, seemingly shocked that I'm walking away from her.

"Calm down," I say, turning and continuing to walk backwards as I speak. "Nothing happened in the past week, did it? Nothing happened in the past ten *years*, so what's another day?" I spin around and head across the marble floor of the main foyer. I reach the grand stairway on the other side and take a step before hearing a commotion somewhere behind me. Glancing over my shoulder, I see two guardians struggling to restrain a man near the entrance to the Guild.

A man I recognize.

A guardian who allowed everyone to believe he died in The Destruction.

The first person who taught me how to fight.

In shock, I grab the banister. "Zed," I murmur. "What are you doing here?"

CHAPTER TWO

I GLANCE AWAY QUICKLY, MY HAND TIGHTENING AROUND the banister. No one can know that Zed and I are connected in any way. It would make things worse for him, and it wouldn't exactly help me either. He'll be in enough trouble for never having given up his guardian weapons without adding the fact that he's secretly been training someone for the past several years.

From the corner of my eye, I watch as the two guardians drag him across the foyer and into a corridor I've entered only twice. There's a well-guarded gate not far along that corridor, and then a glass elevator that drops down, down, down. Then another gate, and then rows of cells separated by thick bars.

How did he get caught? How, after years of staying far from the Guild, did he wind up in the clutches of two guardians?

And what will his punishment be?

Knowing there's nothing I can do for him right now, and fully aware that I'm late to meet my mentor, I hurry up the stairs toward her office. I expect to find her ready to spit fire at me, but instead she raises her gaze from the unfurled scroll in her hands and fixes me with an expressionless stare. "What are you here for?"

"Uh, the assignment you said you had for me?"

"Oh." She returns her attention to the scroll, her thumb running along the broken edge of the red wax seal. "I gave that to Ling."

I stand in the doorway, wondering whether I should dare ask why she gave my assignment to the other fifth-year trainee she mentors. "Um—"

"She's been asking for extra assignments. She was here on time. You weren't." Olive's eyes scan the reed paper, never glancing up at me.

I fiddle with the strap on my bag and try to figure out whether I've been dismissed or not. "So ..."

"No, you don't have the night off." Olive rolls up the scroll and throws it into a drawer, which she slams shut before standing. She combs her fingers through her short hair as she watches me, probably deciding what training exercise I'm least likely to enjoy. She lowers her hands to her sides. "You'll run laps around the old Guild ruins for the next two hours, and you'll wear your tracker band so I know you're not skipping a single second of it."

Terrific. So instead of sitting at home trying not to think of what Chase is doing, I'll be running in circles trying not to think of what Chase is doing. Wondering whether he's been cooking up evil plans since his fall. Pondering what reason he might have had for helping me. Trying to figure out how someone so terrible could seem so ... caring.

STOP. IT.

"Not impressed, I see," Olive says. She sifts through the untidiness of her desk until she finds the box that contains her trainees' tracker bands. "Does the idea of improving your fitness seem like a waste of time to you?"

I carefully arrange my features into what I hope is a pleasant expression. "Of course not. None of this is a waste of time. I appreciate all the extra training you give me."

"I see. Well, since you're so appreciative of the extra training, let's add in some more. You'll do thirty minutes of running and spend the remainder of the time on the obstacle course. The one set up on the ruins. I want it completed perfectly five times in a row before you're allowed to leave."

I nod, relieved that I won't have to spend two hours doing something so mindless. "Thank you." My smile is closer to being genuine this time, which only seems to annoy Olive further.

"You'd better—" A crease forms between her eyebrows as she focuses on something behind me. An annoyed puff of breath escapes her lips. "That time of year again," she mutters.

I look over my shoulder and see two first-year trainees practicing their levitating skills on a large sign that reads *Liberation Day*. The sick feeling I've been trying to escape rises up once more. In trying so hard to forget about Chase, it seems I've forgotten Liberation Day is coming up this week. Now I won't be able to forget either of them.

I turn back to Olive. "Don't you enjoy celebrating our freedom?" I ask quietly.

She tosses my tracker band to me. "I celebrate my freedom every day by simply *being free*. I think it's entirely unnecessary for the Guild to go to such great expense every year to commemorate the day Draven's reign ended."

I've heard about the magnificent balls hosted by the Guilds every year on Liberation Day. I used to dream of attending, but Mom would never have let me, even if I'd been fortunate enough to receive an invitation from a Guild member. This is the first year I'm allowed to attend. This is also the first year I'd rather be anywhere else.

"Am I dismissed now?" I ask as I secure the leather tracker band around my wrist.

"Yes. And don't be late tomorrow night. We've scheduled an assignment race for the fifth years. You'll all begin at the same time and extra points are awarded based on the order in which you complete the assignment and return to the Guild. Now go. You've already wasted enough time this afternoon."

* * *

I enjoy the outdoor obstacle course: vines and broken stone walls and stumps of wood placed strategically by mentors over the years. A still pool of water—formed by rain gathering in the crater left behind from the explosion that destroyed the old Guild—marks the end of the course.

I've just swung across the pool for the second time when I

hear the sound. I drop onto my feet, release the rope-like vine, and squint into the dim blueish light. It was the snap of a branch, as if someone—or something—was moving through the trees nearby.

Of course my first thought is of Chase. It always is these days. Is he hiding amongst the trees, watching me? Has he been waiting for me to show up so he can speak to me? After all, he knows I train on the ruins sometimes.

Then it strikes me, with sickening abruptness, that he was the one who *created* these ruins. He is the *sole reason* this Guild no longer exists. I bend over and breathe deeply, willing the nausea away. How is it that I stood beside, that I spoke to and laughed with—that I *touched*—someone of such evil intent and never realized it? Is he so good at hiding that part of himself?

I straighten and peer between the trees once more. They sway ever so slightly in the chilly breeze, their tangled branches reaching for one another like spindly fingered arms. But I see no other movement. Then, with a sudden rush of wings and a squawk, a large bird detaches itself from the dark outline of the trees and swoops overhead. With each flap of its wings, bright spots of luminous color light up its feathers. I breathe out sharply in relief, one hand against my chest as adrenaline subsides and the pulsing light of the bird disappears into the forest on the other side of the clearing.

When I've completed my five perfect rounds on the obstacle course, it's almost too dark to see clearly. Of course, it's never *completely* dark in Creepy Hollow, not with the glow-bugs and various other night creatures that produce some form of illumination. Or the giant mushrooms that soak up the moon's rays, or the plants that light up if you stand on them. I head back to the Guild, thinking of Zed. We may have exchanged a few heated words lately, but I still care what happens to him. He's done so much for me over the past few years, and now he's locked up in a cell. I doubt there's any way I can help him, but I should at least try to find out what's going on.

As I cross the Guild foyer, I glance at the corridor he disappeared into earlier. Last week, after returning from an assignment with a pyromaniacal, graffiti-loving elf in tow, I stood uncertainly at the base of the main stairway while Olive pointed to that corridor as if she expected me to know what was down there. "Well?" she said. "What are you waiting for?"

The guards didn't stop me when I walked into that corridor. They opened the gate without question. Another guard at the bottom of the elevator shaft took note of my assignment details, then gestured to the gate of solid bars behind him. Not boring vertical bars like those filling Velazar Prison, but bars twisting elegantly into curling spirals, joined by shapes that looked like roses and leaves. As I stared at the closed gate, wondering how I was supposed to get through it, the guard asked, "First time down here?"

I nodded, then frowned at the elf as he rolled his eyes and muttered, "Amateur."

"What year are you in?" the guard asked.

"Fifth."

"Cool. Hold your pendant up to the gate. That'll open it. All guardians and fifth-year trainees have access down here."

So I held my pendant close to the gate, and the metal pieces curled away and disappeared into the walls on either side. It was easy. And four days later, when I went back to deliver the papers detailing the elf's release and community service requirements, no one questioned my right to be there.

Will they question me now?

Without hesitation, I veer toward the corridor as if that's where I intended to go all along. I doubt anyone's watching me, but for those who might be, I'd like to appear confident rather than undecided. Casually, I pull my trainee pendant from beneath my T-shirt and leave it resting against my chest where it's visible. My footsteps sound louder than normal against the marble floor as I leave the expansive foyer behind me and head along the corridor. I tell myself it's only my imagination. *You have every right to be here, remember?* "Evening," I say to the first two guards, stopping in front of them and waiting expectantly.

They nod and open the gate without a word. I walk through, managing to keep my expression neutral instead of smiling jubilantly. The corridor ends with an elevator of glass. Glass walls, glass ceiling, even a glass floor. The view beyond is enchanted to look like soil, as if the elevator shaft has been dug into the earth. As the glass box drops smoothly down, I see glow-bugs and worms and tiny tunnels with minuscule creatures crawling along them. It's rather eerie, and I wonder who decided on this particular enchantment.

At the embellished gate outside the bottom of the elevator, I greet the guard with a smile. "Hey, I'm here to get some extra information from one of my recent assignments."

"Sure, can I see your trainee pendant?" he asks. I hold it up. He reads my name off the back, then checks his amber tablet.

"I don't see any—oh, yes. You've still got someone in here." He steps to the side and nods to the gate.

Trying not to look too relieved, I hold my pendant up a second time and watch the gate uncurl itself and disappear into the wall. I had no idea whether that elf had been processed yet or not. I would have had to act ditzy and apologetic if it turned out he wasn't here anymore.

I walk along the main passageway, glancing into every cell I pass to see if Zed is in one of them. It's a far more pleasant place than Velazar Prison, with cells that are larger and brighter. But then, this isn't technically a prison. Olive called it a detainment area. Fae are *detained* in these cells before their hearing takes place.

A man throws himself at his bars and sticks his arm through, attempting to clutch the sleeve of my jacket as I pass. I shrug away from him and continue quickly. Fortunately no magic can pass beyond these bars.

I throw a quick look over my shoulder as I approach the first side corridor. The guard isn't watching me, so I turn into it to have a look. Four cells along on the right, I see a pacing man with turquoise-streaked blond hair. Zed. I hurry toward him and come to a stop outside his bars as he turns.

"Calla." His eyes widen in alarm, his gaze darting over my shoulder before returning to rest on me. "What … what are you doing here?"

"What am *I* doing here? What are *you* doing here? How did you get yourself caught?"

"I was …" He crosses the cell and grips the bars, looking past me once more. "Careless. I was careless. Just a stupid mistake. But you …" He frowns and shakes his head slightly. "I forgot you were here. At this Guild."

I blink. "You *forgot*?" Joining a Guild is the only thing I've ever wanted, and Zed knows that. It seems impossible he could have forgotten.

"I know, I know, I remember now. It's just … a lot's been happening … and you … well, you haven't exactly been on my mind. I started a new job, and all my focus has been on that. Everything else has faded into the background."

There was a time when it would have hurt to hear that I don't feature in Zed's thoughts, but I'm long past those days. "What job? What's going on with you? What stupid mistake caused you to wind up here?"

"I …" Zed scratches his head, looking rather sheepish. "I was at one of the Underground bars that never closes. I had a bit too much to drink, ended up offending a pair of reptiscillas, and got into a brawl. I was the only one who didn't get away in time when the guardians showed up."

I shake my head, wrapping my hands around the bars as I step closer. "What were you doing in Creepy Hollow? You used to stay far away from any area that has a Guild."

"I have some friends here," he says, looking away. "But it doesn't matter how I wound up getting caught. The fact is that I'm here and they've seen my markings now. They'll look me up, and they'll soon find out that I'm supposed to be dead. They might even find out that I'm Griffin Gifted. And you know what else, Cal?" He places his hands around mine. "They're going to find out about you too. You know that. You won't be able to hide what you can do forever."

A familiar pang clutches my insides as I'm reminded—suddenly, painfully—of the loss of my Griffin Ability. I often reach for it still, automatically, only to find that it's gone. "They're not going to find out," I say quietly.

"They will," Zed insists. "Eventually you'll slip up, and then everyone in the Guild will know you have a Griffin Ability."

I shake my head, readying myself to explain to him that that part of me is gone, but the sound of slow footsteps freezes my tongue. I whip my head around, but I don't see anyone yet.

Zed's grip on my hands tightens. "You have to get out of here," he whispers fiercely.

"I know. I'm—"

"No, I mean permanently. Leave the Guild. You don't want to become like these guardians, arrogant and superior, tangled up in laws and protocols, unable to help those that really need to be helped."

The footsteps move closer, and I can't believe what Zed is asking me. "Zed, this is everything I've ever wanted. I'm not giving it up simply because you have a grudge against a Guild Council that doesn't exist anymore."

"It's not just that Council, it's *every* Council. There will always be—"

"No." I pull my hands free of his clutch and step back. "If there's anything I can do to help you, Zed, I will. But I'm not leaving the Guild." And with that, I walk away. My footsteps carry me to the end of the row of cells and into the main passageway. I nod to the guard as I pass him. He doesn't stop me.

CHAPTER THREE

MY SIX-YEAR-OLD SELF IS LOCKED INSIDE A LAVISHLY decorated bedroom with a towering brute of a man, and I've just convinced him to stab himself in the thigh. He cries out and staggers a few steps before dropping to the ground, blood beginning to pool around him. My hands shake and tears drench my cheeks and I *can't believe* I've done something so terrible. But he's a terrible man, I remind myself, and he was going to hurt me if I didn't hurt him first.

Other men run into the room, some rushing to their fallen comrade, while another grabs me around the waist and lifts me over his shoulder. "Get her down to the dungeon!" someone else shouts. "And don't believe anything she shows you."

The dungeon is fear and sweat and mustiness and names, names, names scribbled across a circular wall that spins around and around me. I hear a clang of metal, and then I'm shut in a cage, hanging above black water that ripples unnaturally. The cage is small, so small, and I shrink into the center of it as the bars press closer.

And all the while at the edge of my vision, in the murky darkness of the dream landscape, someone lingers.

Chase.

Draven.

He hides in the shadows, watching everything, doing nothing. Nothing to save me or anyone else. He hides until the moment he beheads the man we all thought was the real enemy. And then smoke and flame consume the dream world.

* * *

I wake with a start, my body tensing for a moment before I remember where I am. Safe. At home. I relax against my pillows, turning my head to the side so I can see the round clock above my desk. Superimposed above the mishmash of painted numbers, glowing gold digits tell me it's just gone five in the morning. As my heartbeat slowly returns to normal, I try to think of other things. The assignment race tonight; Mom lying in the healing wing at the Guild; my three newest friends who don't seem to mind the rumors that follow me around; Dad and the bribes he made to keep my Griffin Ability secret; Gaius imprisoned somewhere, forced to take Griffin Abilities from others; Chase, who saved my life and found my mother, even though he's supposed to be the villain.

It does no good. It never does any good. I've tried to push

Chase from my mind, but thoughts of him always sneak back in, like smoke slipping through the tiniest gaps. I may as well stop trying to forget him and start attempting to figure him out instead.

I roll onto my side and snap my fingers at the lamp beside my bed. Light ignites a moment later. I blink several times, then lean over the side of my bed and reach for the history textbooks I threw under there last week. My hand brushes over a thick spine. I heave the book onto the bed. I sit up, cross my legs, and open the book to a random page. It's a relatively new textbook, which means it covers everything right up until the present, including, of course, Draven's reign.

I check the contents page, then flip through to his chapter. I've studied these pages before, of course—several of my Guild entrance exams required knowledge of this section—but it didn't mean much more to me than words on a page. Facts to be memorized. Names, dates, events, people who no longer exist. But it's real now. *He's* real.

I start at the beginning, hoping to find something about his childhood, something I must have missed before. But the reason I don't remember reading that part of Draven's story is because that part doesn't exist. Nobody knows anything about his childhood. He first showed up as an apprentice to the Unseelie Prince Zell. He was called Nathaniel then, according to those who were interviewed after Draven's fall.

Nathaniel.

Another name that may or may not belong to him.

I pull the book closer and run my finger beneath the words as I continue following the story. It seems that Zell's followers

25

thought Nathaniel was helping him. He did everything Zell told him to, including finding the Griffin discs and the chest that contained all the power the halfling Tharros Mizreth once had. Nobody knew that Nathaniel had his own plans. Nobody expected him to kill Zell, open the chest, and take all that power for himself. But that's exactly what he did. And it was on that night, the night the Guilds fell, that everyone discovered who Draven really was: A powerful halfling. A Seelie Prince. The son of Princess Angelica, the Seelie Queen's youngest daughter.

The book goes on to detail Draven's mark and the way he brainwashed everyone into following him. It tells of all the areas he conquered and how those who managed to escape him gathered in hiding to form a resistance. The resistance had a weapon, a sword protected for centuries by a group known as the Order of the Guard. It was that sword that finally put an end to Draven and the power he was wielding. The textbook includes the prophecy that was written onto the sword, but as for who the 'finder' and the 'Star of the high land' actually were, the author has only this to say:

When the blinding light and tornado-like winds subsided, Draven, the sword, and the one who delivered the final blow were gone. Witnesses believe that the power released at the moment of Draven's death consumed all three.

I'm one of the few who knows the truth, though. I know that Vi was the finder and that Tilly was the one who, along with Vi's help, delivered that final blow. Together they ended

Draven, but they didn't stick around afterwards to answer questions. Vi had a secret to keep, and Tilly had a normal life to get back to. They left quickly, and Vi's dad, a spy for the Seelie Queen, stayed behind to tell the tale—minus any names—of what happened at the very end.

All brainwashed fae were free of Draven's influence. The winter lifted. The Guilds were rebuilt. Our world put itself back together. The end.

Except that wasn't the end. Because he isn't dead after all. An enchanted necklace saved him, and now I have no idea who he really is.

* * *

I don't stop this time. I don't tell myself I'm a foolish idiot, and I don't consider what I'm going to say when I get there. One foot in front of the other along the stone-paved tunnel of Sivvyn Quarter, each step pushing my anger up another notch. I reach the door behind which I thought I had found someone I could trust. Hurt pierces my chest, but I smother it with anger. Then I raise my fist and bang on the door.

No response.

I wait several moments before pounding my fist against the door again. Then I bend down and bring one eye to the keyhole, just as I did the first time I stopped outside this door. But instead of seeing an old couch and a striped cushion through the gap, I see nothing but darkness. Standing, I take hold of the handle and push down. The door opens easily, confirming what I knew in my heart all along: he's gone.

I push the door open fully and step into the empty room, light from the glowing tiles outside illuminating the bare corners of what used to be Chase's home. Nothing remains aside from the lingering smell of paint. Deep down I know that this is the only thing I could have expected to find here. Of course he's gone. Of course he ran the moment someone found out who he really is. But I still feel an aching disappointment as I stand in the middle of this empty space.

Disappointment that I soon manage to replace with anger. Anger at Chase for having made a fool of me, and anger at myself for letting him. I spin around, walk out of the house, and yank the door shut behind me. Then I lift my stylus to the tunnel wall and write a doorway spell onto it. There's somewhere else I need to go, even though I already know what I'll find there.

I walk out of the faerie paths into another Underground tunnel, this one not too far from a place called Wickedly Inked. My suspicions are confirmed as I round a corner and see that the sign for Chase's tattoo studio is gone. I reach the open doorway and find two women unpacking boxes and organizing the contents on shelves around the shop. Jars of herbs, bottles of colored liquids, bowls of dried flowers, a collection of dragon-eye rings, and an assortment of other ingredients used in potions and enchantments. Their long black dresses swirl around them like smoke, and when one turns to speak to the other, I see her black eyes and pointed teeth.

Witches? In Creepy Hollow?

A tendril of fear wraps itself around the core of anger heating my chest. Witches live in lands so distant that, at least half the time, their existence is thought to be a myth. I've never met one, though I've heard the stories. Stories children whisper to frighten each other.

The younger and prettier of the two women lowers a jar of teeth back into a box and comes toward me. "Can I help you with something?" she asks. Her voice sounds … odd. It's sweet and feminine, but something reverberates beneath it. Something deep and ancient and threatening. It sends a chill crawling up my spine.

"I'm looking for the previous owner of this shop," I say, noticing that the lower part of her dress is, in fact, made of smoke.

"Oh." She scratches her arm with fingernails as pointed as her teeth. "I can't help you then. We moved in yesterday, and the previous owner disappeared days ago. The sale was conducted through a third party."

"Can you point me in the direction of this third party?"

"No, I'm afraid I can't." She offers no explanation, and I don't think I'm brave enough to pry further. Over her shoulder, I notice gouge marks in the wall beside the door leading to the back room. Marks that I'm pretty sure weren't there before.

The chill creeps further up my neck. "Well, thanks anyway." I turn and walk quickly away, waiting until I'm around a corner before hastily writing a doorway onto the tunnel wall. I hurry into it, unable to rid myself of the eerie feeling that someone is about to grab hold of me.

CHAPTER FOUR

"SO I LOOKED IT UP IN THE RULE BOOK," GEMMA SAYS, "AND there's a limit to the number of assignments a mentor is allowed to give you. Not because it's too much work for you, but because of the rankings. You could spend all your free time doing assignments and earning points, and that way you'd be top of the class, even though you may not be the best guardian." She idly drums her fingers across the book in front of her on the library table. "You should find out if Olive's exceeded that limit with all the assignments she's been giving you. If she has, you can submit a formal complaint."

I fold my arms on top of the transformations manual I'm supposed to be reading. "I doubt Olive's breaking any rules. She does *everything* by the book. And she schedules training for me far more than she schedules assignments. Is there a limit on training hours as well?"

"Yes," Ned says from the chair at the end of the table. He's so quiet I'd forgotten he was sitting there writing notes on his amber.

"Yes," Gemma adds. "I mean, if *you* want to spend all your time training, that's fine, but your mentor isn't allowed to give you more than a certain number of training hours per week."

"Well, I'm sure Olive is giving me the absolute maximum," I say as I flip through several more pages without bothering to read them. "I don't mind, though. I like training."

"We noticed," Gemma says, picking up her book once more, the cover of which depicts a woman winking while surrounded by a cloud of sparkling pink hearts.

"Ah, and what do we have here, Gemma?" Perry, who decided it was too boring to wait in the library for our assignments, reappears and drops into the seat beside Gemma. He scoops her book from her hands and reads out loud. "'Her breast heaved beneath the corset as the duke slowly dragged his fingers—'"

Gemma snatches the book from his hands and whacks him with it. "It does not say that."

"Oho, how the lady doth protest," Perry crows. "Perhaps because that's exactly what it says."

"This is an autobiography and step-by-step guide by the runner-up of last year's Create A Potion contest. It's basically a textbook, not a romance novel."

"Oh. Well if my textbooks were full of heaving breasts, I might open them more often."

"There are no heaving breasts in this book!"

"That's disappointing," Perry says. "Why on earth are you reading it then?"

With a groan, Gemma throws the book onto the table and stalks off. Feeling like I need to support her on this, I pick up the book, lean across the table, and smack Perry's arm.

"Hey!" he complains.

"You know," Ned says quietly, "that at some point you should probably tell her you like her instead of teasing her all the time."

"I—what?" Perry looks so startled that I find myself laughing. "What?" he asks again.

"Do you really think it isn't completely obvious?" I say to him.

"What is?" he asks.

I look at Ned for confirmation. He nods. "It's completely obvious."

"You—that's—ridiculous."

Ned sighs. "And you say I'm scared of girls."

"I'm not scared of anyone," Perry protests.

"You really should tell her," I say, "otherwise she'll keep pining after Mr. Perfect from upstairs."

"Upstairs?" Perry frowns. "Who's upstairs?"

Oops. I guess it isn't common knowledge that Gemma has a gigantic crush on one of the Seer trainees. I prepare to give Perry a vague answer, but all thoughts of Gemma and the Seer upstairs vanish from my mind as Ryn and Violet walk into the library and stop beside our table.

"We need to talk," Ryn says.

Shoot. I've managed to avoid him all day, probably because he's been busy catching up on the work he missed while on honeymoon. I had hoped that work would keep him busy for longer.

"Do we really?" I ask. "I have an assignment race just now and I don't want to be late."

"You won't be," Ryn says, putting his hand on my arm. I have a feeling he's going to drag me out of my chair if I don't willingly go with him. I'd prefer not to make a scene, so I stand and follow him and Vi to a quiet corner of the library. Ryn sweeps his arm briefly around us. I sense a ripple of magic.

"Did you just put a shield up?" I ask.

"Yes. A sound shield. I don't want anyone overhearing the conversation we're about to have."

"You're so paranoid, Ryn. No one is anywhere near us."

"It's not the people he's worried about," Vi says. "It's the surveillance devices all over the place." I follow her gaze as she watches an insect with needle-thin legs and a bulbous body zoom past us.

"Oh. I thought that was a real bug. I thought all the bugs I've seen flying around here were real."

"Some of them might be," Ryn says, "but most of them aren't. Now stop stalling and start explaining."

"Explaining what?" I demand. "It isn't my fault this guy turned out to be *Lord Draven*."

"Why was he there? What was flipping *Lord Draven* doing visiting you at our union celebration?"

"We're *friends*, okay? At least, we were before he turned out to be the supreme halfling prince of evil."

"Friends?" Ryn asks, eyeing me closely. "That's it?"

I've never been the blushing sort, but I can't help the heat that rises to my face as I remember Chase taking my hand and sliding his fingers between mine. I so badly wanted it to be more. Ugh, how could I have been so deluded?

"Wonderful," Ryn says with a long sigh, his eyes on the betraying flush in my cheeks. He looks at Vi, who seems to be refusing to meet his gaze. "The awkward moment in which I discover that both my wife and my sister have made out with the same guy."

My brain stumbles over Ryn's words and comes to a horrified halt. "WHAT?"

Vi glares at her husband and crosses her arms. "Thank you, Oryn. Probably not the best time to bring that up."

"Is there a more appropriate time to mention something like this?"

"You *kissed Lord Draven?*"

"Hey, so did you," she replies defensively.

"I did not. I might have wanted to—" Ryn interrupts with a groan "—but fortunately it never happened."

"Look, he wasn't Lord Draven back then. He was just a regular guy I'd saved on one of my assignments."

"Whoa. *Whoa.* One of your *assignments?* How do I not know this?"

"Because you didn't need to," Ryn says. "Barely anyone knows that all of this started when one simple assignment went wrong and a guy who thought he was human accidentally ended up in our realm."

"He … he was …" Words fail to form as my brain rushes to fill in some of the gaps of Chase's story. The gaps I was wondering about just this morning. He grew up in the human realm. He thought he was human. And then Vi tried to save him from something, and he ended up here in our world. "You knew him," I murmur. "You knew him before everything went wrong."

"Yes," she says quietly. "He was a good guy."

Amidst the confusing mess of emotions already pulling me in a hundred different directions, I find myself feeling oddly … left out. As though I've arrived in the middle of someone's retelling of a story and missed out on part of it.

"Okay," Ryn says, his tone suggesting that this is the point where he attempts to take control of the situation. "We obviously have to inform the Council of this, but we need to know more. There's no sense in creating mass panic for no reason. So the question is, what kind of guy is he after having destroyed half our world? Calla?" He looks at me. "You're the one who knows him now."

I lift my shoulders in a helpless shrug. "I don't know. I honestly don't know. He kept a lot of secrets from me, and I don't know if what he did tell me was the truth. The only thing I know is that you won't be able to find him. I went to his house Underground—"

"Underground?" Vi interrupts. "Here in Creepy Hollow?"

"Yes. I went there this morning and he and all his belongings are gone. I went to his tattoo studio as well, and that's also gone. Some creepy witches have a shop there now."

"Witches?" Ryn says. "That can't be right."

I'm not in the mood to argue, so I simply say, "I don't know, Ryn. They looked like witches. My point is that I have no idea where he is, and I doubt you or I will be able to find him. If he's remained hidden all this time, he's obviously very good at it."

"There must be something else you can tell us," Vi says. "Something he said that might—"

"Hey, Calla, we're starting the race now," Perry calls to me as he and Ned head for the library door.

"Great. Gotta go." I slip past Ryn and Vi and hurry to catch up to my friends.

"Everything okay?" Perry asks. "Looks like your brother isn't too pleased with you."

"He isn't, but it's no big deal. I'll talk to him later and sort things out." We hurry down the stairs to the mentors' level. "Do these assignment races happen often?" I ask.

Perry shakes his head. "It isn't often that the Seers See enough things going wrong at the same time."

"And all assignments need to be of similar difficulty level," Ned adds. "That's not something they can control either."

We reach the second floor landing where the rest of our classmates are gathering. I aim for Gemma, who still looks miffed, but someone grabs my arm and pulls me aside. "You're late," Olive says.

"But … the race hasn't started yet."

"Ling was here before you," she says, nodding to the girl standing patiently beside her. "That means you're late."

Ling gives me a sweet smile laced with venom. I choke down my desire to argue with Olive's ridiculous logic and force myself to return Ling's smile.

"Now," Olive says. "If either of you return from this assignment in last position, there will be consequences. I have a reputation to maintain, and I don't need the two of you ruining it."

What reputation? The words almost slip out, but I manage to hold my tongue. I doubt Olive would appreciate me asking what makes her reputation more special than that of every other mentor.

"And please don't forget, Calla—since you seem to have trouble performing this part of your duty—that if you have to kill someone, *don't hesitate.*"

I bristle at her implication that I can't do my job properly. "I won't hesitate. But I won't kill either."

Her lip curls up slightly, almost as if she's snarling. It isn't an attractive look on her. "Don't be stupid," she says. "Innocent people are going to wind up dead if you can't do this."

"I can do it," I say as an image of the boy I forced off the top of the chef school building resurfaces. "But I've chosen not to."

She sighs, her expression turning patronizing. "We all started off with our unrealistic ideals. You'll learn."

I certainly don't want to *learn* that killing is sometimes the only option, and I plan to prove that to Olive by—

My thoughts are interrupted as someone shoves past, knocking me into Olive. "Lo-ser," Saskia sings as she saunters past us.

Olive pushes me away with a growl of annoyance. "Somebody do me a favor and beat that Starkweather girl. Both she and her mentor have become far too full of themselves."

Ling gives Olive a curt nod. "I'd be happy to."

"Thank you, Ling. I don't see Calla succeeding, so it'll have to be you."

I breathe in deeply and count to five. *Don't react, don't react, don't react.*

"Here he comes," another mentor calls out. I look around and see a boy of about fourteen or fifteen coming down the stairs, struggling to balance a pile of scrolls in his arms.

"So how does this work?" I ask.

"They're handed out randomly," Ling says, to my complete surprise. I'm fairly certain those are the first words she's uttered to me.

"And then what? Do we go over the details with our mentors as usual? Or do we read the scroll on our own and then—"

"Stop asking silly questions and get over there," Olive says, pushing me forward into the crowd of fifth years. Scrolls disappear from the arms of the flustered Seer trainee as my classmates jostle around him. As I attempt to get closer, the remaining scrolls slide from his hands and land on the floor.

"Oops!" Saskia says, grabbing a scroll from the floor and skipping away.

I crouch down and help the boy gather the fallen scrolls. "Sorry about that," I say.

His eyes lock on mine as we stand. He frowns, then sifts through the remaining scrolls and hands me one. "Here. This is yours."

"Oh." I wrap my hand uncertainly around the rolled-up reed paper. "I thought these assignments were random."

"No, that one's definitely for you."

Unease pricks at the back of my mind. "How do you know that?"

He shrugs and smiles as the last few scrolls disappear from his hands. "I'm a Seer. Sometimes I just know things."

CHAPTER
FIVE

I STEP TENTATIVELY ALONG THE EDGE OF THE SWAMP, CAREFUL not to slip into the murky water. Insects hover lazily above its still surface, and trees reach over from either side, their drooping limbs tangling with one another. A blueish green haze settles over the scene as daylight disappears bit by bit.

The assignment details were minimal: a swamp, two tourists, a dangerous dare, and a wolf-like creature that neither of them expects. I have to save them, of course. If the creature disappears, that's great. If it fights back ... well, then I hope to be able to restrain it and bring it back to the Guild.

Humidity clings to me, sticking my hair to the back of my neck. I reach for my jacket pocket for something to tie my hair up with, before remembering I left the jacket in Olive's office. After seeing the location of this assignment, I figured I wouldn't need it. I pull a twig from a nearby branch and transform it into a stretchy band. After a quick glance up and down the swamp to make sure I'm still alone, I scoop my hair up and secure it with the make-shift hair accessory.

Much better. I crouch down beside a tree and wait, watching the insects, the misty haze, the occasional ripple across the water's surface. The smell of decaying vegetation fills my nose. *How pleasant ...*

Above the high-pitched singing of insects, I slowly become aware of voices. I tense, readying myself to reach for a weapon. After another minute or so, they come into view on the other side of the swamp: two women who appear to be in their early twenties. They push noisily through the brush, laughing loudly, completely unaware of the danger that lurks within this swampy jungle.

"No way," one says to the other amidst her laughter. "That's got to be the stupidest legend of all. Where did you hear that one?"

"That guy at the restaurant last night. He's a local. He knows these things."

"Yeah, he knows how to tell stories while trying to pick up girls." The two of them lean in to each other as giggles overtake them.

"Fine," the second one says after she's recovered. "I assume you'll touch the water then, since you aren't afraid of the big bad Swamp Monster."

"Of course I'll touch the water. I might die of some horrible swampy disease, but it won't be the Swamp Monster that kills me."

I suppress a groan, hoping her words haven't sealed her fate. *She won't die, she won't die, she won't die,* I chant to myself as the woman leans down and trails her fingers through the dirty water. I picture my bow and arrow—not focusing too hard on the idea—and raise my hands to the space where I imagine them to be. The weapon appears, fitting perfectly into my grip. Chase was right about that: it takes only a brief thought, an expectation that the weapon is already there, rather than a deep focus.

Don't think of him now.

My weapon is brilliant and sparkling, filling the area with its light. The women won't be able to see it, though. My weapons and I are both hidden by glamour magic. The wolf creature, however … Well, if he's anywhere nearby, he won't miss this brightly lit weapon. Perhaps I should have gone for stealth, rather than revealing myself too soon, but I'm hoping he'll come for me instead of the humans.

A shriek pierces the air. I jump to my feet, ready to attack. But I realize a second later that it was only one of the women pretending to push the other into the swamp. The two of them dissolve into giggles once more as I release a sigh of relief. I scan the banks, the trees, the clumps of soggy vegetation growing in the water. Where will he come from? Is he watching already? Is he on *my* side of the bank?

I throw a glance over my shoulder as a shiver crawls up my back despite the smothering warmth of the air. Am I being watched? Or is it simply my imagination, like last night at the old—

Noise erupts behind me. I whip my head back around in

time to see a black shape explode from the water. The wolf, his shaggy, dripping fur flinging water everywhere, collides with both women. Their screams chill my blood.

I don't waste a second. My arrow zooms across the water and finds its mark in the wolf's side before he's finished rearing his head back. With a roaring snarl, he leaps off his prey and swings around to face my side of the bank. Wild, gleaming eyes stare hungrily at me through the hazy air. I discard my bow. It disappears, its glow vanishing in an instant. In the near darkness, I can see little more than those fiery eyes on the other side of the swamp.

The moment he jumps, so do I. With a single bound, he's across the water, but the muddy earth I was standing on is now bare. Those glowing eyes turn upward. He sees me above him, balancing on the branch I launched myself onto. He lets loose a vicious growl. Then his head morphs and shifts and becomes something almost human. "Dinner time," he snarls.

Fear ripples through me, raising the hairs on my arms. I don't show it, though. Instead I reach swiftly for my bow and point an arrow directly at his head. "Try it," I say, hoping he doesn't.

But he readies himself to spring. He's an enormous beast, after all, so of course he thinks he can take down the pesky guardian trainee trying to rob him of his dinner. I get ready to flip backwards out of his way the moment he launches at the tree. He tenses. He leaps—

And from a doorway in the air, a man steps out, knocks the wolf back onto the ground with a mere sweep of his hand, and brings slender branches slithering across the ground to bind the wolf's limbs.

"Who the hell are you?" the wolf demands in rough, grunting tones as he morphs into a shape that looks far more like a hairy man than a four-legged beast. The newcomer sends a stunner spell straight at the wolf's chest, knocking him unconscious.

Good question, I think to myself. Whoever this is, he's interfering with my assignment, and I doubt Olive will be pleased with that.

I drop to the ground, bending to absorb the impact before I straighten. "I'd like to know the answer to that," I say.

The man turns—

—and I feel the air punched from my lungs. "You," I manage to gasp.

"Calla?" He seems as startled to see me here as I am to see him. He can't be feeling what I'm feeling, though. Never in a million years could he understand the way my heart just split. "Calla, what are you—"

"Stay back!" I say as Chase moves toward me. I hold a hand up between us, as though that might keep him away. As though I might possibly stand a chance against the most powerful being our world has ever known. The heavy air seems hard to breathe. The sheen of sweat coating my skin turns icy. "Is it true?" I manage to whisper. I already know it is, but I want to hear him say it. I want him to admit it.

Chase's expression is indefinable as he says, "It is."

I'm shaking, partly in anger and partly in fear. After all, it is *Draven* standing before me. Powerful, dangerous, a killer.

What's wrong with me that I couldn't see that in him? How did I miss it? "You lied," I whisper.

Stupid, stupid. Why are you still here? Why aren't you running?

"I didn't," he says.

"I *trusted* you," I yell. "I told you things I've never told anyone else."

"I know, and I—"

"And then you made a fool of me!"

"No! That was never my intention. I was going to tell you everything."

I choke out a laugh. "Everything? You were going to tell me *everything*?" I shake my head. "You were never going to tell me who you really are. Why would you do that? This is the only reaction you could possibly have expected."

"I was going to start at the beginning." He takes a step closer. "Tell you about the person I used to be. The guy I was before I discovered this world and its magic."

"Is that guy supposed to be different from the guy who caused The Destruction? The guy who killed so many people?"

"Yes."

"How? That guy is *you*!"

"No! Not anymore."

I find myself shaking my head again. "I don't believe you. I can never believe you again after all the *lies* you—"

"I did not lie to you." His voice is fierce as he takes another step closer. "I kept things from you, but you knew that. You knew all along that I wasn't telling you everything, and you agreed with me that it was better to say nothing than to lie."

I know I said that, but this ... who he really is ... it's so much more than any normal secret. "You led me to believe that you were someone else," I say, trying to keep the tremble from my voice, "and that's just as bad as lying."

He looks as though he may want to say something else, but he turns his head away instead, looking out across the murky water.

Leave, that voice inside my head tells me. *Leave now.*

So I do. I ignore that tiny, stupid part of me that still thinks of him as Chase—that still *misses* him—and focus on what my brain tells me: He's a killer. Get. Away. Now.

He doesn't come after me, but I run into the faerie paths anyway. My breath catches, my hands shake, and I stumble out the other side onto the old Guild ruins. A cool breeze curls along my bare arms, sending another shiver through me. I wrap my arms around my body as I pace the ruins. Why, why, *why* did he show up tonight? Why is he still entangled in my life? Why can't I rewind time and pick a different house to break into and never find myself involved with him in the first place?

I press my hands against my face—and then I remember the assignment race. "Shoot," I mutter out loud, dropping my hands to my sides. I'm supposed to be back at the Guild now. I'm supposed to have successfully completed my assignment. And while I did manage to keep the women from becoming the wolf-man's dinner, I'm going to have a lot of explaining to do when Olive puts my tracker band into the replay device and sees another person arriving at the scene, capturing the wolf-man, and then having a tense conversation with me. Replay devices haven't yet advanced to the level where sound can be replayed, but the scene is suspicious enough without our exact words. Olive will want to know who the man is. And I can't tell her that.

Some tiny part of my wonders why. Why can't I tell her? Why can't I tell *everyone* at the Guild what I know? Then they can hunt Draven down, capture him, and hand out whatever sentence he deserves for all the terrible things he's done.

He isn't just Draven. He's Chase. You care for him. You don't want that kind of fate for him.

"Shut up," I whisper to myself. I should *want* him to be captured, but I don't, and that disturbs me. So I push the thought aside, refusing to examine it more closely. With shaking fingers, I remove my tracker band. I place it on the ground. I pick up a rock and bring it down again and again until the strip of leather is battered and perforated. Then I light a fire with a snap of my fingers and watch it burn. It takes a while—probably because of the protective enchantments embedded in the leather—but the flames are magical too, and eventually the tracker band disintegrates.

Then I pull my knife from my boot—the knife from Dad, the one Saber stabbed me with—grit my teeth, and cut a shallow wound into my arm. I spread the blood around a bit, wipe some of it onto my clothes, then wait for the wound to heal.

When I get back to Olive's office—not in last position, she tells me, but close enough—I explain that the wolf bit my arm and tore the tracker band off. She crosses her arms, her expression telling me she doesn't quite believe me. "How fortunate the wolf didn't rip your entire hand off along with the tracker band."

"Yes. It was definitely fortunate that he didn't get his teeth right around my wrist."

"How do you expect me to award you any points if I can't see how you performed on this assignment?"

"I don't know. The two women got away safely, if that counts for anything. But I suppose you'll have to take my word for it."

"Your word," Olive says with a humorless laugh. She shakes her head. "Zero," she snaps. "And be grateful I'm not giving you negative points."

Grateful? I'm grateful I didn't have to kill the wolf-man. I'm grateful Olive didn't see my tracker band. And I'm grateful she knows nothing about Chase. Because despite the fact that it makes me no better than a traitor, I can't escape the feeling that I don't ever want him to wind up in the clutches of the Guild.

CHAPTER SIX

I LOWER MYSELF ONTO THE MAT ON MY HANDS AND KNEES, stretch my legs out behind me, and start my set of push-ups. "Not much," I say to Gemma in answer to her question about what I'm doing later. "Probably just homework and any extra training Olive decides to give me."

"Well, if you don't have extra training, do you want to come over later? We can just chill and chat about girl stuff."

"Okay. Sure." My eyes remain fixed on the section of floor in front of my face as I push against it repeatedly. "I don't think I'll have much to add to the conversation, but we can chat about you."

She laughs. "Okay. I'm hanging out with Rick for a little while after we're done with training, so we can dissect that."

"Cool."

It's our last session for the day and Gemma and I have been assigned to the strength training area. I started with weights and now I'm onto push-ups. Beside me, Gemma is doing lunges while holding a bar across her shoulders. The idea of spending the evening rehashing every word the guy she's crushing on said to her doesn't fill me with a great deal of excitement, but if I were in her shoes—and if the guy I liked hadn't turned out to be an evil, brainwashing, Destruction master—I'd want to do the same thing. Besides, Rick is a Seer, so talking about him might not be that boring after all. There are so many things I've wanted to know since I discovered Mom was a Seer trainee before she fled the Guild years ago.

"How much do you know about Seer life?" I ask Gemma. My arms are beginning to burn and my breaths are coming faster now, but I can keep going for a while. "Has Rick told you lots? Like, what their training is about and … what the process is from the time a vision is Seen … to when it makes its way … downstairs for guardians to take care of?"

"Yeah, some of it. They use special mirrors." She stops her lunges and pulls one leg up into a stretch. "Why don't you ask him? You can come upstairs with me after this session."

"Okay. But won't that be … a bit weird? Just the three of us … hanging out?" It's getting harder to carry on a conversation, but I manage to get my words out at the top of each push-up.

"No, we'll be in the Seer common room. Other trainees hang out there, so it won't be—Freaking heck, will you *stop* already? How many push-ups are you planning to do?"

"I don't know," I say breathlessly, still going. "I don't count anymore. Olive tells me to ... keep going until it hurts ... and then to keep going some more after that."

"Okay, your mentor *seriously* needs to chill out."

"Do I, Miss Alcourt?"

From the corner of my eye, I see Gemma step back quickly. Olive's boots appear in my line of vision. "Um ... oops," Gemma says. "I'm sorry."

I get to my feet, rolling my shoulders and swinging my arms as I look from Olive's crossed arms to Gemma's guilty expression. "Hi," I say to Olive, hoping to break the glare she's currently directing at Gemma.

"I'm just gonna go use those weights over there," Gemma says. She turns and hurries to the other end of the strength training area.

"I have a new tracker band for you," Olive says. "We need to test whether it's working."

I take the tracker band and put it on. "Okay. Is there anything in particular you want me to do?"

After a long exhale of breath that suggests it's the bane of her existence to come up with an exercise for me, she says, "Yes. Do that aerobics routine from the other day. Bring the tracker band to my office when you're done."

I manage to nod instead of groan. I'm one hundred percent certain Olive came up with that stupid routine specifically to embarrass me. With a combination of stepping, jumping, running on the spot, punching the air, and kicking imaginary opponents—all in a repeating pattern—it's easily the silliest thing I've ever done. No doubt Olive's sole purpose was to get me to finally say no to something. I'm pleased to say I managed to resist.

I head to the far corner of the training center where the obstacle course items are stored and attempt to hide myself between some of them. Then I imagine the beat Olive told me to count in my head and get started on the silly side-to-side stepping while pulling one knee up in between each step. I ignore anyone who walks past. I keep going through all the various moves, recognizing that this might actually be fun if I were on my own with some music playing. I'm not, though, and when I feel I've embarrassed myself sufficiently, I bring my little routine to an end.

I slip the tracker band off and walk across the training center. "Come up to the Seer trainee level when you're done," Gemma calls to me as I pass her.

"Okay."

Olive doesn't waste time when I get up to her office. She opens the cupboard where all her trainees' past assignments, recorded onto tiny marbles, are stored in rows. She takes a blank marble from a box and returns to her desk where the replay device is waiting. The replay device—which Ryn told me is new technology; they didn't exist in his day—is a sphere with a flat base on which to sit and a small hollow at the top in which to place the marble. She picks up the sphere, puts it down on top of the tracker band, and places the marble in the top. With her stylus, she quickly draws a symbol onto the side of the sphere. Then she stands back, crosses her arms, and watches. A small three dimensional image of me doing my aerobics routine appears in the air above the device, proving that I did, in fact, look as stupid as I felt.

"Good. The tracker band's working." She removes the marble and adds, "We definitely don't need to keep that recording." She returns it to the box of blank marbles, presumably so she can record over it next time.

"Thanks." I wait for a moment, in case she's about to give me some extra training for tonight, but when she says nothing further, I turn around and leave her office.

I've never been as high up as the Seer trainee level, but I know where it is. When I reach it, I ask a young girl for directions to the common room. She takes me to the end of a corridor and points to the room on the left. I step into a large round space with a rich blue carpet covering the floor and pairs of blue curtains hanging at regular intervals around the room. In between each set of curtains, an oval mirror is attached to the wall, each with a pretty, decorative frame. Couches, tables and chairs are arranged into various different sitting areas.

I walk down a few steps into the room, searching the groups of people until I see Gemma. She's talking with a guy I presume is Rick. As I move toward the two of them, I can't help comparing him to Perry. Rick is almost as tall, but he isn't as lean and muscular—obviously, given that his training doesn't involve anything physical. His face is handsome, but there's something about Perry's smile and that mischievous glint in his eyes that makes him cute. Perhaps I should ask Gemma if she's noticed it. Then I can at least tell Perry if he stands any kind of chance with her.

Gemma sees me approaching and stands. Rick gets to his feet and Gemma introduces the two of us. "Calla's curious about the life of a Seer," Gemma tells him. "I said she should come and ask you herself."

"Oh, sure," Rick says with a good-natured laugh as we sit. "As long as you're not about to ask me why the Seers didn't see The Destruction coming."

"Oh no, don't worry," I assure him. "Gemma explained that one to me already." I rub my hands along my legs, not sure what to ask now that I finally have the opportunity. "So … I was thinking that I don't know all that much about how it works. As guardian trainees, we receive assignment details on scrolls, and that's pretty much all I know about your end of the process. I don't even know what it's like when you actually have a vision."

"It's … disorienting," Rick says. "We get pulled into it, as if we're really there, and then thrown back to the present. We get used to it after a while, but sometimes it still results in dizziness and nausea."

I lean forward on my knees. "And you can't control what you See, right?"

"Well, no, but we can influence it. We have to direct our thoughts a certain way, focus on certain ideas so we're more open to seeing the important things. It's also difficult to control the length of a vision. Sometimes I'll see barely a flash of something, and other times it's longer."

"That's part of your training as well, isn't it?" Gemma says.

"Yes." Rick groans. "We have to try and immerse ourselves in the visions so they last longer and we see more details, but it's tough. Even the instructors can't always get it right. The other day one of them Saw a fire-breathing dragon in a setting that looked like the foyer downstairs, but it was only about two seconds of a vision, so it was totally useless."

"That's a bit scary," Gemma says. "I didn't think anything could get inside this Guild."

"Exactly, which means it probably wasn't the foyer. So with a vision like that where there's no useful information at all, you have to just move on. Hopefully if it's something really important, someone else will See it in more detail."

"And then how do you record these visions?" I ask.

"We have mirrors with special enchantments in them, like these ones here." Rick stands and removes the nearest mirror from the wall. As he sits down with it, I see what I missed before: these mirrors don't reflect anything. "Once I've had a vision," he says, "I just need to recall it while using the right magic, and it will be transferred to the mirror so other people can see it. If it's something a guardian needs to take care of, and if it has enough details to be useful, like place and time, then everything is written down. Then someone higher up, a Seer who's already graduated, decides what level of guardian or guardian trainee the vision is sent to."

"Okay," I say, nodding. "At least I have a better understanding now of how it all—Oh." I stop talking and pull away from Rick as his body goes rigid, his head tilts back, and his eyes flutter back and forth behind his eyelids. Somewhat afraid, I look at Gemma. "A vision?" When she nods, I ask, "Does this happen often?"

"Fairly often, I guess. It freaked me out a bit in the beginning, but I'm used to it now."

Rick recovers with a shake of his head. "Sorry about that,"

he says as he lifts the mirror with both hands. He chants some foreign words while staring directly at it. He turns the mirror to face Gemma and me, and in its surface I see a woman with smudges of dirt on her face and strands of silver in her messy black hair. She laughs—and then she lunges forward, fury flashing in her silver eyes, her arm outstretched as if to grab us. Gemma and I pull back in fright, but the scene vanishes from the mirror. Then it begins replaying.

"That's unpleasant," Gemma says as we watch the woman's snarling face a second time.

"You see?" Rick says to us as he places the mirror flat on his lap once more. "That one really wasn't useful at all. Do either of you recognize that woman?" Gemma and I shake our heads. "And there's no sense of time or place, so … yeah." He swipes his hand across the mirror and mutters a word I've never heard before. "That one gets erased then." He stands and returns the mirror to the wall. As he walks back, he says, "Are you okay, Calla? You still look a bit startled."

"I'm … yes. I've just never witnessed something like that before." My amber vibrates in my pocket. As I remove it, I add, "But it was interesting to see, and thank you for explaining everything. I understand better now." What I mean is that I understand Mom better now. I can see why it might be unpleasant to have visions taking over several times a day.

I read the message on my amber, then look up at Gemma. "I'm sorry. I won't be able to hang out tonight after all. Last minute babysitting emergency."

"Oh. Whose baby?" Gemma asks.

"Friends of my brother's."

"Okay, we can chat tomorrow then."

I nod and stand. "Thanks again, Rick." I head across the common room for the door, trying not to look at the creepy mirrors that don't reflect anything, and trying to forget the image of a woman with savage fury reaching out of the future to grab hold of me.

CHAPTER SEVEN

"THANKS SO MUCH FOR DOING THIS, CALLA," RAVEN SAYS AS she lets me inside. I follow her and her elegant silver dress past the living room and into the dining room. "My parents were going to look after Dash, and then these extra tickets became available so I invited them to come with us instead, but then I had to find a trustworthy babysitter at the last minute."

"It's not a problem at all." I dump my bag of homework beside the messy dining room table. "I'm used to babysitting for Vi and Ryn's other friends, so I really don't mind."

"Oh yes, Jamon and Natesa," Raven says as she leans across the table past rolls of fabric, bottles of glitter and buttons, and open notebooks filled with her neat handwriting. "Their daughter is such a sweet little girl."

I nod and lean my hip against the table as Raven's fingers

finally make it past all the obstacles on the table and grasp a pair of plain white heels. "I thought you had a room upstairs for all your clothes casting stuff," I say.

She straightens and gives me a guilty look. "I do. It's still there. But I haven't tidied it in a while—and I bought a whole lot of new stuff recently—so, it's kind of impossible to work up there at the moment."

With a smile, I say, "It looks like it's almost impossible to work down here as well."

"Don't be silly. This isn't nearly as bad as upstairs."

"She's right," Flint says from behind me. He walks into the room with four-month-old Dash on his hip. "You don't want to go anywhere near that room upstairs. You'll probably end up swallowed alive by fabric."

"Heeeeey," I say, smiling widely at the adorable little boy and opening my arms as I walk toward him. He makes some giggling nonsense sounds and waves his tiny hands, smacking his dad's cheek in the process.

"Hello to you too, Calla," Flint says as he hands the child over to me.

I hug Dash to my chest and kiss his baby-soft cheek before saying, "Hey, Flint. Sorry, you know you're always going to be second when this cute little guy is in the room."

"Yeah, I know." Flint turns to Raven, now sitting on a chair paging through one of her notebooks. "Almost ready?" he asks.

"Yes, I just need to decide what to do with these shoes." She continues flicking through the pages. "I want to do that spell that makes the surface mirror-like, but I'm thinking of mixing it up a bit with that other one that looks like sparkles zipping around beneath the surface."

"Okay. Will that take long? People are going to be here soon."

"I know, I know. Shh. You're distracting me."

With a long-suffering sigh, Flint looks at me and nods toward the living room. I follow him, asking, "People are coming here? I thought you guys were going out somewhere."

"We are," he says as we sit, "but Raven's parents are bringing their carriage for us all to go in. Vi and Ryn are coming too."

"Oh, really? I wouldn't have thought a clothes casting awards evening would be their kind of thing."

Flint laughs. "I don't think it is, but we were given extra tickets, and they're supportive of Raven's career, so they seemed excited to come along."

"Okay. Wait, did you say Raven's parents have a *carriage*? Like, with pegasi and everything?"

"And everything," Flint says, nodding.

"Wow." I bounce Dash on my lap while he watches me with wide green eyes, giving me the occasional smile.

Moments later, a knock comes from outside. Flint jumps up and opens a section of the wall. Vi and Ryn walk in, looking far more smartly dressed than usual. Vi even put on a dress for the occasion. I turn my gaze back to Dash and occupy myself with giving him more wide-eyed smiles and kisses on his nose and cheeks. Hopefully everyone will leave before my brother or Vi manage to interrogate me again. I was supposed to visit them last night after my assignment, but I conveniently 'forgot.' I don't like the idea of keeping things from them, but I also don't want to tell them about my unexpected encounter with Chase. It feels too … personal. A story I don't want to share. My silly heart cracked open again, and I don't want anyone else knowing that.

No such luck. Vi starts filling Flint in on whatever work she's currently doing at the Reptiscillan Protectors Institute, and Ryn heads straight for me. "We didn't finish our conversation yesterday," he says as he sits beside me.

"I know. I'm sorry." I bounce my legs up and down and Dash continues his gurgling. "But if you're hoping to go after him, I can't tell you anything else useful. He didn't exactly leave a forwarding address after vanishing from his Underground home."

"Do you have his amber ID? We can try to track it if you— Vi, are you sure it's okay for you to lift that?" Ryn asks, raising his voice and half rising from his seat.

Vi looks over the top of the box in her arms. Beside her, Flint is holding an even larger box. "Yes, Oryn," Vi says, sounding more than a little annoyed. "The baby and I have no trouble picking up a few old weapons."

"Weapons?"

"Yes. Flint's donating some stuff to the Institute."

"Uh, I'm happy to carry both boxes," Flint says, obviously trying to avoid an argument.

"Don't you dare," Vi says. She walks to the wall where Flint opened a doorway just now and lowers her box to the floor. "There. Now we won't forget to take them later."

Ryn sighs and mutters, "I don't know why she doesn't just use magic."

"Because I'm not lazy like you," Vi calls across the room.

Ryn rolls his eyes, lowers his voice, and says, "Anyway, we were talking about tracking what's-his-name's amber."

"Yes. You could try that. But I'm about a hundred and fifty percent sure he'll have anti-tracking spells on it."

"Hmm. True. Have you tried sending him a message?"

"No, Ryn, I have not. It's rather difficult to sum up one's feelings in an amber message after finding out that the guy one likes is actually an evil halfling prince."

Ryn's eyebrows climb up his forehead, and I want to kick myself for making the moment so awkward. After a pause, he says, "You knows he's too old for you, right?"

"OH MY GOODNESS." I stop bouncing my legs, and poor Dash looks like he wants to cry at my sudden outburst. I lower my voice to a fierce whisper. "*That's* what you're worried about right now?"

"Everything okay?"

I look up and see Raven in the doorway, newly casted sparkly shoes just visible beneath the hem of her silver dress. "Yes. Sorry. Everything's fine." I restart my leg-bouncing. Dash chews on one finger while looking concerned.

"Great," Raven says. "I'm just going to put this little guy to bed." She crosses the room and lifts Dash from my lap. "Hopefully by the time that's done, my parents will be here."

As she leaves the room, another knock comes from the direction of the wall. Vi takes that as her cue to join Ryn on my side of the room. "Anything useful to report about …" She hesitates, then mouths the name *Draven*.

"No," Ryn answers for me. "Calla's being spectacularly unhelpful."

I elbow Ryn. "It isn't my fault he was spectacularly secretive. If I knew something useful, I'd tell you."

Would you really? asks a tiny, traitorous voice at the back of my mind.

"Did you tell Calla about the news from Velazar?" Vi asks.

"Oh, I forgot about that." Ryn leans a little closer to me as Raven's mom hurries upstairs—probably to steal a few minutes with Dash—and Flint chats with Raven's dad. "Someone from Velazar Prison notified the Guild two days ago that the man we told them to look out for, Jon Saber, tried to visit our old librarian friend."

"Amon?"

"Yes. So Saber is now in custody. Turns out this isn't his first time in prison. That's how he and Amon met. Hopefully we can get some information out of him about the man who has your Griffin Ability. Without letting the Guild know exactly what we're asking about, of course."

"Of course." I chew on my thumbnail, then start shaking my head. "This won't stop whatever Amon is planning, though. I'm sure he has plenty of other followers to carry out his dirty work. Other prisoners he's met over the years who have finished serving their sentence."

"The guards have been told not to allow him any visitors," Ryn says, "and to send us all details of those who try to visit him."

"I don't know why they were allowing him visitors in the first place," Vi says.

"I'm sure they didn't in the beginning. They all know he was one of Draven's men. But perhaps good behavior earned him a visitor or two over the years."

"And there's always blackmail," I add. "He seems to be pretty good at that. Anyway, hopefully you'll soon know where Gaius is. It should be easy to get that information, right? Just give Saber a compulsion potion and ask him the right question."

"Yes, well, unless he's been trained to cheat a compulsion potion," Vi says, crossing her arms over her chest.

"Cheat? How? I thought that when compelled to tell the truth, you have no choice but to, you know, tell the truth."

"Yes, but there are ways of ... *bending* the truth," Ryn says. "He might tell us details that are true, but unhelpful. Or, in certain cases, if he can convince himself that something is true, even though it isn't—or if he's been told a lie by someone else, but he believes it to be the truth—then we could wind up with false information."

I flop back against the cushions with a groan. "That sucks."

"It does."

"Okay, let's go," Raven says, returning to the living room with her mother. "We don't want to be late. Calla, feel free to eat anything you find in the kitchen. And if you need any materials for your outfit for the Liberation Day Ball tomorrow night, you're welcome to take what you want, either from the table down here or the room upstairs, if you feel like venturing in there."

"Which I wouldn't recommend," Flint adds. "I'm not coming to find you if you get lost in there."

"Thank you." I stand along with Ryn and Vi. "But I'm not going to the ball."

"What?" Raven looks horrified. "Of course you have to go. The Guild balls are *amazing*. And the theme this year is so much fun."

"I know, I just don't really … feel like it."

"Nonsense," Raven says. "Go play around with all the fabrics and accessories in the room upstairs. You'll soon be in the mood to dress up." She heads to the wall as Flint reopens a doorway. Through it, I see the front half of a pegasus waiting patiently outside.

Vi steps closer to me and touches my arm. "I know why you're not feeling in the mood for a party, but you should go. The sooner you can get over whatever hurt you're feeling, the better."

I nod, not because I've suddenly decided to attend the ball, but because I know she means well. "Thanks. I'll take a few things in case I change my mind."

"Come on, let's go," Ryn says to Vi. "I need to forget about today's drama."

"Today's drama?" I ask as the two of them head for the doorway. "What happened today?"

"Nothing," Ryn says.

"Someone escaped from the detainment area this morning and hasn't been found yet," Vi says over her shoulder.

"*What?*"

Ryn stops to glare at his wife. "Does the word 'confidential' mean nothing to you?"

"Oh, come on. She's your *sister*. And she's a member of the

Guild. I'm sure she'll find out tomorrow."

"Who was it?" I ask, my heart beginning to pound faster as I wonder if it might possibly be …

"Confidential," Ryn says firmly. "Confidential, confidential."

"Hurry up, you two," Raven calls from outside. "We're going to be late."

Ryn and Vi step outside, the doorway seals up behind them, and I'm left standing alone in the quiet of the living room, wondering if it's at all possible that Zed was the one who escaped.

CHAPTER EIGHT

"SO YOU'RE SERIOUSLY NOT COMING?" GEMMA WHISPERS TO me as the mentor at the front of the lesson room, a tall woman named Anise, explains the exact order in which ingredients should be mixed to create the perfect antidote to common poisons.

I add a few details to the scales of the dragon I've been sketching on one of the blank pages at the back of my notebook. I've been working on this one for several days now, half focusing on it while listening to whatever the mentor for that day is talking about. I try not to let any mentor see the sketch, of course. Who knows if they'd believe me if I had to explain that drawing helps me concentrate. "I just don't feel like going to a big party, that's all," I say to Gemma. "As Olive pointed out, we celebrate our freedom every day simply by being free. Why do we have to make a huge deal about it?"

"Oh my goodness. I can't believe you just agreed with your mentor on something." Gemma leans over and touches my forehead. "Are you sick?"

I roll my eyes and swat her hand away with a quiet laugh. "No, I'm not sick." I glance toward the front of the room again, then flip back to the notes section of my book and start copying down the instructions currently being written on the board by an animated stylus.

"Come on, Calla, I need you to be there. I need moral support."

"Moral support for what?" I raise my eyes to the board and continue copying the words.

Gemma leans closer, lowers her voice further, and says, "I asked Rick if he'd go with me, and he said yes!" She lets out an almost inaudible squeal.

I stop writing and look over at her. "You actually asked him?"

"Yes!" Her voice is a high-pitched hiss now. I can tell she's ready to explode with excitement, but since we're in the middle of a lesson, now probably isn't the best time.

"Congratulations," I whisper. "That's wonderful. So you told him how you feel about him?"

"Well, not exactly." Gemma ducks her head and doodles a pattern on the corner of her page. "I might have mentioned going as friends."

"Gemma," I scold, loud enough that Anise looks up from helping someone at the front of the room.

"Miss Alcourt. Miss Larkenwood," she says. "Why do I get

the feeling you're not discussing the lesson?"

I snap my mouth shut, deciding the question is most likely of the rhetorical sort. "Um …" Gemma mumbles.

"Probably because they're not," Saskia says from behind us, loud enough for most of the class to hear.

Since most of the mentors seem to favor Saskia and eat up whatever she says, I expect this comment to land us in even more trouble. But Anise simply crosses her arms over her chest and says, "You're no better, Miss Starkweather. I've heard the words 'secret admirer' at least three times during this lesson, and I have no doubt where they came from."

Suppressed laughter comes from several desks around the room. On the left near the front, though, Blaze crosses his arms and slides further down into his seat with a thunderous expression on his face. Nobody who was in the dining hall for breakfast this morning could have missed his public break-up with Saskia. She kept going on and on about the secret admirer who'd left her a gift of jewelry in her locker yesterday afternoon, along with a note asking her to meet him at the ball tonight. Blaze stood up and shouted for everyone to hear that she could attend the ball without him if she was so intrigued with this secret admirer. I can't say I blame him.

As Anise turns back to the board at the front of the room, Gemma leans over again and whispers, "Please, please, please come. If things get weird with Rick, I need you to rescue me. Besides, do you really want to miss this year's theme? All creatures great and small. It's going to be epic."

"Why would things get weird?" I ask as I continue writing

down potion instructions. "And it's too late for me to find a date."

"You don't need a date. Lots of people don't take dates."

I look at her. "So you want me to be a third wheel to your just-friends date with Rick?"

"No, no. You can just … be near in case I need you."

She looks so desperate, and she *is* my friend. I suppose I can make the effort to get dressed up and go to this ball if it'll help her nerves in some way. Thank goodness I took a few minutes to venture into Raven's cluttered design room last night to choose some items I could reach without having to climb into the mess. "Okay," I say with a sigh. "I'll come."

"Yay!" Gemma squeezes my arm, then lowers her head and scribbles across her page as Anise looks back at us with a frown.

I give Anise an innocent smile. She looks away, and I cover my mouth as a wide yawn takes over. Dreams of my time locked up in Zell's dungeon continue to disturb my sleep every night and it's taking a toll. The dreams always vary slightly. Sometimes Chase is there, sometimes it's the boy I pushed off the top of the chef school building. Last night it was Gaius in the shadows, calling my name in barely audible tones. He struggled against some invisible force, crying out to me again and again. It sends a chill across my skin just thinking about it.

I blink the memory away, then swat at a surveillance insect as it buzzes too close. Honestly, can't they keep those things hovering around the ceiling instead of getting too close to a person's mouth when she's yawning? Do the people who have to watch all these recordings really need to see inside my mouth?

"Ow!" The bug bumps into the back of my hand and stings it before zooming away. I rub at the tiny red spot as Gemma and several other trainees look up.

"Miss Larkenwood?" Anise says. "Is everything okay?"

"Yes, sorry, I'm fine." I rub the red spot that's already disappearing. "The bug just startled me, that's all." I guess it was a real one after all.

"At least it wasn't a mischievous sprite," Gemma whispers. "I was in second year when one of them blew laughing dust into my face during a lesson. I had to be escorted out because my giggling was totally out of control. So embarrassing."

The remainder of the lesson passes without incident. For the next lesson, we all traipse down to the fifth-year lab on one of the lower levels to practice the potion we've just been taught. Our training sessions took place this morning, which means when our time in the lab is done, we're finished for the day. Excited chattering fills the room as we gather our things and head out. Most of us stop by the lockers to grab our training bags, and at least half the class gathers around Saskia to see if she's been gifted more jewelry by her secret admirer. I ignore them all and open my own locker. I reach for my bag, but my hand stills as I see a folded piece of paper on the top shelf. I hesitate, frowning, then pick it up and unfold it.

Calla,

Come to the ball tonight. Meet me beneath the stained glass clock at 9 pm.

Looking forward to a dance with you,
Your secret admirer

I almost burst out laughing. This is *definitely* a joke. I look around to see if anyone's watching me, but all eyes are on Saskia as she hunts through her locker. She steps back and lets out a huff. I guess there's no gift for her today. I look down at the note again, wondering if it's the same as the one Saskia got yesterday. Is this the kind of thing that makes her giddy with excitement? If so, I don't understand it. I find this note creepy, not romantic, and I plan to stay far away from any clock I see at the ball tonight.

I push the note into my bag, shut my locker, and wave goodbye to Gemma. "See you later," I say, trying to sound enthusiastic. I turn and walk past my classmates. Instead of heading for the foyer, though, I walk in the opposite direction toward the training center. Everyone else is rushing off to get ready for the ball tonight, but Olive scheduled an extra hour of training for me. She probably thought she'd be ruining my ball-preparation plans by doing so. Little does she know I'd far rather spend my evening in the training center than in a ballroom.

* * *

I enjoy my workout, so I keep going for longer than an hour. But eventually I have to leave if I'm hoping to look half decent tonight. I don't have much of an outfit yet—just a collection of materials I thought might look good together—and it'll take some time to get the basic clothes casting spells I know to produce something wearable.

I hurry along the corridor and out to the foyer. There's no

one else here except the faerie walking casually down the stairs with his hands in his pockets. Clearly he isn't attending the ball tonight. Or if he is, he's not worried about—

Hang on. I look closer, then freeze on the spot as he reaches the bottom step and keeps walking. "Zed?" I whisper in horror. He looks my way. Panic crosses his face, and his steps falter slightly, but he keeps moving. Toward me. He stops beside me and smiles.

"Calla. What are you still doing here?" Up close, he doesn't look nearly at ease. His shoulders are tense and his smile is strained.

"You ... *you're* the one who escaped?" I whisper, leaning closer to him. No one said a word today about someone escaping the detainment area, so I'd almost forgotten about it.

"Stop looking so shocked," Zed says, never allowing his smile to fade. "If someone walks past, you're going to give me away."

I straighten and look around before returning my gaze to Zed. "How the heck did you escape?"

Quietly, he says, "You're not the only one with a Griffin Ability."

My lips part, but I don't know what to say. We never speak of Zed's Griffin Ability, but I haven't forgotten it. That strange, disturbing power of his. One touch, and he can make a person relive his or her nightmares. Trouble is, Zed gets to feel the same terror his 'victim' is experiencing. It's not the most pleasant of Griffin Abilities.

"I thought ... I thought you said you never wanted to use that power again."

"I had to get out somehow. After I touched the guard, he was disoriented and scared enough that I was able to get the key from him."

"And you? Weren't you disoriented and scared?"

He looks away. "I ... I was scared. But I wasn't seeing the things he was seeing."

I swallow. "So you've been hiding inside the Guild since you escaped?"

"Yes. All over the place. An empty lab, the library, the healing wing, a storage area. Wherever I had to. I've been waiting for a quiet moment to walk out of here without anyone noticing." He looks toward the entrance room at the side of the foyer.

"And when you get in there?" I ask. "You're going to do it again? Scare them, so you can get out without being scanned?"

"Yes." He hesitates. "You're not going to stop me, are you? You'll let me go?"

I feel guilty about letting someone escape the Guild, but it's *Zed*. He's my friend, and he hasn't done anything wrong. "You're not a criminal," I say. "Of course I'll let you go."

"Thank you," he says with such sincerity that I know I've made the right decision. He looks around again—so do I, just to make sure there aren't any surveillance bugs buzzing around—before grasping both my hands in his. "Come with me," he says fervently.

"What?"

"Calla, these people ... you don't want to be one of them."

"I do, Zed. That's why I'm here."

"There's so much you're not seeing," he says with a slow

shake of his head. "Guardians ... the Guild ... it's all a very noble idea, but there's so much wrong with the system. There are so many people to save every single day. How do they choose who's worth it and who isn't?"

"They save as many as they can."

"They don't. They abandoned us. Remember? *So many of us.* You got out, so you don't know how bad it got after that. *The Guild* left us to that fate. These people you idolize."

I want to tell him just how much I *don't* idolize Olive and anyone else like her, but I need to stand by my commitment to the Guild. "I'm one of them, Zed. And if you hate them, you hate me."

"I don't hate you, Calla. That's precisely why I'm begging you to come with me. This is your last chance to—"

"Go." I pull my hands out of his and step back. "Just go before someone figures out that you're the guy who escaped."

His expression is tortured, as though he honestly believes he's leaving me to a terrible fate here amongst the guardians he's grown to hate. But he doesn't see what I see. He doesn't see all the good that comes out of this imperfect system. I know this is where I'm meant to be.

With a final nod, Zed turns and strolls away, pushing his hands back into his pockets, doing his best to look relaxed. I walk back to the training center and wait there for a while, giving him a chance to get away. Giving the guards a chance to recover from their waking nightmares. Giving myself time to smother my guilt.

CHAPTER NINE

THE BALLROOM IS ALMOST FULL BY THE TIME I ARRIVE AT
Estellyn Tower. The Guilds host their Liberation Day cele-
brations at different venues every year—never at a Guild; that
would pose too many security issues—and this year, the Creepy
Hollow Guild has hired the ballroom on the second floor of
the glitzy Estellyn Tower. I remember what Olive said about
there being far too much expense involved in celebrating
Liberation Day, and I find I'm starting to agree with her. Or it
could be the fact that I have negative associations with this
place and I'd be happier if the ball were held pretty much
anywhere else. Because all I can think of as I walk in here is the
party I attended recently on the topmost level of this tower.
The party Chase turned out to be at.

I find myself wishing, *wishing* with an intensity that hurts my chest that he was just a normal guy. Wishing that I could have invited him tonight, so that we might have walked in here together and admired the splendid decor and laughed at the outrageous costumes and danced until our feet hurt.

He is Draven, I remind myself. *Draven. Not Chase.*

I push aside my silly dreams and step into the ballroom. The decor enchantments have transformed the room into a jungle. Instead of walls, I see moss-covered trees and giant ferns and vines draped from one side of the room to the other. Mist creates a subtle haziness near the ceiling, adding to the mood along with the floating lanterns emanating yellow-green light. Musicians on a raised platform on one side of the room keep the music going, and the dance floor is already packed with couples spinning about.

People are dressed like creatures from all parts of the world, both human and fae. I run my hands self-consciously over my dress, hoping I look at least a little bit like a mermaid. That was the plan, but since I didn't put much thought into it prior to this afternoon, it wasn't exactly a detailed plan. My dress is a shimmering aquamarine color with a faint pattern of scales covering it, but the mermaid theme doesn't extend much further than that. I tried to create a fishtail shape at the bottom of the dress, but it ended up being so tight I couldn't move my legs. I also tried to create shoes that appeared to be made of water, but that proved to be far too complex as well. So in the end my dress is a simple style and my shoes are plain silver heels. I pulled my hair over my shoulder and braided it with blue-green ribbons. By that point I'd run out of time to construct a mask, so I finished off my blue eye makeup with some tiny crystals on my lashes and blue, green and purple sequins around my eyes and at the top of my cheekbones.

I look around for someone I recognize. Gemma told me she'd be late, so I don't expect to see her here yet. Saskia is nearby, loudly showing off her new jewelry to a group of her friends. Whatever the jewelry is, I'm not close enough to see it. I get a good look at her outfit, though: a gorgeous red dress that shimmers like fiery coals, and a pair of leathery webbed wings. I think she's meant to be a dragon.

I continue to look around, then twist my hands together as I start to feel awkward. I wonder if I should wait outside the ballroom, but then the current dance ends and Perry waltzes off the dance floor toward me. He looks ridiculous with butterfly wings protruding from his back and a mask the shape of a butterfly covering half his face. It's definitely him, though—I can tell from his height and the green in his hair and, well, the fact that he looks absurd and proud of it. He does a twirl and a bow before reaching me, and I can't help laughing as he straightens, takes my hand, and kisses it. "You're making fun of this whole dress-up thing, aren't you," I say.

"Never," he exclaims. "What makes you think that?"

"I wonder." I reach up and flick his mask. "And were you dancing by yourself, or did I happen to miss your partner?"

"I was practicing," he says, "for when the perfect partner comes along."

"I see. Well, your outfit is extraordinary. I think you should win a prize for it."

"Thank you." Perry does another bow. "And may I say that you make a lovely fish, Calla."

Indignant, I place my hands on my hips. "I'm not a fish. I'm a mermaid."

"Oh, sorry, of course. My bad." Perry laughs, but his smile falters as he focuses on something over my shoulder. "Is that Gemma?"

I turn and see a girl with a delicate silver filigreed mask covering the top part of her face. Her white feathered dress and the feather hair piece pinned into her dark hair make me think of a swan. The overall effect is stunning. "Yes, that is Gemma. And that—" my eyes move to the handsome guy on her arm "—is Mr. Perfect. Your competition."

"That's ... whatever ..." Perry splutters, but he pulls off his butterfly mask and stands a little straighter. Gemma and Rick walk over to us, and Gemma introduces him. She looks a little dazed, as though she's just been handed all the riches of the Seelie Court and can't quite believe it. Perry, on the other hand, can't stop frowning. He greets Rick, then shoves both his hands into his pockets and remains silent. I realize it might be up to me to get the conversation going, but then Rick asks Gemma if she'd like to dance, and the two of them disappear into the crowd.

Beside me, Perry appears to deflate. I lean closer to him. "Still want to tell me it's not obvious?"

He stares at his feet. "I suppose it is obvious. I only considered it recently, though, the night we came to that party here. I realized afterwards that of course I like her. Of course I don't just want to be her friend. But it's too late." He jerks his head over his shoulder and adds, "How can I compete with that?"

"You don't have to compete. Just be yourself and tell her how you really feel, and maybe it'll turn out she feels the same way."

He shrugs half-heartedly and lets out a loud sigh. He pushes his shoulders back and straightens. "Well, after rejection like that, all I have left are my dance moves. May I have this dance, Lady Calla?" He holds a hand out to me as I start laughing at him once more.

"Yes, I'd—" From the corner of my eye, I see Ryn, dressed for a regular day of work at the Guild, pushing past people and waving to me. "Um, in a minute. Looks like my brother needs me."

"Ah, more rejection," Perry says in anguished tones, pressing a hand dramatically against his chest. "My poor heart can barely stand it."

"Your poor heart will be fine." I pat his arm, give him a brief hug, and then meet Ryn near the doorway. "Hey, you're not dressed up at all," I say. "Is everything okay?"

"Yes, but I won't be staying long. I just needed to speak to you and a few other people before leaving."

"Leaving? Where are you going?"

Ryn groans. "Vi had this *fabulous* idea. You know how she wants to keep working right up until the last second, and there are all these things going on at the Institute that she doesn't want to miss out on just because she's pregnant?"

"Yes. It seems to be the cause of every disagreement you guys have these days."

"Right. So she suddenly came up with this plan to go to Kaleidos."

"Kaleidos?" I absently play with the ribbons at the end of my braid. "The floating island Tilly's from?"

"Yes. Time passes differently there, so Vi's hoping she can get through most of her pregnancy on the island. She's hoping that months there will only be weeks here and that she won't miss out on too much of the real world."

My hands fall to my sides. "That's a terrible idea. The time difference is always changing, right? So what if it works out the other way around? Weeks there turn out to be months here? Then she'll be missing even more than she would otherwise."

Ryn crosses his arms. "That's exactly what I said."

"But she doesn't agree with you?"

"She admits it's not the best idea she's ever had, but she still wants to see if it might work. We're going just for this weekend as an experiment."

"But what if it's not just this weekend? What if you're *there* for a weekend, but you miss out on weeks here?"

"I'll be keeping a close eye on the time difference. Kaleidos has this system set up with people just inside the shimmer and people just outside it. They communicate every fifteen minutes or so to keep track of the time difference. That way they know when it's changing one way or the other, or speeding up or slowing down. And the Guild knows we're going, of course. One has to get permission to travel on and off the island."

"Oh." I frown. "The stories Tilly tells about her childhood make it seem as though rules like that never existed."

"Yes, well, Tilly and her brother always managed to find their own way off the island. They didn't exactly follow the rules."

I raise my eyebrows. "I'm sure that's something you can identify with."

Ryn groans. "Yes. Unfortunately, being grown-up and on the Guild Council means I'm supposed to at least *try* to stick to everyone's rules these days." He takes a deep breath and looks around the ballroom. "Anyway, Vi wants to leave immediately, so she's at home packing. I just came to let you and a few other people know what's going on."

"Okay. Well I hope you don't lose any time over the weekend."

"I hope so too." He hugs me, then adds, "And if your, uh, *friend* tries to get hold of you, let me know. Oh, wait. Messages don't go through the Kaleidos shimmer." Ryn frowns and scratches his head. "Just don't do anything silly, okay?"

I roll my eyes. "He and I were friends for weeks without your knowledge. I'm sure I'll be fine."

Ryn nods, although he doesn't look entirely convinced. He squeezes my arm and steps past me to speak to someone else.

"Ready for that dance?" Perry asks, appearing a second later as if he's been waiting for the moment Ryn leaves. "The next one's about to start and it's my favorite."

"Ok, okay." I needn't have bothered replying, since Perry's already guiding me onto the dance floor as the music changes. "This is that one where we dance in rows, right? And we keep swapping partners?"

"Yes," Perry says, his eyes fixed on someone further down the row we've just joined. I follow his gaze and see Gemma. I smile to myself as I realize exactly why he's so eager for this dance. Someone near the end of the row counts us in, and then we all start moving. I concentrate on getting the steps right. I did dancing at junior school, like everyone else—it was compulsory; part of exercise class—but I haven't practiced much since then. I falter a few times, as do several other people, but I manage to keep up with the hand movements and the twirling and the stepping to the side and then repeating it all with the next person in line.

My second partner is someone with sweaty hands and a stiff expression. He doesn't smile once. I'm glad to step to the side and take the gloved hands of my third partner, a man whose face is fully concealed behind a tiger's mask. He leads well, and I find it easy to keep up with him. I twist beneath his arm, his gloved hand slides smoothly over mine, and then I step to the side once more. My fourth partner is dressed in dark clothing with a black panther mask covering his face. Warm brown eyes smile at me from behind the mask, and I can't help smiling back.

Three more partners, and then the dance comes to an end as the music slows to something more intimate. I move quickly to the side of the room, careful not to catch anyone's eye as I go. I don't want to wind up in some stranger's arms as we follow the painfully slow steps of one of the traditional faerie dances. I help myself to a glass of something from a tray as it floats past me. I sip the sweet, fizzy drink, watching couples over the rim of my glass. Gemma and Rick are staring into one another's eyes as they keep up with the dance. Perry's partnered up with a fourth-year girl I've seen in the training center a few times, but he's looking over her shoulder, watching Gemma.

My eyes skim the crowded ballroom, looking for more

people I recognize. I don't see Olive anywhere, but I didn't expect her to be here. I manage to pick out some of the other Guild mentors and Council members, along with most of my classmates. Saskia seems to be gone, though. Is she meeting her secret admirer in private somewhere? Which reminds me ... how long will *my* secret admirer wait before giving up? I'm not planning on searching for that stained glass clock.

Amidst all the colorful outfits, my eyes stop on the black panther I danced briefly with just now. He's in discussion with a woman with rabbit ears atop her head. She gestures to the panther mask with a frown. I can understand that. It's strange talking to a person whose face you can't see. The panther-man removes his mask, and—

My glass slips from my fingers.

Chase?

I duck my head immediately, in case he looks this way, but the sound of splintering glass was barely audible above the music. Several people nearby ask if I'm okay, but I ignore them as I hurriedly brush the broken glass beneath a table with a whispered word and a quick sweep of my hand. I walk along the edge of the room, staring across to the other side with a pounding heart. Draven, the man who destroyed Guilds and brainwashed even the strongest of guardians, is standing calmly amidst a gathering of people who are celebrating the very day they all think he died.

I *danced* with him. I was *in his arms*. Why didn't I recognize him? How did he make his eyes look different?

He raises his gaze. I freeze. His eyes lock on mine.

It would be so easy to shout out his name right now, to reveal to everyone in this room exactly who he is. I could do it. I *should* do it. But something holds me back …

After an infinite moment, he breaks eye contact. He nods to the woman he was speaking to, then hurries away. I push through the crowd, rushing to catch up with him. But everyone seems determined to move as slowly as possible, and after looking away for a moment, I lose sight of him. I stand on tiptoe, scanning the ballroom, but I can't find him. The woman he was speaking to is in the same spot, so I aim for her instead.

"Um, hi, sorry," I say as I almost skid into her. "That man you were just talking to—the one dressed like a black panther—do you know where he went?"

She blinks at me. "What man?" She looks down at the drink in her hand as her eyebrows pull together. "Where did this come from?"

Fantastic. There's probably a confusion potion in there. I put my hand on the woman's shoulder and manage to force out a carefree laugh. "Oh dear. I think you may have had a little too much to drink." Then I step past her and hurry around the room to the door. Chase must have left. He wouldn't stay here, not when I could so easily give him away. Not when there are dozens of guardians present who could overpower him.

Or could they? Exactly how powerful is he?

I look behind me, doing one last brief search of the ballroom, before running out the door. I find the stairway and hurry down to the first floor where it's possible to access the faerie paths. I'm probably too late by now. He's had plenty of time to get away. The only reason he might still be here is if he *wants* me to find him. Part of me is hopeful as I search the lobby. The part of me that refuses to recognize what a dangerous man he is. The part of me that looks at him and still sees Chase.

That part grows a tiny bit smaller as I finally have to admit he's nowhere to be found. I trudge back up the stairs. They don't go any higher than the second floor, so if Chase wanted to go up instead of down, he would have had to take the elevator and pass a security scan before being allowed on any of the upper levels. I suppose he could be hiding somewhere on this floor. I pass the ballroom door and look down the carpeted passageway. A sign tells me it leads to a gym and something called the Phoenix Lounge. No one stops me, so I keep walking. I turn a corner and the passageway continues—and at the far end is a stained glass clock.

I back up. I almost turn away, but then I notice a shape on the ground beneath the clock. A strange red shape, part of it rounded and soft and part of it sticking up sharply. I raise my eyes once more; the clock tells me it's twenty minutes past nine. I take a few tentative steps forward, reminding myself that guardians are supposed to be brave. I should be able to push down the fear crawling its way up my neck. The fear that heightens as I realize that the red at the other end of the passage looks a lot like the red of Saskia's dress. And that Saskia wasn't in the ballroom just now. That she had planned to meet the mysterious person who left a letter in her locker.

The moment my mind makes sense of what I'm seeing, I know it's her. She's lying on the floor facing away from me with one of her dragon wings poking upward, shielding the upper part of her body from view. She doesn't move. I want to hurry over to her, but fear slows my footsteps. It almost freezes them, in fact, but I force myself to keep moving. I hear the tick of the clock and the unnatural pattern of my breaths.

But I hear nothing from Saskia.

Keeping a safe distance, I step around her. I see her hair now, and her—

I can't help the shriek that escapes me. I clap a hand over my mouth. Saskia's skin is a greenish hue with traces of dragon-like scales here and there. On the patches of skin where there are no scales, a fine green powder rests. Her lips are parted, and a smeared pool of vomit lies beside her face. Her hands are swollen and lumpy, pulling her skin tight around the dragon-eye ring on her right hand.

It's rare for disease or sickness to kill a faerie, but one look at her utter stillness and her unfocused, unblinking eyes leaves me with no doubt. Saskia is dead.

A cry from the other end of the passage makes me look up. A small group of people from the ball, including one of the guards who was standing at the door, hurry toward me. To my left, where the passage continues toward the gym and the Phoenix Lounge, I notice more movement. People must have heard my scream.

"What's going on here?" a man demands. It's Councilor Merrydale, the very first Councilor I met at the Creepy Hollow Guild. The one who was in charge of determining all the requirements for me to become a trainee. He was always friendly to me, but he's stern now, a frown creasing his brow as he takes in the scene. "Miss Larkenwood?" he prompts when I can't seem to find my voice.

"I—I don't know what happened," I say, looking at her again, focusing on her hands and not her half-open, unseeing eyes. That ring looks so familiar. "I just found her here like this."

Murmurs and gasps fill the passageway as the crowd grows larger. Someone starts to cry.

"Did you see who did this?" Councilor Merrydale asks.

"No, she was alone. There was no one else here."

"What's that on your hand?" someone says.

It takes me a moment to realize the question was directed at me. I raise both hands, twisting them this way and that. Then I see it: green powder smeared across the side of my left hand. Fear stabs at me. "I—I don't know." I wipe my hand against my dress, but the powder seems to have stained my skin. "It, um, must have got on my hand when I checked to see if she was alive." I didn't touch Saskia, though. That green powder shouldn't be anywhere near my hand.

"You touched her?" someone says.

And then another voice, high-pitched and fearful: "You did this."

"What?" I look around, searching for my accuser, but there are too many people now.

"You killed her," that same voice says, wobbling and tearful. I find the owner, Lily Thistledown, a friend of Saskia's. "We all know you never liked her. We all know the stories about strange things happening to people around you."

"I didn't kill her," I protest. "I found her like this."

But others are whispering now, and I hear the same accusation travel around the crowd.

"I didn't do this!" I shout. I turn my gaze, desperate, to Councilor Merrydale. "I didn't," I repeat, shaking my head.

He glances at the crowd, then back at me. He steps forward and places a hand on my arm. "Miss Larkenwood," he says gravely, "I'm sorry about this." He breathes out long and slow before delivering the final blow: "You are suspended pending further investigation."

PART II

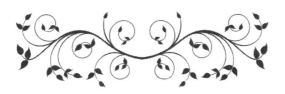

CHAPTER TEN

YEARS. I'VE SPENT *YEARS* WORKING TOWARD MY DREAM OF becoming a guardian. Training in secret, saving lives the Guild never even knew were in danger, and then studying my butt off for all those exams I had to pass before anyone would allow me into fifth year. And then what happens? One moment in the wrong place at the wrong time, and everything I've ever wanted is about to be snatched away from me.

No. That isn't going to happen.

I pace from one side of my living room to the other, refusing to accept that this could be the end of my guardian career. It can't be. It won't be. Not when I look at things logically. There are flaws in the system, but at its core, the Guild represents justice and truth. They don't want to lock up innocent people. They want to find the real criminals. And when they question me under the influence of compulsion potion, they'll realize I'm not a murderer.

"She's lucky they only suspended her," Gemma says to Perry. "They could have expelled her on the spot and taken her into custody."

"No, she isn't lucky," Perry says, slapping his butterfly mask down on his lap. "This is ridiculous. They shouldn't have even suspended her. They have no evidence against her. No reason to suspect she was the one who did it."

"There's that green stuff on her hand," Gemma points out.

"Which, as Calla said, got onto her hand when she was checking to see if Saskia was still alive. Right?" Perry looks to me for confirmation.

I nod, absently rubbing my hand where the mysterious green powder was. But I didn't touch Saskia, and I didn't touch anything else with green powder on it, so where did it come from?

I continue my pacing as Gemma and Perry argue back and forth. After Councilor Merrydale uttered that horrible word—*suspended*—things happened quickly. He conjured up a bubble and placed it over my hand to prevent me from transferring the powder to anyone else. Two Guild guards took me by the arms and led me away. Minutes later I was back in the Guild heading for the healing wing. The guards deposited me in a small room, bare except for a single bed and table. I noticed chains attached to the bed, but the guards obviously didn't consider me dangerous enough to warrant using them. They waited outside the door as a healer—dressed in full protective gear, including a transparent mask over her mouth and nose—

attended to me. She pressed my hand against some kind of sticky pad to take a sample of the powder, then cleaned my skin and asked plenty of questions about Saskia's appearance. She frowned the entire time and showed no sign of recognition at my description of the symptoms.

She left without answering any of my questions. Councilor Merrydale came in and cast a tracker spell over me, which consisted of him drawing a thick line around my ankle with his stylus and joining the two ends of the line by making a locking motion with a tiny key. A key he then hid away in a pocket while the line on my skin slowly faded. He then told me that my father and the two guards were waiting outside the room to escort me home. Gemma and Perry showed up as we were leaving, and Dad—who's probably been wondering for years if his outcast daughter would ever make any real friends—let them come home with us.

"But they have no solid evidence!" Perry repeats.

With a sigh, Gemma says, "If you're found at the scene of a crime, it looks suspicious. You know that. So even though the Guild has no solid evidence, they have enough reason to believe she might have been involved, so they can't just let her go." Gemma looks across the room at me. "No offense. I know you didn't do it. I'm just saying I understand why the Guid has to proceed the way they've proceeded."

"Yeah," I say dully. "Because I might vanish through the faerie paths and never come back, and then a murderer will be on the loose." I finally stop my pacing and flop into an armchair. "I suppose I should be grateful Councilor Merrydale took 'pity' on me, as he put it, and decided on house arrest instead of throwing me into a cell in the detainment area."

"Yes," Gemma says. "That is something to be grateful for."

I stare at the ceiling and murmur, "Saskia is dead." The words sound strange to my ears. "I didn't like her, but I never wanted her to *die*. It's so strange that she's just … gone. I've become used to her constant degrading comments, and now she'll never be there again in the training center or the dining hall or any lesson …"

Perry moves around in his seat and says, "I hope you're not implying that you're actually going to miss her."

Gemma smacks him and mumbles something about being disrespectful of the dead.

"No, that's not what I mean. It's just strange, that's all. A shock. Something so unexpected."

"Yeah," Gemma says quietly. "Do you think she just got sick somehow, or do you think someone actually … murdered her?"

"Who would do that?" Perry asks. "I mean, people might have joked about it, but who would actually go through with it?"

Suddenly, I realize why Saskia's ring looked familiar. I sit up straight as several things click into place at once. Things that are obvious but were most likely overshadowed by shock until now. "That big ring she was wearing," I say. "Is that the jewelry she received as a gift from her secret admirer?"

"Yes," Gemma says. "Didn't you see it this morning when she was showing it off to everyone? That's why she changed her outfit at the last minute. She wanted to match the ring."

"The ring is what made her sick. I'm almost certain of it.

And it wasn't a coincidence that I was the one who found her." My fingers dig into the armrests as I realize the truth of what I'm about to say. "Someone set me up."

Gemma and Perry blink at me. "Set you up?" Gemma repeats, sounding doubtful.

I quickly explain that I also received a letter from an anonymous secret admirer. A letter that told me to come to the stained glass clock at nine o'clock tonight. "Which is exactly where I found Saskia, and it was just after nine. Her secret admirer must have been the same person, and he—or she— gave Saskia a ring with some kind of disease or spell on it. I saw the exact same rings in an Underground shop run by witches. They would know dark spells to create lethal diseases, wouldn't they?"

"Witches?" Gemma looks horrified. "There are *witches* in Creepy Hollow?"

"She had the ring for more than twenty-four hours," Perry said. "Why did it take so long for her to get sick?"

"One of her friends did say that she was already starting to look green when they all arrived at the ball," Gemma says, "but he'd put it down to the green light in the ballroom."

"If it was the ring, then why are none of Saskia's friends dead?" Perry asks. "I'm sure some of them touched it."

"I don't know. Maybe it was a slow-release spell and it only started affecting Saskia this evening while she was wearing it. And maybe it was specific to her, so that's why her friends are fine. Is it possible to make a spell like that?"

"Perhaps," Perry says, "but if I were you, I would not have

touched her. What if you get sick now?"

I rub my hand against my leg. "Yeah. I'm trying not to think about that possibility."

"If only you hadn't followed the instructions in that letter," Gemma says.

"I didn't, actually. I'd forgotten all about it at that point. I was only there because I was—"

Looking for Chase.

My blood turns cold at the realization. Did Chase do this? Did he set me up somehow? And the green powder ... did he put it on my hand while we were dancing?

"Gemma? Perry?" Dad says from the kitchen doorway. "It's getting very late. Thank you for being here for Calla, but I think you need to go home now."

Perry retrieves his butterfly mask and Gemma reaches for Rick's jacket, which he must have wrapped around her before she left Estellyn Tower. "I'm sorry I ruined your big night with Rick," I say to her as the three of us stand.

"You don't need to apologize," she says, pulling the jacket on. "It wasn't your fault. Besides, we got a few dances in before ... you know."

"I know, but if I hadn't just been accused of murder, you and Rick might still be hanging out somewhere."

"Maybe. Probably not, though. I don't think either of us would be in the mood to simply hang out after something so awful just happened."

"I guess not."

Gemma and Perry walk to the wall, and Dad opens a doorway for them. They make a comical pair, Gemma with all her feathers and Perry with his silly butterfly wings still attached to his back. I smile as they wave goodbye and head into the faerie paths. The edges of the doorway melt back together. I lower myself into the armchair, my smile gone. Dad perches on the couch opposite me. "I left a message for Ryn, but I don't know when he'll see it. I don't know all that much about Kaleidos, but it seems the only way of communicating with anyone there is the old fashioned way."

"Well, there's no point in sending a letter. He'll probably be home before it gets there. Besides, it's not like he can do anything about this."

"No, I suppose not." Dad hesitates, then says, "I heard what you said to your friends. Your theory about what happened. Do you really think you've been framed for this?"

"It seems that way, doesn't it?" I rub my hands up and down my arms, feeling colder now that I'm not pacing around the room. "It makes me wonder if it will be harder to prove my innocence than I thought."

"It will be fine, Cal. They'll question you, you'll tell them the truth, and they'll know it's the truth because of the compulsion potion." He gives me an encouraging smile. "Guardians are the good guys, remember? They'll get to the bottom of this."

I try to return his smile. "I know. But in the meantime, what am I supposed to do? I can keep up with lessons if my friends tell me what work they're doing, but I can't train. I'm not allowed to leave the house."

"You could paint," Dad suggests. "You hardly do that anymore."

I shake my head. "Painting isn't going to help me when I get back to the Guild."

"Neither is complaining about the training you can't do. Painting is something you enjoy, so why not spend your free time doing it?"

I consider that, then decide it's time to stop considering things and go to bed. "Maybe," I say as I stand. "I'll see if I feel inspired tomorrow." I hug Dad goodnight, and he tells me once more that everything will be fine. But as I head for the stairs, I glance back over my shoulder; the worry on his face is unmistakeable.

With my hopes dropping lower and lower, I climb the stairs to my bedroom. It's late and my head is starting to ache, so I don't spend long in the bathing room pool. When I've washed off all my glittery makeup, I leave the pool to clean itself, dig out my favorite blue and yellow winter pajamas from the bottom of a drawer—because it really is starting to get colder—and climb into bed.

Then I lie awake thinking about the person I've given up trying *not* to think about. Did Chase kill Saskia? I don't want to believe he could have done it, but it's entirely possible. And why would he frame me? Is he trying to get me in trouble with the Guild before I can tell them he's alive? Discredit me so they won't believe anything I say?

An hour later, I'm burning with anger and no closer to falling asleep. I reach for my amber and consider sending Chase a message demanding to know if he did it. But I force myself to put the amber down. I'm not certain I want to reopen any lines of communication between us, and I doubt he still has the same amber. He probably got rid of it minutes after Vi revealed who he was, just in case someone figured out how to get past whatever anti-tracking spells were on it.

I turn over yet again, breathe in a long, calming breath, and wish for sleep to come.

CHAPTER ELEVEN

I'M TRAPPED INSIDE MY HOUSE. I TRY TO OPEN A DOORWAY to get outside, to breathe fresh air, but something keeps my hand from writing the spell. Even my legs feel like they're stuck in syrupy thickness, unable to move. The walls start sliding toward me. My chest tightens and panic sucks all the air from my lungs. I struggle to breathe as the walls come closer, closer, closer, transforming into the bars of a cage. A scream climbs up my throat but can't seem to make its way out of my mouth. I drop to my knees and curl in on myself as the bars form a cage around me.

I'm hanging above the black water again. I remember escaping earlier after I tricked a man into opening my cage. I showed him an image of his master, the scary Unseelie prince, telling him to let me out. I ran through the other room, the round room with the papers and the table, and tricked someone else into opening the sliding stone door. But outside in the passageway, someone caught me. I was carried back in here, struggling and screaming, and thrown into my cage.

I'll never be free. I'll be locked in this terrifying place forever, listening to the wails of other prisoners and forgetting what it feels like to not be afraid. I hug my knees and shudder as sobs overpower me.

"Hey, it's okay," someone says. "Everything will be all right. They don't want to hurt us." I rub my eyes and see a young man in the cage next to mine. "I'm Zed," he says. "What's your name?"

"Calla!"

The shout isn't mine. I look around and see a lanky man with disheveled hair standing at the edge of the water. Gaius? What is he doing here? Abruptly, I become aware that I'm dreaming. I realize this is nothing more than a mixture of memories that can't hurt me.

"Calla!" Gaius shouts again. "Please don't wake up yet. I'm in—"

* * *

My eyelids slide apart and my blurry gaze tries to focus on my bedroom wall. I blink and rub my eyes and find my body damp with cold sweat beneath my pajamas. *Only a dream*, I remind myself as the fear slowly melts away and relief takes its place. That last part seemed so real, though. I push myself up and rub my eyes again. I lift my sticky hair away from my neck and try to remember the last moments of the dream, what Gaius looked like and exactly what he said. But the details that seemed so clear at first are already beginning to fade, in that way that dreams do.

I drop my head back onto my pillow, closing my eyes and telling myself that it isn't gross to lie here in this cold, sweaty mess and that I don't need to get up and have a bath and that the best thing to do is go back to sleep.

* * *

On Saturday afternoon I'm called into the Guild to have a 'chat' with Councilor Merrydale. The vague memory of my dream comes to mind, and I half expect something to hold my hand back when I try to open a doorway to the paths. Then, as I step into the darkness, I expect some kind of siren or alarm to go off. Nothing happens, though. I wonder if, somewhere inside the Guild, guards have just been alerted that a person under house arrest has left her home.

I direct my question to the guard who escorts me from the Guild entrance room up to Councilor Merrydale's office. "Yes, an alarm goes off at one of the stations in the surveillance department if you cross the tracker spell boundary," she tells me. "But someone will have been informed that you were told to come here, so the alarm would then be disabled. And the spell tracks your location, of course, so the person on duty can check that you're on your way here and not running off somewhere else."

She waits with me outside Councilor Merrydale's office,

saying nothing more. In the expanding silence, I grow more nervous as each second ticks by. When the door opens all of a sudden and Councilor Merrydale calls me in, a spike of fear makes me queasy. His message said this was a 'chat,' but I'm certain it's more than that.

"Please sit, Miss Larkenwood," he says as he returns to the other side of his oversized desk. This office is familiar to me. I came here several times during the process leading up to my admittance to the Guild. Councilor Merrydale settles into his chair and looks at me. His face lacks its usual cheerfulness, but there's still a small smile there as he asks, "May I call you Calla?"

"Um, okay." He's only ever called me Miss Larkenwood, which makes me wonder why he's being extra friendly now.

"Don't look so nervous," he adds. "This isn't an interrogation. I just wanted to explain a few things and give you a chance to tell your side of the story. When something like this happens and there's a hearing to determine whether a person is guilty or not, a Council member is appointed to assist in the defense of that person and represent him or her where necessary. I volunteered to be that representative, and Head Councilor Bouchard approved. If you also approve, then we can proceed."

"Oh. Thank you." I consider his offer for a moment. "I suppose my first choice would be to have my brother defend me, but I assume that won't be allowed."

"Unfortunately not. Family members may not represent one another."

"Then yes, I approve."

"Good. I'll just need you to sign this form then." He slides a scroll across the desk, and I try to keep my fingers from shaking as I find the blank line at the bottom of the page and sign it. I see another line for a parent to sign for those who are under the age of eighteen, but a note beside it says that those who are members of a Guild are able to give their own consent. Good. I'm feeling like enough of a child as it is. At least I don't have to call daddy and ask him to sign a piece of paper for me. I sit up straighter, remind myself that I've done nothing wrong, and push the paper back across the desk. "Thank you," Councilor Merrydale says. "So, do you want to tell me what happened last night? I assume it was simply a case of being in the wrong place at the wrong time, but it does, unfortunately, appear rather suspicious that you were on your own in that corridor instead of in the ballroom like everyone else."

I nod, give myself a moment to consider my words—because I'll probably be asked to repeat this story while being compelled to tell the truth—then start with the anonymous note in my locker. When I get to the part about following Chase out of the ballroom, I carefully navigate my way through the truth. "Then I saw a friend I wasn't expecting to see. I wanted to speak to him, but he appeared to be leaving early. I lost sight of him in the ballroom and assumed he'd left, so I went downstairs, hoping to catch up to him. I didn't find him, though. When I went back upstairs, I saw the sign for the other lounge further down that passage, and I wondered if he'd gone that way. When I turned the corner and saw the stained glass clock, I almost turned back. But then I saw Saskia. I didn't know it was her or that she was dead until I reached her. That's when I screamed, and it was barely a minute after that when everyone else showed up."

Councilor Merrydale nods as he quickly scribbles down everything I say. He looks up and asks, "Was there anyone with you who can confirm that you saw this friend and followed him out of the ballroom?"

I shake my head. "Unfortunately not. My other friends were dancing at that point."

"And the letter you received," he adds. "Do you still have that?"

"Yes. It's in my training bag." How fortunate that I kept it instead of throwing it away.

Councilor Merrydale calls a guard in—the same woman who brought me here—and sends her to my home with a note addressed to Dad, probably telling him to send my bag back with her. "While we wait for Clove to return," he says, "there is something else you need to explain."

I shift anxiously in my chair. "Okay."

"The dragon-eye ring in your locker."

My limbs go still as a chill runs through me. "What ... what dragon-eye ring?"

"Your locker was searched this morning and we found a ring exactly like the one Miss Starkweather was wearing."

"But ... I don't have a ring like that. Somebody must have put it there. It must be part of the set-up."

Councilor Merrydale nods and makes another note on his reed paper.

"You didn't touch it, did you? I think the ring is what made Saskia sick."

"Oh?" He looks up. "What makes you think that?"

I suppose I'll be compelled to answer these questions at some point, so I may as well come clean now. "When I was Underground recently, I saw those rings in a shop run by witches. Their magic is very different from ours, isn't it? And this sickness that killed Saskia isn't something anyone seems familiar with, so it might very well be a witch's spell."

"Witches," Councilor Merrydale murmurs, a frown on his face now. "How odd. What were you doing Underground?"

I hesitate before answering. "It isn't illegal to go Underground, is it?"

"No. Although it certainly isn't encouraged. Where exactly is this shop?"

I explain the location as best I can, and while he writes down my instructions, the guard returns with my training bag. "That was fast," I say to her with a smile. She nods and leaves without a word.

"Okay, let's add this letter to the evidence we already have, and then you can return home," Councilor Merrydale says as he rolls up the reed paper.

I unzip my bag and dig between the books and training clothes. When I don't see the crumpled letter, I start unpacking my belongings. I remove every single item from my bag until all that remains are several bits of charred paper. Like a letter that was burned or had a self-destructing charm applied to it. I breathe out slowly through my nose as I stare at the empty bag and start to wonder just how deep this deception goes. Then I straighten, resigning myself to the fact that this piece of evidence is gone for good. "It's not here anymore," I say quietly, not bothering with any excuses.

Councilor Merrydale nods. "That's unfortunate." He leans back in his chair and sighs. "You understand that none of this looks good for you."

I swallow, feeling sick. "But ... the compulsion potion. You'll know I'm telling the truth then."

"Yes," he says as he pushes his chair back and stands. "Hopefully."

Hopefully? *Hopefully?* What does that mean?

"Thank you for coming in, Calla. I'll be in touch when we're ready to proceed with the next step in the investigation. Clove will see you home now."

CHAPTER TWELVE

"TELL ME AGAIN WHAT WE'RE DOING IN HERE?" GEMMA asks on Monday afternoon.

I lift the goggles hanging around my neck and position them over my eyes. "My dad told me to paint. So I asked if I could paint the walls in the guest bedroom. He said yes."

"I see." Gemma gives me a doubtful look. "I'm guessing he didn't know you meant *this*."

I look around the bare room at the balloons of paint floating in the air. "He didn't ask me to be specific, so ..." I shrug. "I didn't give him specifics."

"Uh huh. Hopefully he appreciates your design style."

"I'm sure he'll be fine with it. Mom, on the other hand, will probably freak out when she wakes up and sees it. Who knows when that will happen, though, so let's not worry about things we can't control." I push my shoulders back and lift my arms into position. A bow glitters in my grip a second later, with an arrow ready to fire. I aim for a balloon and say, "Let's get this redecorating party started."

"Wait." Gemma puts her hand on my arm. "Are you sure it's safe to shoot arrows in such a confined space?"

I lower the bow. "It's not *that* confined. If it was, I'd be having a panic attack." At the questioning look on her face, I add, "Claustrophobia."

"Ah."

"We'll go one at a time, and that way we won't shoot each other."

"Okay. That's comforting."

"And if we make holes in the wall, we'll just fix them."

"Right."

I raise my arms again, pull the arrow back, follow my chosen balloon for a few moments as it drifts lazily through the air, then fire. With a loud *pop*, bright green paint shoots out and splatters across two walls, the floor, the ceiling, and both of us. Gemma shrieks and jumps backward. I laugh as I wipe green paint off my goggles. "I told you to wear old clothes, didn't I?"

"You did. I'm glad I listened." Gemma pulls her arm back as a knife forms between her thumb and forefinger. While she looks around for a balloon to aim at, I free my arrow from the wall it's embedded in and let it vanish. As I skip back to Gemma's side, she aims for a balloon behind me. Her arm flashes forward, and purple paint explodes everywhere. She

squeals again, then laughs and says, "That was oddly satis-
fying."

"I know!" I get as far back as I can, choose a blue balloon,
and line up my second shot. "Where are Perry and Ned this
afternoon?"

"Perry had some extra training. Ned was being weird. He
said he doesn't want to see you at the moment."

"Oh." I try not to be offended by that comment and shoot
the balloon instead.

When it's safe to open our mouths again, Gemma wipes a
hand across hers before saying, "Don't worry about him. It
took him months before he was comfortable around me. I'm
sure he's still just getting used to you. He's strange like that."

"Okay."

"Yeah." She pulls a throwing star from the air this time.
"What's the smoky white stuff in some of the balloons?"

"Mini tornado charms. I thought the wind blasting out of
them might create some cool patterns in the wet paint."

"That sounds ... a little bit destructive. I'm going to leave
those ones to you." She flicks her wrist forward, and pink paint
flings itself across the room a second later.

"What happened at the Guild today?" I ask as I reach for a
knife. "Anything exciting?"

"Not really. Some lessons, some training. Lily and Rosa
were absent, but I suppose that's expected given that Saskia was
their best friend. Oh, there was something interesting." She
ducks her head as I aim at a red balloon. Red paint adds itself
to our canvas, and Gemma continues. "Some genius inventor
guy has finally figured out what combination of spells to apply

to the replay devices so they can now play sound. Apparently these spells have been in the testing phase over the past few months, but now they're ready to sell to the public." She wipes her paint-splattered hands on her pants and reaches into the air for an arrow. "Your friendly mentor read the letter to us this morning. There are teams going around to all the Guilds to add these spells to the surveillance and assignment replay devices. I think they're coming to us tomorrow."

"I'm sure Olive had something negative to say about that."

"Of course. She said, 'I wonder how much we have to pay this teenage know-it-all to add sound to the assignments that are painful enough to watch as it is.'"

I shake my head and laugh. "She is so predictable. And that was an excellent impersonation, by the way."

"Thank you." Gemma pulls her arm back, then throws the arrow at an orange balloon.

We finish up all the paint balloons before I finally pull a throwing star from the air and aim at one of the tornado balloons. "I'm not quite sure what's going to happen with this one, so maybe just … brace yourself." Gemma nods, raises her fists, and bends her knees slightly, as though preparing to fight off a great force. My hand snaps forward, the balloon pops, and a great gust of wind swirls around us. I throw my hands out to keep from falling as the wind spins me around and my ponytail flaps wildly around my face. I can't see anything, I can barely breathe, and I'm wondering if this was a gigantic mistake.

Then the wind vanishes. Gemma and I stumble to a halt and grab onto each other. "Whoa," she says. "Don't do that again. I think one was enough."

I nod, looking around the room. The tornado wind has spun streaks of color around the room so that the splatters all appear to point in the same direction, one color bleeding into the next in an infinite spiral.

After admiring our work, Gemma and I head to my bathing room to clean up. "Oh, I didn't realize my mom was trying to get hold of me," Gemma says after washing her hands and fishing her amber out of the safety of her pocket. She frowns at the screen, then sucks in a shocked breath.

"What? Is something wrong?"

"Oh no," she murmurs. "This is bad. This is really bad." She looks up. "Remember I said Lily and Rosa weren't at the Guild today? It's because they both started getting sick last night. Healers managed to slow down the symptoms, but they both ..." Gemma's voice catches as a sheen of tears appears over her eyes. "They passed away this morning."

* * *

"I leave for one weekend," Ryn says, "and people wind up dying from a disease no one's ever heard of while my little sister is accused of being the one spreading this deadly disease."

I hug a cushion to my chest as though it's the only thing holding me together. "Yes. This is why you shouldn't leave." I clear my throat to try to rid my voice of its wobble. "I hope your weekend was better than ours."

"It was actually two and a half weeks, but yes, it was much better than the weekend you and Dad had."

"I'm so sorry," Vi says. "I wish communication was easier

through the Kaleidos shimmer. We would have come back immediately if we'd known."

"It wouldn't have made much difference," Dad says, returning from the kitchen with a tray of food. It's nothing spectacular, just a few snack items he's quickly gathered together. Normally I'd be happy with this kind of dinner, but right now I feel too ill to eat anything.

"Dad's right," I say as he places the tray of food on the coffee table between the four of us. "You don't work at the Guild anymore, and Ryn isn't allowed anywhere near the case, so it's not as though either of you could do anything to help."

"I may not be allowed near the case, but that doesn't mean I can't gather information so we know at least *some* of what's going on."

I look up from my spot on the floor. "What did you hear today?"

"It wasn't only those two girls who died. One of the night guards and one of the Fish Bowl setting designers, both of whom danced with Saskia at the ball on Friday night, also fell ill last night and passed away."

No, I wail silently. *Not another two people.* I release a shuddering breath and say, "So ... this disease is spread by touch then? And it doesn't act immediately. People become sick a day or two later. So by the time we know who we shouldn't be touching, it's too late."

"Seems to be that way," Ryn says.

"This could be catastrophic," Vi whispers. "This disease is going to spread quickly. Exponentially. Every Guild member and their families could be wiped out within weeks."

Ryn grasps her hand. "You need to go back to Kaleidos. I don't care that the time difference is the other way around at the moment. You need to be somewhere safe, where this disease can't—"

"Okay, let's not panic about this," Dad says. "Healers are working nonstop to figure out a cure for this thing. They've already managed to slow it down somewhat, so they're on the right track. I'm sure it won't be long before they create a cure or an antidote or something."

I shake my head and murmur, "You can't be sure of anything."

"Well, at least I'm looking on the bright side instead of using words like 'catastrophic.'"

"Someone needs to visit those witches," I say. "If they're the ones who made this spell, then they probably know the cure."

"I heard something about that too," Ryn says. "In the lunchtime queue in the dining hall. Someone was telling Councilor Merrydale that his team searched every tunnel in the area you told him about, but no one found any hint of a witch."

My grip on the cushion tightens. "That can't be right. I didn't just imagine them." I stare at the food that no one's eating. "I suppose it has been several days since I saw them. Perhaps they've left already. Or maybe those guardians didn't look in the right place."

"Maybe," Ryn says, but he sounds unsure. As if he doubts the existence of these witches in the first place. I'm about to argue that I did *not* simply make them up when Vi interrupts.

"Why start with that girl in particular? Was it a random

choice, or a calculated move?" She turns to me. "What was her name again?"

"Saskia Starkweather."

"Saskia Starkweather," Ryn repeats slowly.

"Sounds familiar," Vi says. "Oh." She sits up a little straighter. "Back when Ryn and I were trainees, the head Councilor at the time was named Starkweather. She died in the Guild explosion. I wonder if Saskia was a relative of hers."

"Should be easy enough to find out," Ryn says.

"Just don't let anyone know you're looking into this case," Dad warns.

"Genealogy records are public. I won't need permission to see them."

Dad nods, and the four of us stare at the food for a while. "Somebody needs to eat something," Dad says eventually.

"I'm not hungry," I say.

"Cal, you need to eat."

"You didn't bring plates, Dad," Ryn says.

Dad lets out a long-suffering sigh as he stands. "I didn't think we'd need them, but if you insist."

As Dad leaves the room, Ryn leans closer and lowers his voice. "I know we're all thinking it, so one of us may as well say it out loud. Is *he* the one doing this? Has he been waiting all this time to make his move?"

I know without a doubt that the 'he' we're talking about is Chase. "You're right," I say, knowing this is not the time for secrets. "I have been wondering if it's him. He ... he was there that night."

"*What?*" Ryn and Vi's furious whispers coincide.

"Yes. I saw him in the ballroom, but I lost sight of him before I could get close enough to speak to him."

Ryn looks at Vi, then back at me. "That's too much of a coincidence. He must be involved somehow."

"Maybe," I say. "Maybe not."

"How could he *not* be involved?"

"I don't know, but …"

Ryn rolls his eyes. "Right. The two of you were 'friends' so you don't want to consider him capable of doing something this terrible."

"I don't want to believe he could do it either," Vi says quietly.

"But he could," Ryn says. "And he has. He's killed many, many Guild members in the past. Don't forget who he really is."

"Who he *was*," Vi points out. "He may not be that person anymore."

Ryn shakes his head. "We need to go to the Council."

"And tell them what?" I demand. "That Vi and I have seen Lord Draven? Who's going to believe us? They'll think we're—"

Dad walks back in then. Vi grabs an apple from the table, as though that was the reason she was leaning forward. Ryn scratches his ear. I try not to look guilty.

"Perhaps we should talk about something else," Dad suggests as he places a pile of small plates on the table. "This is all getting very depressing." He takes a seat and turns to Ryn and Vi. "Have you thought of any names for the baby?"

CHAPTER THIRTEEN

I'M CLAWING MY WAY THROUGH DARK WATER WITH A serpentine beast chasing me. I can see the edge of the pool, but my arms move in slow motion. The serpent is catching up. I know it; I can sense it. My fingers reach for the edge of the pool, almost there, *almost* there. They graze the edge—and something bites down on my ankle, tugging me back into the depths. I scream in pain and terror, my voice lost in a stream of bubbles. A hand wraps around my wrist and tugs upward. With a great splash, I'm pulled from the water. As I lie dripping wet on the stone floor, looking up at my rescuer, I realize that this is just another nightmare. With the realization, the pain fades away. The edges of the dream become fuzzy, and the person kneeling beside me comes into focus.

"Piker's Inn on Ratafia Island," Gaius says quickly. "If you remember nothing else when you wake up, remember that. Piker's Inn on Ratafia Island. Tell Chase."

I blink at him as he becomes clearer. Why does this part of the dream seem so much more real than everything else? "This is a crazy question," I say, "but are you real?"

Gaius looks startled. "You're still asleep. You're still here."

"I ... I know."

"Yes, yes, I'm real," he says hurriedly. "It's a Griffin Ability. One of the many I've been forced to take. They didn't realize I could use it to travel into dreams. I tried contacting Chase, but he has so much protection around his mind, it's impossible. I tried others on the team as well, but I don't know if they heard enough before they woke."

"This is crazy," I murmur.

"No!" He grips my hand. "It's real. I'm real." He starts to grow fuzzier and smaller, as though I'm being pulled away from him. "Piker's Inn, Ratafia Island!" he shouts. "Don't forget when you wake up! Please don't forget!"

* * *

I'm awake before my eyelids open. I sit up, pushing my hair away from my face and rubbing my eyes. This is the real world. This—me sitting on my bed, my blurry eyes focusing on the clock—is real. And yet ... the end of that dream felt more real than anything else I've ever dreamt. What if it *was* real? I lean over and pick up my amber and stylus from my bedside table. I stare at the blank amber for several more moments. Then, before I can change my mind, I write Chase a message.

You probably won't get this, but if you do, and you haven't found Gaius yet, check Piker's Inn on Ratafia Island. P.S. I don't want to hear back from you.

That last bit sounds rather childish, but I send the message anyway. Chances are that Chase won't even receive it, so there's no point in agonizing over the wording. I drop the amber onto the bed beside me and rub my temples. Dad will be off to work shortly, if he hasn't left already, and I'll be spending another day trapped inside a house that's beginning to feel smaller and smaller. Saturday, Sunday, Monday, Tuesday … and now Wednesday. My fifth day under house arrest. I wonder how long it will be before I start feeling claustrophobic inside my own home.

My amber vibrates and pings, and I open my eyes to see a message from Ryn. I pick up the amber and take a closer look.

Eleven more people dead. The Guild is under quarantine. No one here is allowed to leave. Those still at home have been ordered to stay put and restrict contact with family members. I told Vi to return to Kaleidos. She finally agreed for the baby's sake. She's staying on her own near the island for another twenty-four hours. When she's certain she isn't sick, she'll go through the shimmer. Will keep you and Dad updated.

With shaking fingers, I pick up my stylus and write, *Stay in your office and don't touch anyone. Don't you DARE get sick.* Then I jump off the bed and rush out of my room, calling

Dad's name. Based on the answering silence, he's already left for work. I run back into my room and grab a mirror from my desk. I'm about to call him when my amber emits another ping. I lean over the bed and see a message from Perry. My heart plummets as I read his words.

Gemma's sick. I'm so scared I can't even think properly. I don't know what to do.

A shiver of fear races through me. I drop the amber and press my hands to my face. "No," I murmur. "No, no, no." This is all spiraling out of control *way* too quickly. We need a cure NOW, dammit! If eleven more people are dead, then the healers obviously haven't found one yet, which leaves the witches as the only other option.

I rush to my closet and grab the first clothes I find: a pair of pants, a T-shirt and a hoodie. After dressing, I tug my boots on, then throw all the money I can find into my smallest purse and slide it into my left boot. I fetch my amber and stylus and open a doorway on the nearest wall. Screw the house arrest and the tracker spell. If I manage to get hold of a cure, it'll be worth whatever consequences I have to deal with when I get back. I imagine the Underground tunnel where Wickedly Inked used to be and hurry into the faerie paths.

The tunnel is silent when I step into it, but I know that somewhere inside the Guild, an alarm has just been triggered. I'm thankful for the quarantine. If it weren't for that, guards would probably show up here within minutes, and I doubt they'd give me time to explain that I'm looking for a cure. I hurry toward the witches' shop—exactly where I found it last week—but slow down as I near it. Something tells me it wouldn't be wise to run in there demanding a cure they may not even have.

I wander through the doorway and into the shop as if I'm merely browsing. It's properly set up now, with all the jars and bottles and bowls in their correct places, and candles and lanterns sitting at the end of each shelf. A table decorated with strings of flowers stands in the center of the room with more items displayed upon it. As I walk around, I smell rosemary, lemongrass, cinnamon, and other herbs and spices I can't remember the names of. The witches are nowhere to be seen, but the door to the back room is ajar, so I assume they're nearby. The gouge marks I noticed in the wall last time are gone.

On the table, I find the bowl with the dragon-eye rings. I bend to take a closer look. Each ring is made of silver, and the part that holds the eye is shaped like a claw. The eyes are different colors, but other than that, the rings are all the same. Saskia's ring looked exactly like these.

Having no idea what kind of dangerous spells could be on the rings, I refrain from touching them and move on. Near the back of the room, on a wooden podium, I find an old leather-bound book. The gold embossed title has faded with age, but even up close I'm unable to read it, given that it's written in a language I don't recognize. After looking around to make sure I'm still alone, I carefully lift the cover. It appears to be a spell book. Tiny hand-written letters beneath each title give the name of the spell in English, but the instructions are in another language. The accompanying pictures give me a good idea of what each is about, though. Disturbing pictures detailing strange, dark spells. Magic that should never be performed. Communication with the dead, piecing different body parts together to form new creatures, a summoning spell, a changeling spell, a—

"You again."

Startled, I almost knock the book off the podium as I swing around. "Oh, I'm sorry." I hurriedly reposition the book and close the cover.

"See anything you like in there?" the woman asks with a twisted smile, her black eyes seeming to gleam. She's the younger witch, the one I spoke to last week. Her dress today is deep red instead of black, but the bottom of the skirt seems to shift from fabric into smoke in the same way the other dress did. She watches me as she runs her tongue over her pointed teeth.

"No." I cross my arms over my chest so she can't see my hands shaking. "I didn't like anything in there."

"You're from the Guild," she says. That strange, deep vibration that rumbles subtly beneath her sweet voice sends a shiver up my arms.

"How do you know that?"

"I didn't know the first time," she says, "but I do now. You're wearing something that gives you away. Something that reeks of Guild magic."

My trainee pendant. I can feel the metal resting against my chest beneath my T-shirt. I remind myself that the pendant contains protective enchantments. I hope they're strong enough to protect me from this witch. "If the stench of Guild magic is so strong, then I assume you're aware that guardians were in the tunnels yesterday looking for you."

"Of course."

"Why couldn't they find you?"

She tilts her head and says simply, "We didn't want them to."

"So you used some sort of glamour or trick to keep them away?"

"Yes."

"But you have no problem with *me* finding you?"

She moves closer, and I take a step back. "You're not here to threaten us," she says. "You want something from us."

I swallow and remind myself that people are in the process of dying *right now*. I need to hurry up. "On Friday night, a girl wearing one of those rings—" I point at the bowl "—died. Her skin turned green and scaly, she became ill, and then … she died. Do you know what I'm talking about?"

"Ah, the dragon disease," the witch says. She walks to the bowl of dragon-eye rings and dips her hand into it, sifting through the rings. "Just so you know, these rings are harmless. They're simple trinkets. It was the client's idea to place a spell on one of them."

"Who was the client?" I ask immediately.

"That," she says, "is none of your business. Our client information is strictly confidential."

"Fine. All I need to know then is whether you have a cure

for this dragon disease. It's spreading quickly."

She gives me a calculated smile and says, "We had a feeling someone would come in search of a cure soon. How fortunate we cooked up a pot last night."

"A pot? So you have a lot of it then?"

"I have enough for your Guild, if that's what you're asking."

"Of course. I'm not going to save only a few and leave everyone else to die."

She smiles once more. "How noble of you." She disappears into the back room while I bounce impatiently on my feet. Moments later, she returns with a black pouch, the contents clinking together within it. "The disease begins with a potion made from Lisorna dragon venom mixed with a few other secret ingredients," she says as she places the pouch on the table beside the bowl of dragon-eye rings. "It's lethal to most magical beings. Contact with the potion is enough to begin poisoning a person immediately, but the symptoms only become visible and take full effect a day or two later. The first girl would have died the fastest, since she received the most potent dose—we dipped the entire ring in the potion. Green powder exuding from the pores is the first visible symptom. It changes the skin's color, subtle at first, which is why many don't notice until hours later, when the scales start to form and the nausea takes over. Death isn't far off after that. Then the disease spreads to anyone who comes into contact with the green powder, which contains the same poisons as the original potion."

I'm horrified by the witch's calm, detached explanation. "Do you not feel guilty at all? Knowing that you're responsible for the deaths of almost twenty people so far?"

She seems confused. "I'm not responsible for anyone's death. I serve my clients by doing my best to give them exactly what they ask for. It's up to them what they choose to do with the resulting product."

I let out a shaky breath. I open the pouch and find a number of small glass bottles containing a clear liquid. "How much of the cure is needed to heal someone?"

"A drop on the tongue will suffice. If a person's mouth can't be opened, then a drop injected beneath the skin works just as well."

"And how do I know this really is the cure for dragon disease? You could be selling me bottles of water."

She narrows her eyes at me and something seems to flash across them. With an annoyed huff, she returns to the back room. When she walks out again, she's holding a cage with a rat inside it. The cage looks like a miniature version of the cages Prince Zell hung his prisoners in. I immediately feel sorry for the rat. From a hidden pocket in the folds of her dress, the witch produces a tiny vial containing a translucent green liquid. She taps a few drops between the cage bars onto the rat, then returns it to her pocket. "Since the creature is small and the dose is large," she says, "it won't take long."

Every second of waiting is painful as I wonder if it might be too late for Gemma. I need to be certain this cure is legitimate, though, otherwise I may not be helping anyone. After a few minutes, the rat begins scratching. Its hair starts to fall out, and the skin beneath has a green tinge. Tiny scales start to form.

I rub my left hand, thinking of the mysterious smear of green powder that somehow found its way there just before

Saskia was killed. "That powder got onto my hand when the first girl died," I say to the witch. "That was over four days ago, so why am I not dead yet?"

"The cure must have already been in your system."

"But I didn't take any cure."

"Then it shall remain a mystery," she says as she allows a drop of the cure to fall onto the rat. "One I'm not particularly interested in solving." The rat rolls onto its side, breathing erratically for several more moments before the scales vanish. After another minute, its skin becomes pink once more. "Good enough?" the witch asks.

"Yes." I close the pouch and pick it up. "Thanks." I turn to go, but she grabs hold of my arm with a grip far stronger than I would have imagined.

"Not so fast," she says. "You haven't paid yet."

"Oh. Right." I place the pouch on the table and reach into my boot for my purse. "How much?" I'm willing to spend everything I've got if I have to. People's lives are at stake.

She gives me that calculating smile once more. "We don't deal in money here."

I hesitate. "Okay. What do you want then?"

She purses her lips and walks slowly around me, examining me as she goes. She touches my hair and I try to repress a shudder. "So pretty," she murmurs. "Like real gold."

"So … you want some of my hair then?"

"No. Perhaps another time. I want some of your blood."

"My blood?" A quiet warning ripples through me. It doesn't sound like a good idea at all to hand my blood over to a witch.

"That's the price. Take it or leave it."

Dammit. "What are you going to do with my blood?"

"Does it matter?"

"Of course it matters. What if you use it to weave some kind of dark spell over me?"

"So what if I do? Does that change how badly you want the cure?"

I press my lips together and breathe out sharply. She knows it changes nothing. She knows she can ask for anything and I'll give it to her.

"What we do with your blood needn't concern you," she says, her tone businesslike. "All that should matter to you is that your friends are dying. Are you willing to take a risk for them?"

Of course I am. Everyone I care about is connected to the Guild in some way, and they're all going to wind up dead if they don't get this cure—as am I. Which means that either way, whether I hand over my blood or not, I'm in danger.

"Fine," I say. "But do it quickly. I've wasted enough time here already."

The witch's hand disappears into the smoky folds of her dress, and when it reappears, she's holding a small knife. She takes my arm and pushes my sleeve back. I look away and clench my teeth as she cuts a line into my forearm. When I look again, I see blood dripping from my arm into a glass vial.

"*Are you crazy?*" A voice demands from behind me. In the next second, a powerful gust of wind sweeps through the shop, forcing the witch to stumble back and drop the vial. It smashes onto the floor, creating a splatter of blood around it.

"You pesky nuisance," the witch growls. "I should have finished you off last time."

I spin around, though I already know who I'll see in the doorway. "Funny," Chase says. "That's exactly what I was thinking about you."

"Oh, of *course* you're here," I yell as the witch conjures up dark smoke that transforms into ferocious pecking birds. Chase sweeps aside the birds—and half the contents of the shop—with more hurricane-like wind. As jars and bottles shatter all around me, I grab the pouch of cures and drop to the floor, shouting, "Why can I never seem to get away from you no matter where I go? Are you stalking me or something?"

He holds his hand up and moves into the shop, forcing the witch and her cloud of pecking birds back against the wall with a strong shield. "You call it stalking, I call it saving your life. Again." He sweeps his hand through the air in a quick circle. Snow descends, whipping into a blizzard within seconds. I feel a hand on my arm, tugging me toward the door. I stuff the pouch into my hoodie's front pocket, jump to my feet, and go with him. "You were giving your blood to a *witch*?" he demands as we run from the shop. "What is wrong with you?"

"I'm trying to *save* everyone!" I yell at him. "Dragon disease, remember?" I'm about to accuse him of being the one who put this entire plan together when it strikes me that it's highly unlikely Chase is one of the witch's clients, given the confrontation he just had with her.

"What the hell are you going on about?" He stops running and lifts a stylus to the tunnel wall. "I don't know anything about a dragon disease," he says as he writes a doorway spell.

The sound of flapping wings reaches my ears. I look over my shoulder and see the screeching flock of birds flying toward us. They morph together into a hairy beast with curved silver talons that roars as it leaps toward us. But instead of being devoured by this monster, it's the faerie paths that swallow us up as Chase wraps his hand around mine and tugs me into the darkness.

CHAPTER FOURTEEN

WE HURRY OUT OF THE PATHS INTO A MOONLIT LIVING room. I step away from Chase, looking around to get my bearings. Through one of the large windows I see a bright moon reflected on a lake, and there's that distinct magic-less feeling in the air that I've come to associate with the human realm. Whose home are we in? What time zone are we in? I don't have time to ask, though. Chase unlocks a door and pulls me through it—but instead of entering another room of the house, we're inside the faerie paths once more, running again, as though it's possible the witch might be following us.

I slam into the back of Chase as he stops abruptly. A moment later, a door opens in front of him. We run into an empty room with stairs and Chase slams the door shut behind us, locking it with the gold key I've seen him use before. I realize we're in the entrance hall of Gaius's mountain home.

"No, no, no," I say breathlessly, wringing my hands and ignoring the cut on my arm. It's still bleeding, but I'm not too concerned about it. It'll heal soon. "What are we doing *here*? I need to get to the Guild."

"We're here because it's safe."

"It isn't *safe*." I back away from him. "*You're* here." The hurt in his eyes is unmistakable, but I don't have time to regret my words. I take the key from his hand and turn back to the door. "I need to get to the Guild."

"Wait." He catches my arm.

"I can't *wait*! People are dying! Weren't you listening to me?"

"Calla, just calm down for a minute and—"

"Let me *go*!" I tug my wounded arm out of his grip and run back to the faerie door.

"Wait!" a different voice shouts, but I ignore it. I don't have time to wait for anything else. But as I turn the key, a hand that isn't Chase's wraps around my wrist. I try to pull away, but Gaius—Gaius! Alive and safe!—holds on. "It'll only take a moment." He closes his eyes and frowns in concentration.

I realize what he's doing. My magic, my Griffin Ability. He's giving it back to me. Oddly enough, I suddenly feel like crying.

"Go," he says, releasing my arm and stepping back. "And I'm sorry you found out about Chase the way you did. He didn't want it to be that way."

I risk a brief glance over my shoulder and meet Chase's gaze for a second. Then I pull the door open and run into the darkness.

Being a faerie door, it has a fixed destination, so I wind up back in the dark, quiet house beside the lake. I leave the key in the faerie door for Chase or Gaius to find, noticing as I turn to face the rest of the room that some of the furniture looks oddly familiar. *Not important right now*, I remind myself. With one hand still holding onto the pouch inside my hoodie's front pocket, I lean against the wall and write the spell for a normal doorway. Seconds later, I'm running into the Guild's entrance room, pulling my sleeve down over my bleeding arm.

"Whoa, hold on." Two guards, both of whom seem to be surrounded by a transparent, body-hugging bubble, block my way. "Didn't you hear about the quarantine? You're supposed to stay at home."

Another two bubble-covered guards join the first two. I wonder how they breathe inside those things. "No, wait," one of the new guards says. "This is the girl they want. The one who set off the house arrest alarm."

"Yes, that's me," I pipe up, pulling the black pouch out of my pocket. "I heard that more people were getting sick, so I went and found a—Whoa!" Four sets of guardian weapons are pointed in my face. I hold my hands up, being careful not to let go of the pouch. "A cure," I say carefully. "This is a cure. It's nothing dangerous."

"The Council will decide whether it's dangerous or not. We've been ordered to deliver you straight to them."

"Oh. But there's no time to waste. Can you take this—" My words are cut off as two guards grab me by the arms and drag me into the foyer. As I struggle to break free of their grip, I notice the carpet covering the grand stairway. Instead of its normal green, the carpet is black. The color of mourning. "You need to take the cure to the healing wing," I say with more urgency. "Please. I'll go wherever you want if you—"

"Our orders are to take you to the Council. Nothing more."

"But people are dying! Please!" My struggling turns to thrashing as I think of Gemma. I don't know where she is, but I *have* to get this cure to her before it's too late.

Behind the guards, I see a flicker of an image of Gemma. My flailing stills for a moment as I hastily slam a mental gate down around my mind. *Be careful*, I remind myself.

"Calla!" I hear a shout behind me as I'm dragged toward the stairs. I look over my shoulder and see Perry hurrying across the foyer. He must have arrived here this morning before they announced the quarantine.

"Perry!" I yell. I manage to twist out of one guard's grip for just a moment. I drop to my knees, pull a bottle from the pouch with my free hand, and slide it across the floor toward Perry. "Give that to Gemma," I shout as someone yanks me to my feet again. "Just a drop."

I'm lifted up and tossed over a guard's shoulder, and the last I see of Perry is him fighting off another guard before diving across the floor to retrieve the bottle. Which tells me that wherever Gemma is, she's still alive. I almost laugh I'm so relieved.

Instead, I grunt as the guard carrying me starts running up the stairs, his shoulder digging repeatedly and painfully into my abdomen. The other guards remain around him, making sure to keep their weapons trained on me. Anyone would think I was the biggest threat this Guild had ever seen. I suppose from their point of view, I very well might be.

I'm gasping for air by the time the guard sets me down in front of a door. I don't know which level we're on, but it felt like it took forever to get here. The guard knocks on the door, opens it, then pushes me into the room. I stumble forward as all the guards follow, their weapons still trained on me. Inside the room, I find seven members of the Council—and Olive. She's the only one standing. The others are seated around a long rectangular table with at least one empty chair between each of them—probably to remind them not to touch each other. In the center of the table is a replay device similar to the one Olive keeps in her office to watch our assignments.

A guard edges forward and lowers the pouch onto the floor beside me, then steps hastily backward as though the pouch might explode. Councilor Merrydale stands and nods to the guards. "Thank you. You may leave now."

"Are you sure?" one of the guards asks. "She could be dangerous."

Dangerous? I want to ask the guard what he thinks I might do, but I manage to keep my mouth shut and my eyes pointed forward instead of rolling toward the ceiling.

Councilor Merrydale seems to agree with me because, after looking around the table, he says, "With eight fully trained guardians in the room, I think we can handle her."

"We'll be just outside then," the guard says. As they leave the room, Councilor Merrydale points toward the empty chair at the far end of the table. "Please have a seat, Calla. You have excellent timing. We've been discussing your case."

"And your law-breaking," Olive adds. "I see you have as

much regard for house arrest as you have for all the other rules of the Guild."

I meet Olive's gaze for a moment before taking a seat at the table. It's the first time I've seen her since before the ball. Is she disappointed in me? No. Disappointment would imply that she cared in some way, and I know that isn't true. She seems almost smug. As if she always knew we'd wind up in this position. As if she's finally been proved right.

I'll try not to enjoy it too much when I instead prove her wrong.

I pull my chair in, then start speaking quickly. "Before you ask me anything, can you please send this pouch of bottles to the healing wing. It's the cure for the dragon disease. I know you probably don't believe me, and you can fetch a compulsion potion right now to see if I'm telling the truth, but in the meantime, please get this to the healers." When the only responses I receive are expressions of concern and doubt, I lean forward and add, "Please, I'm begging you. People are dying. This can save them."

A round-faced woman stands. "I'll take it. Kassia, you can get the compulsion potion." Another woman stands, and the two of them leave together.

After the door closes, Olive points to the replay device and asks, "Shall I proceed?"

"No, let's wait for the others to return," Councilor Merry-dale says. "In the meanwhile, it seems only fair to let Calla know where she stands at this point."

"All right," Olive says with a nod. She doesn't appear to be bothered that I've interrupted whatever she was planning to show the Councilors before I walked in. She settles into her chair as though getting ready to watch a show.

Councilor Merrydale examines the papers in front of him. "There's quite a list of evidence against you, Calla. Each item on its own is circumstantial, but together, these pieces of evidence paint a rather damning picture. So, let's see." He frowns at his notes. "You were found at the scene with no other witnesses. There was powder on your hand, suggesting you touched the victim. The disease seems to be spread by direct contact, yet you're still healthy while everyone else is getting sick. A ring exactly like the one the victim was wearing—and from which the sickness spell allegedly originated—was found in your locker. And …" He shuffles through his papers.

"And the handwriting," the man on his left says.

"Ah, yes. The anonymous letter the victim received was compared to a sample of your handwriting and found to be almost an exact match."

"But that's impossible," I interrupt before I can stop myself.

The man who mentioned the handwriting frowns at me. "It certainly isn't. I checked the comparison myself."

"But—"

The door swings open and the woman who took the pouch of cures rushes in. "It worked," she says breathlessly. "It worked. I took the cure straight to Marina at the end of the corridor. She's healed already."

"Yes!" I want to jump out of my chair I'm so happy, but when the Councilor looks at me, it isn't with gratitude or joy or relief, but with something like fear.

"I still have to get to the healing wing," she says to the

others. "I'm going now." And with that she takes off, the door banging shut behind her.

In the ensuing silence, the remaining people in the room look at me with expressions of mistrust and uncertainty. *What's wrong?* I want to say to them. *Isn't this a* good *thing?*

They start whispering to one another. "Remember all those stories?" the man who mentioned the handwriting murmurs to the woman beside him. "The stories we heard about when she first applied here? I wrote them off as ridiculous rumors, but now I wonder ..."

"I know," the woman whispers with a quick glance in my direction. "All this talk of witches. Perhaps she *is* one."

Unable to stand an accusation like that, I smack my hand down on the table. "I am *not* a witch."

Olive, the only person who seems bored by all of this, says, "Witches have black eyes and pointed teeth. Of all the things Calla may be, a witch is not one of them."

I look at her, surprised to find her agreeing with me for once. She stares back with the smallest of smiles. A knowing smile. A smile that scares me. For the first time, something occurs to me: could *she* have done this? Could she have bartered with a witch for a dangerous ring that would kill a trainee she dislikes while framing a trainee she hates? But what about everyone else who's dying? She wouldn't want to wipe out the entire Guild, would she? Perhaps she didn't know it would spread. Perhaps that was a side effect the witches conveniently forgot to mention.

I'm trying to decide whether it's worth accusing her out loud, just to see her reaction, when the other Councilor, Kassia, returns. In her hand is a small vial; a compulsion potion, I presume. "The cure is genuine, Kassia," Councilor Merrydale tells her as she sits. "Pepper ran back to tell us Marina was healed before taking the cure to the healing wing."

"Oh. She didn't wait for confirmation?" Kassia gestures to the tiny vial. "That seems irresponsible. What if it wasn't a cure but a poison instead?"

Councilor Merrydale's voice is quiet as he says, "Marina was close to death. I suppose Pepper thought it worth the risk."

"Well, that's wonderful news," Kassia says, "although I'm not sure what it says for Miss Larkenwood's case that she knows exactly how to make the cure for a disease she supposedly knows nothing about."

I rein in my frustration and manage to keep from slapping the table again. "Please, Councilor …" I don't know her last name, and I suspect it may be rude to call her Kassia. "Please, Councilors," I say, addressing them all instead of just her. "Give me the potion and question me. Then you'll know it wasn't me who made the cure *or* the sickness spell."

Councilor Merrydale nods and reaches for the vial of compulsion potion.

"I don't think that's necessary," Olive says, standing and speaking loudly. "We all know that anyone intelligent enough can twist their answers to disguise the real truth. Nothing Miss Larkenwood says now, whether under the influence of compulsion potion or not, can convince me of her innocence. Once you've seen what I'm about to show you, I think you'll agree with me."

Oh shoot. What has she found? Is this why she's been

looking so pleased with herself? Councilor Merrydale considers Olive's request with a frown. He looks around at his fellow Councilors, and, after several nods and shrugs, he says, "All right. Proceed."

With a barely concealed smile, Olive reaches across the table with her stylus and turns the replay device on with a quick spell. There's already a marble sitting in the top, so an image lights up in the air above the device. The scene is of the Guild stairway. It moves by quickly, and I imagine the little surveillance insect zooming through the air above it.

"This replay was skipped over at first," Olive says, "because nothing about it is immediately suspicious. But after the audio spells were installed yesterday, the surveillance team went back through some older replays, just to check that everything was working properly. That's when they found this." The surveillance bug reaches the bottom of the stairway and flies across the foyer, stopping above two people standing close together. My heart drops like a leaden weight.

The two people are Zed and me.

My hands are clasped in his, and I realize the surveillance bug caught the end of our interaction. "Go," I hear myself say to him. "Just go before someone figures out that you're the guy who escaped." Then Zed turns and heads for the entrance room, and I walk in the opposite direction, making no attempt to alert anyone to the fact that a criminal is escaping the Guild.

Olive waves her hand, and the replay freezes.

Holy. Freaking. Screw-up.

She was right. No clever twisting of the truth can get me out of this one.

"That's not all," Olive announces. She removes the first marble from the replay device and drops a second marble into the hollow at the top. "After the audio spells were added to my replay device yesterday, I watched a few older assignments to check that everything was in order. I also happened to put in a marble from one of Miss Larkenwood's extra training sessions last week. I hadn't checked it at the time. I trusted she'd done the training she was told to do. But since she's shown herself to be ... less than trustworthy over the past few days, I decided to take a look at this one."

I twist my hands together in my lap, trying to figure out what I've done wrong. I've never missed an extra training session, and I destroyed the tracker band that showed Chase at my assignment last week. So what did Olive see that's supposedly so incriminating?

"I assumed Miss Larkenwood had returned directly to my office after her additional training at the ruins," Olive says as she writes the activation spell onto the replay device. "She did not. She took a detour and had a private conversation with someone. A conversation that will shock you."

My hands freeze in my lap.

No. Nonononono.

The scene is close up this time because it came from a tracker band, not a surveillance bug flying overhead. Zed and I are standing close together, separated only by the cell bars between us. We're speaking quietly, but the new audio spells on the replay device pick up every word. "You know what else, Cal?" Zed says as he places his hands around mine. "They're going to find out about you too. You know that. You won't be able to hide what you can do forever."

After a moment of hesitation, the tiny little me floating above the replay device says, "They're not going to find out."

"They will," Zed repeats.

Don't say it, don't say it, don't say it.

"Eventually you'll slip up, and then everyone in the Guild will know you have a Griffin Ability."

The replay stops.

All eyes focus on me.

And with a shuddering breath, the world drops out from beneath my feet.

Voices surround me, hollow and distant. "It was never witchcraft or Unseelie magic. It was a Griffin Ability."

"Why didn't we figure this out sooner?"

"Her parents have obviously hidden it well."

"And she hid it too, making this number one on her list of crimes against the Guild."

"Miss Larkenwood." Councilor Merrydale's booming voice stands out amongst the rest. He rises to his feet, quickly hiding his confusion and disappointment beneath a hard exterior. "You've left us with no choice." He meets the gazes of his fellow Councilors, who nod to him in confirmation. He looks at me once more, and where there was once warmth in his eyes, I see only a cold detachment. "You are expelled from the Guild of Guardians. And for the suspected murder of Saskia Stark-weather, for aiding in the escape of a criminal, and for knowingly deceiving the Guild with regard to your Gifted status and Griffin Ability, you are placed under arrest."

CHAPTER FIFTEEN

BEFORE MY BRAIN HAS HAD TIME TO PROPERLY COMPRE-
hend Councilor Merrydale's words, the guards are back in the
room tugging me to my feet. They drag me out to the corridor
because apparently my slow, stumbling footsteps aren't fast
enough for them. Or perhaps my feet aren't moving at all. It's
hard to tell when my brain seems stuck in that room listening
to Councilor Merrydale's words on repeat.

There's shouting all around me as people emerge from
offices and lesson rooms and wherever else they've been hiding.
Some of the shouting is about the cure and some of it's about
me, and I hear the words 'Griffin Ability' thrown around
several times. I'm starting to regain my senses by the time we
reach the bottom of the stairs and the foyer. The guards, with
their arms hooked tightly and painfully beneath my arms, lead

me across the foyer toward the corridor that will take us to the detainment area. That's when I start struggling. I have no hope of fighting off all these guards—or every guardian inside this Guild—but I know I can't go down there. I'll be locked inside another cage, and this time my brother won't be able to save me. Not without breaking the laws he works every day to uphold.

I wriggle and kick and even try biting, but every time I break one guard's hold on me, someone else is there to take his or her place. I scream out in frustration and continue fighting back. I end up tossed over someone's shoulder again, tasting blood on the inside of my lip. Amongst the people streaming into the foyer, I see Perry and Ned. I go limp for a moment, wondering why Gemma isn't with them. Was I too late? Did I take too long getting the cure to Perry?

The world spins around and, with a painful thud and an "*Oof*," I find myself on the floor. Arms pin me down. Enchanted guardian ropes wrap around my arms and legs. I look up at the domed ceiling with the swirling enchantments I may never see again after today and realize there's only one way out of this. And since most people know my secret already …

My mental walls are down in an instant as my imagination sets to work doing what it does best—creating a scene that doesn't actually exist. High above me, the domed glass appears to shatter as a dragon dives through it, plunging down toward the crowd on the foyer floor. The shrieks and screams around me become deafening. The dragon pulls out of its dive seconds before hitting the ground, and I add in the rush of wind from its wings as it swoops by. The guards jump up, already shooting arrows into the air. Mentors and other guardians add their weapons to the mix, and the great foyer becomes a melee of sparkling weapons, shouting guardians, running trainees, and scorching dragon breath.

I struggle against my bonds as part of my mind remains focused on the dragon illusion. Unfortunately, these are the kind of ropes that aren't broken by simple magic. A guardian blade would do the job, though. I squirm out of the way before I'm trampled by a guard, then twist my hands as far apart as they'll go while still being bound at the wrist. Then I think of one of my knives and pull it from the air—just as someone else's glittering knife sweeps toward me. I jerk away, but not before the knife swipes at the rope around my ankles, cutting it loose. The person moves around me and slices cleanly through the rope binding my wrists before pressing something small into my hand. In the tangle of people above me, I can't see who my liberator is. The rope falls away. I roll over and push myself up in time to see Perry running away with a knife in his hand.

I close my palm around the tiny key he gave me, then turn and push through the crowd toward the entrance room. Maybe I'll get the chance to thank Perry one day, but now isn't the time. Or maybe he'll never want to speak to me again once he discovers I'm Gifted and have essentially been lying to him, Gemma and Ned all along. I make sure to keep the illusion going as I head in the opposite direction. In my mind, I see the dragon letting loose a stream of fire. I add some smoke into the mix to decrease visibility and help me get away without being stopped. When I finally reach the entrance room, I find there's only one guard left there. I imagine the dragon reaching around the doorway with a clawed foot. The guard rushes at it with a glowing sword.

I turn to the wall and open a doorway there with a shaking hand and stylus. Then I freeze as I try to figure out where to go. I can't go home. I can't go to Ryn's. I can't go to Raven's or the old Guild ruins or anywhere else I might normally hang out. A sob rises in my throat as I wonder if I'll *ever* be able to safely visit these places again. Everything has changed. Everything is ruined. I'm a criminal on the loose and the Guild will never let me—

"Hey! Stop her!"

I whip my head around and look beyond the imaginary dragon claw. A small group of guards has abandoned the assault on the dragon and is coming for me instead. The guard fighting the dragon claw swings around and lunges at me. I twist out of the way, picture a place no one in the Guild knows about, and dive into the darkness.

Seconds later, I stumble to a halt in the Underground tunnel outside Chase's old house. I spin around quickly, but there's no one else here. It's empty, dim, and quiet except for the sound of my gasping breaths. I sit down immediately and pull up the bottom of my right pant leg. I'm not sure exactly where the line is that Councilor Merrydale drew around my ankle, so I hold the tiny key just above my skin, hoping that will help. When nothing happens, I move it around a bit. Slowly, the thick line becomes visible. I find the point where the two ends of the line overlap. Feeling stupid, I place the end of the key on my skin and turn it, just as Councilor Merrydale did. The ends of the line spring apart, like an animated tattoo, before the entire line quickly fades away.

I drop the key and stand. I can't bare to keep still, so I pace the paved tunnel floor, walking back and forth past the front door that once belonged to Chase.

I don't know what to do.

I don't know where to go.

I press my hands to my face as tears well up. This is such a mess. Almost every guardian in Creepy Hollow now thinks I'm an enemy when all I've ever wanted is to be one of them. How did everything go wrong so quickly?

Somewhere behind me, in a nearby tunnel, I hear footsteps. Lots of them. I drop my hands and turn around, listening carefully. "… must be here somewhere," a voice says. "Split up and find her."

Oh crap. Oh CRAP! How did they find me?

My amber.

I don't have the best anti-tracking spells on it. It's not as though being tracked is something I've had to worry about since Draven's reign ended. I slip my hand into my back pocket and pull out the amber. I toss it onto the tunnel floor, and then, just in case there's anything on it that might give away how much my family knows about me, I bring my heel down on it, smashing it in half.

Then I run.

Blindly, from one tunnel to the next, with no thought for which direction I'm going in. The tunnels must be teeming with guardians, though, because no matter where I turn, I still hear their voices, their footsteps. And if these tunnels are all connected, then pretty soon I'm bound to run right into a group of them.

"Oh!" I turn a corner and slam into somebody. I push backward against him, slashing the air with a knife the moment there's space between us.

"It's me!" a familiar voice says, backing up with raised hands. "It's just me," Chase says.

My shoulders droop with relief, although I can't help wondering if I might be safer locked up at the Guild than in the company of the man once known as Lord Draven.

"Why haven't you opened a doorway instead of running mindlessly around the tunnels?" he asks.

"I didn't think I had time to stop and—"

"Come on." He takes my hand in one of his while writing a doorway spell onto the tunnel wall.

"No." I pull my hand away and step back as a doorway to the faerie paths materializes. "I ... I don't want to go anywhere with you."

"Are you serious? You don't have time to stop and open a doorway, but you have time to stop and consider whether it's safer to come with me or wait here until whoever's chasing you catches up?"

"I don't trust you," I whisper fiercely as footsteps grow louder and then softer; a group of guardians running along a nearby tunnel. "I know who you are and what you've done. I'd be crazy to go anywhere with you."

"Did I ever hurt you when you didn't know who I was? No. How many times have I saved your life?"

"Um ..."

"Exactly. You *know* I'm not that guy anymore. If you thought I was, you'd have set the Guild on my trail the day you found out who I am. Or you'd have told your mentor after I turned up at your assignment, or shouted it out at the Liberation Day Ball. But you've kept quiet. You're angry with me—and I don't deny that you have the right to be—but you can't honestly tell me you think I'm a danger to you."

"Stop telling me what I should and shouldn't be thinking and where I should be going!" I whisper-yell. I swipe at the moisture beneath my eyes, looking behind me as footsteps and shouts grow louder once more. As mad as I am at Chase, I have to admit that he's right. There's a reason I've kept quiet every time I could have told the Guild about him, and he knows exactly what it is: I don't believe he's that person anymore. But he *was* that person, and he *did* kill countless people, and just because I choose to go with him now doesn't mean I can ever forget that.

I see the first guardian run around the corner and I make my decision. "Fine. Let's go." I put my hand into Chase's and hurry through the doorway with him. As darkness fills the space around us, I keep my mind blank. Dim light appears ahead: another Underground tunnel, but, judging from the silence that greets us as we step into it, it's far from the one we were just in.

"Are you sure they have no other way of tracking you?" Chase asks, walking out of the paths and turning to face me.

"I'm sure."

"Okay." He turns and opens another doorway. "Let's get—"

"There!" comes a shout from nearby. Noise fills the tunnel suddenly, as though every guardian chasing me has just arrived. Arrows whizz past us. I flatten myself against the tunnel wall as Chase holds his hand up, raising an invisible shield. "How are they tracking you?" he demands.

"I don't know!"

"You'd better figure it out quickly," he says, his voice strained. "I may have a lot of power, but I can't hold off this many people forever. And if we jump through the paths they'll simply keep following us. They shouldn't be able to track you once you're inside the mountain, but I'd rather not risk—"

"Oh." My hand flies to my neck. "My trainee pendant. They must be tracking that." My fingers feel for the chain. I lift it over my head, my heart clenching as I silently whisper goodbye to this one last part of my guardian life. Then I throw it down the tunnel.

My hand is in Chase's and we're in utter darkness once more. Then another tunnel, silent again. "Give it a minute," Chase says, holding his hand up and listening carefully. A quiet pair of footsteps moves toward us, but it turns out to be a reptiscillan girl wandering along with her nose in a book. She looks startled when she glances up and realizes she isn't alone. Her gaze turns suspicious as she passes us, quickening her pace.

Chase lifts his hand and his stylus moves quickly across the wall, writing the words for yet another doorway. I follow him, forcing my mind back to that blessedly blank state where all I think of is the darkness of the faerie paths surrounding me. But the blank state can't last, and the moment we step into the quiet living room of the lakeside house, every weight of the past few days drops on top of me again. All the people who've died, my biggest secret out in the open, my guardian future ripped away from me, losing my friends, leaving my family to be interrogated by the Guild.

With a barely stifled sob, I walk to the front door, unlock it, and step out onto the porch. The moon is higher now than when we ran through this house earlier. Wisps of cloud drift slowly across it, growing blurry as tears gather in my eyes. I wonder if my guardian weapons are gone, or if I still have access to that one piece of the life I've now lost. The weapons are tied to guardian markings, but I don't have those yet, which means they're probably linked to my pendant in some way. So if the Guild destroys my pendant … I reach slowly into the air and try to grasp a knife.

Nothing.

I tilt my head back and squeeze more tears from my eyes. "Gone," I whisper.

Exhaustion adds itself to the weight I'm carrying. Where I couldn't bear to keep still earlier, now even standing feels like too much of an effort. I move to the side of the porch and sit down, pulling my knees up to my chest and leaning against the railing.

Chase walks onto the porch and stares at the lake. "Those were guardians who were after you," he says quietly. "What happened?"

I press my lips together as hot tears travel down my cheeks. "They know about my Griffin Ability," I murmur. "They expelled me."

I sense Chase turning to look at me, but I keep my eyes pointed at the floor in front of my feet. "Calla, I'm—"

"Don't." I don't want to hear anyone say they're sorry. It makes no difference. It doesn't fix anything.

He walks to the other side of the porch and back. He rubs his neck. He looks at me again, but says nothing. I guess he can't figure out what to say. I don't ask him to leave. I don't ask him to stay. I want both. Neither. I want him to fix this unfixable mess so I can go back to the life I've always wanted. The life I came so close to getting. No one can fix this, though. Not even him.

Finally Chase lowers himself to the floor. He leans back against the wall beside the front door. He stares at the lake, and I stare at the floor, and the only sound is the occasional whisper of leaves rustling against each other in the nearby trees. I run my tongue along the cut on the inside of my lip as silent tears continue to wet my cheeks. I feel brittle and alone, and all I want is someone's arms around me, promising me that everything will be okay. But it seems I'll never have anything I truly want.

More silence. More tears. The moon climbs a little higher.

"I really liked you," I whisper after an indeterminate amount of time has passed. "Why did you have to turn out to be … *him*?"

He rubs a hand over his face and says, "I'm sorry. I wish every day that I wasn't. I wish I could go back and choose a different path."

I wipe my tears away and wrap my arms around my legs. Quietly I ask, "How can you live with what you've done?"

His jaw tenses. He takes a shuddering breath. "With great difficulty." He presses his trembling lips together, and when he turns his head the other way, I wonder if it's to hide tears. "There is blood on my hands that can never be washed off," he says in a raspy voice. "I will spend the rest of my life trying to make up for what I've done, and it will never be enough."

No, I think to myself. *It won't be.* How can one person ever make up for that much wrong?

Appearing to have his emotions under control, he looks back out at the lake again. There are so many things I want to ask him. So many things I want to understand. And talking about him is easier than talking about me. "You're a halfling," I say. "Why do you look like a faerie?"

He turns his gaze to me and says, "It's simple. The pale color in my hair is a result of bleach. The pale color in my eyes is due to contact lenses. I could never find quite the right color to match my hair, but this seemed close enough."

"Contact lenses? Those things humans put in their eyes to help them see better?"

"Yes. They aren't only to correct vision. Some are colored. It's a simple camouflage faeries wouldn't expect."

I watch him for a moment, then say, "I want to see your real eyes."

Without a word, he stands and goes back into the house. He walks out a minute later and, instead of returning to his spot against the wall, he sits in front of me, close enough that I can properly see his face, but leaving a comfortable amount of space between us. He looks into my eyes, and I look into his. They're a warm, rich brown. These are the eyes I saw behind the panther mask at the Liberation Ball. These are *his* eyes.

"No more deception," he says.

I nod. "No more deception." I hug my knees closer and say, "Tell me the truth. All of it."

"All of it? We may be here for some time."

I shrug and try to push my sadness aside. "It doesn't matter. I have nowhere else to go."

CHAPTER SIXTEEN

MY NAME IS NATHANIEL AARON CHASE. I WAS BORN IN THE human realm twenty-eight years ago to a faerie mother and a human father. Her name was Angelica, and she disappeared not too long after I was born. After my dad recovered from his broken heart, he met and married the woman who became my real mother.

I lived a sheltered life. I had no siblings, and my parents provided me with pretty much anything I wanted. I wouldn't say I turned out to be a spoiled brat, but I certainly knew nothing about suffering. I was innocent, naive, and I'd never had to make a difficult choice in my life. Then one night a faerie girl showed up in my bedroom, and everything changed.

I was totally unprepared for the world I discovered. This world of magic where almost anything I'd thought impossible suddenly became possible. I thought it was amazing at first, the forest and the colors and the creatures and the spells. And the faerie girl—Violet—was even more incredible. I fell for her quickly. I even thought I loved her.

But things went wrong almost immediately. There was a prince, an Unseelie prince, and he wanted things he shouldn't want. He wanted his mother's throne, he wanted an army of Gifted fae—along with the guardian whose special ability allowed her to find them—and he wanted the power that once belonged to the infamous halfling, Tharros Mizreth. This power was locked in a chest, and only Angelica knew where the chest was. She also knew how to unlock it.

So how did I end up entangled in this Unseelie prince's plot? Well, I had a connection to Angelica *and* to the Guild. I could help Prince Zell get everything he wanted. And once it turned out that I had magic of my own—and not only magic, but a Griffin Ability too—Zell used that as his bargaining chip. I had no hope of controlling this power that had suddenly awoken within me, but Zell introduced me to someone who could help. A girl who called herself Scarlett. A girl who was half siren and had no problem using her enticing powers on me or anyone else. I learned to protect myself from her influence eventually, but back then, lost as I was in this new and dangerous world of magic, I found her powers hard to resist.

I wound up stuck in the middle then, with the girl I loved on one side and the guy who threatened my family and promised to teach me about my magic on the other. It was a dangerous game to play, trying to keep both sides happy. Zell watched my every move, so I couldn't tell Violet about him.

And I didn't tell Zell that Violet was the guardian he was looking for. Instead I hoped to find my own way out of this mess before he could get his hands on her. But it wasn't long, of course, before Zell found out that I'd been lying to him and that she was the one who could find people. After punishing me, he told me I had to deliver her to him. He threatened my parents so that I'd have no choice but to comply. But I loved Vi, and I didn't want to simply hand her over.

I came up with a plan. It was stupid, barely a plan at all, but I thought it would be enough to keep everyone safe. In the end, it did, but Vi hated me after that. I knew she'd never trust me again. Zell refused to let me go—he wanted to use me for my power over the weather—and even if he had allowed me to leave, where would I have gone? He was right when he said I'd never belong in the human world again. Not with all that power waiting to erupt from me at any moment. There was no one in my old life who could possibly understand what I had been through and what I was still going through. I watched my parents from a distance, hurt and confused and heartbroken with no idea as to why their son had simply disappeared one day. But at least they were safe.

I was forced to watch Zell's plan coming together. I was even forced to help bring in some of the Gifted people he was hunting down. Not you, though I remember seeing you there. I remember looking into that dungeon and hating it. Hating myself for being part of it and doing nothing to stop it. When I could take it no longer, I ran. I had no plan at all. I simply left. I cast some protective spells around my parents' house, and then I fled into Creepy Hollow, looking for Vi. She was my last hope. I knew she hated me, but I had nowhere else to turn, and I hoped she would hear me out and somehow forgive me.

She didn't. She told me she never wanted to see me again, and it hurt more than I expected. The decision I made then changed the course of history: I went back to Zell. I shouldn't have. I should have gone off on my own. I probably could have made it work. I could have found some community of kind people willing to help out a halfling still learning about his terrifyingly destructive power over the weather.

Or perhaps not. I'll never know.

I didn't believe I could do it on my own. I thought Zell and Scarlett were the only ones left who could help me. So I returned to the Unseelie Court, hoping Zell hadn't noticed my brief disappearance. He had, though. He dragged me off to the human realm, to my parents' house, where he easily broke through the protection I'd put around them. Then he murdered my parents while I was forced to watch.

Something inside me broke that day. I had nothing left to fight for. On the one hand, I had my unbearable grief, and on the other, my boiling hatred for Zell—and for Violet, who could have prevented this by forgiving me and taking me back into her life. It seemed to me I had a choice: death or revenge. Unfortunately for the entire fae realm, I chose revenge. I kept my mouth shut and did everything Zell told me to. In order to gain his trust once more, I finally told him where Angelica was hiding, in the center of a labyrinth she'd built to keep the chest of power hidden. Then I helped Zell find the last griffin disc. To him, I seemed like a loyal servant.

But in the end, when we opened the chest, I killed him and

took all of that power into myself. And the plan that I'd carefully and secretly been putting into place, the plan that only Angelica knew about, began to unfold. The Creepy Hollow Guild exploded because of a device Violet had unknowingly planted there for me. The Gifted army was now mine to control—with an enchanted mark I placed on everyone's palm—and one of those Gifted fae started the enchanted fire. The powerful winds I set in motion helped to spread the fire quickly. We attacked the Unseelie Palace, the Seelie Palace, all the Guilds across the realm. By morning, our world had changed completely. Everyone knew of The Destruction and Lord Draven.

There was so much power contained within me. Everything was so easy. I could do *anything*. But there was something else that was different aside from the increase in power. I didn't quite feel like the same person. As time passed, there seemed to be less of me and more of ... *him*. Tharros. His ideals and his desires. In the beginning, my plan had been about destroying Zell's world. Destroying Violet's world. Pain and the desire for revenge had led me there. But once that ancient power was within me, influencing me, taking over, I wanted more. I wanted our entire realm to kneel at my feet. I wanted the *human* realm to kneel at my feet. And that didn't come from me—it came from him.

Scarlett noticed the change first. Before I did, in fact. It worried her. After Zell killed my parents, we'd become friends of sorts. Well, I'm not sure 'friend' is the right word, but we looked out for each other. I admitted to her that I wasn't as loyal to Zell as I let on, and she confessed that she'd made a mistake becoming involved with him and his horrible schemes. She confessed her guilt at helping Zell get hold of *me*. She didn't quite appreciate the way I took Zell down, though. After The Destruction, she told me I was even worse than him. Angelica said I should have killed her for making a comment like that, but it was early on still; I hadn't become quite that heartless yet. Scarlett left soon after that. I could have put more effort into tracking her down, but it didn't seem worth it. I think a tiny part of me still cared enough to let her go.

And so my reign continued. Angelica stayed by my side through everything, as we rebuilt the Guilds and the Unseelie Palace for our purposes. As we hunted down unmarked fae and cast our brainwashing spells over them. As we threw the enemies we particularly wanted to punish into her labyrinth to be driven to insanity by the endless passages and the confusion spells. Amon was also there from the beginning, a trusted follower of mine since the moment I betrayed Zell. He did anything I asked. Looking back now, I don't remember much of it. I think it got to the point where there was barely any of me left. There was only Tharros and his power and his desire to rule over every living thing.

My memories of the end are unclear as well. Violet confronted me, along with the weapon I'd read about. The only weapon that was supposed to be able to truly destroy me. Well, not me, but this being I'd slowly become after fusing my power with someone else's. I'd read the prophecy. It said someone else was supposed to kill me, and I'd already marked that someone else, so I was convinced I was safe. Though I don't remember much else, I remember that feeling. The certainty that I was invincible.

Vi and I spoke, though I don't know what we said. We fought and that, too, is hazy. And then, right at the end, everything became clear—because she did what only she could do: She *found* me. The real me, beneath all that power I'd consumed. It was like waking up after a long sleep. Like breathing again after being trapped under water.

And that was the moment she killed me.

I don't remember pain; I only remember light. I don't know how long it blazed for, but when it subsided … I wasn't dead. I was lying on the grass near a waterfall. The Infinity Falls, I discovered later on. I remembered the eternity necklace—the necklace I'd stolen from Vi—and found it still around my neck. The white teardrop pendant was cracked down the middle, and I was fairly certain it had performed the job it was created for: It saved me from death.

But I was me again, and I remembered all the atrocities I had committed, and the weight of my countless wrongdoings was almost too much to bear. How unfair was it that this second chance at life had been given to *me*, a selfish coward who'd turned the world into a terrible place, rather than someone else far more worthy? I wanted to end my life. I came close to doing it, but as torturous as I found my waking moments, I was too afraid of death to choose that route.

I dragged myself through life for those first few weeks, existing more than living. So many fae were putting the scraps of their lives back together then; I was just one more struggling, homeless, broken-hearted person, surviving on handouts from the very people I had forced into hiding during my reign. Slowly, as if it was a subconscious idea rather than an intentional plan, I made my way back to Angelica's labyrinth. I didn't know what had happened to her. She'd been living at the Unseelie Palace, and, from the bits of information I'd picked up, almost everyone there had been arrested. When I found her labyrinth deserted, I assumed she had met the same fate. I continued on until I reached her chamber in the center, where I found everything I could possibly need: stores of food, money, spare styluses and other magical supplies. I took what I needed and left.

I holed up in an abandoned room Underground. I drowned my misery in the bliss of confusion spells and alcohol from the nearby pubs. My life had no meaning other than surviving from one day to the next. I wasn't brave enough to face what I'd done and move on, and I wasn't brave enough to pull the plug and end everything. And in that miserable, self-destructive state is where Scarlett found me.

She wanted to help me fix up my life and move on. I essentially told her that I wasn't worth her time and to get lost. She kept trying, but I made no effort whatsoever, so eventually she left, saying it was up to me to pull myself together.

I didn't. I passed out in a tunnel one night after too much drinking, and when I woke up, I was in a home I didn't recognize. A little Underground home filled with old fashioned furniture and the smell of paint. An elf woman with wisps of grey in her hair was the one who woke me up and fed me—and then told me that collapsing in a drunken state outside old ladies' front doors was a waste of a perfectly good life. I told her my life wasn't perfectly good. It was a black hole and I was happy to waste whatever was left of it. She told me to stop being an ungrateful child. That shocked me enough into telling her the truth, or part of it, at least. "I did terrible things after The Destruction. Terrible, horrendous things you can't even begin to imagine."

Not looking disturbed in the slightest, she leaned closer and said, "So did everyone else. Now get off your self-pitying backside and do something to make up for it. You can start by helping me carry this pot to Sivvyn Quarter's homeless shelter."

I didn't know what she saw in me. I didn't understand why she cared. But something about her tough-love approach made me get off that couch and help her. Her name was Luna and she cooked food and sewed clothes for the nearby homeless shelters when she wasn't painting. It turned out she was more familiar with those shelters than she originally let on. She was an orphan who married later in life than most elves. Tragically, her husband died early on in their marriage, leaving her alone with the baby they had adopted. She numbed her sorrow with illegal-strength pain-killing spells to the point where she became addicted. Due to her neglect, her son wound up malnourished and ill, and by the time Luna sought help, it was too late. He was too young and weak, and the illness finished him off within days.

Luna lost herself in her addiction, burying her sorrow where she could no longer feel it. It was only due to the kindness and persistence of a woman at one of these Underground homeless shelters that she eventually managed to crawl out of the darkness and piece her life back together. She turned to her art and found that she could make a living that way. I don't know if she ever forgave herself for letting her own child die, but she somehow found a way to move on. Years later, as a tough but kind old woman, she managed to help me do the same thing.

It was hard, so hard, facing every day with a smile when just beneath the surface was the burning guilt of all the ruin I had caused. And there were constant reminders of it at the homeless shelters we helped out at. Their purpose wasn't simply to provide food or a safe place for people to spend the night; they also served to connect people. Family members or friends who'd lost touch with each other after The Destruction, after fleeing into hiding or being captured and marked and forced to work for me. I always kept quiet as Luna chatted to everyone, passing on messages to friends of friends, helping people find one another. She had some sort of Seeing ability, dampened by her years of addictive spell use, but still there. Sometimes she'd See things about people's lives, things that would help them find their loved ones, or things that gave them hope for their futures.

And then, just as I came to care for this tough, gutsy old lady, I lost her. What she hadn't told me was that the illegal spells she'd been addicted to years before were the kind that slowly poisoned the body long after she stopped taking them. She knew she was dying, but she had hoped old age would catch up to her first. In the end, though, it was the poison that took her. She left her house to me because she thought it was about time I moved out of 'that dingy little hole,' as she called it. And just before she died, she gave me her artistic ability. "So you can always paint your way out of the darkness," she said.

And there was plenty of darkness after she died. I never allowed myself to be completely sucked under again, though. I felt I owed Luna that much. I waded through the darkness, pulled myself together, and contacted Scarlett. There was no way I could ever seek forgiveness from all the people I had wronged, but I could at least start with her. We had looked out for each other before The Destruction, but now we became genuine friends. I told her about my life before, and she told me about hers. Where she came from, why she'd run away, what her real name was. I told her the plans that had been slowly forming in the back of my mind. My plan to help people in the same way guardians did. To try and make up for all the wrong I'd done.

I wanted to fit in more easily than a halfling, so she helped me with my hair and eyes. And of course, neither of us ever mentioned the name Draven. Everyone called me Chase by then. It was the name I gave Luna when she asked. Calling myself 'Nate' felt like a lie. I wasn't that guy anymore. I never would be.

I started paying more attention to what was going on around me. I'd listen to the whispers in the bars and the clubs Underground. If something wound up stolen, I'd find it. If someone planned to hurt someone else, I'd be there to stop it. If guardians showed up, I'd keep out of the way, but often they didn't. It felt good to be helping people instead of hurting them. It felt good to make a difference. Initially, I worked alone, acting in secret wherever I could. But as time passed, I found people I could trust. People who had almost as much to make up for as I did. Somewhere along the line I became a tattoo artist as well. I loved drawing, and I needed an income—as well as the appearance of a regular, Underground day job—so it seemed like a good choice.

Years passed, and that brings us to the present, when a girl with gold hair accidentally stumbled into my life and became entangled in my dangerous endeavors. It began with a chance encounter but, in the end, I think we would have met anyway, one way or the other. In the beginning, you were just another person to protect, but you soon came to mean more to me than that. You were brave, honest, idealistic, strong. You were the bright palette of colors in a dark world. You told me your secrets, and I wanted to tell you mine. I wanted to tell you everything. But with a secret as great and terrible and ugly as the one I hid, would I ever have been brave enough to tell you? And if I had, would you have been understanding enough to hear me out without running away screaming?

We'll never know …

CHAPTER SEVENTEEN

CHASE'S HANDS ARE CLASPED TIGHTLY TOGETHER IN HIS LAP when he finishes. I wonder if he's ever told this story in its entirety to anyone else. It must be draining to relive it all. The pain and the suffering and the guilt. When we've sat in silence for a while, he raises his eyes and whispers, "Please say something."

Say something? There are so many 'somethings' running through my head, it's hard to know where to begin. "Um ... thank you?"

He gives me a half-smile. "I suppose there are far worse things you could say."

"It's just ... a lot to think about."

"I know. I've never told anyone all of it. Not in detail like that. Most of the time I just get on with life. I protect whoever needs to be protected and then move onto the next project or mission without allowing myself any distractions."

I play with the laces on my boots and ask, "Where did the name Draven come from?"

He looks down. On the back of his right hand, sticking out below his sleeve, is part of a tattoo I haven't seen before. "It's silly," he says. "It was the name of the street I lived on. Vi called me Mr. Draven Avenue back when I was just an assignment to her. When she didn't know my name yet. I chose that name so she'd know exactly who it was that caused The Destruction." He swallows. "That's how full of hate I was. I wanted her to suffer, to believe that everything I did was her fault."

I nod to show that I'm listening, but I don't know what to say to that. I know he isn't like that anymore, but it's hard to hear that these monstrous feelings were once the motivation for everything he did. "Um …" I clear my throat. "How did you find me earlier? When I was with the witch, and then just now, in the tunnels."

"Do you remember my assistant at the tattoo shop? She's been hanging out in that area, looking out for any of my old clients so she can warn them away from the witches. She told me when you went there the first time, last week. It scared me to know how close you were to danger, but at the same time I was so happy you'd come looking for me. Part of me thought you were probably only there to yell at me, but at least you weren't staying away anymore. I wondered if I should look for you so I could try to explain everything, but when I saw you later that night at your assignment, you made it clear you didn't want to talk to me."

"Well, I was still very angry."

"Yes. I noticed. Anyway, that's how I knew you were there earlier. My assistant told me you'd been inside the witches' shop for far too long. And then later on when you were in the tunnel outside my front door … well, you didn't think I'd leave my house unwatched, did you? I left a surveillance device there. I wanted to know who would come looking for me."

I see beyond his words to the real meaning. "You wanted to know if I'd give you away to the Guild."

He hesitates a moment, then says, "Yes. I didn't know if I could trust you not to. And I would have understood if you had."

I bite my lip—noticing that the cut from earlier is now healed—and shift my position on the floor. I'm not sure how to explain why I never gave Chase away to the Guild. I was angry and upset and confused, but something about handing him over didn't feel right. "Why were you at my assignment anyway?" I ask. "What did you want with that wolf-man? And what were you doing at the Liberation Day Ball?"

"That was all part of finding Gaius. I tracked down anyone who'd been seen in Saber's company recently. That's what led me to the wolf-man who was part of your assignment last week. I questioned him, and his answer—that Gaius was being held on Ratafia Island, though he didn't know exactly where— led me to the woman at your Guild's Liberation Day Ball. She owns Ratafia Island, and I needed access to all the documentation that details who owns which properties. She unknowingly told me where I could find all those documents.

"By the time you sent a message to me this morning, I had

narrowed it down to six different locations on the island. Your message confirmed that it was Piker's Inn, and I left immediately to find Gaius. The rescue mission was quick, and we were back at the mountain in under an hour—just in time for me to find out you were with one of the witches."

"And just in time for Gaius to return my Griffin Ability to me so that when my delightful mentor revealed it to a roomful of Guild Councilors, there was no way I could truthfully deny it." An ache expands across my chest as I relive that moment.

"Oh." Chase looks up as guilt crosses his face once more. "Damn. That was exceptionally bad timing on our part."

I shake my head and look out across the grass. "It wouldn't have made a difference, I suppose. She had a recording of me admitting it, along with a recording of another crime. They would have expelled and arrested me anyway. My Griffin Ability was the only thing that got me out of there, so I'd say it was exceptionally *good* timing on your part."

"Oh," Chase repeats, looking relieved. He watches me, but when I meet his gaze he looks away. He swallows and says, "Can I ask you something?"

"Yes."

"Do you think you'll ever trust me again?"

I lace my hands over my knees, considering my answer before giving it to him. "I don't know. On the one hand, it's so hard to look at you and imagine *Lord Draven*, the brainwashing dictator who now fills the pages of so many history books. But on the other hand, it's impossible to look at you and *not* remember him now that I know the two of you are the same person."

He nods slowly. "I understand."

I rest my chin on my hands and stare past him at the other side of the porch. There's a swing there, and for a moment I allow myself to imagine a different life where Chase is a normal guy and I'm a normal girl and we can sit together on that swing without a care in the world.

"Calla?"

I blink. "Yeah?"

"I know you didn't want to hear me say it earlier, but I really am sorry about everything that went down at the Guild today. I know how badly you wanted to be a guardian. I know this is a huge loss for you."

I squeeze my eyes shut before more tears can come. I breathe slowly until I'm sure I can speak without too much of a quiver in my voice. "I can't believe it's just ... over. My future. Everything I've ever wanted. And not only that, but having my Griffin Ability exposed. I'll be on the list by now for sure. At least I got away before they tagged me. They won't be able to track me, but they'll always be on the look out for me." I lift my head and cover my face with my hands as I groan. "Ugh, my mom is going to be so mad when she wakes up. This is why she didn't want me joining the Guild in the first place. Now my whole family's going to be in trouble. She ran away when she was supposed to tell them her vision, I turned out to be Griffin Gifted, and my dad's been hiding both of these secrets, so there are bound to be consequences for that.

"Oh." I drop my hands, realizing suddenly how worried Dad will be. "I need to let my dad know I'm okay. Or Ryn. Wait, why hasn't Vi found me yet? Oh, she might not even know about all of this yet." I shake my head and rub my hands over my face. "I'm so tired. I just want to sleep and forget for a while that any of this happened."

Chase stands. "You can stay at the mountain if you'd like. It's the safest place to be. Protected against magical influence and tracking and all of that. Vi won't be able to find you if you're there, though. And if you're not comfortable with me being there ... I mean, if you'd rather stay somewhere else—"

"No, it's fine, I—Gaius is also there, right?" Chase nods. "Okay. Yes, I'll stay there." Chase extends his hand to help me up just as I push myself to my feet. He ends up hiding his hands awkwardly in his pockets.

"Um, I can send a note with a messenger to your father," he suggests. "Old school style. We can't say where you are, of course, but we can at least let him know you're okay."

I nod. "Thank you." We walk back inside and Chase closes the door behind us. I realize that I'll probably never return to my own home again—that I essentially have no home now—and I wrap my arms around my chest to keep myself from falling apart again. As Chase pulls out the gold key for the faerie door, I look around and realize why part of this room looked familiar earlier. "This is the furniture from your old house Underground."

"Yes. Luna's furniture. It doesn't fit in with everything else here, but I guess I'm too sentimental to get rid of it."

"So ... this is your house?"

"Yes. I've had it for some time, though I don't use it much. It's similar to a house my parents and I used to stay at during vacations when I was growing up. I moved the faerie door here after I vacated the tattoo shop, but before that, this house was completely separate from any of my work. I used to come here sometimes to just … get away."

He unlocks the faerie door and we head through the vacuum of time and space to the entrance hall inside the mountain. We walk up the stairs and along a carpeted passage, where Chase opens a door to a bedroom. It looks similar to the one I wound up in last time after taking a nauseating trip back in time—four-poster bed, wardrobe, thick rug on the floor—but I can't tell if it's the same one. "Thank you," I say to Chase. "I don't know where I'd go if it wasn't for this place."

"Well, you're intelligent and resourceful, so I'm sure you would have figured something out, but this way you don't have to. One less thing to worry about."

I nod. There are already too many things buzzing around my tired brain without adding the stress of finding a safe place to hide for the night.

"I'm sure the Guild will be watching your family closely over the next few weeks in case you try to contact them," Chase says, "but I can probably organize a way for you to safely meet with them."

"Really? That would be amazing."

"It may take a little bit of time, but it's definitely possible."

"Okay." I rub my hands up and down my arms. The air is colder here than at home. "Why … why would you go to all that trouble? I mean, I'm sure you have plenty of other stuff going on."

"Well …" He takes a deep breath. "I've got a lot to make up for, haven't I?"

I'm not sure if he's talking about me specifically or the entire world, but either way, that's an understatement.

"And … um … " Chase looks down at the floor, then shakes his head. "Anyway, I hope you're able to sleep." He closes the door, and I'm left alone with my memories of the Guild turning on me and the knowledge that nothing will ever be the same again.

I go into the adjoining bathing room and clean the dried blood off my arm. Then I drag myself to bed. I have no idea where in the world we are or whether it's night or day, but I want to sleep, sleep, sleep and hope that everything is somehow okay when I wake up.

CHAPTER EIGHTEEN

PERHAPS IT WAS MY EXHAUSTION, OR PERHAPS IT WAS THE fact that all the mystery, shadows and questions surrounding Chase were finally removed, but I managed to sleep without being woken by nightmares of the past. I opened my eyes to find that my world had not magically fixed itself while I was sleeping, though I didn't feel quite as awful as I felt before I fell asleep. Chase was gone, but I wandered around until I found Gaius in an indoor greenhouse up another flight of stairs. As if sensing I was in desperate need of a distraction, he put me to work.

"Is this the right one?" I ask, holding up a large jar of clear liquid and walking between the rows of plants toward Gaius. He's kneeling on the ground beside a prickly bush with dark blue thorns.

He looks up. "Yes, that's the one. We'll soak the thorns in there first."

"Okay." I sit beside him and unscrew the lid. The liquid within smells unpleasantly sweet. "What does it do to the thorns?"

"It draws out the poison, leaving only the beneficial compounds. After the thorns dry out, they're then ground into a powder. You've probably used it before. The end product is called Blue Shade."

"Oh yes. I think my mom uses it in some of her sleeping potions." Sleeping potions that landed her in a prolonged enchanted sleep. Perhaps it's best she wasn't awake for all the drama that took place yesterday. She would have completely freaked out.

Gaius hands me a pair of tweezers. "Only the dark blue thorns," he reminds me. "If they're pale blue, they're too young. Drop them straight into the jar."

"Do you ever use the thorns as they are? With the poison still in them?"

"I don't. Chase, however, has found them to be useful in conjunction with a blowgun. They have a temporary paralysis effect. Great when you don't want your enemy running away from you."

"That does sound useful." The two of us continue removing thorns. After working in silence for some time, I say, "Thank you for letting me stay. I know it was … unexpected. I'll be gone as soon as I figure out a few things."

"Don't be silly. You can stay as long as you like. There are plenty of rooms, as I'm sure you've noticed. And I'll make you a key for the faerie door. I should be thanking you too, in fact. You passed on my message so Chase was able to find me. I'd probably still be locked up in Piker's Inn if it weren't for you."

"Was it very horrible?" I ask carefully. "They were making you take abilities from people, weren't they?"

"Yes. Not many. They located only four Gifted people in the time I was there. I'm not sure if we'll ever find those people again, so for now, those abilities have been added to our collection."

"Your collection?" I pull back from my task for the moment. "You mean you've taken other people's abilities as well and kept them?"

"Yes. Our collection of Griffin Abilities, all stored within various objects, is in a room downstairs. Oh, they weren't taken by force," he adds quickly at the look of horror on my face. "They were all freely given up. Not every Gifted person wants to be different, and many of them don't want to risk winding up on the Griffin List."

"But why do you keep them?"

"In case people change their minds and want their magic back."

"And you're not worried you might run into the same problem you had with Saber's time traveling bangle? Someone else getting hold of all of them?"

Gaius drops a particularly large thorn into the jar. "The only reason we had that problem was because Chase removed the bangle from the mountain. That's how people found out about it. He obviously shouldn't have done that."

"It still seems dangerous keeping them all in the same place.

What if someone breaks in here?"

"Well, good luck finding the right room in this giant mountain," Gaius says with a chuckle.

I return to my work on the thorns, thinking about the size of this place. "How did you wind up living in a mountain anyway?"

"It's been in my family for centuries. Ever since Tharros—" He cuts himself off. "Oh, um, perhaps I shouldn't talk about him. Given recent, uh, revelations, it might be a bit awkward."

"It's okay. It's not like it's a forbidden subject or anything just because of Chase. We should be able to talk about Tharros, and other history, without things getting awkward." What I don't add is that I'd rather talk about this than be left to depressing thoughts about my messed-up future.

"You're absolutely right, Calla," Gaius says with a nod. "We should be able to talk about these things. So, this place has been in my family ever since Tharros began his attempts to bring down the veil between the human and fae realms. People were building secret shelters and hideouts all over the place, and one of my wealthy ancestors decided to buy a mountain."

"As one does in times of uncertainty."

"Of course. He had a large part of the inside excavated so it would be habitable, which was a process that turned out to be rather lengthy. By the time it was completed, Tharros had been defeated and no one felt the need to live in hiding anymore.

"It wasn't used much after that. It ended up being passed down to my father, who kept his dragon hidden here because he didn't have a permit. After I lost my job at the Guild, I came here because I had nowhere else to go. That was back in the day when some of the Guilds had employee housing, so no job meant no house. Oh, careful, you almost got poked there. Here, put some gloves on. They're a bit big, but you can shrink them." Gaius digs around in the box of instruments, spray bottles and tubes sitting on the ground beside him until he finds a pair of gloves for me. "Then my father died in a dragon racing accident, so it was just me in this great big mountain. I did some odd jobs over the next few decades, but nothing that paid particularly well. So … that's when I wound up using my botany and potions knowledge for less than legal means."

"Oh. Really?" I finish shrinking the gloves and pull them on. "Are you serious?"

"I am. Illegal potions and ingredients and enchantments and all that. I even invented a few new substances that had never been on the market before. They became quite popular. I did pretty well for myself."

"That's … really … I would not have guessed that about you, Gauis."

"You're shocked. I can tell. But weren't you just saying we shouldn't feel awkward to talk about our history? Besides, I know your secret; it's only fair you know mine."

"Um …" If he's referring to my Griffin Ability, it doesn't feel as though it's on quite the same level as an illegal magic operation.

"Anyway, it all got messed up after The Destruction. I was away from the mountain when our dear friend Lord Draven started that storm within the faerie paths, so I had no way of getting back here. I went from having a fortune to being homeless. And that is when …" He takes a deep breath and stops pulling thorns, staring past the bush at memories only he can see. He swallows. "That's when I saw the real fruit of my work for the first time. I saw people who were nothing more than shells, barely existing, their minds utterly lost to their addiction. Lives ruined, long before The Destruction hit any of them."

"Gaius ..." I don't know what to say. All I know is that my simple question has led us into far darker and heavier territory than I could ever have guessed, and I don't know how to get us out.

"I know, I know," he says, still staring somewhere past me. "I should have realized, right? I should have known the lasting effects my substances and spells were having on people. And I did, to a certain extent. I had a vague idea of it in the back of my mind, but it was never *real*. I simply produced the enchantments and potions, that was all. Then I sold them to distributors. I never saw the end users."

"You don't have to tell me this stuff, Gaius," I say quietly.

With a sigh, he looks down at the jar of floating thorns. He tilts it to the side, examining it. "Yes, we can fit some more in here." He returns to his work pulling thorns from the bush, and I'm about to ask if we've moved on to a different topic of conversation when he starts speaking again. "I never sold another spell after that. It made me sick to even consider it. When I eventually got back to the mountain after Draven had been defeated, I set fire to my greenhouse and my laboratory. Destroyed everything. And then, after plenty of time pondering what an awful person I had become, I decided to build another greenhouse, fill it with plants that would be useful in everyday potions, and send the resulting herbs and powders and other ingredients to where they were actually needed.

"Chase and I met some time after I got that up and running. He'd been looking for me for months. He knew about my Griffin Ability from the information Zell had gathered on the Gifted, and he'd thought of a way I could use it that would be helpful to others."

"So he told you who he was, and you trusted him just like that?" I ask, my tone skeptical.

"He didn't tell me right away. But from what he said he'd been involved in, I suspected he was high up in Draven's circle. And it's not as though I was innocent. I had ruined lives just as he had. Lives like ... like Luna's." Gaius lowers his tweezers to the ground and screws the lid back onto the jar. Quietly, he adds, "I understood the need for atonement." He packs the bottle into his equipment box and stands. I get to my feet, brushing sand off the back of my pants. The box floats ahead of us as I follow him to another part of the greenhouse where a mirror berry bush is growing. "Anyway, that's how I wound up living in a mountain," he says with a chuckle. "Bit of a long-winded answer, but there you have it."

"Thank you for telling me. I appreciate knowing the truth."

"Now you know I'm not such a good guy after all," he says with a teasing grin.

"Maybe. Maybe not." I look at my distorted reflection in one of the larger mirror berries. "Maybe there's no such thing as good guys and bad guys after all. Not when the good guys fail to see what's wrong, and the bad guys are the ones who end up helping you."

"Ah," Gaius says as if he understands. He pats my arm awkwardly. "Your guardians are not the bad guys just because they failed you. They're trying to fix up all the mess in the world, and they don't always get it right. They make mistakes too."

"I suppose. That's just not the way I imagined the Guild to be." I clear my throat, deciding we need a change of subject. "Um, so, are we picking berries now?"

"Yes, just a handful. They're part of an experiment I'm working on at the moment."

Gaius fills a small bowl with berries, and I grab a few to munch on as we leave the greenhouse. Instead of walking back downstairs, we head right, and it turns out there's a laboratory next to the greenhouse. Half of it is filled with potion ingredients and equipment. The other half is dedicated to the construction of various gadgets. The counters are covered in cogs, levers, pipes and various mechanisms I've never seen before. "I guess you had to rebuild this as well after you burned the previous one," I say.

"Yes. I probably should have considered my options more thoroughly before setting fire to all of my equipment. I was rather annoyed with myself when I decided I still needed a laboratory after all."

He places the jar of thorns and the bowl of berries on the nearest counter while I look around. "So the greenhouse and the lab are up here. The next floor down is for the bedrooms and your study—which is like another greenhouse—"

"Hey, it's not that bad."

"Not that bad?" My eyebrows lift. "Gaius, one day the plants in that study are going to take over completely. They'll devour all the books and the furniture, and then they'll move on to the rest of the mountain."

Gaius scratches his head. "Now that you mention it, there is one shelf I haven't had access to since the dragonwing snapping pods matured. I really should take care of that."

"You should. Okay, so then below the bedrooms is the level with the faerie door and the mountain ledge entrance Chase brought me through the first time I came here."

"The kitchen, dining room and living area are down there too." He sets a balance scale down on the counter beside the berries. "And a storage room."

"Okay. Is that all, or is there more?"

"There's a lot more, actually, and there are other people who come and go, but I'm not sure I should be telling you about any of it, seeing as how … well, you might not be with us for that long."

"And if I end up in the hands of the wrong people, you wouldn't want them getting any important information out of me about this place."

Gaius gives me an apologetic look. "Yes. You understand, don't you?"

I nod, but I hate that that's something we have to worry about. I'm curious about this mountain and I wish I could see all of it.

"Hey," a voice says behind us. I look around and see Chase walking into the lab. "The secret ingredient you requested," he says to Gaius, handing him a brown paper bag. Now that he doesn't have a jacket on, I can see the new tattoo marking his right arm: a long feather, the top of which disintegrates into small black birds flying away.

"Oh, fantastic." Gaius opens the bag. I lean closer to get a look at this secret ingredient. I'm expecting a vial of liquid or a bottle of powder or a bunch of exotic herbs, but instead Gaius pulls out a glazed piece of bread in the shape of a ring. He takes a bite, then holds it out toward me.

"Um …"

"It's called a bagel," Chase says. "I introduced Gaius to them a while back. Apparently he can't survive without them now."

"Mmsogood," Gaius mumbles through his chewing.

I look at Chase. "And here I was thinking you were out on a secret save-the-world mission."

"Oh, I was. I just picked this up on the way back."

"Right."

"And while I was picking it up, I had an idea about how you can see your brother without anyone at the Guild knowing about it."

"Oh." He has my full attention now. "What is it?"

"You won't like it. You'll most definitely say it's too dangerous, but it will work. Trust me."

CHAPTER NINETEEN

I CLENCH AND UNCLENCH MY FISTS AS ANXIETY BUILDS IN-side me. "It's been half an hour."

"I know," Chase says. "We agreed we'd give it at least an hour, didn't we?"

"I know, but I thought he'd be here by now."

"Relax and have some patience."

"It's a little difficult to relax when we're hiding *inside the Guild*."

Through the dim light in the back corner of the library, Chase looks at me. "Nothing's going to go wrong. And even if it somehow does, you and I can easily fight our way out of here together."

I pull my knees closer and lean my head back against the wall. I let out a long, slow breath. "This is just a little bit insane. You know that, right?"

"Yes. And that's exactly why we're safe," he says. "Because no one would ever expect it."

"Let's hope not."

Chase's brilliant plan involved me using my Griffin Ability to help us walk right into the Guild this morning without anyone ever knowing. I was terrified to come back here, but getting inside was as easy as Chase said it would be. My illusion made the guard in the entrance room think he was seeing two of my classmates instead of Chase and me. To get safely to the library, I projected images of empty space onto the people we passed, which took a little more concentration but seemed to work fine. I kept my hood up to conceal my hair and face from anyone who might see us on a surveillance device, and we walked at an unhurried pace, despite my instinct to run.

On the way up to the library, Chase stopped a messenger dwarf and asked him to deliver a note to Ryn. Presumably the dwarf thought Chase was just another guardian because he took the note without question. Chase's initial plan was for us to go straight to Ryn's office and talk to him there. That would cut out the need for Vi to find me. But I didn't think that option was nearly as safe as meeting at the back of the library where hardly anyone ever goes. Ryn's office door is usually open. His team members come and go, along with other Council members. It would be far too easy for someone to walk in and see us. And even if we could easily fight our way out, Ryn would still be in trouble.

My right heel bounces up and down. "If we hear someone, I'm going to hide us with an illusion, okay? In case it isn't him."

Chase nods.

"What if someone's checking all messages going to Ryn? They wouldn't let this one through. It's far too suspicious."

"If the message came from outside the Guild, then it would probably be checked, but I highly doubt they're checking internal messages."

My leg continues bouncing.

"Calla." Chase puts his hand on my knee to stop my leg moving. "Do you really want someone coming back here to find out why the floor is vibrating?"

I roll my eyes—then I realize his hand is still on my knee. I give him a pointed look and he quickly removes it. "What if Ryn doesn't figure out what the message means?" I say. "Or maybe he can't get hold of Vi at the moment because she's on Kaleidos, so the message doesn't help him at all."

"He'll figure it out," Chase says. "It wasn't exactly cryptic. And your brother's supposed to be intelligent, isn't he?"

Something in Chase's tone tells me he doesn't think very much of Ryn's intelligence—and that's when I realize something. I turn and look at him properly. "You've met my brother." It comes out sounding like an accusation, which I suppose it sort of is. "I mean, aside from when he was captured and marked. You met him before that, because of Violet." I was so shocked to discover that Vi knew Chase back before The Destruction that I never asked if Ryn knew him too.

Chase keeps his eyes averted. "Yes, I've met him. We had a few ... less than friendly encounters."

"Well," I mutter. "This is just wonderful."

Chase seems to decide it's in his best interests to keep quiet, so we sit in awkward silence until we hear footsteps coming our way. We stand quietly as I let go of the mental barrier keeping my thoughts in. I picture the wall behind us and focus hard on pushing the image outward onto whoever's about to walk around the nearest book shelf.

Ryn. And Violet.

I pull the image back and raise the protection around my mind. They see us—and within a second, two sets of weapons are pointed at Chase. He raises his hand, but it's more of a greeting than a surrender. "Hi," he says. "I'm flattered, but that isn't necessary."

"He's right," I say, moving in front of him. "He isn't who he used to be. He helped me get away from all those guardians who were chasing after me, and he gave me somewhere safe to stay." My eyes move to Vi. "That's why you haven't been able to find me until now."

Still looking uncertain, they lower their weapons. The moment Ryn's bow vanishes, I run and throw my arms around him. "I'm so relieved you're okay," he says as he hugs me tightly. "But are you *crazy*?" He pulls back and takes hold of my shoulders. "What are you doing here? And with *him*! You!" He points at Chase, then takes in a deep breath, as though barely managing to hold back from throwing himself at the guy. "You should be in prison for everything you did. You should be dead. That's what was supposed to happen when you were stabbed with that—"

"Ryn!" I whisper furiously. "Stop it! That's not why we're here."

"It's fine," Chase says. "He's right. I should be dead or in prison. I should be suffering every day for all the pain I caused others. If guilt counts, then I'm suffering every day already."

I look back and forth between the two of them, waiting for some kind of explosion on Ryn's side and hoping it doesn't come. When neither of them says anything further, I step in front of Ryn again, trying to bring his attention back to me by answering his question. "No, I'm not crazy. I thought the Guild might somehow be monitoring your house. And our house. Or that someone might be following you to see if you met up with me somewhere. So it seemed like the safest place to talk to you would be here. And Chase ... well, like I said, he's different now. He explained everything that's happened since we all thought he died." I look over my shoulder at him. He's watching Vi, and she's staring back with a stunned expression.

"I know it will never be enough," he says quietly, "but I'm so sorry. I'm so, so sorry for everything."

"I thought I killed you," she whispers.

He presses his lips together before being able to answer. "I'll admit there were many times I wished you had."

"So ... you really are Nate again? There's no part of Tharros left in you?"

"There's nothing left of him. You may not have killed me, but you certainly eliminated his power that night. I, uh, I go by Chase now. It's my surname."

I turn back to Ryn. "So you obviously got my note then."

He holds up the piece of paper with the words 'She can find me now' written in Chase's handwriting. "This was a big risk," he says.

"I know, but no one else would have known what it means if they'd seen it."

"I guess not. Anyway, it worked. I contacted Vi immediately. She hasn't been at Kaleidos since this happened, so she was at home. She searched for you, then came straight here."

I glance at Vi again, now speaking quietly with Chase. I wonder if he's giving her the shortened version of what he told me. I look back at Ryn and say, "I … I'm sorry I'm putting you in such an awkward position by being here. I know you made an oath to the Guild and the Seelie Queen, and I'm a criminal and you're obligated to turn me in. So if you need me to stay away from you then I—"

"Calla, listen to me." He grasps my shoulders once more. "You are my sister and I will *never* hand you over to these people. You've done nothing wrong and you don't deserve to be hunted like this. If I'm going to stay on the Council—and I think I should, not only so that I know what they're up to, but so that I can attempt to influence things in the right direction—then it will have to appear as though I've cut ties with you. But you will always be my sister and I will always do everything in my power to protect you."

I nod in gratitude, blinking away the moisture in my eyes. "Thank you."

"If anything," he adds, "it's *him* I should be handing over. He's right here. *Inside the Guild.* Every logical, responsible part of my brain is screaming at me to stun him and drag him down to the detainment area. Then we'll finally have justice. We'll finally have Lord Draven."

I give him a sad smile. "But you won't. Draven is gone. This is someone else."

Ryn shakes his head, his eyes downcast and his brow furrowed, as if this is something he can't quite accept.

"Have they questioned you about me?" I ask in an attempt to bring this conversation back to the situation at hand. "Are you in trouble?"

"They have, but I'm not in trouble. I told them I didn't know about your Griffin Ability. Since we weren't brought up in the same household, it was a believable story."

"But didn't they compel you to tell the truth?"

"They did. And I chose my words extremely carefully."

"But ... surely you can't *lie*, no matter how careful your words are?"

"They don't actually know what you can do, Cal. Because of all the stories about strange things happening to people around you, and because of the dragon disease they've never come across before, they believe you have the ability to cause illness in others. As long as I kept that very specific detail in mind, I was able to truthfully answer that I didn't know you had that Griffin Ability."

I shake my head in disbelief. "So that's what it means to twist the truth. But what about that giant dragon illusion I created in the foyer? They must have realized it wasn't real."

"They decided it must be connected to the dragon disease, as if it was a hallucination people saw once they were sick. They thought you were trying to make everyone sick at the same time. After you got away and everyone had calmed down, they gave a drop of that cure to everyone, just in case you had somehow cast this unknown sickness spell over the entire Guild."

I close my eyes for a moment. "It makes me feel ill to know they believe all these terrible things about me. They'll never accept that I only ever wanted to be one of them, will they?"

Ryn shakes his head, his expression sad. "Probably not. They don't trust Griffin Abilities, so they'll never trust you."

Anger flares up inside me, but I push it aside. There are more important things to talk about than my current feelings for the Guild. "Is Dad okay? Have they questioned him as well?"

"Dad is ... in a little more trouble than I am. He'll probably wind up having to pay a gigantic fine for not registering you on the Griffin List, since the law states that he should have done that as soon as he became aware of your ability. But hopefully it won't be any worse for him than that."

"Ugh, this is all such a mess." I run my hands through my hair, pushing it away from my face. "All those poor people who died. And the real criminal is still out there! Why is the Guild being so *useless*?" Okay, so I guess I couldn't keep my feelings contained after all. "They're supposed to be the good guys who fix all the problems, and instead they're—"

"Shh." Ryn holds his hand up. Vi and Chase stop talking. All four of us look toward the bookshelves as footsteps approach the back of the library. I quickly picture an empty space here, wiping away the image of four people and their shadows. It's such a simple projection, but I concentrate fiercely on it, making sure not to drop it for a second. The assistant librarian reaches the end of the row, searches a shelf briefly before pulling a book out, and leaves without a glance in our direction.

We remain frozen until her footsteps are gone. "That was close," I whisper.

"Well, not really," Ryn says. "Your illusions are pretty good. I couldn't even see myself standing here for a while."

"See?" Chase says to me with a smile. "I told you nothing would go wrong with this plan." Then he goes back to telling Vi whatever he was telling her before the librarian showed up.

Ryn glares at Chase, as though he can't believe the guy has the audacity to agree with him on something. He puts his hand on my arm and lowers his voice. "Can you honestly say that you trust him?"

I bite my lip as I try to figure that one out. I told Chase I didn't know if I'd ever trust him again, but then I took him up on his offer to stay at the mountain, and I agreed to go through with today's crazy plan. "Since I met him, he's only ever tried to help me. He's the one who found my mother and returned her to the Guild, and he's saved me from death on more than one occasion. So ... I think I do trust him." With my life, at least, if not my heart. That will remain firmly guarded from now on.

With a resigned sigh, Ryn says, "Then I suppose I'll have to somehow find it in myself to trust him as well. Doesn't seem possible at this point, but I can work on it."

"Thank you. But Ryn ..." I look down as the fear and uncertainty I keep pushing aside threaten to overwhelm me. "I don't know what to do now," I whisper. "Everything I really wanted is gone, and neither of the options ahead of me are ones I want to choose. I could turn myself in, but even if the Guild does eventually figure out that I'm not the one responsible for the dragon disease, they'll still tag me because of my Griffin Ability. I'll never truly be free. Where will I work? What will I do? The Griffin List is public and no one will want to hire me for anything. And if I *don't* turn myself in, then I'll be on the run for the rest of my life. And there's still the question of what I'd actually *do* with that life."

"Hey." Ryn takes my hand in his. "You've been through a lot of unpleasantness in your life, and you've somehow never let it get you down. You can get through this too. You'll figure something out."

"But this is the thing I wanted more than anything else, and now I'll never have it."

After a pause, Ryn says, "Was it the Guild you really wanted, or was it what the Guild represents?"

I frown, not entirely sure where he's going with that question. "Isn't it the same thing?"

Ryn shrugs as he pulls his amber from his pocket. "I guess you'll have to figure that out." He looks down at the amber's screen and reads a message. "Someone's looking for me. I need to get back downstairs."

"Okay. And take a book with you so it looks like you had a reason for coming up here."

Ryn smiles. "Of course. And just one more thing." He leans closer to me. "I don't want to know exactly where you're staying in case I'm interrogated again, but ... is it with him?"

Terrific. Hello, awkwardness. "We're both staying with a

friend of his, so you don't have to worry about anything inappropriate, Ryn. It's not like I'm shacking up with the ex-dark lord."

"Look, I know you had feelings for him before, so I was just checking if—"

"You have nothing to worry about, Ryn. Didn't you say you need to go?"

"Right, yes. V, are you ready to go? Someone's looking for me downstairs."

"Oh, yes, okay," Vi says. "I think Nate—Chase—has told me everything important."

Chase nods. "And … congratulations." He gestures toward Vi's stomach, where a slight bump is now visible. "I'm glad things worked out for the two of you."

Ryn frowns. Vi smiles, then hugs me quickly and says, "I'm so happy you're all right. I didn't want to go back to Kaleidos until we knew for sure you were okay."

Chase steps closer to me. "Did you give Ryn the amber?"

"Oh, I forgot." I remove a thick rectangle of amber from my hoodie pocket and hand it to Ryn. He runs his thumb over the rough surface and raises an eyebrow.

"This looks like something you used to have, V."

"Shut up," she says. "My amber wasn't nearly that old."

"Yeah, this one's practically an antique," I tell them. "It's from long ago when they'd make two devices from the same piece of amber, and those ambers could only send messages to each other. It's so old that tracking spells don't work on it. I've got one and now you have the other, so we can safely communicate."

"This is yours?" Ryn asks, looking up at Chase.

"It belongs to a friend. He's been around a while. He's practically an antique too."

"Well ... thanks," Ryn says with some awkwardness. He takes Vi's hand.

As the two of them walk away, I hear her whisper, "That was so weird."

Chase looks at me. "She's right. That was weird. The last time I saw her, she put a sword through my chest."

I push my hands into my hoodie pocket. "You kinda deserved it, though."

"Yes," he says with a nod. "I did." He tilts his head back and stares at the library ceiling. "I wasn't sure if she'd be here. I wasn't quite prepared. So many things to say, so much to apologize for."

I feel as though I should say something now, but I'm not sure what. It's strange thinking of him and Vi and what they meant to each other once upon a time, years ago. It makes me feel small and insignificant, as though I'm standing on the outside of someone else's story looking in. It's the same feeling I had when walking into the Guild earlier, watching all these people who have the one thing I want but will never have: the guardian life.

"Let's go," I say quietly, walking forward and trying to shrug off this feeling of aloneness. "I don't want to be here anymore."

CHAPTER TWENTY

GAIUS AND I SIT IN COMFORTABLE SILENCE IN THE MOUN-
tain's living room. He's making notes in his lab book about his
most recent experiment—the one involving mirror berries—
and I've got a sketchbook open on my lap. Flames crackle in
the fireplace on one side of the room. It's nice. It's quiet. So
much quieter than the desperate screaming uncertainty in my
head.

With a wordless groan, I throw the sketchbook onto the
floor. "I don't know what to do, Gaius. *I don't know what to
do!*"

Startled, he looks up. "Uh ... do you mean you don't know
what to draw?"

"I have to make a decision about what to do with my life. I
can't simply do *nothing*, and I can't stay here forever, but my

brain feels paralyzed. So paralyzed I can't even draw." I stand up and retrieve the sketchbook so I can show him the blank page. "Nothing. Absolutely nothing. That's *never* happened to me. Normally I can sketch for hours while somewhere in the back of my mind, my problems work themselves out. Now all I have is a blank piece of paper and an empty future."

"It's only been a few days. You don't need to decide immediately."

"But I do. My life needs purpose."

"You could … be my apprentice."

I sink back into the armchair. "That's very kind of you, but I find plants to be rather boring."

"Oh." Gaius looks confused, as if the idea of anyone finding plants boring is an unfathomable concept.

"I'll probably have to do something art-related. I still enjoy that—well, if I can ever get past this blank page." I wave the empty sketchbook before dumping it on my lap again. "So maybe I could go somewhere far away where there are no Guilds and start over. Chase could probably help me with some fake identification."

Gaius nods. "I'm sure he could."

"I can find an art school to finish off at. And my Griffin Ability is under control now, so that wouldn't be a problem. It wouldn't be so bad, I suppose." I slide further down in my seat. "I wouldn't really feel like I'm making a difference to anyone's life, though."

"Well, in that case," Gaius says, "there is one option that seems obvious to me."

"And that is?"

"Work with Chase. Do what he does. It's what you're trained for after all."

Work with Chase? I remember him suggesting the idea to me once, but we both decided it wasn't a good idea. I couldn't very well assist a vigilante while also working to uphold the Guild's laws. But now ... well, I still don't feel comfortable with working outside the law, and even if did, I probably shouldn't do it with the ex-Lord Draven. "No, I ... I think I need to start over somewhere else." I tap the end of my pencil against the blank page, hoping for inspiration now that I have at least a fraction of an idea for what I might do when I leave here.

Still nothing.

Aware that throwing my book a second time would make me no better than a child having a tantrum, I settle for glaring at the sketchbook instead. "I think the creative part of my brain is broken."

"Well, until you figure out how to fix it," Gaius says, snapping his notebook shut and sitting forward, "I have something for the rest of your brain to work on. Have you ever tried exercising your Griffin Ability?"

I frown. "Meaning ..."

"Testing the limits of it. How far do your illusions extend? Is it by distance? By number of people? Have you ever tried to show two different illusions to two different people at the same time? That kind of thing."

I remember wondering why I'd never tested my illusion ability when I was at Lucien de la Mer's party at the top of Estellyn Tower, but I haven't thought of it since then. Too many other things going on in my mind. "That's a good idea, actually. I've spent so long simply trying to get it under control that I never thought about testing it or even … having fun with it."

"Great, let's do it now." Gaius stands and walks to the other end of the room. He stops in the doorway. "We can test distance first. I'll start here."

"Oh, that's easy."

"Well, go ahead then. Show me something."

I leave the sketchbook on my chair and stand in front of the fireplace. I think for a few moments, then release my hold on the imaginary wall around my mind. I picture a floating mirror berry bush on fire. It appears in the air in front of Gaius, who grins the moment he sees it. I'm not sure what happens to mirror berries in real life if they're burned, but in my imagination, I decide they're going to burst. I see them exploding all over the bush, sending their purple juice flying out in all directions. Gaius jumps back, shielding his face for a moment before dropping his hands and laughing at himself.

My laughter joins his as I allow the image to vanish. "Come on, you've used this ability before. I could have imagined an ogre running at you with a club and you should have been able to calmly stand your ground."

"Instinct," he says, attempting to defend himself with a straight face. "It was pure instinct. I saw the berry juice coming and I had to protect myself."

"Whatever you say. Okay, how far are you going now?"

Gaius moves next door to the kitchen. When I produce another burning bush illusion, he shouts to tell me he can see it. Next, he moves one floor up to where the bedrooms are. He waits at the top of the stairs and I head back to my spot by the fireplace. I picture a floating bagel this time. When I hear the laughter, I know he's seen it.

"If only it were real," he shouts down to me.

I run to the doorway and peer out. "Okay, go up another level to the far corner of the greenhouse. That's quite far away, isn't it?"

Gaius nods and disappears. I sit on the nearest couch and picture all the plants in the greenhouse burning. Then I realize that might not bring up the best memories for Gaius, so I picture rain pelting down instead. I keep the image going until I hear his footsteps on the stairs. "I didn't see anything," he says when he reaches the doorway. "What image were your projecting?"

"Rain. Can I try again?"

"Yes, of course. That's what this is all about." He hurries away.

I close my eyes so I can focus properly. I imagine holding it back, like clouds building as a storm gets ready to unleash itself. The sky darkens and the clouds swell and then … *Rain.* Everywhere. Every floor. Every room. I don't know what's below me, but I picture the rain in that space, and if there's anything above the greenhouse level, I imagine the rain there too. My face scrunches up as I pour every ounce of energy into it, as if I could actually make the rain come into being.

Then I let go and flop back against the cushions. When I hear Gaius hurrying back down the stairs, I push myself up out of the chair. "Well?" I ask as he appears in the doorway.

"Were you trying to flood my greenhouse?" he demands in mock annoyance.

"Indeed I was. The whole mountain, actually."

"Well done. You did an excellent job then." He walks back into the living room and picks up his notebook. "We'll have to go somewhere else in order to test the distance further."

Hurried footsteps in the entrance hall make me turn back to the doorway. "Was that you?" Chase asks, holding a towel against one arm and looking concerned.

"Yes. Where were you?"

"Downstairs. With the gargoyles."

"Gargoyles?" I ask, noting his use of the plural. "You have more than one?"

"All the way down there?" Gaius asks. "That's amazing. Calla, that's even further than the greenhouse."

"No wonder I'm feeling tired all of a sudden," I say with a small laugh. "Oh, but your arm," I say to Chase, noticing something dark and wet seeping into the blue towel clutched against his arm. "What happened?"

"Oh, nothing too serious. The gargoyles reacted quite wildly to the sudden downpour, and I was standing a bit too close. But Gaius is right; that's very impressive."

I clasp my hands together as awkwardness creeps into the space between us. That feeling of isolation followed me back here after our visit to the Guild, and I haven't said much to Chase since then. "Thank you. And I'm so sorry about your arm. Can I ... do anything?" I'm not sure what I'd do, but I feel like I need to offer since it's my fault he wound up clawed by a gargoyle.

"No, don't worry, it'll be fine. I'm sure it's started healing already."

"Okay." I look around for my sketchbook and find it on the chair I was sitting on earlier. Perhaps I can think of something to draw now. Something like exploding berries.

"Calla," Chase says. "Would you like to see where the gargoyles are kept? I know you're not particularly fond of them, but it could be interesting."

"Oh, yes, all right." Maybe a real conversation with him will help me to stop picturing him with Violet. Stupid, stupid thoughts. I should instead be picturing him as Lord Draven and reminding myself that he's too dangerous to get close to, even if he's a 'good guy' now.

We cross the entrance hall and walk around the back of the stairs where I notice, for the first time, another flight of stairs leading down. "How did you manage to see my rain projection?" I ask. "I thought you kept your mind shielded. Gaius said that's why he couldn't get into your dreams."

"Most of the time I do, but not always. If I know there's nothing I need to shield myself against mentally, then I don't always bother." We reach a landing with a door. Chase places his hand on it. I hear a click somewhere, and the door vanishes. There are more stairs on the other side of the door, so we continue going down. Eventually Chase asks, "Are you okay? You haven't said much since we returned from the Guild this morning."

"Well, to be fair, I haven't said a great deal to you since the day of the wedding."

"That's true. Well, except for when you shouted at me."

"Except for that." We pass a floor with a wide corridor leading off in both directions and numerous closed doors. But the stairs keep going down, and so do we. I decide to be honest with Chase, since that's our thing now. "The truth is, you and I almost had something. Something more than just friendship. And then to discover that …" I take a breath, trying to find the best way to say this so I don't sound petty.

"Yeah," Chase says with a resigned sigh. "The evil Lord Draven thing."

"Well, no. I mean, yes, obviously, but I was actually referring to the fact that you and Vi—you and my *sister-in-law*—were together. It's just strange."

"Oh. I didn't even think of that."

Right. Of course I'm the only one upset by this trivial bit of information from the past.

"Why is it bothering you?" Chase asks. "That was over ten years ago. You were just …" He trails off, perhaps realizing that he's hit on the real problem.

"Exactly," I mutter. "Just a child." So not only am I standing on the outside of someone else's story looking in, I'm a *child* standing on the outside looking in. And while Chase never treated me like a child before, how can he help but see me as anything else now? And why do I even care? "But you're right," I add quickly. "It shouldn't bother me. It doesn't really. I'm just being silly."

We reach the bottom of the stairs and Chase turns to face me. "Calla—"

"So where are these gargoyles?" I ask, looking around the bare room we're standing in. It's more of a cave, actually, since there are no floorboards or wooden panels covering the rough-hewn rock.

Chase decides to take the hint and drop the awkward conversation. "There's a narrow passage over there," he says, pointing to a tall shadow in the corner. "We keep more than just gargoyles, and we don't want to risk any of them getting out through a door, so a passage works well. None of the creatures are small enough to fit through it."

My heart rate kicks up a notch as I take a few steps toward the passage. It's little more than a slit in the rock. "I think narrow is an understatement," I say with a forced laugh. "How does anyone fit through there?"

"It's not that bad. It barely brushes my shoulders on either side."

His description causes a breathy laugh to escape me. No way. No. Freaking. Way. "I'm not going through there," I tell him.

"Why? It's really not that bad. No one's ever got stuck in there."

"No."

"Come on." He reaches for my arm. "I'll go first and you can follow—"

"No!" I shrink away hurriedly before he can touch me, already feeling the panic rising in my chest.

"Okay." He holds his hands up. "Okay, I'm sorry." He looks away, but not before I see the hurt in his eyes. Hurt? As if I'm shrinking away from *him*? I should explain. I should tell him it isn't him or his touch, it's this stupid fear of mine, but this room is getting too small, and just looking at that narrow slice of space is making me panic.

I step past him and aim for the stairs. *Must get out*, my brain tells me. *Get out. Find space.* I run all the way back up to the entrance hall before I stop and remind myself to breathe. This is okay. It's open and spacious and I'm not *trapped* here. I look back down the stairs, but I don't see Chase following me. I close my eyes and breathe some more. Then I continue up to my bedroom.

I sit on the edge of the bed and stare at nothing for a while. I think of moving on and starting over in a new place, and it makes me feel empty. I think of trying to return home, and it makes me scared. The Guild probably isn't allowed to monitor the inside of the house—I assume that would violate some kind of privacy right—but wouldn't they find out somehow if I was hiding there? Perhaps they do random checks with a search warrant or something. But I could hide myself with an illusion then. Or get away through the faerie paths. That would leave Dad in trouble, though, if the Guild found out that I'd been there.

So. I can't go home. I don't want to leave here, but I don't particularly want to stay either. If I sleep, will my subconscious figure out the answer for me?

I get up and walk to the two bags on the floor in the corner of the room. Chase took me into a shopping mall in the human realm after we left the Guild this morning so I could get some clothes. I've been using a few laundry spells on the clothes I ran away in, but those spells never seem to work out properly for me. Not the way Mom does them. I dig through the bags until I find pajamas. They're soft and warm and comforting, but the most important part is that they're dark blue covered in large yellow stars, making them so similar to my favorite set at home that I almost cried when I saw them.

Hours later, instead of being lost to blissful sleep, my back-and-forth thoughts are still torturing me: The look on every Council member's face when the recorded version of me said the words 'Griffin Ability.' The Guild foyer full of guardians fighting me and my imaginary dragon. Not knowing whether Gemma survived the dragon disease. That flash of hurt in Chase's eyes.

I climb out of bed and walk to the door. He's probably asleep, but if he isn't, I can explain myself. He has enough to feel guilty about as it is without adding anything unnecessary to the load. The passage is almost dark now, with only one lantern lit. My feet are silent on the carpeted floor as I walk slowly, checking for light shining out beneath any of the doors. I reach the end of the passage and find that it extends around the corner. Further along, on the right, a strip of light glows at the bottom of a door.

I don't know if the room belongs to Chase or Gaius, but if it's Gaius who opens the door, I'll just apologize and go back to bed. I walk the last few steps toward the door and tap lightly against it. I hear movement inside, then quiet footsteps. The door opens, and Chase stands there, looking surprised to see me. He's still in his clothes, but they're rumpled and creased, as though he may have fallen asleep in them at some point. His hair is on the messy side, but, considering I spent the past few hours tossing in my bed, my hair probably looks a lot worse.

"Hi," he says. "Is everything okay?"

"Yes, um … I just wanted to apologize for earlier. My mini freak-out downstairs. It didn't have anything to do with you."

With a small frown, he says, "Okay."

I tuck my hair behind my ears, mainly so that my hands have something to do. I'm starting to feel silly now, as though I've been worrying for nothing. Perhaps I imagined the hurt I saw in his eyes earlier. He's probably forgotten the incident already, and here I am making a big enough deal out of it to get up in the middle of the night in my pajamas and come and apologize. "Uh, anyway, I'll just—"

"Wait, hang on," he says as I turn to go. "I wanted to talk to you about something. Do you want to come in?"

I look past him uncertainly. "All right."

He pulls the door open fully and steps back. I walk inside. His room looks far more lived-in than mine. The old writing desk that stood in his Underground home is here, along with some of his paintings. A second table holds closed jars of paint, paintbrushes, dirty rags, and all his tattooing ink and equipment. Breathing in, I catch a faint whiff of paint; it smells like home. The covers on the bed are pushed back, confirming my suspicion that he fell asleep in his clothes at some point this evening. Or perhaps he was asleep now. "I didn't wake you, did I?"

"No." He leaves the door open and crosses the room. "I fell asleep earlier, but … I couldn't stay asleep." He pulls out the desk chair for me and sits on the edge of the bed. "So, I'm still investigating Amon. We may have delayed his plans by getting your mother back, but I'm sure we haven't stopped them."

"Oh, did you know that Saber is in the Guild's custody

now?" I ask as I pull my legs up and cross them. "And that Amon isn't allowed any visitors? The prison is supposed to notify the Guild if anyone asks to see him."

"Yes, I know, but I don't think that's made much difference to Amon. There's another prisoner at Velazar who's begun receiving visitors recently, and I'm almost certain that's the channel through which Amon is now receiving information and issuing instructions."

"How do you know that?"

"I have a contact who has access to the records at Velazar."

I narrow my eyes at him. "Do you have contacts everywhere?"

"Yes," he says, then frowns. "Almost."

"And do they all know who you really are?"

"No. Most of them don't. Anyway, I want to get into Velazar and speak to this prisoner. Find out how much she knows of Amon's plan. I've wanted to visit before, but I decided Velazar Prison might not be the best place for me to be caught."

With an expression of mock bemusement, I say, "Now why on earth would you think that?"

He gives me a wry smile, then continues. "No one knows who I am simply by looking at me, and it would be easy to provide false identification. But I don't want there to be a record of me—even a false version of me—anywhere. So I've avoided Velazar Prison."

"Until now," I say, figuring out where this conversation is heading.

"Until now," he repeats. "I know you're probably planning

to leave soon, and I know you're not interested in working with me on a permanent basis because you're worried about laws and all of that. But I wanted to ask you anyway." He leans forward, resting his elbows on his knees and watching me intently. "Will you help me get inside Velazar Prison?"

I look down at my hands. I probably shouldn't get involved in this stuff, but Amon is a threat to Mom as long as he still wants information from her, so that immediately makes me far more interested in this situation than I would otherwise be. And even though sneaking into Velazar Prison isn't legal, we'd be doing it for the right reasons. We'd potentially be stopping a far greater threat.

Dammit. This is like when I talked myself into stealing that bangle back from the Guild. And when I convinced myself to allow Zed to escape because I know he isn't a criminal and doesn't deserve to be locked up. "I used to see clearly in black and white," I murmur, "but now all I see are shades of grey. I don't like it."

"That's the way the real world works, though. Nothing is ever truly black and white."

I stare at my hands as they twist together. The moral debate aside, at least I know Chase doesn't view me as a child. He wouldn't ask for my help with something so important if he did. He says nothing more as he waits for my answer. The silence builds, and eventually I make my decision. I force my hands to be still and look up. "Okay. I'll do it. And if there's anything else involving Amon, I'll help with that too. I don't ever want him getting close to my mother again."

"Thank you," Chase says. "I'll try and organize for us to go tomorrow. The sooner we find out what Amon's been up to since your visit with him, the better."

As we stand and walk to the door, I say, "How exactly do you think this other prisoner is passing information to him? The prisoners are kept in floating cells that move continually. What if their two cells never happen to pass each other?"

"There's a pattern to the way the cells move, so Amon and this other prisoner pass one another at regular intervals. I'm sure by now they've developed a system of exchanging information as quickly as possible."

I turn in the doorway to face him. "And why would this prisoner want to help Amon?"

"Because," Chase says with a heavy sigh, "this prisoner is my mother."

PART III

CHAPTER TWENTY-ONE

I'M STANDING IN CHASE'S LAKESIDE HOUSE PREPARING MY-self mentally to meet the runaway Seelie princess who betrayed her family, personally hunted down a terrible and dangerous power, and stood alongside her son as he consumed that power and proceeded to bring our world to its knees. A woman who, unlike her son, most likely feels not a shred of remorse for the things she's done.

I hear the front door open behind me. I turn immediately, knowing that it can't be Chase. He went back through the faerie door to the mountain. To fetch something, he'd said. Before I can reach for the knife in my boot, I see who it is. Elizabeth, the woman I saw in Chase's past. The woman I met at Estellyn Tower.

"Hello," she says. "Where's Chase? I thought we needed to

leave now."

Her question confuses me, and for a moment I can't think what to say. "He—uh—he went back for something. What are you doing here?"

"Didn't Chase tell you? I'm coming with."

"Oh." Chase did say he would find someone to play the 'visitor' while he and I sneak in under the illusion of invisibility. He hadn't said who that person would be, though, and I didn't think to ask. "Why did he ask you?"

She gives me her sultry smile. "I can be very, *very* persuasive."

"Oh." Then it hits me. "*Oh.* You're Scarlett."

She seems surprised for a second, but she recovers quickly. "I am." With a roll of her eyes, she adds, "Chase seems to prefer my real name." She tilts her head to the side as if considering me. "I take it he told you everything."

"Yes."

"Not a pretty story, is it."

I shake my head. "No. I didn't expect it to be. But thank goodness for Luna. Things might have turned out differently if not for her."

"Indeed." Elizabeth watches me closely as she asks, "What did you think of her vision?"

Confused and hating the fact that I have to admit it, I ask, "What vision?"

She frowns. "You said Chase told you everything."

"He did." At least, I thought he did. "He said Luna had a Seeing ability, but he didn't tell me about any specific vision of hers."

"Oh. Well, never mind then." Elizabeth smiles, not un-kindly. "It probably wasn't right for him to share it. Forget I said anything."

I don't like the fact that she knows more than I do, but she's been part of Chase's life far longer than I have. There are probably many things she knows that I don't. I look down at her hands and find myself distracted by what I see there. "Why do you always wear gloves?" I ask. I'm certain I've never seen her without them.

She lifts her hands, turning them over and splaying her fingers. "My hands are a little ... dangerous. I don't intend for them to be, of course," she adds innocently, "but they do seem to have the unfortunate habit of sucking the life out of people."

"Sucking the—wow. So that's your Griffin Ability?"

"No. I don't have a Griffin Ability. This is what siren magic looks like when you can't turn it off. That turned out to be my *unpredictable* side effect of being a halfling. For the first few years they thought I had no magic. Then, after it appeared, I couldn't turn it off. So while most sirens don't generally practice the age-old art of sucking the life out of men, I didn't really have a choice. And, unlike the rest of my persuasive siren magic, this part works on women too. In case you were wondering."

"I ..."

"Ah, you're here," Chase says from behind me, walking through the faerie door. He shuts and locks it. "Ready to go?" he asks the two of us.

Elizabeth nods. I'm not sure if I'll ever be ready to face the inside of a prison in the company of the two women Chase was closest to when he became Lord Draven, but I nod anyway. "Yes."

* * *

We make it inside Velazar Prison without a hitch. Elizabeth charms the guard into allowing her in without putting one of those magic-inhibiting rings on her finger, while I remain fully focused on imagining an empty space wherever Chase and I are standing. My heart pounds furiously the entire time, but I don't allow my fear to take up any room in my brain. I need all my attention on this illusion. We make it through the confusing network of damp corridors and stairways and eventually find ourselves on the bridge spanning the cavernous space where the prison cells are kept. I watch them all floating past one another in eerie silence, wondering which one contains Angelica.

The guard who led us here presents a piece of paper to the guard standing at the gate halfway across the bridge. They exchange a few words before the gate is opened for us and we pass through. The guard leads us across the bridge to the other side of the cavern where we head down another corridor and stop outside one of the visitation rooms. As the guard lifts his hand to open the door, Elizabeth steps closer to him. "Why don't we stay out here for a little while," she purrs. She slides her gloved hand around his neck and whispers into his ear, "I'd like to get to know you better."

He turns his head and swallows, his eyes focusing on her

lips. I can already see there's no hope for him. "What if …
what if another guard walks past?" he asks.

"Then I'll have a little chat with him or her. I promise you
won't be in any trouble." She leans closer and presses her lips
again his jaw.

The moment the guard's eyes slide shut, Chase steps
forward and opens the door. We walk quickly into the room
that's split in half by vertical bars. Bars made of the metal that
doesn't allow magic to pass beyond them. This visitation room
is a little different from the one I was brought to last time,
though. Or perhaps they've all been changed since then.
Instead of a wall and a door on the other side of the room,
there's an open space. And into the space slides an entire prison
cell.

"Remember to keep yourself hidden," Chase murmurs. "It'll
be simpler if I don't have to explain who you are."

We walk toward the bars as the cell comes to a halt. There
isn't much inside it: a narrow bed, a small toilet and basin, and
a table with a few books and a picture frame standing on it.
After hearing Chase's description of Angelica, I wouldn't have
thought of her as sentimental, but I suppose everyone has
someone to care about. I wish I could see the picture in that
frame, but it's turned at just the wrong angle. I wonder if
perhaps it might be Chase.

A woman in prison overalls rises from the bed and comes
toward us. As she pushes her dark hair away from her face, I see
her properly for the first time.

And I stop.

The woman from Rick's vision. This is her. Long, messy

black hair with silver strands twisting through it. Bright silver eyes. I swallow past the dryness in my throat and tell myself that just because she showed up in a Seer's vision doesn't mean things are going to go wrong here. Even if she does strike out at Chase the way she did in the vision, she can't reach further than an arm's length past the bars.

I remain standing where I am and remind myself to focus on projecting my illusion.

"Hello, Angelica," Chase says.

Her hands come up slowly to grasp the bars. She stares at him with a stunned expression on her face and an almost-smile on her lips. Seconds tick by before she murmurs, "I knew it. I knew you couldn't be dead. You had the necklace."

Chase nods. "I'm sorry I didn't come before now. I've been in hiding, and I didn't know until recently that you were here."

She smiles. "There's no need for you to apologize. Seeing you again is enough to make me happy."

"It isn't enough," Chase says. "I'm going to get you out of here."

I'm glad I don't have to be part of this conversation. Chase sounds so sincere, but I know his words are only part of the plan to get Angelica to trust him once more. If she could see me and speak to me, would I be able to lie as convincingly as Chase?

"Oh, how thrilling!" Angelica says. "An escape plan!"

"Yes. I'm still working on the exact details. There are many obstacles between here and the exit."

"I have no doubt you'll figure it out," she says.

"In the meantime," Chase continues, "I wanted to speak to

you about whatever you and Amon are planning."

Angelica's expression becomes unreadable. "What do you know of that?"

"Only the rumors I've heard amongst those who visit you and Amon. It sounds like something big."

"And you want to be part of it?" Angelica asks carefully.

"Yes. In fact …" Chase hesitates, and I know this is the dangerous part. The part where he attempts to split an alliance that's bonded Angelica and Amon since they were thrown in here. He steps closer to the bars, and his tone becomes more fervent. "It was always you and me from the beginning. We took Zell down together. We destroyed the Guilds together. We hunted down unmarked fae and brought thousands to their knees. Amon was the one who messed up in the end. He was the one who found the Star and brought her to me, and that's how she was able to destroy all that power you and I worked so hard for. We don't need Amon this time. We can do this without him."

Angelica appears to consider Chase's words. "Amon knows more than I do, though. I'm not sure this plan even exists without him."

"Of course it does. He's locked up in here and I'm not. Anything he knows, I can find out. Just point me in the right direction."

After several moments of indecision, Angelica gives in. "All right. Let's do this together. After all, it's my son I've always wanted to see at the top, not some old librarian. I'll find out what I can from him, but you'll need to do the rest."

"Of course," Chase says. "Just tell me where to start."

"Amon's plan hinges on three visions from three different Seers. He had all three of them until one—the only one who hadn't told him her vision yet—was rescued. I don't know what information he learned from the first two, but if I tell you where they are, you can find out."

"I can. And recapturing the third Seer should be easy enough. Amon's men don't have the kinds of resources I have access to."

"Well then," Angelica says. "The two Seers are being kept in the center of my labyrinth. I obviously don't have the access stone anymore, so I can't help you get straight there. But it shouldn't be too difficult for you to get past the various obstacles in the tunnels. After all," she adds with a smile, "you helped me put most of them in there."

Chase hesitates, and I wonder if he's remembering the minotaur and the strange rainbow colored water and the chasm we fell into. When he speaks, though, he sounds confident. "That's true. I commanded the labyrinth creatures just as much as you did."

"You shouldn't have any trouble then."

Chase reaches through the bars and takes his mother's hand. "I've spent so much time alone, so much time wondering if it would have been better to die than live such a purposeless life. I'm so glad I've found you again."

She smiles at him. "I've been waiting for this too."

"Oh, and I have a way for us to remain in contact." Chase pulls his hand away and takes something from his pocket. Confused—I don't remember him mentioning this part when we were discussing the plan—I take a step closer. On his palm are two simple silver rings, a blue stone set in one and a green stone in the other. "Telepathy," Chase explains. "While we're both wearing these rings, we can communicate through our thoughts."

Angelica looks impressed. "I didn't realize a spell existed for such a thing." When Chase shows no sign of explaining where he got the rings from, she adds, "What if I don't want to hear your thoughts all the time?"

"Then don't wear it all the time. Besides, you won't hear *all* my thoughts, only the thoughts I choose to direct at you."

She eyes the rings. "It's a clever idea, but far too obvious. We're not allowed jewelry. The guards will see it and confiscate it."

"Then wear it on your toe."

"We're usually searched after we receive visitors. I'll most likely be asked to remove my shoes."

Chase smiles. "You and I both know what you're capable of. I'm sure you can figure out a way to hide it until after you're searched."

"You know me so well," she says. Then she laughs, and it's the same laugh I saw in Rick's vision. I tense, getting ready to tug Chase back the moment she lunges at him. But instead, she reaches calmly through the bars and takes the ring with the green stone. I exhale slowly, wondering what changed between Rick's vision and this moment. Perhaps Chase was originally planning to say something different. Something that would have angered her.

"I need to go," Chase says. "I have someone outside distracting the guards, but I don't know how long that will last for." He says goodbye to her, promising to let her know as soon as he figures out the details of an escape plan.

I keep myself hidden as the two of us walk back to the door on our side of the room. As Chase opens it, I look back over my shoulder at Angelica. A small smile lifts one side of her mouth as she watches her son leave, and I'm left with the unsettling feeling that we may end up regretting this.

CHAPTER TWENTY-TWO

"DO YOU REALLY THINK WE CAN TRUST HER?" I ASK CHASE as he closes the faerie door behind us and locks it. "What if she doesn't intend to help you?"

We cross the entrance hall and climb the stairs. "I think we can trust her. She's a bit of a slippery character, but she was honest about one thing at least: she has always wanted to see me at the top. Since I stumbled into the fae realm and she discovered I had far more power than she ever guessed, she's been devoted to seeing me rule over the rest of this world."

I pull a face. "That's some seriously misguided devotion."

"I know, but it makes me fairly certain she'll align with me rather than with Amon."

We stop outside my open bedroom door. "What was that ring you gave her? You didn't mention that before."

"I remembered those rings at the last minute and went back for them," he says, looking down the passage and pushing his hands into his pockets. "It seemed a convenient way to stay in contact with Angelica. We don't have to sneak back into the prison every time we want to discuss something with her. And it's harder to be deceptive with thoughts than with words. This will help me to distinguish the truth from any lies she might feel like telling me."

I wait for him to mention the most important thing about those rings. When he doesn't, I cross my arms and say, "And?"

With a small frown, he looks back at me. "And what?"

"That was a Griffin Ability, wasn't it? One of those from the *collection* you and Gaius have. And you know he won't approve of you removing the rings from the mountain, so you didn't say anything to anyone about taking them."

A moment passes before Chase answers. "Gaius told you about the collection."

"Yes." I walk into my room and sit on the edge of the bed, my arms still crossed. "He told me his whole story, in fact."

Still standing in the doorway, Chase says, "Then you understand where all the abilities in that collection come from. The majority were voluntarily given to us by those who, for whatever reason, don't want their abilities. The telepathy came from a pair of twins. Their minds were linked in such a way that they could communicate without speaking. Convenient at times, I'm sure, but they wanted to live their own lives without being so closely connected. It's a very useful ability, and its magic doesn't seem to cling to people the way the time traveling ability did. Most of the abilities don't stick, actually. I've told Gaius many times that we would benefit from using some of them on occasion."

"And he disagreed, so you're now using this one without telling him."

"He already knows. He was there when I took the rings."

"Oh." Feeling awkward, I focus on my boots and tap one against the other, activating the spell that makes them unlace themselves.

"You're right that he wasn't happy, though," Chase adds. "But he understands that it makes the communication in this current mission a lot simpler."

"I guess it does." I lift up my legs and cross them beneath me. "So ... the labyrinth. When are you going? And you don't have to hang around in the doorway, you know," I add. "You are allowed to walk into this room."

Looking amused, he takes a few steps forward. "I'm going now."

"Now? Like right now?"

"Yes. I don't have any other urgent matters to deal with at the moment, so why wait?"

"I ... I don't know. I suppose I just picture these things taking longer. If this were the Guild, the request to go into the labyrinth would probably take at least a day to get up the chain of authority, and then after permission is granted, they'd need to make sure the right team is pulled together and that everyone is on the same page for whatever the plan is."

Chase spreads his hands out, palms up. "And here we have the benefits of working outside the law."

I purse my lips and don't bother replying. He already knows my thoughts on that subject.

"Well, I'll see you later," he says, "hopefully with two rescued Seers in tow."

I stand quickly. "Do you need me to go with you?"

He considers my question before answering. "You probably shouldn't. It's quite dangerous, remember? I don't have Angelica's access stone, which means I can't simply picture the chamber in the center and get there through the faerie paths. She built it that way. I can take myself to a tunnel close to the center, but with all the confusion spells and the repeating passages, it could still take some time to find the chamber. That would be the dangerous part. As Angelica pointed out, I'm familiar with many of the creatures and spells, but I'm sure there are new ones, like that rainbow water we encountered last time."

"Would my Griffin Ability be of any help?"

"Possibly. It would depend on what kind of obstacles we come across."

"Then I should go with you," I say, stepping back into my boots. "And don't tell me it's too dangerous. Those Seers and their visions are linked to my mother somehow, so I want to get them away from Amon and Angelica just as much as you do." The boots lace themselves back up while I stare Chase down, daring him to try and stop me.

"Fine then," he says eventually. "But please try not to get yourself hurt. I can only imagine what you brother would do to me then."

"He would do nothing," I snap as I stalk past Chase,

"because I would remind him that I'm old enough to make my own decisions and that neither you nor he get to decide whether I walk into a dangerous labyrinth."

* * *

Two hours later, I'm beginning to regret my show of bravado. Not because I'm afraid of any creatures we might come across, but because I'd forgotten how narrow some of these tunnels become. I can deal with the one we've just walked into through the faerie paths, but if it gets any tighter than this ... *Then you'll stay calm*, I instruct myself. *You made a show of being a big, brave girl. Now you have to live up to that.*

"So," I say out loud as Chase finishes lighting the lantern we brought with us. "Here we are again. In a labyrinth you actually know far more about than you let on last time." I turn to him as another piece of the Chase-puzzle clicks into place. "Hold on. You're very powerful, right?"

"I am," he admits, sending the lantern into the air above us. "Not as powerful as Tharros was, but considerably more powerful than most."

I cross my arms. "Powerful enough to fight a minotaur?"

His eyes meet mine. In the light from the floating lantern, I can see he understands where I'm going with this. Quietly, he says, "Yes."

"So the last time we were here and you told me to run, it wasn't because you were afraid of the minotaur. You were afraid of what he would reveal about you."

Silence passes between us before he once again says, "Yes."

"Another deception," I murmur, looking away. It makes complete sense now why the minotaur's first words to Chase were, 'We meet again.' How could I possibly have forgotten to ask him about that after we ran? Probably because we fell into a chasm and almost met our deaths at the bottom.

"You might see it as a deception," Chase says, "but it wasn't meant that way. Surely you can understand the need for me to protect my identity at that point. You and I had only known each other a few days. Yes, it felt as though we had ... connected, but there was no knowing if our acquaintance would continue after we got out of here. It didn't make sense for me to tell you the truth back then."

I know Chase is right, but I still feel foolish looking back at all the clues I was oblivious to at the time. "Fine. So it wasn't a deception, it was you protecting your ass. But here's another question: If you're actually the master of that minotaur, then why did he try to attack us?"

"He didn't." Chase raises the floating lantern with a flick of his fingers and looks both ways down the tunnel. "We ran away, remember? Only then did he begin chasing us. Perhaps because he wanted to tell me something. Something about what's going on in these tunnels."

"Well, whether he's on your side or not, I hope we don't meet him again." I peer into the darkness beyond the reach of the lantern's glow. "You said the chamber should be nearby."

"Yes. I pictured it when we came through the paths, but without the access stone, we couldn't arrive exactly inside it. I think it should be close. It will suck, though, if we end up going the wrong way."

"How will we know if it's the wrong way?"

"If we don't find the chamber within a few minutes, we turn back. We'll mark our way so we don't get lost, and hopefully some labyrinth trick won't erase it."

"Hopefully. Okay, well, I vote for that way." I point to the right where the ceiling looks higher.

"All right." Chase places a piece of chalk against the wall and leaves it to travel along with us, marking our way. Then he directs the lantern ahead of us.

"So ... we're going to fight our way past anything that tries to stop us as we make our way to this chamber, we'll stun anyone who happens to be guarding it, we'll rescue the Seers, and then we'll safely leave the labyrinth through a hidden exit in the upstairs part of the chamber. Correct?"

"Yes. "

"Sounds simple enough. We should be home by dinner, right?"

Chase shoots a glance my way. "I can't tell if you're being sarcastic or overly optimistic."

"Sarcasm," I tell him with a sigh. "That was definitely sarcasm." I push my hair over my shoulder, then decide to quickly braid it so it won't get in the way when we have to fight something.

"I think optimism looks better on you," Chase says, his tone cautious. "In fact, last time we were down here, you told me how you choose to look at the bright colors of the world instead of the dark ones."

I secure the end of the braid, cross my arms, and point a glare in Chase's direction. "After dumping a gigantic, horrible

231

truth on someone, you don't get to tell them when to be optimistic."

He says nothing to that. I start wishing I could take my words back, or that I could say them differently. But then I remind myself that I'm not in the wrong here. He's the one who placed a great wedge between us. A wedge with the label *Lord Draven*. And as much as I wish we could go back to the easy banter we had before, I don't see how that's possible. Besides, I'll be moving on when this business with the Seers is done and I'm certain Mom isn't in danger anymore. Then I can finally begin to mend the split in my heart that doesn't seem to be able to heal as long as I'm around—

The ground shudders, throwing me off balance. I throw my hands out and catch myself against the tunnel wall as sand rains down from the ceiling. *Oh no no no.* If this tunnel ends up collapsing and we're trapped with no way out and no air and—

"It's fine," Chase says, pushing himself away from the wall beside me. "We triggered an earthquake enchantment. It's meant to send us running in fear down the tunnel, hopefully straight into the arms of some creature. Or simply to add to whatever terror we've already experienced at the hands of this labyrinth."

"S-so the tunnel's actually fine?" I ask, taking a step and then bracing myself against another jolt.

"Yes, just keep walking. We'll soon be past it. And be ready to use your magic or a weapon."

"Right." I've got a knife in my boot, throwing stars inside my jacket, and several other weapons in a belt around my hips.

I'm as prepared as a non-guardian can be. "Are there any other enchantments or illusions you'd like to warn me about?" I ask as we follow a bend in the tunnel.

"Uh, I remember one that makes you think you're being attacked by bats. There's a mirror where the reflection looks like an aged and dying version of you rather than the real you. There was something with falling rose petals that burned … Oh, there's a wall of water that floods parts of the labyrinth every few hours. That one's real, not an illusion. And various other spells that make you forget where you are or why you're here."

"Fantastic," I mutter. The tunnel curves sharply to the right, and we peer carefully around it before continuing. "Now that we're down here and I'm thinking of all the ways this could go wrong, I wonder if Angelica sent you here just to wind up lost and confused."

"Well, I'd ask her," Chase says, lifting his hand and wiggling his pinkie finger where the telepathy ring is, "but she doesn't seem to be wearing her ring at the moment."

I stop and face him. "This is actually incredibly stupid. You don't remember where all these enchantments or obstacles are, or they're creatures that move around, or they're new obstacles you don't know anything about. And there are countless enchantments that could leave both of us without any clue as to what we're doing here. How exactly did we think this was going to work?"

Instead of reassuring me that of *course* this will work, his lips twitch with a suppressed smile. "Is this the point at which you tell me you wish I'd made you stay home?"

Furious that he's making light of this situation, I open my mouth to yell at him.

"I know, I know," he says before I can get a word out. "Gigantic, horrible secret. How dare I attempt to joke with you, blah, blah, blah." He throws his hands up. "Can I just say that I kinda wish I was here with the Calla I was stuck with last time?"

"Well maybe I wish I was with the Chase I first met and not the Chase you turned out to be!"

He stares back at me, any hint of humor gone from his face. His voice is quiet when he says, "If you still can't see that the Chase you met is the same Chase you're with now, then I doubt anything will ever convince you."

My anger vanishes as if swept away on one of his storms. My shoulders droop. I shake my head. "No, that's ... I didn't mean it that way." How do I explain that when I look at him, I *do* see the same Chase I met, and that's the problem? Shouldn't I see the person he really is? The *whole* person, the guy who's caused murder and ruin and pain? Isn't it safer to never let myself forget what he's capable of?

"What did you mean then?" he asks.

I continue shaking my head and staring at the bare ground at our feet. "I don't know. I'm sorry. Forget I said anything."

After a long pause, he says, "Okay." I look up as he attempts a smile. "Just so you're aware, the situation isn't as dire as you think it is. The confusion spells aren't strong enough to affect me, so at least one of us will still be sane at the end of all this."

I blink at him—and then I allow myself to smile. "Well,

thank goodness for that." I swing my arms at my sides and breathe in deeply. "Okay, let's do this."

We turn to keep walking—and the strangest thing happens. The walls begin to melt away as ferns, trees, vines and flowers push their way out of the ground, unfurling, curling, reaching, growing, like the formation of a forest sped up so it takes place over a matter of seconds instead of months or years. Soon enough, we're standing in a lush forest scene, color splashed all over it like one of Chase's paintings. When I look over my shoulder, the tunnel is gone.

"Calla?" Chase says.

"Another illusion," I whisper.

"What illusion?"

"Can't you see it? It's a forest. It's so beautiful." I stretch my arms out and watch the dappled pattern of sunlight and shadows moving across my hands.

"What are you doing?" Chase asks. "Don't touch anything you see."

"Why would it matter what I touch if it isn't real?"

"Because it—oh, hell." Then he swears far more colorfully, grabs my arm and pulls me back.

"What? What's wrong?" With fear coalescing inside me, I search the forest until I see it: a shapeless mass of black smoke. It twists and curls and slowly moves through the forest toward us.

"Dammit, *dammit*," Chase says, pulling me around and tugging me in the opposite direction. "Of all the things we could come across down here, it had to be that." He looks over his shoulder, then pulls me faster. "I thought it was gone. We don't have the right weapon, and there's no time to transform anything. We need to run."

"What's the right—"

"Something loud and ringing like a bell." He tugs me behind him, but I struggle to keep up.

"What is that thing?"

"In smoke form it can incapacitate us. In bodily form it will bite us. And then the horror begins."

"What—"

"Our magic can't stop it when in smoke form, so just *run*, okay? Run!"

CHAPTER TWENTY-THREE

I PUSH MYSELF FASTER, BUT I CAN NEVER BE AS FAST AS Chase. The forest flies past me. I wonder at what point the illusion will end. I throw a glance over my shoulder and—smoky tendrils are *right there*. Fear tears its way up my throat.

"Chase—"

Black smoke envelops me. My body goes numb and the illusion vanishes. I hit the stone floor on my side and roll to a halt on my front. I don't feel any pain. Chase is nearby, groaning something. The smoke lifts—and the pain slams into me. The screaming ache where my left side hit the ground. I manage to lift my head and squint past a bright spot of light. The lantern on the ground, I think. Fortunately it didn't go out.

With another groan, Chase rolls onto his side and gets

awkwardly to his feet. The smoke hovers, still shapeless, but almost as though it's *watching* him. I sit up, clutching my aching left shoulder. I feel oddly sluggish in the wake of the numbness, but I slide my hand into my boot and pull out my knife. Chase sends a gust of wind sweeping along the tunnel. It's almost strong enough to push me over, but it has no effect on the smoke hovering in the air. It swirls and shifts, and then it seems to pull together in a rush and shoot toward Chase. Seconds before reaching him, it materializes into a gruesome creature.

I don't have time to look closely. I kick Chase's leg as hard as I can. He goes down and the creature misses him. It springs off the wall with spindly legs and lands beside me in a crouch. I jerk away, seeing black skin dripping like ink and a mouth too big for its face, stretched wide to reveal jagged teeth. Its large eyes are milky white, but I'm willing to bet it can see everything it needs to see. Feeling stronger than I did a few moments ago, I slash at it with my knife. It jumps back, then launches at me. I swing my arm out, knocking the creature off me, but not before it tears through my sleeve with its ink covered teeth.

One of Chase's knives spins past me and lands in the creature's upper arm. With a high-pitched shriek and a snarl, it tugs the knife free and tosses it away. It jumps up, its body shifting into smoke again. I'm on my feet now, backing away, moving closer to Chase. My arm burns, and a quick glance down reveals gashes in my skin where my jacket is torn. My vision blurs. I blink and shake my head. Looking up, I find the smoke rushing at me. It twists into the demon creature again, baring its fangs and reaching for me with clawed hands. I raise my knife and—

Chase slams into the creature. The two of them strike the ground, the demon flickering between smoke and bodily form, paralyzing him in bursts. Then it snaps together fully and pounces on top of him. A scream fills the tunnel as teeth rip into Chase's neck. My scream, I realize, as I run forward and tear the creature off him. I swipe across its chest with my knife. It screeches out at me as it leaps over Chase to where I can't reach it.

A blast of fire shoots up between us, but it disappears moments later as Chase's hand falls weakly to his side. The demon crouches, takes hold of Chase's shoulder with its teeth, and begins dragging him away. I try to run after them, and I'm vaguely aware that I'm yelling, but I can't seem to manage more than a few stumbling steps. The tunnel tilts dizzyingly. I find myself leaning against the wall, watching Chase as he's dragged to the edge of the light, almost into darkness. I push myself away from the wall and stumble another few steps. Why can't I *run*, dammit?

"Calla?" From the shadows steps a person who no longer exists outside of my nightmares. Goosebumps rise across my skin. It's him. The boy. The one I forced off the edge of the chef school building. The one who fell to his death because of me. "How could you do something so wicked?" he asks, moving slowly toward me. "Have you always had a murderer's heart?"

The guilt I manage to keep pushed deep down erupts from that dark place within me and twists itself nauseatingly around my heart. "You're not real, you're not real," I whisper, managing to lurch past him. I can still see Chase. I just need to get to him. Blinking against the blurriness, I try to move faster.

"You deserve to rot in that faraway prison," the boy says. He's there again, in front of me. "Not for your Griffin Ability or for helping a criminal escape, but because you're a *murderer*."

I recognize the truth of his words and my resulting despair is almost debilitating. I want to curl in on myself and never face the world again. How can anyone ever bear to look at me when all they're able to see is the blackness of my soul blotting out everything else about me? But through this haze of anguish, something inside me knows that none of this is real.

"Stop it, *stop* it," I tell the hallucination. "I know you're not real."

"But your guilt is real," he says, and as he turns away from me, I see the back of his head covered in blood.

"Go away!" I swing my arm at him and he vanishes. My shuffling steps carry me forward. I may be guilty and I may be a murderer, but I still need to get this black smoke monster off Chase. I can see it sitting on top of him, biting his arm and then moving down to do the same to his leg, as if it's trying to puncture him everywhere.

Something loud and ringing. That's what Chase said. I need something loud and ringing like a bell. I pull a knife from the belt around my hips. How long would it take me to transform the metal into a bell? Too long. And in my current weakened state, focusing enough magic to make that happen seems impossible. All I can think of is to increase the size of the blade.

I take a second knife from the belt and let my magic trickle into both of them. As my slow, lurching steps carry me closer to Chase, the blades grow longer and wider.

As if sensing my presence, the creature jumps off Chase and faces me. I pull my arms apart, then strike the blades against one another. A loud clang issues forth, but it doesn't resonate the way a bell would. I have nothing else, though, so I do it again. And again and again. The creature twitches, and bits of its body seem to pull away before snapping back against it. I slam the blades together harder. The creature shudders and shakes its head. It cries out and jumps at me, but I swing the blades up in an X and shove the demon away. I stumble backwards, barely able to keep myself from falling. I prop myself against the wall and *clang, clang, clang*. I'm nauseous and the tunnel is tilting again and a boy on a bicycle rides past me, screaming as a harpy tries to catch him, but *I will keep hitting these blades together*.

The creature twitches and convulses until suddenly it explodes apart, transforming into wisps of black smoke that scatter on an invisible breeze. The wisps quickly come together into one swirling mass, but I keep striking my blades against one another. The swirling becomes writhing. The twisting mass moves past Chase and disappears into the darkness beyond.

I lower myself to my knees and scramble toward Chase, dragging my blades with me. He's been bitten in numerous places—the worst being the lacerations on the side of his neck—but he's still alive. His eyes are closed, his face twisted into an expression of anguish as he mutters words I can't decipher. I try to rouse him, but he doesn't respond.

"It's gonna … be okay," I say, even though the gashes in my arm are burning fiercely, and the tunnel feels as though it's spinning, and small children who aren't real are running around us crying in fear. Soon they vanish, but they're replaced by a young boy with his hair on fire, screaming on the other side of Chase. They're all my fault, I know they are. People I've hurt with my Griffin Ability, whether intentionally or not. Guilt rips through me at the sight of them, but I remember the words Chase reminded me of earlier and manage to hold onto those instead. "Choose … the bright colors," I say out loud. "Bright colors. Not the dark ones. Okay?" My trembling fingers touch his face and find it burning hot. "Bright colors. I know there are so many dark ones, but … just …"

I'm starting to forget why we're here, but I know we need to leave. I manage to get my stylus out of my boot and Chase's amber from his front pocket. Thinking of Gaius, I manage to make my shaking fingers function well enough to write one word: *Help*.

Black smoke materializes around us. I can't tell if it's real or another hallucination, so I scramble for the two blades and bring them clanging together. I lean over Chase, as if my small frame could possibly protect him, and continue hitting one blade against the other. I can barely hold them up, and they're making more noise scraping against the floor than anything else, but I don't stop. "Go away," I gasp amidst my misery. "Go away, go away, go away …"

My hallucinations crowd around us: the boy who fell, his weeping parents, the crying children, a harpy and a bicycle.

They mingle together with black smoke and gliding wings and a figure with dark skin and impossibly white hair. I try to cling to the bright colors, but they're gone. All that remains are two murderers lying on the ground enveloped in darkness.

CHAPTER TWENTY-FOUR

I WAKE FROM NIGHTMARES MORE HORRIFYING THAN ANY I've had before. My brow is damp, my pajamas cling to my body, and my entire being feels like it's trembling. I push myself up quickly—which causes my head to throb—and realize I'm in my bedroom inside the mountain. I pull the bedcovers up to my chin and spend several minutes staring at the tall lamp in the corner while quietly repeating *It was just a dream* inside my head.

Then the questions begin:

What was that smoke creature?

How did we get out of the labyrinth?

Is Chase okay?

I push the covers back and climb out of bed. I feel weak and wobbly, but I make it to the door. Out in the passage, I walk slowly in the direction of Chase's bedroom, keeping my hand against the wall in case I feel a sudden need to be horizontal. I'm only about halfway there when I hear footsteps behind me. "Oh, you're awake!" Gaius exclaims. "What are you doing out here? You must be feeling terrible."

I turn around and lean against the wall. "I wanted—" I stop to clear my croaky throat. "I wanted to see if Chase is okay."

"Chase hasn't woken up yet, but he'll be fine." Gaius reaches my side and slips an arm around my back. "Why don't you get back into bed and I'll ask Lumethon to come over. She knows far more about healer things than I do."

"Lumethon?"

"She's one of Chase's friends. She went into the labyrinth with the tracking owls and found you and Chase."

"Oh. How did she get us out?"

"Levitating stretchers. The expandable ones. They're part of most healers' emergency kits."

I cross my bedroom and climb back into bed. "I actually meant how did she get past the horrible creatures and hallucination spells."

Gaius purses his lips in thought. "Hmm. She didn't say. But you were quite close to the entrance she went through, so perhaps she didn't have to contend with much."

Quite close to an entrance? Chase and I must have chosen the wrong direction. Or perhaps not, since we ran back at some point. Maybe we ran further than I thought, toward one of the entrances. Or maybe the tunnels rearranged themselves while we were fighting that *thing*. That's probably the most likely explanation.

"Do you remember what attacked you?" Gaius asks. He sits on the edge of the chair beside my bed. A chair that wasn't here before. "Chase was quite certain he could handle anything he might come across in that labyrinth, but when Lumethon returned with you both, he was covered in bite and claw wounds, and he's been in a feverish state ever since."

"A feverish state? I thought you said he'll be fine."

"He will be. You were in a feverish state too, and now look at you. All better."

"Well, except for feeling shaky and unsteady."

"Oh! The tonic potion." Gaius reaches over to the bedside table where a collection of bottles I didn't notice until now is gathered. "Lumethon's been injecting you with something to keep you hydrated while you were sleeping, but she said you'd feel quite weak once you woke up and that you should drink this."

"Why would I be dehydrated?" I unscrew the lid of the bottle and sniff the contents. "Did I throw up?"

"No, no, but it's been three days, so you—"

"Three days?" I lower the bottle so quickly that the liquid inside almost sloshes out onto the bed.

"Yes, it's, uh …" Gaius pauses for a moment. "Tuesday. It's Tuesday today."

"Seriously? Ugh, no, where's that antique amber thing? My brother and my father have probably been trying to contact me."

"Yes, uh …" Gaius becomes very interested in his hands. "The amber was here beside the bed. I saw some messages from your brother. He became quite concerned when you didn't reply, so … I replied on your behalf. I'm sorry. I didn't mean to invade your privacy, but it seemed—"

"No, that's fine, thank you. You did the right thing." I take a sip of the tonic and try not to gag. "What did you say to him?"

"Well, I was very polite, and I didn't share any of the upsetting details. I simply wrote, 'Hello. Calla and Chase are unwell after a run-in with an Underground inhabitant. They will be fine within a few days.'"

"Oh dear. I can't see that going down well. What was his reply?"

With some hesitation, Gaius says, "It's probably not necessary to repeat it."

I lower the bottle and fix him with a stare until he relents.

"Fine. He said … 'I'm going to kill him.'"

I nod as I swallow my second disgusting sip of tonic. "That sounds like my brother."

Gaius stands. "I should return the amber to you now that you're back." He hurries out of the room, leaving me to wrinkle my nose at the rest of the bottle's contents and decide to just down it. I finish swallowing the nasty liquid and place the empty bottle on the bedside table as Gaius returns with the old amber. "It's nice to have someone looking out for you the way your brother does," he says, leaving it beside the empty bottle

"I think overprotective might be a better description—for all the members of my family—but yes. It is nice. I should probably stop complaining about it."

"Probably. Are you feeling any better? The tonic is supposed to work quickly."

"Yes, I am actually." I push myself to the edge of the bed. "I'm going to go see Chase now."

Gaius puts his hand on my shoulder. "Why don't you have a relaxing bath and then rest for the remainder of the day?"

"You know, you sound exactly like those fussy healers," I say with a chuckle, "always telling people to *rest*."

"Well, they do have a point," he says, not removing his hand. "I think it would be better if you stayed here and rested."

I pause, my smile slipping as I look up at him. "What's going on, Gaius? Why don't you want me to see him?"

"It isn't that. It's more … well, in his current state, it might be upsetting to you."

"Why would I be upset? It's not as though I care a great deal about him or … anything like that."

With his expression turning to one of doubt, Gaius says, "Then why do you want to see him so badly?"

I don't feel as though that question requires an answer, so I step past Gaius and head for the door. I'm more stable on my feet now, so I make it down the passage without using the wall to hold myself up. Chase's door is ajar. I slowly push it open and step inside. He's sleeping restlessly amongst tangled sheets and bedcovers. His breath is uneven, and his occasional twitches are accompanied by mutterings of unintelligible words. I walk to the bed and gently pull aside the neck of his T-shirt, feeling his burning skin and checking for that terrible bite at the same time.

"The wounds have all healed," Gaius says, joining me at the bedside, "but we think there may still be some poison in his blood."

"Poison?"

"Yes. A black substance that was around all the wounds. It was the same as on your arm. He had far more bites and scratches, though."

"It's my fault," I say quietly. "I couldn't run fast enough, which is why it caught up to us. And then Chase jumped in front of me when the—the *creature*—tried to attack me."

"What was it?"

"I don't know. But I can show you." I picture the swirling black smoke and project the image above the bed. "Part of the time it was just smoke," I say, "but then it transformed into this." My picture changes to the demon-like creature with the gangly, dripping wet body and the eyes and mouth too big for its face. "The smoke paralyzed us so that we couldn't move while it surrounded us, and then after the creature bit us, that's when the hallucinations began. They were all people I've hurt in some way. It was horrible. All that guilt flooding to the surface."

"I've never seen anything like it," Gaius murmurs, still watching my projection.

"Me neither," says a voice from the doorway. The creature vanishes as I hurry to reinforce the imaginary barrier around my mind. "Sorry if I startled you," the woman says as she enters the room. I recognize her as the dark-skinned, white-haired figure who melted into my hallucinations just before I blacked out. I can see her better now: taller than normal, long, straight hair the color of clean snow, and unnaturally pale eyes. "I'm Lumethon." She holds her hand out to shake mine. "Chase has told me a little bit about you."

"Oh. Hi." I shake her hand.

"Gaius asked me to come and check on you now that you're awake, but you seem to be doing quite well. Did you take that tonic I left by your bed?"

"Yes. I'm feeling much better."

"No more hallucinations?"

"No. And my magic seems to be working fine, so that wasn't affected."

"Good. Well, there isn't much else I can do," she says. "I'm not actually a healer. I just know more about these things than Gaius, which is why he always asks for my assistance in these matters." She steps closer to Chase and lays her hand on his brow. "Still burning. Looks like his healing will take a bit longer than yours, but I suppose that's to be expected given the extent of his wounds."

I nod, telling myself that her conclusion seems logical. Of course Chase will take a bit longer to heal, but he will be fine. He has more power than anyone else I know, so how could he not be? I turn to Lumethon and say, "Thank you for coming into the labyrinth to find us. There's absolutely no way we would have got out on our own."

"Oh, of course," she says with a wave of her hand. "Chase would have done the same for me." Before I can ask if she encountered any dangerous beast or spell while she was in the labyrinth, she steps away from the bed. "Can I take a look at some of the books in your study?" she asks Gaius. "I think I may have seen a reference to a creature that feeds on despair."

"Yes, certainly."

They walk to the door, but Lumethon looks back over her

shoulder. "Calla, it was nice to properly meet you. Soak in a pool and then take it easy for a day or two, but I think you're probably fine."

"Okay, thanks." She walks out while Gaius gives me a look that says, *See? I told you to have a bath and rest.* I sigh and wave him away.

Once Gaius and Lumethon are gone, I walk around to the other side of the bed and climb onto it so I can sit beside Chase. I watch him for a while, wondering what nightmares he's caught up in and if he's aware of anything going on around him. Eventually, when I've thought about my words long enough, I decide to speak.

"So there we were," I say quietly, "lying on the ground with our hallucinations of despair consuming us, and I realized something." My hand inches forward until it rests lightly just below the dark markings on his left arm. I've figured out by now that this tattoo is permanent, the vine of thorns that twists around his arm. I wonder why he chose this pattern to permanently ink his skin. "This is my realization," I say. "I can't judge you for what you've done. I'm no better than you are. Whether I've killed one person or thousands, I'm still a murderer. And that twisting, sickening guilt that made me never want to face the light of day again—you were feeling that a thousand times over. You're probably still feeling it." My hand slides down toward his. "I can't imagine what you're suffering through, lost in nightmares I wish I could pull you free from."

"Calla?"

I snatch my hand away as if I've been caught doing something wrong. "Yes?" I ask as Gaius walks back into the room.

251

"We couldn't find that smoke creature in any of my books, but there's a reference to something that may be it. Lumethon's going to do some more research. Anyway, I just wanted to inform you that I'll be in the greenhouse if you need anything."

"Thank you." I climb off the bed. "I was thinking I should visit my mother. I can sneak into the healing wing the same way Chase and I got into the Guild last week. Then I can see my dad as well, if he's able to leave work. We've been in contact using that old amber, but I haven't actually seen him since I fled the Guild."

Gaius tells me he thinks that's an excellent idea, as long as I don't get caught, of course. I assure him I won't. As I walk to the door, I look back over my shoulder at Chase. It doesn't feel right to leave him alone with his nightmares, but Dad must have been horribly worried about me over the past few days, so I need to see him. Hopefully I can put on a brave face and reassure him that everything will be fine, despite my fugitive status and uncertain future.

I pick up the amber beside my bed to write a message. I'm not sure if it's Ryn or Dad on the other end, but I'll assume it's Ryn, given the recent messages Gaius told me about.

I'm awake now and much better. No, you don't have to kill Chase. It isn't his fault I've been unwell the past few days. Please ask Dad if he can visit Mom in the healing wing during visiting hours tomorrow. Thanks.

Then I take Gaius and Lumethon's advice and soak in a hot pool of bubbles, trying not to imagine Chase's nightmares.

CHAPTER TWENTY-FIVE

I'M BECOMING QUITE PROFICIENT AT HIDING MYSELF WITH the illusion of empty space. It was a challenge at first, picturing the absence of something rather than an actual *thing*, but with all my recent practice, it's definitely easier than it used to be. I didn't even have to pretend I was someone else when coming into the Guild. I simply made the guard see a closed wall and only himself in the room instead of a girl with a hood over her head walking in through the faerie paths. It's a little bit thrilling, in fact, to walk freely around the Guild knowing that no one can see me. But I remind myself to be careful and head straight to the healing wing, because overconfidence is what lands people in trouble.

Mom is being kept in a long room that houses a row of beds on either side. Curtains float around each bed, giving patients privacy if they require it. It's a good thing I don't drop my illusion the moment I slip between Mom's curtains, because it turns out her friend Matilda from the library they both work at is visiting. She's chattering away to Mom, telling her about the young couple she found getting far too intimate on the top floor of the library and the resulting awkward situation as she tried to explain to them how inappropriate their behavior was.

I choose to wait outside, keeping myself hidden in a corner while watching the blue-uniformed healers bustling around. I see Dad arrive. He's trying to be casual with his hands in his pockets, but I can tell from the way his eyes dart around, probably looking for signs of me, that he's anxious. Shortly after he goes into Mom's cubicle, Matilda comes out. I wait another minute or two, just in case she left something behind and suddenly comes rushing back to fetch it. When I'm certain she's gone, I walk to Mom's curtains and step between them, trying to move them as little as possible. I pull the protection back around my mind. The moment Dad sees me, he strides across the space and wraps me in a tight hug. "What a relief to know you're okay," he says as he steps back. "I mean, of course you are. I shouldn't have doubted it for a moment. You're far more capable of taking care of yourself than I give you credit for. But when Ryn said you weren't well, all I could think of was the dragon disease, and I didn't know if we'd ever see you again—"

"Dad, I'm fine. I'm *fine*." I take his hands and squeeze them. "I'm so sorry you had to worry like that, but I'm better now, I promise. And I'm going to figure out … something. For what to do next. An art school far away where no one knows me and there are no Guilds nearby. And I'll visit you like this, in secret, now that I know I can comfortably conceal myself. Everything will be okay." I nod continuously as I speak, willing myself to believe my own words.

As if Dad can sense my doubt—as if he knows I need his reassurance as much as he needs mine—he squeezes my hands in return and says, "Of course everything will be okay. This isn't the way you wanted your life to turn out, but life seldom works that way. This is just another challenge, and I know you'll pick yourself up and make it through to the other side like you always do."

I nod and press my lips together. In an attempt to keep my emotions at bay, I walk to the edge of Mom's bed and clasp one of her hands in mine. "How's she doing? Do the healers have any idea yet when she'll wake up?"

"No. There's been no change in her condition."

I look around, happy to see that the area is cozier than the last time I was here. A blanket from Mom and Dad's bedroom at home is draped over the pale blue sheets, a pretty tablecloth covers the little cabinet beside the bed, and on top of the cabinet is a picture of Mom, Dad and me from when I was about fifteen. Beside it is another frame housing a painting I did years ago. "Where'd you find that?" I ask, pointing to the painting with a smile. "I haven't seen it in ages."

Dad frowns. "Neither have I. I know your mom loved it, though. I think she kept it on her desk at work."

"Matilda must have brought it. That was nice of her. Too bad Mom isn't awake to see it."

Dad moves to the opposite side of the bed. "I suppose these

things are more for the people who sit in here with her. We're the ones who don't want it to feel so bare and clinical." Dad glances at the curtain, then looks across the bed at me. "If someone comes in here now, will they see you?"

"Yes. I don't know yet if it's possible to show an illusion to some people and not others, so if you can see me, everyone else can too. But I'm getting much faster at it, so I can conceal myself the moment anyone walks in here."

"Okay." Dad looks over his shoulder again, then positions himself between me and the gap in the curtains. "So, Ryn said you're staying with a friend you met Underground. As your father, I should probably be concerned that you've spent time Underground, but we both know there are more important things to worry about, so all that matters is that you're staying somewhere safe."

"My friend and I are actually both staying with another friend of his, and it's definitely safe. The area surrounding his home is inaccessible from the faerie paths. You have to use a faerie door, which is obviously locked, and you'd have to know where the faerie door is. I doubt the Guild even knows this place exists."

"Good."

"I assume it's not safe for me to come home?"

"Unfortunately not. By law, the Guild is allowed to track fugitives. It's a similar spell to the one they put on the house when you were under house arrest, but this one will detect when you enter our home. They're allowed to put it on any home they can reasonably prove you'd be likely to try and hide at. So there's one on our home, Ryn's home, your grandparents' home, and the homes of the trainees you've made friends with at the Guild. Oh, and even Zinnia's home," he adds, referring to his first wife, Ryn's mother. "Someone at the Guild found out you used to stay there occasionally with Ryn when you were little and your mom and I were away. They seem to think you might try to hide there now."

"Sounds like they're going a little overboard just to find one Gifted person."

"Well, they need to make it look like they're doing everything they can to find the person who brought the dragon disease to the Guild, and you're still their top suspect."

I shake my head, but I don't bother pointing out how useless the Guild is being about this whole dragon disease thing. Dad already knows. Outside the curtain, I hear a healer telling the people next door that visiting hours are almost over. I let go of Mom's hand and quickly make it appear as though I'm not here. When the healer pops her head in to tell Dad the same thing, she sees only him and Mom.

When the healer's gone, I reveal myself once more. I lean over and give Mom a quick kiss on the forehead. "I hope you wake up soon," I whisper. "There's a lot for us to talk about." I give Dad another hug and promise to stay in contact.

"If you need another safe place to meet," Dad says, "Ryn has friends who've offered their home. Flint and Raven. They said we can meet there any time. They wanted to offer you a room in their home so you'd have somewhere to stay for a while, but since they have a little boy—"

"Oh, I understand, you don't have to explain. It's too much of a risk if someone found out. They wouldn't want guardians rushing through their home shooting weapons and magic all over the place when they have a child to protect."

"Yes. But let's try to meet there soon. If you want, I can bring some of your things so you can at least feel a little more at home where you're currently staying."

"Thank you."

After a final goodbye, Dad leaves. I decide to wait a few minutes until the rest of the visitors have made their way out. It'll reduce the likelihood of someone walking into me. I pick up the frame with the painting so I can have a closer look at it—and that's when I hear movement behind me. I drop the frame and spin around, projecting my illusion of nothingness in an instant.

"I saw her!" Gemma whispers in excitement.

"Me too," Perry says. "That's incredible. She just vanished. Calla, are you still here?"

I'm thrilled to see that Gemma is alive, but I'm terrified my two friends are about to shout out that they've found me. I remain frozen and try not to breathe. My furiously pounding heart might give me away, though. Besides, if Gemma and Perry walk any closer, they'll be able to touch me. Then there won't be any doubt as to whether I'm here or not.

"Come on, we're not about to give you away," Perry says, lowering his voice. "We could have done that before; we already knew you were Gifted."

"*What?*"

"Oh! You're still here," Gemma says, her eyes searching the air where I'm standing.

Carefully, I let go of the illusion and close up the barrier around my mind. I watch their eyes widen as I come into view. "What do you mean you *knew*?"

"Well, we didn't *know* know," Perry says. "but we always suspected. I mean, when you put all the stories together, it's kind of obvious, isn't it?"

"It … it is?"

"Yes. Well, it's obvious to anyone with more than half a brain," he says. "All those other dumb-asses came up with stories about Unseelie magic and dark spells." He shrugs. "We figured there was probably a much more sensible explanation."

"Yeah," Gemma says. "I don't know why the Council didn't figure it out ages ago."

I think I know. Something to do with Dad bribing certain people to keep quiet. "And … it doesn't bother you?" I ask carefully.

"Why would it?" Perry asks. "I don't have anything against Griffin Abilities."

"Me neither," Gemma says. "One of my extended family members is Gifted. I'm not supposed to know, but I've overheard things. And seen things. Those Griffin discs …" She shakes her head in wonder. "There were only six of them, but they sure did get around."

I hesitate, looking back and forth between the two of them. "So we're all good? You're not about to follow your guardian training and hand over the criminal you just found?"

"Of course not," Gemma says with a quiet chuckle. Then she skips over to me and gives me a hug. "I'm so happy you got away safely."

"I'm so happy you're *alive*," I say as her hair tickles my cheek.

"Group hug!" Perry throws his arms around both of us.

"Shh," Gemma tells him. "The healers will hear us."

"Thanks for that cure, by the way," Perry adds as the two of them step back. They immediately put some distance between each other, and I realize now that they haven't made eye contact once. I wonder if something happened between them. "The rest of the Guild seems to view it as confirmation that you were responsible for the dragon disease," Perry continues, "but there are some of us who are very grateful you went looking for it."

"Me," Gemma says, sticking her hand in the air. "I'm one of those grateful people."

"Thank *you* for getting that key away from Councilor Merrydale," I say to Perry. "I never would have got the tracker spell off otherwise."

"Well, you know, he just happened to fall down during the big fight in the foyer, and then my pickpocketing fingers just happened to find that key inside his jacket."

"Pickpocketing? How impressive," I say with a grin.

"Thank you. My next mission is to figure out who killed Saskia and framed you for it."

"Wait, hang on." My smile fades. "What exactly are you doing to figure that out, because you could wind up in serious trouble if you're found sticking your nose where it shouldn't be."

"My nose is perfectly fine," Perry says, rubbing it. "We've just done a little digging in Olive's office so far. We found scrolls with non-Guild seals on them."

"Are you *insane?*"

"We haven't managed to open any yet," he continues, ignoring my question, "but they look suspicious. Like she's receiving instructions from outside the Guild. And she didn't like you or Saskia, so she had motive to get rid of both of you."

The thought crossed my mind too, but I don't want Perry and Gemma trying to prove it on their own. "Seriously, Perry, you do not want to be caught looking through Olive's stuff."

"Don't you want to know if she's the one who did it?" Gemma says. "Don't you think *everyone* should know?"

"If she is the one who did it and she finds out you're trying to prove it, the two of you could wind up dead."

"Possibly," Perry says, looking unconcerned. "Well, the three of us. Ned's obviously in on it too."

"This isn't a joke, Perry."

"We know that," Gemma says gently. "We're being careful. But isn't this the kind of thing we're training for? As guardians, we're all about justice and truth and finding the real criminals. Whoever the real criminal is in this case, he or she needs to be found."

"Okay, but since you don't have permission to work on this case, you should take your suspicions to someone higher up. A mentor you trust, or my brother. He'll listen to you."

With a dramatic sigh, Perry says, "Fine. We'll take your thoughts into consideration. But when we prove your innocence, I hope you'll say thank you."

I chuckle. "Of course." I look down at Mom's sleeping form, wondering if there's any way she can hear all of this. Then something occurs to me. I turn back to Perry and

Gemma with a frown. "How did you know I was here?"

"Gemma's a genius, that's how," Perry says. Gemma's cheeks turn pink as she smiles, but she's still refusing to look at him. I decide that something has definitely happened between the two of them. "We knew you must be communicating with your family somehow, but all our houses are being monitored, and they've got Guild people following us everywhere."

"Seriously," Gemma says. "That's not an exaggeration. I went shopping last night and this Guild woman followed me the entire time. She did a terrible job blending in with everyone else."

"So we were going down to the dining hall when your dad passed us on the stairs, and Gemma said—"

"*That's* how you've been meeting up with them, right here inside the Guild, where no one would think to look."

"So we waited until your dad left, and then we ran in here when the healers weren't looking."

"It was so—"

"Shh," I say as footsteps move closer. A shadow passes by Mom's curtain, then stops. "Don't make a sound," I whisper as the person walks closer. The curtains move and a healer's face looks in. He frowns at Mom, then shakes his head and leaves.

A wide grin stretches Gemma's lips. "He didn't see us," she whispers.

"Nope. I imagined we were invisible and made him see that instead."

"Amazing," Perry murmurs.

"We need to go before we all wind up in trouble," I tell them. The three of us shuffle toward the curtain and Gemma

262

peeps out. "I can conceal all of us until we're out of the healing wing," I say.

"That is *so cool*," Gemma says, barely managing to keep her voice below a squeal. "Please can we be friends forever."

I can't help smiling at that. It's a smile that remains on my face the whole way back to the lakeside house. And it's a smile that turns thoughtful as I walk through the faerie door to the mountain. How many friends would I have kept in the past if I'd simply told them the truth instead of allowing them to believe horrible rumors? Or, conversely, how much sooner would I have wound up on the Griffin List?

It doesn't matter. I only care that I've finally found the right kind of friends. Friends who not only accept me as Gifted, but who love me for it.

CHAPTER TWENTY-SIX

"ARE YOU MOVING IN PERMANENTLY?" GAIUS ASKS THREE days later as I walk up the stairs with several boxes floating behind me. I look up, expecting to find him annoyed or confused. After all, I didn't mention this to him before I left for Raven and Flint's house this morning. Instead, I find him looking pleased.

"Not exactly," I say, drawing the words out, hoping he isn't too disappointed. "I just thought it would be nice to have some of my things here for now. You know, until I figure out what my next move is."

"Ah, I see."

I climb the remaining stairs, making sure to concentrate on the boxes so they don't bump into each other. Inside my temporary bedroom, I lower them to the floor. Then I open one, take Chase's coat out—the one he put around my shoulders after Ryn and Vi's wedding—and walk to his room with it. I find him in the same condition as when I left this morning. After hanging his coat over the back of the desk chair, I fetch the sketchpad I've been using and sit on the edge of the bed. This is what I do these days when I'm not arranging to visit my family in secret. I sit in here and draw. Or I practice projecting my illusions, seeing how detailed I can make them or how quickly I can change from one to the next. Or I read through the information Gaius found on various distant art schools. Lumethon says she doesn't think Chase is aware of whether anyone is in this room with him, but I hate thinking of him lying here alone in his distressed, nightmare-consumed state.

"Calla?" I hear Lumethon's voice out in the passage. "I think I found it," she says, walking into the room with Gaius behind her. I leave the sketchpad on the bed and walk to her side so I can see the book she's holding. She points to a page with a drawing of a cloud of smoke alongside a drawing that looks very much like the demon labyrinth creature. "It's a morioraith. They're only supposed to be found in the Dark North. First, in smoke form, it paralyzes its victim. Then it shifts into bodily form so it can bite and scratch. Its venom causes hallucinations based on any wrong you've ever caused anyone, which is exactly what it wants because then it shifts back to smoke form and feeds on its victim's despair, guilt and shame. Once satiated, it leaves the victim to die from the poison." She looks up. "Sounds like it's one of the few things that can actually defeat Chase."

"Morioraith," I say, testing the word out. "Where did you find this book?"

"Underground. At the witches' shop."

My mouth drops open. "You went in there? Are you crazy?"

"I believe I asked her the same thing," Gaius says, taking the book from Lumethon and paging through it.

"No, I'm not crazy." She walks to the side of the bed. "The witches have no reason to hurt me. They don't know who I am or who I'm connected to. I found a book that was for sale, so I bought it, and that was that." She places her hand on Chase's brow. "I think his skin is cooler than before. Still warmer than normal, though."

"Okay, so we know what this creature is called now," I say, "but that doesn't tell us why Chase isn't awake yet. It's been a *week* since he was poisoned. His magic is far more powerful than mine, so why hasn't he recovered? This feels like it's taking too long."

"He was bitten far more than you were," Gaius points out.

"I know, but ... a *week*? A normal bite would heal within hours."

"It isn't just the physical effect of the poison," Lumethon says. "I think his body has dealt with that already. It's his mind that's still fighting. We're all aware of Chase's past. If he's facing the guilt of everything he's ever done wrong, then he could be battling nightmares for some time still."

I push my hands through my hair. "That's so horrible to think of. I wish we could wake him up somehow."

"I know," Lumethon says. Then she asks, "What's the time?

I think I'm supposed to be downstairs now. Darius finally got the Terrendales out, and now he doesn't know what to do with them."

"Oh, yes, I found a location," Gaius says. "I'll give you the details."

I wish I could ask them what they're talking about, but I know it's all part of that Downstairs Stuff I'm not supposed to know anything about. I've seen a few people coming and going —always down the stairs and through that door Chase opened with his handprint—but they never do more than nod in my direction and continue on their way.

"Um, I won't be here for dinner," I call to them as they turn to leave. "I'm meeting my dad and my brother." Gaius waves to show me he's heard, and he and Lumethon continue discussing the Terrendales, whoever they are, as the two of them leave the room.

I climb onto the bed, but I don't open the sketchbook yet. I watch Chase for a while before my eyes fall, as they always do, on the telepathy ring sitting on the low table beside the bed. I've contemplated putting it on several times, but I know that accusing Angelica of sending Chase to his death inside the labyrinth wouldn't exactly be helpful. Looking at it now, though, I'm filled with a sense of restlessness. The days are moving by, and I've made no effort to find the Seers because Chase hasn't woken up yet. But why do I have to wait for him? Surely I could do something useful on my own.

I reach over Chase and pick up the ring. I place it on my palm and stare at it as I think. Angelica said she no longer had an access stone to give Chase, but perhaps she knows where I can find it. If I can get my hands on it, then Chase and I can easily go straight to the labyrinth chamber when he wakes up. Or I could go with Lumethon if Chase doesn't wake in the next few days.

Before putting the ring on, I decide what my story will be. I need to know exactly what I'm going to tell Angelica so the wrong thoughts don't end up coming to mind. When I'm clear on the details, I pick up the ring and slip it onto my left forefinger.

Hello? I wait for an answer, but none comes. Louder, as if I'm shouting the word, I say it again. *Hello?*

I count to six before—*Nathaniel! Why the hell did you stop communicating? Did you forget all about your prison break-out plan for me? Was your goal simply to use me to get information and then leave me here?*

I focus on thinking each word clearly, as if I were saying them out loud. *Hi, Angelica. I work for Ch-Nathaniel. I'm aware of his plan to get you out of Velazar. I'm working on it at the moment. I just thought you should know that he's unconscious after an attack from a morioraith in your labyrinth. He's been like this for a week now, which is why you haven't heard from him.*

Silence is my only answer. For a few moments, I wonder if she's taken the ring off. Then she says, *I thought you sounded different. Who are you? What's your name?*

My real name comes immediately to mind before I've even had a chance to think of the fake name I chose just minutes ago. Chase was right about deception being difficult when you're communicating with thoughts.

Calla, she says. *Why should I trust you?*

Do you want to get out of prison or not?

Of course I do, but how exactly are you going to make that happen?

Unbidden, the thought of my Griffin Ability rises to the forefront of my mind. I tug the ring off my finger before I can give away anything more about myself, but then I decide that this is actually a good thing. If Angelica senses my honesty, hopefully she'll trust me. I quickly put the ring back on.

What a fascinating Griffin Ability, she says.

It's what helped Nathaniel get into Velazar to see you.

Thank you for that. And I'm sorry about the morioraith. I didn't know it was still there. The men who've been running things on the outside for Amon and me are in control of the labyrinth now. It turns out Nathaniel needn't have gone in there. When the prison cell cycle took me past Amon's cell again, I discovered the Seers are no longer there. They've been moved to a lighthouse. Brigham Lighthouse just outside Kagan City.

I tug the ring off again to hide my immediate reaction. Chase is trapped inside his nightmares for no reason. *No reason!* We could have both *died* because Angelica gave him the wrong information. I force myself to calm down before putting the ring back on. *You had better not be lying about this.*

Why would I lie? Nathaniel and I have an agreement. We're in this together now, which is why you're going to be freeing me from prison. If you don't believe me, go and find the Seers first. Then you'll know I'm telling the truth.

Fine. Nathaniel or I will be in contact soon.

I remove the ring and clench it in my closed palm. Angelica seemed quite certain her new information is correct, but what if Amon was lying to her for some reason? Only one way to find out, I suppose. We need to go to Kagan City.

CHAPTER TWENTY-SEVEN

I PULL SEVERAL BOOKS OFF THE PLANT-LADEN SHELVES IN Gaius's study, but none of them mention Kagan City. There are hundreds of books in here, though, so I probably just haven't found the right one. After stepping around a small, wheeled contraption that glides in random patterns across the study floor while stabbing the air with a hairpin, I head out to the lakeside house and then to Creepy Hollow forest.

I come out of the faerie paths a short distance from Raven and Flint's tree. I don't want to arrive directly outside it in case someone from the Guild happens to be watching their house. I also want to spend a few minutes out in the open with the endless forest stretching for miles in every direction. I miss it. I miss breathing in fresh air, watching glow-bugs come out as darkness settles, and walking between giant mushrooms and luminous flowers and plants hiding exotic creatures. Now that I think about it, most of the forest should be safe for me to walk through. I only need to avoid the places where guardians are likely to be—the old Guild ruins, the homes of the people closest to me, the shoppers' clearing. Of course, the rest of the forest is home to all kinds of potentially dangerous creatures, but as far as I'm concerned, they aren't nearly as much of a threat to me as guardians are.

I don't notice anyone lurking near Raven and Flint's tree, but I decide to conceal myself anyway. It's good practice, if nothing else. I reach their tree and bend closer to blow gently against the rough bark. As I straighten, gold dust floats away from the tree to reveal a door knocker beneath. I take hold of it and knock twice. Moments later, a doorway-shaped portion ripples and vanishes. Flint looks out. "Hello?"

I slip quickly past him into the house before dropping my illusion. "Hey, it's me. Just taking precautions."

"You know," Dad says, crossing the room, "I'm really glad you didn't figure out you could make yourself appear invisible when you were younger. You would have got up to all sorts of mischief."

"Me? Never. Ryn was your naughty child, remember?"

"I heard that," Ryn shouts from another room.

"Ah, you're here," Raven says. She stands up and shifts Dash to her hip. "Dash has been waiting for a goodnight kiss from you."

"Oh, you little charmer." I kiss Dash's pudgy cheek, and he rewards me with a shy smile. Then he spreads out both hands and reaches for me.

"No, no, no, it's bed time for you," Raven tells him. To the rest of us, she adds, "I'll be back down just now." She heads for the stairs, and Flint follows her.

"Cool. If you need us to help with the food or any—Whoa." My eyebrows shoot up and my jaw threatens to hit the floor as my gaze lands on Vi standing in the kitchen doorway. "Ho-lee pregnant lady. You're enormous."

She places her hands on her hips. "Thanks. That makes me feel so much more attractive than I already feel."

I slap my hands over my mouth, then say, "No, sorry, that came out wrong. I'm just … a bit shocked. I mean, it looks like you could go into labor *right now*. How the heck did that happen? You've only been gone—I don't know—a week?"

"Four and a half months," Vi says. "Approximately. It's the first time in six years that the time on Kaleidos has slowed down for so long. It's just changed the other way, speeding up on their side. That's why I came home." She walks across the room and sits down, rearranging the cushions behind her before leaning back. I sit opposite her. "There's also this ceremony thing at the Institute next week. I'm one of the people they're honoring for all the work I've done there. It would be rude to miss it. I've got about a month left, but I'm happy to spend it here. I've missed Ryn," she adds as he joins us. "More than words can describe." Ryn takes her hand and kisses it as he sits beside her.

"Why did you do it then?" I ask. "Are you really so work obsessed that the idea of spending months alone on a faraway island seemed better than missing a few months of work?"

"Calla." Ryn frowns at me.

"I'm sorry." Darn my stupid runaway mouth. "I didn't mean for that to sound rude. Never mi—"

"It's fine," Vi says. "You're not the first person to ask. Before we knew about the baby, I committed myself to being part of some important changes that are soon coming up at the Institute. I don't want to let down all the people I love working with so much by stepping out, but I also don't want to miss out on time at home with the baby when he or she comes along. I didn't want to have to choose, so I found a way to have both."

"I honestly didn't think it was going to work out," Dad says.

"Neither did I," Ryn says.

I give Vi an apologetic look. "Neither did I."

"Thanks, everyone." Vi pretends to be offended. "It's nice to know that Tilly is the *only* one who thought my idea was a good one."

"Of course she did," Ryn says. "We all know Tilly's just the tiniest bit crazy."

"The best kind of crazy," Vi says with a smile.

"Oh, Dad, where's that letter for Calla?" Ryn asks.

Dad removes a small folded piece of paper from his pocket and leans over to hand it to me. "It came by private messenger this afternoon." It looks like he might be about to say something else, but then his focus shifts. "Flint, is that the new KarKnox multi-tool?" He stands up and crosses the room to examine whatever it is Flint is bringing downstairs. I unfold the paper.

Calla,

I'm sorry about everything. Please meet me on Saturday night at 10 pm where we used to do our target practice. Z

Saturday. That's tonight. Zed obviously assumed Dad would be able to pass this message on quickly.

"If this Z person is a friend from the Guild," Ryn says, "then I'd say don't go. There's a chance he or she is luring you to this meeting on behalf of the Guild."

I cross my arms and frown at him. "You read my letter?"

Ryn's eyes shift to the side before returning to me. "Dad read it first."

I puff out my breath. "You're so immature sometimes."

"Only sometimes?" Vi asks innocently.

"This guy isn't from the Guild," I tell them. "I trust him, but I'll go with caution."

"I think I should go with you," Ryn says.

"No thank you." I stand and walk away quickly before I can get into an argument with Ryn. I think I can handle a meeting with Zed on my own. Besides, Ryn probably wouldn't be pleased to discover that 'this Z person' is the prisoner who escaped the Guild while I watched and did nothing.

* * *

Zed and I used to do our target practice near a deserted beach somewhere in the human realm. We felt safe there. We were invisible to human eyes, and the chances were slim that anyone from our world would come across us. I arrive there ten minutes late so I can sneak up on him rather than the other way around. I walk quietly between trees that bear the scars of our many hours of practice. Knives, daggers, throwing stars, axes, spears. I learned them all out here.

Where the trees end and the dark earth mingles with light beach sand, I stop. I see a lone figure sitting just out of reach of the waves, watching the moon hanging above the water. I look both ways along the beach. Finding it deserted, I walk across the sand to join Zed. He stands the moment he sees me. "You actually came," he says. "I thought you might be too angry after the conversation we last had. And then with everything that's happened to you since then …"

I look around once more to check we're still alone. Then I sit. "You know about what happened?"

"Yes. People talk." Zed sits beside me. "I don't think there's anyone in Creepy Hollow who doesn't know what went down at the Guild."

"Terrific," I mutter.

Zed looks at me and says, "I'm really sorry about all of it, Calla."

I meet his turquoise gaze. "Why? You never wanted me to be part of a Guild."

"I know, but I didn't want it to end this way for you, with your name on the Griffin List and your ability revealed for half the Guild to see."

I let out a long sigh. "Well, that's the way it happened. I can't change it, so now I have to move on."

"You've always been the optimistic type," he says with a smile.

I lift my shoulders. "Not as much these days, but I'm trying."

"I sent you a lot of messages, but when you didn't reply, I realized you'd probably thrown your amber away."

"Yes." I scoop up a handful of sand and let it run between my fingers. "I had anti-tracking spells on it, but I don't know how good they were. I still need to get a replacement, actually. I've been using one that's so old it only communicates with one person."

Zed laughs. "I thought ambers like that only existed in museums."

"Apparently not."

"Well, do you want one of mine?" Zed asks. "I have two."

"You have two? Why?"

"I've always had two. One's personal and one's for business."

I can't help laughing. "Business? What business?"

He shrugs. "Maybe I just like having two."

"Well you won't have two anymore if you give me one."

"I'll get another one. It's fine. Besides, my ambers have the most superior anti-tracking spells on them, which you definitely need." He leans to the side and reaches into his pocket to remove a rectangle of amber far slimmer and smoother than the one I've been using. "I'll delete all my stuff off it." He takes out his stylus. I watch the waves tumbling onto the shore while he deletes any information left on the amber. Messages from his girlfriend, perhaps, or from those guardian-haters he seems to like hanging out with these days. "Here." He hands it to me. "It's been wiped totally clean. It even regenerated a new amber

ID so you won't be bothered by messages from all my business associates."

"Business associates," I say with a snort. "Right. Well, thank you. Once I've disguised myself and changed my name and moved far away and started making new friends, then maybe I'll start using social spells again."

"Is that what you plan to do? Move away, I mean?"

"Yes. It's sad to leave, but I'll probably visit my family a lot. In secret, of course. My brother and his wife will be having a baby any day now, so I don't want to miss out on that."

"So soon?" Zed asks in surprise.

"Yes." I frown at him. "Did I tell you they were having a baby?"

"No, but I overheard your brother talking about it at the Guild. You know, during my many hours of hiding."

"Ah, yes." I sift more sand through my fingers. "And now you and I are both fugitives."

"Yes. Here's to the fugitive life." He raises his other amber like a champagne glass. I lift the amber he gave me and tap it against his.

"To the fugitive life," I say with a laugh, because I may as well embrace it. "And to friendship."

"To friendship," Zed repeats. Then he leans over and kisses me.

CHAPTER TWENTY-EIGHT

I TRY TO JERK AWAY, BUT ZED'S HAND IS ALREADY AROUND the back of my neck, pulling me closer to him. I place both hands against his chest and push hard. As he falls back, I scramble to my feet. "What are you doing?" I gasp.

"I thought … I thought you wanted this." He stands up.

"I did, but that was months ago, and you told me I was too young for you. And don't you have a girlfriend?"

"Not anymore. And I know I said you were too young, but … I don't know." He lifts his shoulders. "You seem different now."

"Different?"

"Yes, like … you don't seem like a little girl anymore."

I cross my arms tightly over my chest, still clutching the amber he gave me. "Well, thanks, but when I said 'to friendship,' I meant it."

"Are you sure?" He steps closer to me. "Are you sure you don't want something more?"

I look into the blue-green eyes I used to daydream about and wait for my heart to start pounding or shivers to race across my skin or sprite wings to stir deep inside me.

Nothing.

Absolutely nothing.

"Zed," I say. "I'm sure. I'm happy we're friends again and that we're not arguing about the Guild, but … that's all I want. Just friendship." I swing my arms awkwardly at my sides. "I think I should go now. Good night."

I walk quickly away toward the trees.

"Calla?" he calls after me. I look back. "I'm sorry if I made you feel awkward. I'm happy with friendship. Seriously."

I dip my head. "Okay. Thank you. And thanks again for the amber."

I return to the mountain via the lakeside house. It's late, but I'm not tired yet. I need to get my mind off Zed and all that awkwardness. How odd! What could possibly have made him think I still feel the same way I felt all those months ago? I rub the back of my neck and shoulders as I step out of my shoes, trying not to dwell on the way his lips felt odd against mine. It isn't a memory I want to keep.

I pad along the passage in my socks and walk into Chase's bedroom. A lamp is still on, so I move it to the empty side of the bed where I like to sit and draw. I open my sketchbook and page through it to the one I'm currently working on: a section of the old Guild ruins covered in creeping vines and star-shaped flowers. This book is full of drawings now, ranging from brief, abandoned outlines to detailed, nearly finished pictures. Since my initial shock at having been kicked out of the Guild has worn off, I'm finding it easier to turn to a new page, place my pencil on the paper, and watch something take shape.

Every now and then my hand stills as I look down at Chase. He seems a little calmer tonight. Less tossing and fewer mumbled words. I touch his skin. It isn't burning the way it was a few days ago, but I can't tell if it's back to a normal temperature or not. "What are you dreaming?" I whisper.

I turn back to my drawing and decide it needs some color. In fact, this whole book needs some color. Everything is black and white and grey so far. I set the sketchbook aside and stand up. There must be some color pencils in this bedroom. I walk to the table covered in jars of paint, tattoo ink, a pile of loose sketches, and other art-related bits and pieces. Beside several small canvases stacked on top of each other, I see a jar with pens and pencils sticking out of it like an artist's version of a bouquet. I reach for it, but then my attention is caught by something else: The tiny ship inside the glass bottle.

I carefully pick it up and take a closer look. The ship is sailing on stormy waters with minuscule raindrops pouring down and the occasional flash of lightning zigzagging across the scene. The first time I saw this bottle, I had no idea of the significance of this enchanted object. No idea that it was a tiny clue to who Chase really is. But now I know exactly what it represents: his powerful ability to create storms and control the weather. I try to find some part of me that's still angry with him for not telling me the truth, but I don't think there's any anger left. I understand now why he had to keep his secret until he knew if he could trust me. I just wish there had never been any secret to keep in the first place.

I lower the bottle gently back onto the table. Then I pull the jar closer and look through the pens, charcoal sticks and bits of chalk until I find a single rainbow pencil. I shake it to check that it's still working, and it changes from orange to yellow. Perfect. Before I head back to the bed, I glance down at the pile of sketches. The one on top is of the greenhouse. Sliding it to the side, I see an ink drawing of a phoenix on the next page. Underneath that is a charcoal moon reflected on rippling water, and under that—a sketch of me.

Surprise jolts through me, followed quickly by guilt. I shouldn't be looking through Chase's sketches. These are personal. I wouldn't like it if someone went through my sketchbook without my permission. But I can't help lingering for another few moments to examine the sketch more closely. With yellow and a bit of orange, he's colored my eyes and parts of my hair, but the rest of the drawing is in varying shades of grey. There's a shy smile on my lips, and I wonder what moment he was trying to capture in this drawing.

As I shuffle the papers back together, I see the edge of a worn notebook sticking out from underneath the pile. I slide it out. I know I shouldn't, but I'm so curious, and what's another few moments of snooping? I open the notebook and find pages and pages of Chase's handwriting. It isn't a journal, though. This looks more like ... assignment details. Names, dates, places. A tick next to every person who's been saved or aided in some way. A record of all the good Chase has done since he left his dark past behind.

I close the book and slide it back beneath the sketches, then return to the bed with the rainbow pencil. But my focus has shifted entirely, and I don't feel like drawing or coloring anymore. I look at Chase. I place my hand gently on his wrist. I've avoided holding his hand so far. It seemed too … intimate. It made me think of that moment after the wedding when he slid his fingers between mine and my heart expanded to fill my entire chest because I believed, for just a little while, that happiness was ours.

With my heart pounding heavily and my throat strangely dry, I lift his hand and fit my fingers between his. "Please wake up," I whisper. And then quieter, almost inaudibly, as if it's a secret no one else should ever hear: "I miss you. I probably shouldn't, but I do. I miss you a lot. I missed you even when I was angry with you. And after you finally explained everything and we began talking again, I missed you even more because nothing was the way it used to be after that." I rest my forehead against our clasped hands and close my eyes. "Is it crazy that I don't want to leave you?" I murmur.

Bright specks of light flash on the other side of my eyelids. Confused, I pull my head back and open my eyes. A haze of golden sparkles drifts around our interwoven fingers. I snatch my hand away in fright. Across the room, the pile of sketches on the table is swept into the air, while next to me, the flame in the lamp flares suddenly, setting the lampshade on fire. I extinguish it with a quick shield spell thrown over the fire to smother it. Darkness descends upon the room. I cup my hands together and coax a ball of light into being. I expand it until a warm glow illuminates the room, then send it higher up so it floats near the ceiling.

Then I sit with my hands tucked firmly beneath my arms, watching Chase while my heart rate slowly returns to normal. This hasn't happened to me before, these sparkles, these uncontrolled bursts of magic. But I know what they are. Mom and I had a horrendously awkward conversation once where she explained the magic of physical attraction and ... other things.

"I'm not supposed to feel this way about you," I murmur. "I'm supposed to keep reminding myself who you really are, and then I'm supposed to leave."

Instead of answering me, Chase remains lost in his dreams. I tell myself that this is a good thing, because do I really want him knowing how I feel? No. Not when he once crushed and nearly destroyed a world and could potentially do the same thing to me.

I pick up my sketchbook and the rainbow pencil and begin adding color to my drawings. I'll go to bed at some point, but for now, I need to let my mind drift.

* * *

I feel disoriented when I wake up. I'm on the wrong side of my bed and there's no bedcover over me. Then I open my eyes enough to realize that this isn't my bed. After blinking some more and sitting up, I find the sketchbook and rainbow pencil next to me. I must have fallen asleep here instead of going back to my own room. I rub my eyes before looking across to Chase's side of the bed.

He isn't there.

Startled, I look up and find him sitting at the desk, staring at nothing. His hair is wet and his clothes are clean. "You're awake!" I almost jump up and run over to him, but I manage to restrain myself. I crawl to the edge of the bed instead. "When did you wake up?"

He slowly turns in his chair to face me. "A little while ago. I had a shower. Now I'm ... thinking."

"About?" I ask carefully.

"The torture I just lived through."

I swallow, then say, "You've been unconscious for a week."

"Is that all?" he says with a humorless laugh. "It felt like forever."

"It was the morioraith."

"I know." He lowers his head into his hands. "I'm so sorry, Calla. I should have remembered it. I should have been prepared. But Angelica and I used to travel straight into the chamber and out again. And the morioraith ... I never dealt with it directly. Angelica found it somewhere. She used to control it with a gong. A great big one with a deep resonating sound. The morioraith couldn't stand it. But even without a bell or a gong, I could have done so much more. I should have been ready with magic the second it shifted into bodily form, but it all became confusing so quickly. I couldn't do anything, and I'm so sorry."

"*You're* sorry?" I ask. "*I'm* the one who's sorry. I was slowing you down. You could easily have got away without me. And then you jumped in front of that thing so it wouldn't bite me and you wound up with your entire body poisoned. That's why I'm the one who's apologizing."

"It would have taken me anyway," Chase says. "I have far more to sate a morioraith's hunger than you do." He opens the top drawer of the desk and places something inside it. "I've spoken with Angelica," he says. "She told me what she told you."

I bite my lip, then ask, "Are you mad at me for using the ring?"

"No. I assumed you were only trying to help." He doesn't look at me when he speaks, though, so I can't be sure if he's telling the truth.

I stand up and cross the room. I stop in front of him, but still he doesn't look up at me. "Are you okay? I mean, are you *really* okay?"

He rubs a hand over his face and stands. He looks over my shoulder as he says, "It feels like the past ten years never happened. I feel like the monster who woke up beside the Infinity Falls. The monster who could barely face living because of all the terrible things he did. All the memories are *right there*, just below the surface, so raw, so near. It's all I can see. It's all I am."

"No." He still won't meet my eyes, so I reach up and touch his face. The smallest of touches, just along his jaw, but enough to make him look at me. "You are so much more than your past. You're this—" I pick up the nearest canvas, one of my favorites: sprites dancing in the rain "—and this—" I grab a few sketches from the floor "—and this—" I hold up the tattoo machine "—and this. *This* is what you are now." I pick up his notebook and wave it in front of him. "And yes, I know I shouldn't have looked at it, but it's amazing. You've helped *so many* people."

He quietly takes the book from me and returns it to the table. "I think you should leave," he says.

I open my mouth, but I can't come up with a response. Hurt stabs me in the chest, but I tell myself he didn't mean it that way. I've been in his room from the moment he woke up, so it makes sense that he'd want a little bit of time a—

"The mountain, I mean. You shouldn't be around here anymore. You're planning on leaving anyway, aren't you? It may as well be now."

The imaginary knife in my chest starts twisting. "You're … kicking me out?"

"Calla." He gives me an agonizing look. "You shouldn't be around me. How have you not realized this already? *I am a monster.*"

"No you're not!" I run my hands through my hair in frustration. "A week ago you were the one trying to convince me that you're not that person anymore, and now I'm the one trying to convince you. Thank goodness one of us came to our senses during this whole morioraith ordeal, otherwise we'd both be calling you a monster."

"As we should be," he mutters.

I grab his notebook and push it against his chest. "Read this."

"Calla—"

"Read it! Then tell me you're a monster, after all the good you've—"

"This will never make up for everything I've done!" he yells, tossing the book onto the floor. "I can never go back to all the people I've wronged and apologize to them. I can never ask for their forgiveness."

"No, you can't. And you can never change what you did either. So I'm going to remind you what you told me not too long ago when I was the one who needed to be pulled from the darkness: *The only thing you have control over now is your future.* So are you going to wallow in self-pity, or are you going to make a difference?" I bend and pick up the notebook. I push it into his hands. "And you really shouldn't just chuck this around," I add quietly. "It seems like something you probably want to keep." And then, since I can't think of anything else to say, I turn around and leave.

CHAPTER TWENTY-NINE

CHASE IS GONE WHEN I WAKE THE NEXT MORNING. I GO hunting for some food in the kitchen, and that's where Gaius finds me to tell me the news that Chase has recovered and is out on another mission already. "I'm sorry you didn't have a chance to speak to him before he left," he says to me. "I know you've been waiting anxiously for him to wake up."

"That's okay. I actually spoke to him during the night."

"Ah, wonderful. Did he seem all right to you? He was very quiet this morning. I couldn't get much out of him."

"Um …" I pick up an apple from the bowl on the kitchen table and roll it around in my hands, wondering how much Chase would want me to reveal. "Well, he did just spend a week trapped inside nightmares of the past. He probably needs a little time to get his head back in the right place. Did he say where he was going?"

"To find the lighthouse outside Kagan City."

"Oh. I thought—I mean, I assumed—we'd go there together. But ..." I shouldn't be surprised. He did tell me I should leave the mountain because he doesn't want me anywhere near him, so I suppose that includes this little mission to find the Seers. Too bad he didn't stick around long enough for me to tell him I still want to be involved until we're certain we've stopped Amon's plan. I continue rolling the apple between my palms. "Um, anyway, do you know Kagan City? Have you heard of it before?"

"I haven't, but we managed to find it in one of my books this morning. Have you seen this convenient little device for peeling apples?" He puts a ring down on the table, takes the apple from me, and places the apple in the air above the ring. Before I can tell him that I don't usually peel my apples, the glossy red fruit begins spinning faster than my eye can follow. When it wobbles to a halt, the peel is gone.

I pick up the apple and examine it with a frown, wondering where the peel went. And wondering why Gaius changed the subject so abruptly. I lower the apple and look at him. "Did Chase tell you not to let me follow him to wherever this lighthouse is?"

Looking cornered, Gaius says, "Well, uh, we don't think you should be getting too involved, seeing as how you're leaving soon."

"So that's a yes?"

"Have you chosen where to go yet?" he asks innocently.

With a groan and a roll of my eyes, I walk out of the kitchen.

Two days later, Chase still hasn't returned. Gaius tells me not to worry about him, so I try to ignore the insidious voice that says, *What if he never comes back?* I choose some art schools and start getting a portfolio organized. We're two months into the school year, but hopefully arty people aren't as strict about those sorts of things as guardians are. I'll show them what I can do, and hopefully one of the schools will accept me. I ignore the teeny, tiny part of me that hopes I don't get into any of them.

In the afternoon, I go into the human realm for some exercise. I jog around a park alongside the humans, comfortable in the knowledge that they can't see me. When I pass someone eating a bagel, I start laughing and almost trip over my own feet. Then I wish I had human money so I could buy one for Gaius. After my warm-up, I stand in the middle of the park and practice fighting using a stick I've transformed into a long, straight staff. I spin it in front of me and behind my back and over my head. I sweep it through the air and then lunge forward to smack it down against the ground. I repeat every single move I know. It feels so good to be active that I can barely stand the thought of spending the rest of my life in front of a canvas or bent over drawing paper. I wanted art to be a hobby, not a career, and now everything is going to end up the wrong way around.

I console myself with the thought that at least I'm not in prison. At least I don't have a Griffin List tag embedded magically beneath my skin so the Guild can track my whereabouts for the rest of my life. At least I have the chance to start over.

* * *

I wake up and reach clumsily for the two ambers beside my bed. My hand finds the new one first, and I look at it through one blurry, half-open eye. It's blank. No surprise there. Zed's the only one who has the ID so far, and he and I aren't in the habit of sending too many messages to each other. The noise that woke me must have come from the older, heavier amber. I pick it up and squint at the words on its surface as they swim into focus.

Congratulations, you're an aunt!

I blink. "What?" Then I sit up straight. "*What?*" I jump out of bed and grab my stylus, which rolls off the bedside table and disappears beneath the bed. After scrambling underneath it to retrieve the stylus and muttering about how this would all be a lot easier if I could just mirror-call him, I reply to Ryn's message. Then I hastily change out of my pajamas and into some clothes. I drag my fingers through my hair and dash into the bathing room to brush my teeth. When I come back out, there's another message from Ryn. I slide my amber into my back pocket and run to the door, then run back because I've forgotten to put shoes on.

Through the door, I hear a familiar voice. I pause in the middle of pulling on a sock, just to make sure I've heard correctly. Yes, that's Chase, speaking with Gaius—something about confirming that the Seers are indeed imprisoned at the lighthouse. Relief floods me. *He's okay!* He probably won't be pleased to find that I'm still here, but we can have that discussion later. Shoes on, I jump up and hurry out of my room. I run along the passage and reach the top of the stairs as Chase turns at the bottom and walks back up.

"Hi, good morning, goodbye," I say as I rush past him.

"Hey, hang on. Where are you going?"

I stop at the bottom and look up. "Creepy Hollow. Vi had her baby!"

"What? That's impossible. She's barely pregnant."

"No, no, she spent some time on Kaleidos. It's all fine. A little bit early, but Ryn says Vi and the baby are both fine."

"Oh, that's good." When I turn away, he adds, "Wait, can we just—" He jogs down and stops beside me. I notice now that he's wearing the coat I finally returned to him. "Can we talk for a moment, or are you needed there urgently?"

"Well, no, it isn't *urgent*. I'm excited to get there, that's all."

"This won't take long. I just wanted to apologize for—" He cuts himself off as Lumethon walks out of the living room while flicking through messages on her amber. She heads for the stairs without a glance in our direction. Chase clears his throat. "I'm really sorry that I—" The faerie door swings open and a bald man I'm almost certain is a drakoni walks through it. He locks the door with a gold key, nods to us, then greets the spiky-haired elf who walks out of the living room. The same elf who worked as Chase's assistant at his tattoo shop and then showed up in the healing wing after I woke from my

Velazar Prison ordeal.

The two of them begin chatting. Chase sighs, takes my arm, and opens one of the doors leading off the entrance hall. He pulls me into the room, which turns out to be piled high with old furniture as well as broken gadgets and half-constructed weapons that probably began their life in Gaius's laboratory. Chase closes the door, leaving a small circle of light in the ceiling as the only source of illumination.

"Sorry," he says. "I forgot this was the storage room."

"You were saying something about not taking long?"

"Yes. I'm sorry about the other night. I shouldn't have spoken to you so soon after I woke up. I wasn't in the right frame of mind, and everything felt a bit ... hopeless."

"Well, to be fair, I was the one who fell asleep in your bedroom. You wouldn't have had to speak to me if I hadn't been there."

"True." After a pause, he asks, "Did you sit next to me a lot while I was asleep?"

I shrug, grateful for the gloomy light that hides the heat rising to my face. "Every now and then."

"Well, thank you. My dreams were ... horrendous. It was a great comfort to wake up and find I wasn't alone. And thanks for throwing my book at me. It helped."

"I didn't really *throw* it at you."

"You should have. It might have knocked some sense into me while you were still in the room instead of a day or two later."

"Well, you know, I guess you needed a little more time to remember that you're not a monster after all."

"Yeah. Being out in the light of day helped as well. Oh, and I'm glad to see you didn't listen to me when I told you to leave. I've checked out Brigham Lighthouse, and it looks like a rescue attempt will go more smoothly if we have your illusions to help get us in and out."

"Of course." With a smile, I add, "I never planned to listen to you when you told me to leave, by the way."

"Good. Because it's also …" He takes a deep breath and rubs the back of his neck. "Well, it's nice to have you around."

"It's, um, nice to be around." Fantastic. Now my face is definitely heating up.

"Anyway, I'll let you go now." He opens the door, and the bright light that streams in is jarring. His hand brushes my arm briefly as he adds, "Please pass on my congratulations to Vi and Ryn."

Somewhere behind him, sparks shoot from a watering can spout and cartwheel through the air. I hurry away before he notices.

* * *

I sneak into the curtained healing wing cubicle where Vi is in bed with a little bundle in her arms. She looks up at me with shining eyes, and the first words out of her mouth are, "Isn't she the most beautiful thing you've ever seen?"

I manage to contain my squealing as I fling my arms around Ryn and squeeze him tight. "Congratulations, big brother." Then I hurry to the side of the bed and gaze at the little wrapped-up bundle. I brush my finger gently against her soft cheek. I look at her tiny eyelashes and sweet rosebud mouth. "She's perfect," I breathe. "What's her name?"

"Victoria Rose," Ryn says, standing beside me and putting an arm around my shoulders.

"So pretty," I murmur. "Are they family names, Vi?"

"Rose was my mother's name," she says. "And Victoria …" A sad smile crosses her face. "She was my mentor, but she was like family. She died in The Destruction. I only ever heard people call her Tora, but her full name was Victoria. I'm not sure what we'll end up calling this little one. Victoria, Tora, Tori …"

"Vicky? Vix?" I suggest.

"Well, she'll be Victoria when she's in trouble," Ryn says, "which is bound to be often, if she's anything like me."

"Victoria Rose," Vi corrects with a laugh. "Didn't your parents always use at least two names when you were in trouble?"

"So Victoria Rose when she's in trouble," Ryn says, "and perhaps Tori the rest of the time."

"And maybe she'll be Ria to her friends," I add, "because that sounds cool and exotic. What do you think her color will be?"

"It's too early to tell," Vi says, stroking her hand over Victoria's fine, dark hair. "It usually takes a few weeks to settle, doesn't it?"

"Yes," Ryn says. "But I have no doubt she'll be just as beautiful as her mother, no matter what her color."

Vi shakes her head as she smiles at him. "Always trying to be Mr. Charming."

"Hey, it's true," he tells her, his smile matching hers. Then he sits on the edge of the bed and looks at me. "I'm sorry I didn't message you sooner. Don't hate me, but ... she was actually born yesterday afternoon."

"What?" I give him my best glare. "And you waited until this morning to tell me?"

"I knew you would have wanted to come here immediately, but the healers first needed to check that she was healthy—which she is; plenty of strong faerie magic pumping through that tiny body of hers, despite her early arrival—and then all the visitors started arriving, and it seemed easier to wait until after the initial rush. I knew it would be safer for you if there were fewer people coming and going."

"And safer for you," I add. "I definitely don't want you to wind up in trouble, which we both know you would be if someone saw me in here. Speaking of which," I add, throwing a glance over my shoulder as footsteps approach the curtain. I quickly project the illusion that I'm not here.

A healer looks in and says, "Ryn, is your father still around?"

"No, he went back to work. Is everything okay?"

"It's better than okay," she says with a wide smile. "His wife just woke up."

PART IV

CHAPTER THIRTY

I REMAIN HIDDEN IN VI'S ROOM CHEWING IMPATIENTLY ON my fingernails while Ryn checks out what's happening with Mom. He comes back to report that the healers going in and out of her room keep shooing him away. I pace around, my brain repeating, *She's awake, she's awake, she's finally awake!* Nerves shoot through me. There's so much I have to ask her. So much she needs to explain.

Dad arrives. I want to rush into Mom's room with him, but Ryn holds me back, telling me to give them a little bit of time alone. "He needs to explain all the things that have happened while she's been asleep. The fact that we know about her being a Seer, and how she was abducted, and then your expulsion from the Guild. Just give her a few minutes for things to sink in before you go rushing in there. And while you're waiting, make sure you're still focused enough to conceal yourself. You don't want to ruin everything now and wind up in a detainment cell downstairs."

"I hate it when you're so sensible," I mumble.

He pats me on the shoulder. "I know."

Eventually, after about the fourth time Ryn disappears to see what's happening, he returns to tell me I can go through to Mom's cubicle. I take another moment to be certain I'm concealing myself properly. Ryn says, "Perfect. You're completely invisible. I'll come with you so I can stop anyone who tries to enter while you're in there."

My heart flutters on anxious wings as I walk past all the floating curtains to the ones behind which Mom has been sleeping for the past six weeks. As we step between the curtains, Ryn sweeps his hand through the air. "Sound shield," he murmurs to me.

I stop just inside the curtain. Mom is sitting up, dwarfed by the oversized healing institute pajamas. Her wispy hair, white blonde and yellow, is tangled, but someone's made an effort to tame it since she woke up. "Calla." She smiles and reaches her hand out to me. Dad sits on one side of the bed, so I rush to the other side and take hold of her hand. My words tumble from my mouth. "Are you okay? How do you feel? Is it confusing to wake up after so long?"

She places her other hand over mine. "I hardly feel any different than I would after waking from a normal sleep. A little bit confused at first, but otherwise normal. That's the sign of a high-quality sleeping potion," she adds, lowering her gaze as her expression turns to one of guilt. She shakes her head.

"I'm so sorry I did this to you. It was the only thing I could think of at the time. I couldn't let him know what I'd ..." She trails off, then grasps my hand tighter and looks up. "Is it safe for you to be here? What if someone sees you?"

"Ryn's standing close enough to the curtain to intercept anyone who tries to walk in. That'll give me time to conceal myself. I can do it quickly now. I've been practicing a lot lately."

She nods. "I know why. I'm so sorry. You know I didn't really want you to be a guardian, but I never wanted it to end this way for you. Never."

"That's not important now. Yeah, it sucks, but ..." I push away the ache that resurfaces every time I'm reminded of my expulsion. "I'm just so glad you're awake. I was really mad at you at first, but then ..." I squeeze her hand as I feel tears threatening. "Why didn't you tell me, Mom? About being a Seer. I wish I had known. It would have helped me to understand you better."

"It's ..." She shakes her head and looks away. "It isn't a gift, it's a curse. I've Seen so many horrible things. And it's so disorienting, so ... upsetting. I hate it. I've always longed to be rid of it. I just wanted to be normal, so I did my best to pretend that I was."

"But now that I know," I say, looking down at our joined hands, "will you explain everything? The vision you had that made you run away, and why someone came after you for it, and why there are two other Seers involved in all of this? Please?"

"I'll have to tell the Guild anyway," she says quietly, "so I should get used to talking about it. And you deserve an explanation, since you were abducted and almost killed because of me." When she manages to meet my eyes, I see tears and the enormous weight of responsibility in her gaze.

I give her a brave smile. "It really wasn't that bad." I don't know how much Dad has told her, but she doesn't need to know how truly horrifying that experience was.

"Well then," she says. "I should probably start at the beginning. I was born a Seer. I hated my visions from the moment they first began. My parents understood and they only ever wanted me to be happy, but they were aware that any respectable faerie born with the Seeing ability should be trained to support the guardian system. So they sent me to the Estra Guild.

"It wasn't all that bad. I had friends. Tamaria and Elayna and I did everything together. Near the end of first year, we were in the library one afternoon when all three of us were struck by a vision at the same time. Different, but all related to the same event. The head librarian was there. Amon. He saw us collapse. He must have heard whatever we said while we were experiencing the visions.

"When we woke, Amon rushed off to call one of our instructors. The three of us sat together, trembling, and we shared what we'd seen. We used to carry little hand mirrors around with us so we could practice transferring visions if we had them. So we did that, and we watched the horror of our future. Then I told Tamaria and Elayna that we couldn't let anyone at the Guild see these visions. After all, guardians were the ones who were going to make this future come about.

"I don't know if they agreed with me. I don't know what they planned to tell the Guild. But I took those three little mirrors and I ran. Guardians came to our house, of course, but I refused to tell them what I'd Seen. They tried to threaten me, but my father made them leave. When we were alone, I showed him and my mother the three visions. Then he understood. He packed up all our things and we were gone before the next morning.

"Years later, he revealed to me that he had never destroyed those mirrors. I thought he was crazy to have kept them, but he said, 'What if this future comes to pass one day, and the only way to fix it is from the scraps of information within these three visions? You will always know yours, but what if you need to be reminded of the other two? Don't destroy them.' I didn't want to listen to him, but as scared as I was, I recognized that he was probably right."

Mom pulls her hands away from mine and slips her wedding ring off her finger. "I hid the mirrors away. I never even told your father I still have them." She takes hold of the diamond on top of her ring and twists it. She twists until the diamond comes away from the ring. "I'm sorry," she says, looking at Dad now. "I'm sure you never meant for this ring to be used for such a purpose."

"Uh ..." Dad stares at the two parts of the ring, looking perplexed. "No."

Mom rubs her finger in circles over the diamond until it loses it sparkle and its shape. It melts away to reveal three tiny discs piled on top of each other. As she recites an enlargement spell, the discs expand. Within seconds, three small round mirrors—the non-reflective Seer kind—sit on her palm. "Still quite small," she says. "Let me make them a little bigger." She applies another enlargement spell, then lifts one of the mirrors so I can see it better. "This was Elayna's vision," she says as Dad's quick strides carry him around the bed to stand beside me. She touches the mirror's surface and the first of the three visions comes into view.

A full moon hangs in a starry sky. A night creature chirps, and two sprites flit across the scene. Without warning, a jagged lightning bolt splits the sky in half, bringing with it a horrendous ripping sound that shatters the quiet of the night. When the bright light has subsided, I see a great tear in the fabric of the sky. The tear grows wider, and beyond it is … a different world. A different realm. The scene darkens and a shadowy figure appears. All I can see of his face is the green light glowing in his eyes. His quiet voice sends a chill along my skin: "The veil has fallen."

The mirror returns to its silvery non-reflective state. "The veil," I repeat softly as I stare at its blank surface. "Meaning … the one between our realm and the human one?"

Silently, Mom nods. She picks up the second mirror. "This is what I Saw." Once again the scene is a night sky, but in the foreground is a stone statue of a trident pointing upward. The trident appears to be rising out of rough ocean waves also carved from stone, which in turn are mounted atop a wide cylindrical base with patterns carved into it. As I watch, a man walks to the statue and climbs easily up onto the stone waves. He stands beside the trident and wraps one hand around it as he gazes up at the sky. I can't see his face properly, but I can just make out the green glow where his eyes are.

Two men walk up to the statue carrying a woman between them. They lay her on top of the stone waves. Another two men carry a second woman and lay her beside the first. They're still alive, but they seem to be barely conscious. The four men stand guard, two on either side of the statue. When they train their weapons on the women, I realize with a jolt that these men are guardians. Into the view of the mirror steps a witch hefting an axe in her hands. She nods first to the men on the right and then to the men on the left. "We thank the Guilds for their assistance. You have helped to make this possible." She walks to the statue, looks down at the women, and then up at the trident. The man holding onto it appears to go rigid. The trident glows. The witch calls out, "From the magic of the depths to the magic of the heights, with blood from one side and blood from the other. Together with the greatest power nature can harness, we shall tear this veil asunder." Then with a barbaric cry, she swings the axe down onto the first woman's neck. I gasp and clap a hand over my mouth as blood gushes down the side of the statue. The witch moves to the second woman. As she cries out and brings her axe down again, I clench my hand in a fist over my mouth. Then bright white light obliterates everything.

The vision is over.

"That … that was horrible," I whisper. "And those guardians just *watched*."

Mom swallows. "And this," she says, picking up the third mirror, "is what Tamaria Saw." The vision begins with a view of the outside of a tower, but it quickly zooms in, flies through a narrow window, and focuses downward. On the round floor of the tunnel is a writhing mass of bodies. Hundreds of people, all tied up and screaming. The vision rushes down, flitting past people, focusing on individual faces. "Not that one," a voice says, and a person is pulled free. "Not that one either. Didn't I tell you not to use the special ones?" A man is pulled free, and then a boy with tattoos on his face, and a crying woman, and a girl with—gold hair? My heart leaps into my throat as the vision pulls back and up, and I watch as a great boulder roughly the same shape and diameter as the inside of the tower falls with blinding speed and crushes the mass of screaming people. In a flash of light, everything turns white and disappears.

I breathe out slowly. "That … that was me. As a child. And that man with the glowing eyes. Was that Draven?"

"Yes," Ryn answers from near the curtain.

"So this was all supposed to happen during Draven's time, but it didn't."

"No, it didn't," Mom says. "Something must have changed. Or perhaps many things changed. But if Ryn hadn't rescued you from the Unseelie Prince, you might have ended up with all those people at the bottom of that tower. And if Draven hadn't been killed, then this vision might have become reality."

"But it didn't, so what use are these visions to Amon?"

Mom lowers the mirror onto the bed. "I think he believes that this could still happen. He probably thinks that if he can bring all the right elements together the way they are in this vision, then he can bring down the veil at any time. There's nothing to indicate that it was restricted to that specific time in history."

"But ... how could he ever get all the right elements together? I assume that lightning bolt came from Draven, and he's ... well, he's supposed to be dead."

"I don't know," Mom says. "All I know is that Tamaria showed up out of the blue several months ago. I don't know how she found me. I've had nothing to do with the Seer life or the Guild since I left. I went to business school and then I ended up as a librarian at Wilfred because I just wanted something quiet. I thought I'd hidden myself perfectly, but she managed to track me down.

"She told me a man had approached her about the visions the three of us had. A man who knew Amon. He wanted her to tell him exactly what she'd seen, and he also wanted to know where he could find Elayna and me. She refused to tell him anything, and eventually he left. She searched for me because she wanted to warn me. She believed this man was trying to piece together the information from all three visions so he could bring about this fall of the veil.

"I told her she should never have come. What if this man was tracking her and now he knew where to find me? Anyway, she left, and I lived in fear for several weeks. But nothing happened, and I forgot about it. Then that man broke in and fought you, and afterwards you mentioned the name Tamaria, and I knew. I knew that's why he'd come, and I knew he would be back. That's why we had to move. And that's why I finally let you join the Guild. I knew we were no longer safe. I wanted you to spend as much time away from home as possible, and I wanted to know you could properly defend yourself if you were at home when he broke in again. I've always hated the Guild, but I had to put that aside knowing you'd be safer there."

"And in the end, the Guild is exactly where they abducted us from," I say quietly. "How is it even possible," I ask as I begin to think these visions through, "for two realms that overlap to suddenly exist in the same space because magic is no longer separating them? Would they kind of ... meld together? Would one destroy the other?"

"Hopefully we never find out," Mom says. "But do you understand now why I didn't want the Guild to know what I'd Seen? They *helped* with everything you saw in those visions. And even though many guardians would have tried to stop it from becoming reality if I'd shared the vision with them, I didn't even want to put the *idea* into anyone's mind in case that's what caused the entire thing to come about."

I lean my hip against the bed. "Do you think that's how it works sometimes? The act of trying to prevent something is what causes it to happen?"

"Yes. Maybe I'm wrong, but I do think that."

"I wonder if it's at all possible," Dad says, frowning as he stares at the mirrors, "for someone to actually make these visions become reality. The consequences would be unspeakable."

I run through the details of Mom's horrible vision again. A tower, a witch, an axe, someone from this realm, someone from the human world, a spell that's probably not too difficult for any witch to discover, a trident statue, and a powerful bolt of lightning produced by the guy who happens to not be dead.

Yes. Someone could definitely make this happen.

"We've been told we can take Victoria home," Ryn says, walking back into the cubicle. I hadn't noticed he'd left. "Cal, you probably shouldn't stick around much longer, not unless you remain concealed. You never know when a healer might walk in here."

"I know. You're right." I take Mom's hand again. "I'm sorry I can't stay."

"It's okay, I understand. I don't want you having to project an illusion the entire time and then accidentally slipping up because you're tired. Besides," she adds with a groan, "I'm sure there are several guardians waiting to question me about the vision I refused to show them so long ago."

Worry clenches my insides. "Just questions? Or will it be something worse?"

"I don't know. But I'm not a child anymore, so I should probably stop hiding." She takes a deep breath that sounds just a little bit shaky. "Whatever the consequences are for running from the Guild all those years ago, I'll face them now." She attempts a smile and adds, "Hopefully one day I can be half as brave as my beautiful daughter."

"Mom …" My throat tightens and unshed tears ache behind my eyes.

"Okay, enough of this," Dad says. "Let's be positive. Everything's going to be fine. Soon you'll be home," he says to Mom, "and you can admire the redecorating mess Calla made of the guest bedroom."

"Hey, that was some of my finest work," I protest, allowing

a smile to mask my concern. Mom chuckles, but I can tell it's half-hearted.

I say goodbye to the two of them. Then I remind myself to be as brave as Mom thinks I am as I hurry downstairs and out of the Guild. Chase and I have work to do if we're going to stop Amon from turning these horrific visions into a reality.

CHAPTER THIRTY-ONE

"MY MOM WOKE UP!" I SAY AS I RUN INTO THE STUDY WHERE Gaius and Chase are bent over a map.

They both look up. "That's wonderful," Gaius says.

"She showed me her vision. And the other two visions as well. The ones from the two Seers who are supposedly in that lighthouse by Kagan City."

"Wait, hang on." Chase holds his hands up. "Are you serious? You've seen all three of these visions Amon is after?"

"Yes. And now you're about to see them." I turn around and focus on the space above the center of the room. "I wish I didn't have to watch these again, but here goes." I project my memory of the three visions into the air. I want to look away from the horrible details, but I don't think that would work. So my eyes stay peeled for everything: the split in the sky, the beheaded women, the writhing bodies about to be crushed. When I'm done, the three of us stand in silence. A dragonwing snapping pod smacks closed around a bug. Chase rubs a hand across his brow.

"It's a little bit horrifying to know that I could have made that happen," he says eventually. He clears his throat. "But now we finally know what we're trying to stop."

"I know this is asking a lot," Gaius says, "but could you show us again?"

So I do. When I'm finished for the second time, Chase squints at the empty space and murmurs, "Angelica knows."

"Knows what?" I ask. "That my mother woke up?"

"I don't know. Maybe it was something else, but when I spoke with her a little while ago, I sensed some kind of excitement in her."

"But how could it be this? Even if there are healers at the Guild who are actually working for Amon or Angelica, they'd then have to go to Velazar Prison to pass on the message. It would take a few hours at least. And she can't know that we spoke about Mom's vision. No one else was there to see it, and Ryn put a sound shield around the cubicle."

Chase paces around the room, swatting various hanging plants out of his way. "I don't know. She's happy about something, and that's not good for us. We need to stop this before it even begins."

"Wait," I say. "Just wait. Is it actually possible? Do you think Amon could force you to provide that lightning bolt of power?"

"I don't plan to let him do anything of the sort, but I

wouldn't put it past him to find another source of power."

"Like what?"

Chase looks at Gaius. "Good question."

Gaius scratches his chin. "Why did all those people have to die?"

"Another good question," Chase says. "And I know what you're thinking. Is that the power that was harnessed?"

"What are you talking about?" I ask them.

"It's not important right now," Chase says. "Let's start simple. That statue. If we destroyed it, would that stop all of this from happening, or could any stone statue take its place?"

"You might be onto something," Gaius says. "That isn't just any statue. I've definitely seen it before. It's … oh, I know it. Um, um, um. Oh!" He snaps his fingers. "The Monument to the First Mer King."

"'From the magic of the depths,'" I recite. "So does this monument have some kind of power?"

"I believe it does. It stands guard over the entrance to the mer kingdom."

"Then I'm guessing the merpeople wouldn't take too kindly to us destroying it," I say.

"We can organize some kind of extra protection around it while we inform the mer king of the threat," Chase says.

"Okay. So where exactly are we going?"

"Um …" Gaius clicks his fingers another few times and looks at Chase. "It's in some subterranean river, isn't it? At the mouth, where the river meets the ocean?"

"Don't look at me," Chase says. "I didn't do my schooling in this realm."

"It wouldn't have helped if you had," I say. "We learned all about the Seelie and Unseelie Courts, but barely anything about the lesser royalty. I've never seen this monument before."

"I'm sure I can find it," Gaius says, moving to the nearest shelf and examining the spines of the books there. "Just give me half an hour."

Chase sighs. "Internet would be so helpful right now." He looks across the room at the cuckoo clock, which tells us it's almost midday. "Okay, I'm calling a meeting. We can send two people on the Seer rescue mission, and the rest of us can handle this mer king monument. If Angelica does somehow know what's going on, I don't want any of her people getting there first. I'll see you downstairs in an hour, Gaius."

"Mm hmm," Gaius says absently, pulling a book from the shelf.

Chase nods toward the door, indicating I should walk with him. "Are you in for this one?" he asks once we're out of the study. "You can get back to your art school applications and fake identity plans when we're done."

"Of course I'm in," I tell him as the same kind of excited anticipation I felt at the start of every assignment stirs within me. "I wouldn't let you leave me out of this even if you wanted to."

* * *

An hour later, I find myself in the area of the mountain I haven't been allowed to explore yet. The area where everyone else who comes into this place seems to disappear to. The only time I've been down here was when Chase offered to show me the gargoyles, and that visit didn't last particularly long.

I walk with Chase along a wide corridor past rooms I'm intensely curious to know more about. I hear voices as we approach a half-open door. Unable to contain my enthusiasm, I find the words "This is so exciting" slipping past the grown-up air I'm attempting to portray.

Instead of looking at me as though I'm a tiresome child, Chase grins. "Imagine if you could do this every day." Then he pushes the door open fully and gestures for me to walk in ahead of him. I enter the room and find five people seated around an oval table. I know Gaius and Lumethon, and I briefly met the elf girl when she was posing as Chase's assistant at Wickedly Inked. The bald drakoni man is the one I saw earlier before Chase pulled me into the storage room. Now that I see him up close, I realize he was also at Wickedly Inked the day I went there to find Chase. The only unfamiliar person is the faerie guy who crosses his arms and frowns at me.

"Thanks for coming, everyone," Chase says as he takes a seat at one end of the table. I slip into the chair on his left. "I know I usually give you a little more notice, so I apologize for that, but we finally know what our favorite Velazar inmates are up to, and we need to intervene quickly.

"Uh, introductions first. Calla, you already know Gaius and Lumethon. That's Ana—" he gestures to the elf "—Kobe—" the drakoni "—and Darius. Everyone, this is Calla. She knows all about the Amon-Angelica situation. Okay, so ..." Chase reaches across the table and pulls one of Gaius's maps toward him.

"Dude," Darius says, "you can't just bring some random chick into the circle. We deal with highly confidential stuff here."

Chase looks up with a frown. "She isn't some random chick."

"Fine. You can't just bring your *girlfriend* into this."

"I'm not his girlfriend," I say immediately.

"Whatever." Darius turns his dark blue gaze to me. "Ana saw you go into the storage room together."

I cross my arms. "We were having a private conversation."

Darius snorts. "Is that what they call it these days?"

My skin heats up, and I will the flush to stop before it reaches my face. "You're really quite rude, do you know that?"

Darius smirks. "So I've been told. And I'm not judging, by the way. We all think it's about damn time Chase got some—"

"Look, Darius may be rude," Ana interrupts, "but he also has a point. She isn't part of the team, Chase."

"Yes I am," I say before I can stop to think about the words. Once they're out, though, I realize that I mean them. Of course I mean them. Why would I want art school when I could have *this*? Being part of a team, making plans, fighting bad guys, pulling apart dangerous plots, and saving people's lives. It's everything I've ever wanted.

I realize everyone is staring at me, including Chase. I clear my throat. "I am part of the team. Chase extended the invitation, and I accepted." I keep my gaze averted from his, though, because I'm not sure if he ever actually did extend the invitation. It was Gaius who suggested I stick around and work with him, wasn't it?

Instead of contradicting me, though, Chase says, "Yes, sorry, I should have lead with that." I sense a change in his voice. "Calla is the newest member of our team."

Darius leans back in his chair, still watching me. "Well then. Since we all have our areas of expertise, what exactly do you plan to bring to the party, Calla—aside from a pretty face?"

I blink at him. A second later, a manticore drops out of the air and hits the table. Shrieks and gasps fill the room as the manticore scrambles to its clawed lion feet and opens its mouth to emit an inhuman roar. Darius jerks out of the way and falls from his chair as the manticore's scorpion stinger flashes forward to strike at him. He throws his hands up to release magic—

And the illusion is gone.

Heavy breathing is the only sound in the room. I lean back in my chair and cross one leg over the other. "I think my usefulness extends beyond a pretty face."

Darius slowly turns his horrified gaze to me. Then he starts laughing. He points to the empty air, looks at Chase, and says, "You might have wanted to lead with *that*."

Chase, the only one who didn't freak out at the sight of the manticore, says, "I wasn't sure we had time for dramatic demonstrations, but I see now that it was necessary. Anyway, let's get back to the part where Amon and Angelica plan to bring down the veil that separates the fae realm from the human one."

Everyone's attention snaps back to Chase.

"What?" Darius demands, quickly returning to his chair.

"You're kidding," Ana says. "Surely that's not possible."

"According to three separate visions, it is. Calla's seen them all. Unfortunately, so has Angelica."

I suck in a breath. "You're sure?"

"Yes. I don't know how, but she knows. Perhaps someone with illusions or an invisibility gift was hiding in your mother's room while she showed you the visions." Chase removes the telepathy ring from his pocket and places it on the table in front of him. "I spoke to her just now. She told me she'd received word that the third Seer, the one who was rescued, had unknowingly revealed her vision. Angelica then said that if I still want to be part of her plan, I need to meet one of her minions at the Monument to the First Mer King tonight so I can help him steal it."

"I assume that's a detail from the vision?" Lumethon asks.

"Yes."

"So Angelica still trusts you," Gaius says. "That's good."

"Yes. So we need to get there first, make sure the monument is secure, then ask for an audience with the mer king so we can convince him that it would be in the best interests of the entire fae world that he order his monument destroyed."

"Great," Darius says as he places his hands behind his head. "I love an easy Tuesday afternoon mission."

"You're not going," Chase tells him.

"What?"

"You and Lumethon are going to rescue the other two Seers. If Angelica and Amon think they have all the information they need now, then what reason do they have to keep the Seers alive? Since we don't like to leave people to die, you two will be taking care of that." He slides a map across the table to Darius. "I've confirmed that they're in the lighthouse," he says, tapping an area of the map before leaning back.

Grumbling under his breath, Darius takes the map and shifts closer to Lumethon so they can examine it together.

"Gaius, did you find out where the monument is?" Chase asks.

"Yes. It's at the mouth of the bottommost Wishbone River, where the fresh water joins the ocean current." Gaius turns an open book around and pushes it toward Chase so he can see the illustration on the page. "It's a system of parallel subterranean rivers, one on top of the other. Since the rivers are considered part of the merpeople's territory, they're inaccessible from the faerie paths. The only way to get to the bottom is to drop through the enchanted whirlpools from one river down to the next. The whirlpools form in different places in each river, but the idea seems to be fairly simple. You let the current carry you along until a whirlpool sucks you down. You land in the next river and repeat the process until you get to the bottom."

Silence greets Gaius's explanation. Then Chase says, "Well, I can't say I've ever traveled like that before, but I suppose it's entirely normal for a merperson."

"Probably," Gaius answers. "When you get to the bottommost river, you let it carry you along until the cave system ends. At that point you're actually beneath the ocean floor." Gaius points to a part of the illustration. "If you let the river carry you further, you'll wind up in the ocean in mer kingdom. You don't need to go that far, though. In the final cave is where you'll find this monument. And there are warriors or guards or whatever they call themselves swimming around in this area, so you can speak to them about seeing the king."

"And how exactly do we get out?" Ana asks.

"Ah, yes, I saw something about that." Gaius pulls the book back around and pages through it. "Something about a portal ..." He turns another page. "Yes, here it is. At the end of the final river, just before it goes into the sea, there's this shallow bit on the right where these rocks are. A permanent whirlpool exists there which is actually a portal. You jump into it and wind up in the top river again, which is open to the air, so you can easily get out and open a doorway to the faerie paths."

"Sounds like fun," I say, pulling the book closer so I can take another look at the drawings. The cave systems seem fairly large, so I don't have to worry about confined spaces being a problem. And while the idea of being sucked into a whirlpool seems somewhat frightening, it can't be too bad if merpeople do it all the time.

"Kobe, Ana, Calla," Chase says. "You can all swim, right?"

The three of us nod.

"Then let's be on our way." As the five of us stand and push chairs into place and help gather up books and maps, Chase lowers his voice so only I can hear. "I knew you'd stay." His gaze is focused on the map he's folding, but I can see his lips pulling up on one side.

I remember Ryn asking me if it was the Guild I wanted so badly, or what the Guild represents. I smile to myself as I reply, "I think I did too."

CHAPTER THIRTY-TWO

WE PICK OUR WAY THROUGH TANGLED, OVERGROWN bushes along the bank of the topmost Wishbone River as the sun moves closer to the horizon. "Your team is ... interesting," I say to Chase, keeping my voice low so Ana and Kobe, walking a little way behind us, won't hear.

"It's your team now too," Chase says. "Unless you've changed your mind. You haven't gone through the initiation blood ritual, so technically you're not bound to us yet."

My steps slow as I frown up at him. "Blood ritual?"

His straight face breaks into a grin. "I'm kidding."

"Darn." I manage to keep myself from cracking a smile. "Here I was looking forward to spilling my blood as a way of demonstrating my commitment."

"If that's how you'd like to prove your commitment, I have

no doubt you'll soon get the chance." His expression turns serious and his eyes find mine as we stop walking. "This isn't exactly a safe game we're playing."

"It never is when people's lives are at stake."

He looks out across the water. "This is a dangerous life you've chosen, Calla."

I place my hands on my hips, ready to do battle with him if he goes anywhere near overprotective territory the way Ryn does. "So is the life of a guardian, and I was happy to choose that one. I've never wanted to walk the safe path."

"I know. I'd never dream of telling you that you can't choose this life because it's too dangerous. Your choices are your own. I just wanted to remind you to be careful. There are people who would be shattered if anything happened to you."

"Chase." I place my hand on his arm so he'll look at me. So he'll know how serious I am. "I'm not sure if you're aware of this, so let me be the one to tell you. There are people who would be shattered if anything happened to *you*. We both need to be careful."

It looks like he wants to say something, but Ana and Kobe have caught up to us now. "Is this where we get in?" Kobe asks.

I remove my hand from Chase's arm, glad that I managed to refrain from spontaneously emitting magic that might have knocked down a tree or set his clothes on fire or sent a wave of river water splashing over us. That would have been awkward to explain. I rub my hand across the back of my neck as Chase says, "Yes. That boulder is the marker." He points behind us to a smooth, oval rock with markings on it sticking up from between the bushes. "The whirlpools appear from here onwards."

We skid down the muddy part of the bank and into the water, which is cold enough to raise a shiver across my skin. There are numerous spells I could use right now—waterproof clothing, warming up the water around me, a bubble of air around my entire body—but I'd rather conserve my energy. This is only the start of our mission, after all.

We wade out to where it's no longer shallow enough to stand and let the current pull us along. "So now we just wait for a whirlpool to appear and suck us down?" Ana asks.

"That's the plan," Chase says.

"What if it doesn't happen?" I ask. "Is there a waterfall at some point along this river before it meets the ocean?"

"Yes, but the diagrams showed numerous whirlpools appearing before then."

"What if these whirlpools only appear for merpeople?" Ana says. "We'll only find out when we reach the waterfall. I don't have the kind of magic you have, and I don't particularly want to wind up crushed on the rocks at the bottom of a waterfall."

"Ana," Chase says. "Have I ever let you fall down a waterfall before?"

"Well, no, but I've never—"

"Exactly. You have nothing to worry about."

"Women," Kobe mutters. "Always worrying."

Ana pulls herself sideways through the water until she's close enough to Kobe to punch his arm.

I start thinking about what magic I'm going to use if we do

wind up at the edge of a waterfall, but I've barely come up with a plan when I suddenly feel myself tugged sideways by the water.

"This is it!" Chase shouts.

"Oh crap, oh crap," I gasp as we're tugged violently into the swirling current of the whirlpool and I become abruptly aware of what a bad idea this is.

"Stop, stop, stop!" Ana shrieks. "I don't want to do this anymore!"

"Just go with it," Chase yells.

The whirlpool forms quickly, creating a hole at its center larger than I'd imagined. I fight the panicked urge to magically launch myself out of the water and instead let it pull me down into the vortex. I spin around and around and down, completely out of control, the current terrifyingly strong, my claustrophobia screaming at me that I'm being sucked into a hole with no air, and then—

I'm falling.

A second later, I plunge into a river colder than the one I just left. I pull upward amidst the rush of bubbles, again and again, until my head finally breaks the surface of the water. I suck in air along with intense relief. I don't know why I didn't consider how terrifying that would be before it actually began, but it's probably a good thing I didn't.

I swim toward Chase and Kobe just as Ana surfaces. I look around as I go, taking in the beauty of the vast underground cave this river flows through. The ceiling and walls are covered in specks of purple light, filling the area with a purple glow.

The rock itself is dark, and I can almost imagine I'm looking up at a night sky.

"That was awful," Ana says after several gasps of air. Her short dark hair, normally sticking out in all directions, is flat around her face. "How many more do we have to do before we get to the bottom?"

That's exactly what I was trying *not* to think about.

"Four more," Chase says as the current pulls us gently along. "But was it really that bad?"

"It was rather terrifying," I admit, mainly so that Ana doesn't think she's the only one who was afraid. Based on the few interactions we've had, she doesn't seem to like me all that much. Since we're going to be seeing far more of each other now, I'd like to change that.

"Sorry, but I don't think you can leave without first going all the way to the bottom," Chase says.

"I don't want to *leave*," Ana says. "I committed myself to this mission. I'm just warning you that I'll probably scream going down every single w—Oookay, here we go again."

With no warning, the gentle current suddenly sweeps around into a spinning circle, taking us with it. Even though I tell myself repeatedly that this isn't going to kill me, it's still terrifying being sucked around and around in an ever decreasing circle until the sudden drop comes. The cave we fall into this time is green. There are no specks of light, but a green shimmer in the cave walls reflects off the water. It's also warmer than the first two, which I'm grateful for. Kobe and Ana surface further ahead. Chase and I join the current behind them, floating on our backs and staring up at the shimmering walls as the water pulls us along feet-first.

"Anyone want to take a bet on what the color of the next river will be?" Chase calls out.

"Can we just bet that we all make it to the bottom alive?" Ana's answering shout comes.

"So that's a no?" Chase asks.

"Noooooononono!" Ana squeals, which most likely means another whirlpool has begun. I don't feel any pull in the water yet, though. I lower my legs and body below the surface so I can look ahead.

"Come on," Chase says to me, pulling at the water with strong strokes. "Don't want to miss the ride down, do you?"

Ana and Kobe vanish into the vortex as Chase and I swim toward it. The swirling current catches us—and then it slows, the hole closes, and within seconds the sloshing water becomes a gentle current once more. "Shoot," I murmur. "That didn't just happen."

"It's okay. There'll be another one," Chase says. "We'll just keep going."

We continue floating downstream, the current a little faster now than it was before. Chase is watching the ceiling pass by again, but I've got my eyes fixed firmly ahead this time. It looks to me as though the cave ends abruptly up ahead, but that can't be right. I squint through the green glow and realize the cave doesn't end—but it does become extremely narrow, forcing the river to flow through three gaps that are little more than cracks in the stone wall.

"Oh no." I start pushing against the current. "No no no.

I'm not going through there." I can handle the whirlpools because they're over so quickly I barely have time to panic, but not this. Not these dark slits in the wall.

Chase floats past me as I turn myself around. "Hey, it's fine," he says. "Gaius checked the entire route. He said there's no part of any river that's too narrow to get through."

"Not happening." I begin swimming in the other direction, pulling at the water with as much strength as I have.

"Calla, there's nowhere else for you to go," Chase says from somewhere behind me.

"I don't care. I can't do that." My voice sounds just the tiniest bit panicked as I struggle against the current.

"What do you mean you can't ..." He trails off as I continue pawing at the water and getting nowhere. "Are you kidding?" he asks. "Claustrophobia? That's your issue?"

"Yes! And I'm not going—"

"Just relax and float."

"I can't relax!" Wait, I can use magic. Add strength to my strokes—swim all the back to where we fell in—wait for the next—

"Stop," Chase says, pulling himself closer to me and catching hold of my arm. "Just float, okay?"

"I can't just—"

He grips both my hands. "Why don't you float backwards, and that way you don't have to see—"

"No!" I don't know why, but it'll be even worse if I can't see where I'm going.

"Okay, okay. I'll go backwards and you just look at me, not the walls."

I shake my head furiously as I watch the river narrowing and the three gaps coming closer. We're heading for the middle and there's no way we can stop now.

"Hey, you never told me about Vi and Ryn's baby."

"What? That's ... so not ..." The horrible slit in the wall comes closer and closer.

"Is it a girl or a boy?"

"Um ... a girl."

"Hey, look at me," Chase instructs. "What's her name?"

"Victoria." The name comes out in a rush of air as the water sweeps us into the gap. I force myself to look at Chase, but the shimmering green walls are *right there*. "We're gonna be squashed, we're gonna be squashed, we're gonna be squaaaaashed!" My voice rises into a squeal and I shut my eyes tightly as the current increases. We shoot into the air and lose hold of each other's hands. I open my eyes in time to see the continuation of the green river before I plunge beneath its surface.

I fight my way through the bubbles until I find air and an enormous cave and space, space, space. "I made it," I gasp as I pull myself away from the three waterfalls. "I'm not squashed. I'm not crushed. Oh, space is so amazing." I look around and find Chase nearby.

"So let me get this straight," he says as I swim toward him, his voice only just audible above the thundering water behind me. "You have the most powerful imagination of anyone I've ever met, but you can't imagine your way out of a small space?"

"It ... just ... doesn't work that way." This part of the river seems to barely be moving, so without a current to carry us, we continue swimming away from the falls.

"But all you have to do is picture it, right?" Chase says. "Then that's what you'll see."

"Not when I'm freaking out! I can't focus when I'm panicking."

"Then you have to decide not to panic."

"It's not that simple. You don't know what it's—"

Water erupts between us, throwing us into the midst of two separate whirlpools. "See you in the next river," Chase shouts as I feel myself tugged irresistibly into the vortex. This one becomes wider and deeper than the others, flinging me around until I can barely breathe before finally dropping me into the next river. I'm so disoriented I don't know which way is up. As I run out of air, I try to form a bubble over my nose and mouth. Then I sense myself slowing rising, so I direct my hands behind me instead. With a spurt of power, I shoot up to the surface.

Delicious air fills my lungs as I tread water and look around. I'm in a red cave with a smooth wall on one side and a collection of rocks on the other. Red light seems to come from somewhere beneath me. The riverbed, probably. I turn in the water, looking for Chase, but I don't see him. I don't see Kobe or Ana either, which I assume means the next whirlpool has already taken them.

"Chase?" The current wants to pull me away, but I'm not going anywhere without him. I kick against the water until I reach the rocky side of the river so I have something to hang onto. "Chase!" I call again. He should have come up by now. Trying to beat down my panic, I slap the water with my palms and yell, "Where are you?"

"Hey, calm down, I'm over here." I twist around and see him dripping wet and climbing over one of the rocks beside the water. "Sorry, I got washed under here after I fell through and it took me a while to navigate my way out." He climbs back into the water and swims toward me. "You weren't seriously panicking about being all alone down here, were you?"

"No, you idiot." I splash water at him. "I was scared you were *dead*."

He splashes water back at me, although not as harshly. "Don't worry, it's gonna take a lot more than a subterranean waterfall to end me. Not even a morioraith could finish the job."

"Yes, well, that might have ended differently if I hadn't draped my very confused self over you while banging magically lengthened pieces of metal together like someone in a crazed trance."

He stops treading water and wraps an arm around the rock I'm clinging to. "That's what happened before Lumethon got there?"

"Yes." I look away, embarrassed now that I've shared the finer details of that experience. "I'll admit it's not my most heroic rescue ever, but it did the job."

"Heroic or not, I'm very grateful. I don't think I ever thanked you after I woke up."

"No." I focus on the red water lapping between us. "I think you just told me you were a monster and that I should leave. Oh, and you apologized. And I apologized. There was a lot of apologizing going on." I add in a smile as I look up at him, so he knows we don't need to make this a heavy, serious conversation. I notice then that his eyes are brown instead of the light grey-green of his contact lenses. I'm about to comment on it when a whirlpool swirls into existence not far from us. "Quickly," I say, diving toward it.

This one is faster than the last, spitting me out the bottom before I've had a chance to become too dizzy. A split second before I hit the next river, my body stops, as if sus-pended in the air by an invisible rope. Then I drop the final distance. Standing up, I realize why. The water—warmer than any of the rivers so far—is shallow here, lapping just above my waist. Falling into this water from a great height wouldn't end well.

"This is incredible," Chase says, looking around as he stands.

I have to agree with him. The water looks like liquid gold or gold paint. But when I scoop it up and let it trickle between my fingers, it leaves my hands clean, so perhaps it's only a reflection of the gold cave walls. "Beautiful," I murmur, "and very, very warm." So warm I can see steam rising. "Does it still count as a river if it isn't moving?"

"I think it is moving just a tiny bit," Chase says. "But hey, none of these are normal rivers, so who knows."

"Yeah." I smile at him and find myself noticing his eyes again. "What happened to your contact lenses?"

"They don't do so well in water. I lost them after the first whirlpool."

"Well, I prefer seeing your real eyes," I tell him, and then wish I hadn't because it seems to have led us to a conversation dead end. Awkward, since I can't seem to pull my eyes away from his. The seconds pass, and something in his gaze changes. Something that makes me feel ... "Flip, it's hot in here. I can't handle this anymore." I hastily undo the buttons of my jacket as heat threatens to overwhelm me. How fortunate that I chose to wear a tank top underneath instead of something with longer sleeves.

"Yeah," Chase says, tugging his jacket off. "Definitely too hot."

"You know, I've been thinking about getting a tattoo," I say as I peel the wet sleeves of my jacket off. I leave it floating in the water beside me.

"Ah, time for the giant dragon across your back."

"Close," I say with a chuckle, "but not quite. I saw something on your desk that I really liked. An ink drawing of a phoenix."

"A phoenix," Chase says, nodding slowly. "New life, new beginning."

"I know, it isn't exactly an original idea, but I want something that symbolizes *my* new life. And your drawing is unique. No one else will have anything like it. I mean, if you'll let me use it."

"Of course I will."

"I was thinking across the top half of my back, reaching up to the base of my neck." I pull my wet hair aside and reach back to touch the top of my spine. "And then the wings extending up to my shoulders on either side. What do you think?"

Chase nods. He clears his throat and says, "It would be perfect."

Again, something feels different between us. I know what it is. I know exactly what it is, and I'm expecting fountains of gold water to start spurting up around us at any point. I should say something, but I don't know how or where to begin, and I don't know if I'm brave enough. I breathe in deeply—because, seriously, what happened to the air in here?—and look around. Where is this darn whirlpool? Only one more to go, right? "Um, why do they call these the Wishbone Rivers?" I ask, relieved that I've come up with something to talk about. "Do people think wishes come true here?"

Chase scoops gold water into his hands and lets it run out between his fingers. "Perhaps they do, but the system was named after the top river, which is shaped like a wishbone. It's actually two rivers, joined at the mouth where they go into the sea. Only the right side has whirlpools, though, and parallel rivers beneath it." He looks up and adds, "I checked with Gaius before we left, just in case there was some kind of strange wishing magic we'd have to deal with here."

"Wishing magic," I say, pondering the idea as I trail my fingers slowly through the water. "If wishes could come true, what would you wish for?"

"I would wish ..." He looks away down the golden river. "I would wish I were someone else. Just a normal faerie guy instead of the person who messed up so badly. I'd wish that I could meet you under completely ordinary circumstances, and I'd wish that you could still see me the way you saw me in those last minutes under the flower canopy before everything fell apart." He smiles as he returns his eyes to mine. "Is that too many wishes?"

I hold his gaze while considering my words carefully, and I realize that I am, after all, brave enough. "Perhaps some wishes do come true," I tell him, my words leaving my tongue slowly. I want to make sure he hears every single one. "Or perhaps you simply haven't realized yet that some things don't need to be wished for." I look down and reach for his hand in the water. I slide my fingers between his before adding, "I mean, why would you wish for something you already have?"

Tiny gold beads of water rise out of the river and string themselves around my arm and around his. Gold lights flash in the cave walls around us. My heart thunders, and I'm wondering what happened to the air again. I have no hope of finding it, though, because when I raise my eyes once more, Chase's burning gaze is enough to steal my breath away and send fiery warmth rushing through my insides.

He raises our clasped hands and lets go. He traces his fingers up my arms, turning the fire on my skin to a shiver. His hands still as they reach my neck. He leans forward, his face stopping inches from mine. "Do you mean that?" he asks, his voice hoarse.

With sprite wings fluttering wildly in my stomach, I press a kiss to his jaw, and then another one higher up. When I reach his ear, I say, "I wouldn't wish you to be anyone else. Why would I, when it's *you* that I want?"

His lips find mine, and the world of gold and flashing lights disappears as my eyes close and my fingers spread through his wet hair, pulling him closer. His hands slide around my back, knotting in my hair before tracing down my spine and into the water to press against my lower back. Our bodies fit perfectly together. My arms twine around his neck and sparks skid across our tongues and droplets of magic-infused water rain down on us, mingling with our kisses.

And that's when the world gives way beneath us and a whirlpool sucks us down.

CHAPTER THIRTY-THREE

The final river feels like ice against my burning skin. I rise to the surface, gasping against the cold as well as for air. As the rippling waves around me subside, I notice the water glowing faintly. Blue gems stud the rough cave walls, glinting with wintry beauty, and between them, patterns and pictures have been carved into the stone.

"Calla!" I look around and see Chase behind me. The current, stronger in this river than in the others, is already pulling me along. He joins it, swimming with quick, strong strokes toward me. I reach out for him as the current drags me along. I don't know why, but I feel a need for physical contact with him in the same way I need air. A clasped hand, linked arms, an embrace, *anything*. Something feels incomplete without his touch. He catches my hand, then points past me.

"Look, we're at the mouth already. There's the monument."

I turn, never letting go of his hand. Up ahead on the right, just before the cave ends, I see the monument. A round base, motionless stone waves, and the trident rising up. It seems bigger in real life. "Where are Ana and Kobe?" I ask. "They should be there waiting for us."

"Something doesn't seem right," Chase says, pulling at the water to move us forward faster. "Do you see figures lying down beside the monument?"

I squint though the dim bluish light. I see two shapes on the ground, and fear sends another shiver through me. "I … I think so."

I have to let go of Chase's hand as we kick against the current and move diagonally toward the shore on the right. Once the water becomes shallow enough to stand, Chase pushes us forward with an extra spurt of magic. I almost stumble and fall over as he runs across the pebbles toward the monument. "Be careful!" he shouts back to me. He raises his hand in a sweeping motion, and I sense a shield surrounding me. Hopefully he's done the same for himself.

With no warning, nausea rises within me and spreads a sickening ache across my stomach. Dizziness consumes me. I bend over and lean on my knees, breathing heavily. By some miracle, I don't fall over. "Chase," I gasp. "Chase!" His head whips over his shoulder just as everything becomes black.

I find myself floating in a void of nothingness as my body is squeezed and squeezed and *squeezed*, until finally the pressure releases me and I gasp for air as I stagger toward the light. A tangled nighttime forest greets me. Confused, scared and cold, but longer attacked by nausea, I look around. Is this Creepy Hollow? I hear movement behind me and turn as quickly as my remaining dizziness will allow.

Magic. A swirling ball of it hovering above a pair of hands. And beyond that, the face of a person I recognize. Without hesitation, Zed hurls the magic at me.

I throw myself to the side and land behind a tree. Telling myself that I'm *not* dizzy and that I *can* stand up, I scramble to my feet. I raise shield magic around me as I hear Zed's footsteps crunching over fallen leaves. "Now that was a waste of stunner magic," he says.

"What the flipping heck, Zed?" I shout. "What did you … did you *summon* me here?" Summoning magic isn't something we learn. It isn't natural. It isn't right. And what happened to me just now definitely didn't feel right.

"Yes," Zed says, still walking toward the tree I'm hiding behind. "Difficult spell, but I had help. And you'd be surprised at how straightforward it actually is if you've been able to tag the person you want to summon."

"Tag?" I focus on the illusion of invisibility and drop my mental wall.

"Neck been feeling itchy lately?" Zed asks. He swings around the side of the tree, his arm raised and ready to attack. His brow puckers in confusion when he finds the space behind the tree empty.

I try not to breathe, not to move, as my mind races back to the last time I saw Zed. He tried to kiss me, and his hand was around my neck, pressing tightly as he drew me toward him. He must have done something then. Something I was too shocked to notice because all I cared about was getting him off me.

A shiver raises the hairs on my skin. Being wet and without a jacket on an autumn night isn't ideal.

"I gave you the amber as well," Zed says, turning away as his eyes dart across the area around the tree, "but it turned out I couldn't track that for some reason. Fortunately the tag charm hadn't worn off yet by the time I did the summoning spell."

With my dizziness finally gone and adrenaline rushing through my limbs, I jump to the side and run. *Invisible, invisible, invisible,* I remind myself. Sparks fly past me. I guess he can see the leaves my shoes are kicking up. I stop, skid to the side, and leap. Magic shoots me upward. I land on one branch and grasp at another to keep from falling.

"This will be a lot easier if you just give in now," Zed shouts as turquoise sparks flare past me.

I abandon the illusion and reinforce my shield. "Dammit, Zed, I don't know what game you're playing, but you have *exceptionally* bad timing."

"My timing is perfect," he says, stalking toward me.

"I was in the middle of something important!"

"Exactly. That was the moment at which I was told to summon you. They didn't want you and your illusions interfering with their plans."

"They? Are you ... are you working for Amon and Angelica?"

"No." He stops beneath the tree and starts to gather more magic above his palm. "But I found myself in need of assistance, and so did they. You know what people say: The enemy of my enemy and all that."

"Zed, NO! That is a *terrible* idea! *They* are the real enemy. They're the ones who locked us up in the first place. Why would you take their side now?" Part of me knows I should be running. I should be throwing everything I have into an illusion that will give me enough time to open a doorway and flee. But this is *Zed*. He's been helping me ever since we found ourselves hanging beside one another in cages. We have a friendship that goes back years. There must be a way I can talk him out of whatever he's about to do.

"Firstly," he says, "they weren't the ones who locked us up. Prince Zell was, and everyone admits he was a little crazy. Secondly, I'm not on their side. This was a once-off arrangement that benefited both parties."

A chill courses down my spine. "What did you have to do for them in exchange?"

"Come on, Calla. You know I can't tell you that."

"Is that why I'm here? Have you been told to hand me over to Amon's men?"

He chuckles. "Nothing like that. My work for them was done after I escaped the Guild."

Cogs turn in my brain. "You allowed yourself to be caught," I say softly, "so you could get inside the Guild."

"Yes."

My mind runs through the possibilities. Vi said someone escaped the detainment area in the morning. I came across Zed the following afternoon. That means he was on the loose inside the Guild for almost two days. What terrible things could he have done in that time? "Zed," I say carefully as I pump more magic into the invisible shield surrounding me. "Whatever it is that you want with me, you don't have to do it. What happened to us being *friends*?"

He doesn't answer. Magic crackles above his palm. Enough to break my shield? Possibly. But then what? He won't have time to strike me with anything before I get away. We watch each other, his gaze locked on mine, each waiting for the other to make a move.

His hand flashes toward his pocket. I imagine invisibility and jump. I hit the ground and roll to the side. He tosses something, a small dark ball that explodes inches away from my shield. I throw my arm up as my magic shatters and vanishes. Then he raises his arm and slams his magic at me.

* * *

I awake slowly, my thoughts as lethargic as my limbs. I can't remember where I was when I fell asleep. I try to turn over, but my arms seem to be held together by something. With a groan and a great deal of effort, I manage to peel one eyelid open. I see Zed—and I remember everything.

"I'm sorry I had to stun you," he says, "but there's no way you would have come with me by choice. You haven't been out for long, though. I didn't have time to gather a great deal of stunning power after you made me miss with the first shot." He bends down over my feet. Glittering ropes, the kind that can't merely be cut free, appear in his hands. "This isn't personal,

Calla," he tells me as he winds the rope around and between my ankles. "I've never had anything against you. I haven't forgotten our years of friendship, and I actually care about you a lot. That's why I had to get you out of there."

I blink and shake my head. "What are you going on about?"

He pulls the final knot tight. "I gave you a chance to see things clearly, but you kept refusing. I didn't want you to wind up dead from the dragon disease, though, so I found a way to remove you permanently from the Guild."

My sluggish brain doesn't want to connect the dots, but they're too obvious for me to avoid. "*You're* the one who got me expelled?" The shocking truth wakes my brain up. I wriggle against my bonds and shout, "How could you do that to me?"

"I was *helping* you, Calla."

"Helping me? You almost got me thrown into prison for murder!"

"That wasn't supposed to happen. I needed someone to take the fall, and you needed to get out of there. I planted enough evidence that they'd suspect you, but not be able to prove it for certain. You were supposed to be expelled, not charged for murder. I even gave you the cure before I left so you wouldn't get sick. I *saved* you, Cal."

"You never gave me the cure."

"I did. With one of those surveillance devices. They all have their own control enchantments, and I stole one while hiding in the Guild. I made it inject you while you were in a lesson. By the time we danced at the ball and I left that streak of powder on your hand, you were already immune."

"You ... you were ..." I shake my head and whisper, "You

killed Saskia. And all those other people who wound up sick. How did you turn into this person? This *murderer*?"

He grabs my arms and pulls me closer. "Because it's about time the Guild started paying for everything they've done to the Gifted. For everything they've done to *you* and *me* and people just like us. A whole lot more people were supposed to die, in fact. We—the group I told you about, the group I wish I could convince you to join—had planned to send a very clear message, starting with that Starkweather girl and then letting it spread through every Guild. We were then going to stand up and claim what we'd done so that everyone left would know exactly what crimes they were paying for. But *somebody* interfered by running off and finding a cure."

"Well, if I do nothing else right for the rest of my life, at least I'll know I successfully *interfered* with the mass killing of thousands of innocent people."

Zed lets out a long sigh before standing. "My friends are very angry about your interference."

"Ah, the lovely friends who've deluded you into hating the wrong people. So you decided to summon me, tie me up, and deliver me to them?"

"Of course not," Zed says, looking genuinely upset. "I know you're not the one who's at fault here. You thought you were doing the right thing saving everyone." He lifts his hand, and I feel myself slowly rising from he ground. He walks through the forest, his hand pulling me along by an invisible thread of magic. "I do wish you'd kept your interfering ways to yourself, though, because now we have to do something that's going to make you very upset."

I struggle and kick, but it only causes me to roll around in the air. I pull repeatedly at the ropes around my wrists, hoping to loosen them. "You don't *have* to do anything, Zed."

"I do. People have to pay for the suffering they caused us."

I give up my useless struggling, deciding to save my energy. And it's then that I realize, with chilling clarity, exactly where we are: in a part of Creepy Hollow very close to Ryn's home. My throat goes dry and shivers run along my skin. "Zed? Where are we going?"

"As I said before, Calla, this doesn't have anything to do with you. You're a good person, a sweet girl. But the fact remains that your brother and his wife left me and dozens of other people to be tortured and locked up in a dungeon. Those of us who got away before The Destruction only had to survive the torture. Those who didn't had to commit atrocious acts they had no control over."

I don't bother to answer. I'm already lowering the barrier around my mind and picturing a group of guardians running toward us. They shout at Zell, raising their weapons and firing at him. He falters, but then he shakes his head and laughs. "You and your illusions," he says, continuing to walk straight through the imaginary arrows and sparks. "I know exactly how you work. Show me whatever you want. I won't believe any of it."

"Zed, please," I say, my voice desperate. "It wasn't Ryn's fault. It wasn't Vi's fault. They told the Council about Zell's prisoners as soon as they could."

"And what did Head Councilor Starkweather and the rest of

her Council choose to do? Nothing. *Telling* the Council resulted in nothing. Your brother should have freed us while he was there."

"But he *couldn't* get everyone out—"

"Why not? He got you out easily enough."

"There wasn't time. Zell was already there. He—"

"There was time to break open another few cages at least. Then we could have fought him and got everyone else out."

"How?" I twist in the air, trying to get closer to Zed, trying to make him *see sense*. "You all had those metal bands blocking your magic. If Ryn had let you out, Zell would have stunned you and locked you up again."

"Not all of us. He couldn't possibly have fought all of us. No, the fact is that your brother only cared about saving you, and because of his selfish decision, the rest of us had to suffer. Gifted people did terrible things they never wanted to do. And what did the Guild say when it was all over? Did they apologize for abandoning us? No. They labeled us 'dangerous' and tagged us so we'd never be truly free again. And none of it was our fault!"

"They didn't tag you," I point out.

"Because I've been hiding from the Guild ever since. I've been living like a coward in the shadows, waiting to take vengeance on those who ruined my life."

"No you *haven't*!" I yell. "You were fine until those guardian haters twisted your brain into thinking you needed to do this. And it wasn't my brother who ruined your life, it was Zell!"

"Well, it's a little late to go after him, isn't it." Zed stops in front of Ryn's tree. I feel my feet slowly lowering until they touch the ground. Now that I'm upright, I see a crackling ball of power floating above Zed's hand. He must have been gathering it while we were walking. "You don't have to do anything more than knock, Calla. That's the only reason you're here. They'll never open a doorway for me, but they will for you."

"Please don't do this," I whisper.

Zed separates his swirling ball of power into two smaller spheres, one above each palm. "Your begging isn't helping."

"Please, they don't deserve this. They didn't do anything—"

"Just knock, Calla. And no illusions," he adds as he steps to the side. "You can't run away while your hands and feet are tied, which means the only way any illusion can end is with you and me still standing outside this tree. Except I'll be a whole lot angrier than I am now."

I swallow and stare ahead. "You can't make me do this. The worst thing you can do is kill me, but then you'll still be stuck outside this tree."

Zed sighs. "Do you really have to be so dramatic?" He bends in front of me and blows against the bark until the knocker appears. He lifts it, knocks a few times, then steps to the side. "And don't even think about—"

"DON'T OPEN!" I yell. "IT'S A TRAP!"

"Dammit, you stupid—Fine. We'll do this the hard way." In a second, Zed is behind me, holding a sphere of crackling, sparking power against either side of my head. And when Ryn—my loyal, caring, protective brother—comes to the wall and looks through a peephole, he *will* open a doorway because he'd never leave me out here on my own with someone who's threatening to hurt me.

I squeeze my eyes shut, expecting Zed to take his fury out on me at any second, and shout, "Seriously, Ryn! Do not open a doorway. He's going to—"

"Calla!"

My eyelids spring open as Zed's right hand shoots forward. Ryn, standing in the doorway with a glowing guardian dagger in one hand, collapses onto the floor. A gasp sounds from somewhere behind him, followed by Vi shouting, "Ryn!"

And suddenly, I remember the tracking spell that will set off an alarm in the Guild if I enter this house. I jump forward on my bound feet and throw myself through the doorway just as one of Vi's knives flashes past me and Zed's second ball of power flies the other way. I land on top of Ryn and struggle to look up. I hear Zed's cry of pain behind me. Raising my head, I see Vi collapse against the couch and flop onto the floor.

"Well," Zed says, crossing the threshold. "I expected that to be far more difficult." A glittering knife smeared with blood clatters to the floor beside me. A second later, it vanishes.

"Wait," I say as Zed walks past me. "Wait, please. What are you going to do to them?" I roll off Ryn and manage to sit up.

Zed stands in the center of the room, looking around. He reaches inside his jacket and pulls out a knife.

I start to lose it. "Nonono, Zed, please. Please don't kill them," I beg. "Please, please, please. You don't have to do this."

"I know," he says. "I didn't come for them."

"But … then …"

Zed looks at me, then uses his knife to point first at Ryn and then at Vi. "These two people destroyed lives. Now I will destroy theirs." With that, he crosses the room and climbs the staircase.

Then it hits me.

Victoria.

CHAPTER THIRTY-FOUR

"NO!" I SCREAM. "DON'T TOUCH HER, DON'T *TOUCH HER*!"
I fight desperately against the enchanted ropes. I pull my legs
up and work at the knots around my ankles, but they're so
tight they don't budge. I writhe and tug and twist but it's so
damn *useless*. "Zed! ZED! Don't do anything to her, PLEASE!"
I roll and squirm my way toward the stairs. I have no way of
cutting these ropes and no plan of any sort, but I can't just *sit*
here. "Zed, please," I sob. "Please don't do it, please don't do
it." How can he think that taking a life so pure and innocent
could possibly right any kind of wrong?

Before I reach the stairs, footsteps descend. Zed appears at
the bottom, carrying a wrapped up bundle of blankets in his
arms. I can see Victoria's perfect little face, her closed eyes. She's
still asleep despite all my shouting. "Zed, what are you doing?"

He walks past me without a word. "Where are you going? Where are you taking her?" He steps over Ryn, still lying across the open doorway, and disappears into the night. "ZED! Come back!"

Another wordless cry of rage and desperation leaves my lips—and that's when the guardians choose to show up. Four of them, rushing into the house with weapons raised, each one jumping over Ryn as if touching him is against the rules of some game they're playing. "It's her!" one of them shouts.

"Don't touch her," another says.

"Please," I gasp. "Go after that man who just left. He has the baby!"

"This is a bit of an odd situation," one of the guards says, taking in my stunned brother and sister-in-law, and then the enchanted ropes around my wrists and ankles.

"Please!" I yell. "Didn't you see him? He took Victoria. He's getting away."

"As if we'd believe anything you say after the exit stunt you pulled at the Guild," one of them says. "Bloomhove, Crawdale, check upstairs."

"Does she have to touch us in order to make us ill?" another one mutters as two of the men head for the stairs. "What if she's doing it already?"

"ARGH! You guardians are so *useless!*"

I squeeze my eyelids together and tell myself to breathe, to calm down. *You can do this. You can get out of here.* I open my eyes. Only a guardian blade can cut the glittering ropes that bind me, and there are two guardian swords pointing directly at me. I concentrate on projecting an image of me sitting in the same spot I'm already in. Then I move. Quietly, inch by inch on my backside, toward the nearest sword. Making sure to keep myself concealed, I raise my arms over the sparkling blade, hold my breath, and pull my arms down quickly. Then I lean back and freeze.

The man jerks away. "What just happened?"

I look back at the image of me sitting in the same spot and give her a confused expression.

"I don't know," the second guard says. "What are you talking about?"

Now for my ankles. I stand slowly, wondering how I'm going to make this happen.

"Hey, she was right!" one of the men upstairs shouts. "The baby's gone!"

Both guards look to the stairs. I grab the nearest guard's hand and swipe downward with the sword, slicing the rope and cutting into my left boot. Then I turn and run.

I leap over Ryn and dash into the forest, the excess pieces of glittering rope falling from my arms and ankles. "Zed!" I shout. *Where is he, where is he, where is he?* He's probably long gone through the faerie paths, and I'll never find him, and we'll never see Victoria again, and Ryn and Vi will never forgive me. A sob rises in my chest, and I have to stop running so I can breathe. Why did I ever let Zed escape the Guild? *Why?*

I've barely moved any real distance from the house, but it's so pointless to run anywhere that I don't. I'm too late. I've failed. Which is why, when I notice the figure kneeling on the ground nearby, I believe for a moment that I'm imagining it. Zed wouldn't stop right here, would he? I step quietly toward the figure—and it *is* him, his hands hovering in the air above the tiny body wrapped in blankets.

"Hey!" In a rush of anger and fear, I push my hands through the air toward him. My released power slams into his chest, knocking him onto his back. He rolls and jumps to his feet. "What have you done?" I demand, closing the distance between us while keeping a shield up. I need to get myself in between him and Victoria.

"Nothing. She's fine, I swear."

"She'd better be." I drop the shield and throw a stream of flames at him.

"You don't want to fight me," he says, deflecting the flames with a swipe of his hand and sending a cloud of sand my way.

My shield is almost instantaneous; the sand blasts against it before vanishing. "I do, Zed. I really, really do." I push at the air. A cloud forms between us, impairing our view of one another. His sparks zoom through it, heading straight for me. I drop down as they pass, then jump up again, showing him an image of me leaping across the branches above him. He aims for the trees instead. My cloud becomes a flock of birds, screeching and pecking, and the image of me in the trees jumps down and swipes at him. Then the birds shift into real blades, slicing at him as he throws up a shield, and the illusion of me morphs into imaginary blades that pass through his shield with no problem at all.

From magic to illusions and back again, I throw everything I can think of into a confusing mess, flicking from image to image to image. He doesn't know what's real and what's imagined, what he needs to block and what he can ignore. And with every new illusion, I move another step closer to him. Keeping part of my mind focused on the projections, I raise my hand and shoot a stream of sparks at the nearest branch. It splits and falls to the ground beside me. I lean down—fire and bats and raining blood—and pick it up—shards of ice and pieces of bone—and swing it at Zed's head with all my might.

He falls to the ground and doesn't move.

I drop the branch and run back to Victoria. With a final glance over my shoulder to make sure Zed isn't moving, I scoop her up and run. She starts crying as my feet pound the forest floor and my running body jerks her up and down. It's the most welcome sound in the world right now.

Ryn's doorway is still open because nobody seems to have moved him yet. I jump over him into the house—and find at least twenty guardians pointing their weapons at me. I freeze. Victoria continues to scream her tiny lungs out.

"What have you done to the child?" a guardian demands. The one who was giving orders when the first four arrived.

My eyebrows pinch together as I say, "I did what you should have done and rescued her." I move toward the nearest piece of furniture—an armchair—and lay the unhappy baby carefully down on it. Then I step back with my arms raised. "If you'd like to redeem yourselves," I add, "the man who stole her is lying unconscious in the forest not too far from here."

No one says a word. No one moves. Far too many weapons are pointed at me. I breathe slowly and calmly, giving myself just a few seconds of rest. Then, with one last effort, I push my final illusion out as fast and as far as I can. Blackness. Everywhere. All-encompassing.

I turn around and run blindly as cries of confusion erupt behind me. I trip over Ryn. Something skims past my right arm before I hear a heavy handled weapon clatter across the floor. Something sharp slices across my shoulder. Footsteps move toward me. I pull myself over Ryn and into the forest. Shifting the illusion from one of darkness to one of invisibility, I tear between the trees. I zigzag and duck under bushes and finally come to a stop on the other side of a fallen log.

I hear no voices or footsteps. I tilt my head back against the log and allow relief to flood my body. "She's okay," I murmur to myself. "She's okay, she's okay." Ryn and Vi will wake up soon, and they'll find their little girl safe, and everything will be fine.

My eyes slide shut. I'm exhausted. Mentally drained. Cuts and burns mark my arms from the magical fight with Zed, and blood oozes from a wound on my shoulder where an arrow or blade didn't quite miss me in the darkness just now. I cup my hand over it, sending a tiny bit of healing magic to the spot.

I wish tonight was over, but it isn't yet. I left Chase in the bottommost Wishbone River with two fallen companions and who knows what other threats. I have to go back. I have to help him. I pick myself up, open a doorway, and drag my tired limbs into the faerie paths.

I walk out of the darkness onto the tangled moonlit bank of the top river where the four of us waded into the water earlier. If only wishes really did come true here, and I could wish my way to the bottom without having to pass through every river above it. The thought of all those whirlpools makes me want to cry. And what if he isn't there anymore? What if it's all over and he's back at the mountain? But what if it *isn't* over and he's locked in a battle with Amon and Angelica's men?

I press my hands against the sides of my head, trying to ease away the coming headache. I decide to check the mountain first. It'll be quick. Faerie paths, lakeside house, faerie door, mountain. I can be there in under a minute. I turn around to find a surface on which to write a doorway.

"Hello."

My breath catches at the unexpected sight of a woman leaning against the boulder that marks the beginning of the whirlpools. Unease curls around me. I flex my hand, wondering if I should grab my knife from my boot.

"I thought you might come back at some point," she says, pushing away from the boulder and moving toward me. It's her hair that gives her away first, long dark locks mixed with silver cascading over her shoulders.

Angelica.

I feel as though I've been immersed in ice-cold fear. "H-how did you get out of Velazar?" I ask, taking a step back.

"Calla, right?" she says, ignoring my question. She wipes her hands on her prison overalls before crossing her arms over her chest. "You're the one who spoke to me with the telepathy ring, claiming to be working with my son to free me. The one Amon told me he tried to get rid of. The one who then showed up beside the third Seer's bed when she awoke."

"How do you know about that?"

"I've been keeping an eye on things." She chuckles, as if she's said something amusing.

"How did you escape Velazar?" I demand.

"Oh, I didn't escape. The Guild let me go free."

"What? They would never do that."

"They would," she says, her lips curling into a smile, "if I found the right bargaining chip."

"Bargaining chip?"

"If I found someone they want more than me."

My breaths come faster. A sense of foreboding nudges my thoughts. "There isn't anyone they want more than you and Amon."

"There *wasn't*," she says slowly, "until I told them that the one they've always wanted most is actually still alive."

Blood pounds in my ears. "*What did you do?*"

"I traded his life for mine."

I stop breathing. When I find air again, a painful gasp of it, I manage to say, "You didn't. He's your son. You wouldn't do that."

"How could I *not* do that?" she counters. "He left me rotting in a prison cell for over a decade. And then to come crawling back with lie upon lie about wanting to be part of my plans? Ha! He is no more a son to me than I ever was a mother to him. I knew he was alive all this time. I had no doubt. I waited and waited for my son to come and get me, until the crushing moment I realized he had chosen to leave me suffering behind bars for the rest of my life. Since then I've been waiting every day, *every single day*, for the moment I could repay his treachery in kind."

I shake my head in disbelief. "Where is he?"

She lifts her shoulders in a careless shrug. "I can't be certain. He ran off in that direction with a hoard of guardians on his tail." She gestures vaguely over her shoulder into the thick forest of bushes and trees. "Something tells me he won't have the strength to get far, though." She lifts her hand as if holding something invisible. Slowly, a large metal disc appears, suspended from a cord in her grip. A gong. Which can only mean ...

"The morioraith," I murmur.

"Oh, don't look at me like that," she complains. "I had to give the guardians a fair chance, didn't I? And he's still conscious, although—" she lifts her hand, displaying the telepathy ring on her finger "—I can't discern much from his thoughts. It's all pain and despair and misery." Lightning crackles nearby, followed by the dull boom of thunder. "Ah, it sounds like he's putting up a bit of a fight. How fun."

My face scrunches up in anger, in loathing. "You're despicable."

She laughs—and then she lunges at me, her face twisting with rage. In a split second, I realize this is the moment. The moment I saw in Rick's vision, with her hand reaching out to claw at me. I embrace it, throwing myself at her and knocking her arm aside. We fall to the ground and I pin her down, surprised to find that she isn't nearly as strong as I imagined. I expected a powerful foe, an invincible force, but she's nothing more than a regular opponent. Her fist swings at me, but I catch it, tearing the ring off her hand before she throws me off her with a push of magic. My body rolls to a halt against a bush. I climb to my feet as she rises to hers. I push the ring into my pocket while distracting her with an illusion of the nearest bush catching fire. Then I spin and kick. She goes down a second time, and I don't hang around. I jump past her and run.

I hear her laughing behind me, making no attempt to chase me down. My feet carry me as fast as they can, which isn't nearly fast enough amidst the thick tangle of bushes. I push between them, slashing with magic at the branches in my way, relieved when I finally reach an area that isn't so dense. My arms pump at my sides as I race toward the storm. It isn't as powerful as I imagined Chase's storms to be, and that fills me with terror. What state is he in if his sheets of lightning barely brighten the night sky and his thunder doesn't even rattle the ground?

I run into a long, narrow clearing and see motion up ahead. With a cry, I push myself faster. My breath burns in my chest as my feet fly across the ground. The shapes ahead of me take form. A carriage, wide and solid. Something moving on the other side of it. Wings? Pegasi? I see bars across the back of the carriage as I near it, and the emblem of the Seelie Court. *Run!* I scream at myself. *Faster!* Then the carriage begins moving, and I know with crushing, heartbreaking certainty that I'm too late.

"No!" I shout, racing after the carriage with a burst of magical speed. I fling myself at it and grab onto the bars. "Chase!" I see him inside the carriage, heavy chains attached to his arms and legs. Chains that are no doubt blocking his magic. He droops between them, the picture of defeat. When he looks up, his eyes are focused far away on distant nightmares. "Chase. Chase! It's me!"

He blinks and frowns. Confusion turns to recognition. "Calla?"

I push one arm through the bars, but I can't reach him.

"Tell me what to do. Tell me how to get you out." With a lurch, the carriage lifts off the ground. I cling more tightly to the bars.

"We're flying," Chase says, shaking his head and becoming more alert. "You have to let go. We'll be too high soon, and then—"

"No!"

"Hey!" I look up and find a guard in a smart uniform frowning down at me. "Get off," he commands, pointing a stylus. Instantly, he's joined by another three guards, all balancing atop the edge of the carriage with practiced ease.

Ignoring them, I look back through the bars. "I can't leave you," I yell in desperation.

"You have to. Everything will be okay, I promise."

"Chase, I—" A spark strikes my right arm. Then my left. I cry out as I lose my grip on the bars. I tumble through the air and hit the ground, rolling several times before coming to a stop. My body aches and the burns on my arms sting like hell and all the air has been knocked from my lungs. I lie on the ground gasping for breath and watching the sky until the carriage is long gone.

Until Chase is long gone.

I roll onto my side and hug my knees, and my tears soak into the ground as the cold night wraps itself around me.

CHAPTER THIRTY-FIVE

I RETURN TO THE MOUNTAIN IN THE EARLY HOURS OF THE morning to find Ana and Kobe pacing the living room while Gaius sits with his head clasped in his hands. I stop in the doorway. They look at me, the same question of each of their faces. My voice is dull as I say, "He's gone. Seelie guards took him. Angelica gave him up in exchange for her freedom."

Ana's hands rise to cover her mouth. Gaius seems frozen in place. Kobe shakes his head and says, "I knew something was off. I knew the moment we got down to the bottom river and there wasn't a single merperson to be found. Then Angelica's people showed up, hours earlier than planned and far more of them than expected. We knew instantly that she'd set us up."

Ana's hands turn to fists, clenching tightly against her chin as she looks at Kobe. "If only Darius and Lumethon had been with us instead of saving the Seers. If we'd hidden amongst the rocks instead of climbing out of the water, we could have waited for Chase and Calla to arrive. We could all have fought together. We could have prevented this."

Kobe crosses his arms and turns away, his voice gruff as he says, "Instead we wound up passed out and useless."

"This isn't right," Gaius says, sounding lost. "Chase doesn't get caught. He just doesn't."

I lean against the doorway as my body sways with exhaustion. My eyes, burning from all the tears, slide shut. "He did this time," I whisper. Then I turn and slowly climb the stairs to my bedroom. Cold and tired and drained, I get into bed and pull the covers over my head. There are thoughts at the back of my mind—thoughts about guardians torturing Chase, about the execution they no doubt have lined up for him, about never seeing him again—but I refuse to let them take center stage.

I fall into fitful sleep filled with muddled dreams. Some time later, I wake with one thought at the forefront of my mind: the telepathy ring. With a sudden spike of hope, I tug it out of my pocket and push it onto my left forefinger.

Chase?

Chase!

I don't know if he has the other ring. I assume he took it with on our Wishbone Rivers mission so he could speak to Angelica if he needed to, but I don't remember seeing it. I don't remember feeling it as our fingers laced together or when his hands trailed up my arms. I press my eyelids shut, clinging to the memory.

Then I lie down again and hug one of my pillows, silently calling his name and waiting for a response that may never come.

* * *

Later in the day, I hide in the Creepy Hollow healing wing until a healer and a guard escort Mom to one of the bathing rooms. She'll soon be dressed and ready to head downstairs for further questioning. No one knows yet if she'll be allowed to go home after that.

I slip into her cubicle and begin my hurried examination of the room. My fingers slide over the wall and along the frame of the bed, feeling for markings or signs of magic. I crawl under the bed and find nothing. I scan both sides of the two picture frames before removing them, along with the tablecloth, from the cabinet and pulling all three drawers out. My inspection of every inch of the wood reveals nothing. I straighten and place my hands on my hips, considering whether to rip the pillows apart in case there's some kind of charm hiding inside them.

Then my eyes fall on the painting in the second picture frame. I didn't bring it here, and neither did Dad. Perhaps it was Matilda, like I suggested to Dad—or perhaps it was Zed, who said his job for Amon and Angelica was done after he escaped the Guild. I pick up the frame and remove the back piece—then drop the two halves onto the bed in fright. Staring up at me from the back of the painting is a drawing of an eye. It glows faintly.

I rip the painting out of the frame and tear it in half. Then I tear it again and again into dozens of tiny pieces. I scoop them into a pile on the floor and set fire to them with a snap of my fingers. I watch them burn, feeling a tingle across the back of my neck as I imagine Angelica in her prison cell watching us through the little picture frame I saw sitting on her table.

The curtain moves. I quickly conceal myself and the pile of ash. I asked Ryn to meet me here, but it might not be him. A healer sticks her head between the curtains and says, "She isn't back yet."

"That's fine. I'll wait here," Ryn says from the other side of the curtain.

"I know I've had to tell you this before, Ryn. Visiting hours are—"

"This isn't a visit. I'm here to take her downstairs for questioning."

"Well, perhaps you should wait in—"

"Can you smell something burning?" Ryn asks. "I think you need to check on that."

The healer disappears and Ryn enters the cubicle. I drop the illusion and hold up the two pieces of the empty picture frame. "Angelica was watching everything that happened in this room. She saw and heard all three visions." I point to the floor and add, "I burned the painting that had her spell on it."

Ryn walks over to me and takes the picture frame. "I still can't believe they let her go. I'd love to know exactly who approved that decision. The Council is supposed to decide these sorts of things together with all its members, but I've heard nothing." He adds the picture frame to the pile of ash and sets fire to it. "May as well burn the entire thing." He stands and watches the flames consume the wooden pieces.

"Is Victoria all right?" I ask.

"Yes, she's fine. A healer came over and checked her out. And Jamon sent a few reptiscillan guards to the house to keep Vi company, in case anything else happens."

"I'm so, so sorry, Ryn."

"Why? You have nothing to be sorry for. You stopped a delusional man from hurting Victoria."

I wrap my arms around my chest and look away. "That delusional man ... I know him. I met him when we were both prisoners in Zell's dungeon. I saw him again years later, and that's when I asked him to teach me how to fight. He's the one who trained me. Then he ended up with the wrong crowd of people, and now he believes he has to exact vengeance on the Guild—and you in particular—for leaving all those Gifted people in Zell's dungeon to be tortured and used. I had no idea he'd end up like this. I'm so sorry."

"So that's the guardian who trained you," Ryn says quietly. He shakes his head and adds, "His delusions aren't your fault."

"But ..." I keep my eyes fixed firmly on the floor as I admit what I've done. "I saw him when he was escaping the Guild, and I didn't stop him."

"He's *that* man?" Ryn says. "The one who escaped the detainment area recently?"

I nod. "He's also the one who killed Saskia and spread the dragon disease, but I doubt we can ever prove that. Or catch him." I risk looking up. "You said the guardians didn't find anyone in the forest near your home?"

"No." Ryn sits on the edge of the bed. I lower myself to sit beside him, waiting for him to explode. Waiting for him to shout at me, to blame me for everything that's gone wrong. Instead, he quietly says, "This man sounds highly dangerous, Cal. I know you're feeling guilty that you didn't alert anyone when you saw him. You're expecting me to be angry with you. But my guess is that you couldn't have stopped him if you'd tried. He would have made sure he had a way to get out."

"I suppose so. It seems he had everything else planned out."

Ryn places his hand over mine. "Do you want to talk about … the rest of last night?"

"Only if you've heard something."

"Not a word. If the Seelie Court has custody of a man they believe to be Draven, they haven't told anyone yet. Normally he'd be at Velazar by now, but we haven't heard from them either. There are other prisons he may have been sent to, but Velazar makes the most sense. It's the most secure. And then, of course, there are the rumors about a hidden prison controlled by the Seelie Queen for personal enemies of hers who never end up anywhere near the official Guild system. But that's completely illegal, so of course there's no proof that it's true."

"He could be anywhere," I murmur. "He could even be … dead."

After a long pause, Ryn says, "He could be."

I shut my eyes and say, "Please don't tell me he's getting what he deserves."

"Calla—"

"I know you don't like him, and I know he's done terrible things in the past, but I happen to care a great deal about him. You don't know how my heart aches to think of what they're doing to him. To think that I'll never see him again."

"Calla." Ryn tightens the hand that's clasped over mine. I open my eyes and look at him. "I was only going to say how sorry I am for how this all turned out. I wish there was a way I could fix it for you."

I hear Mom's voice out in the passageway as she speaks with a healer. I stand, whisper goodbye to Ryn, and slip between the curtains before Mom and the healer reach the cubicle. I carry Ryn's words with me all the way back to the mountain, not because I want him to find a way to fix this, but because if a way does somehow exist, *I will find it.*

* * *

I dream of our kiss. I dream of him being so near that no space exists between us. His arms, my heartbeat, his lips, my breath. Magic radiates from my body, causing fountains of golden water to arc through the air all around us. In one moment I'm joyfully happy—and in the next my heart breaks, because I know what's about to happen. The whirlpool begins. It sucks all the water away, leaving me standing alone on dry earth watching a carriage disappear into the distance.

"Calla!"

I press my hands against my ears because I can't bear to hear his desperate cries.

"Calla!"

I shake my head, squeezing my eyes shut.

"Miss Goldilocks."

* * *

I jerk awake, leaving the dream world behind. I rub a hand across my eyes and sit up. I stare at the bedcover, feeling the thud of my heart and trying to forget that horrible feeling of loss that pervaded my dream, blotting out everything else. Perhaps I should have taken something to help me sleep, but—

Calla?

I gasp out loud and clap a hand over my mouth.

Calla?

It's his voice, inside my head. I look down at my left hand where the telepathy ring encircles my forefinger. *Chase?*

You got the ring back, he says.

You're alive! Unimaginable relief explodes inside me.

Of course. Didn't I tell you it would take a lot to finish me off?

Questions stream through my head too fast for me to stop them. *What happened? Where are you? Are you okay? Did they hurt you?*

Are you *okay?* he asks. *You just vanished. I was so worried.* When he mentions worry, it's almost as though I feel it. And then a great weariness and a sense of defeat. I know it's difficult to hide emotion when communicating like this, but fatigue seems to make it even harder for him to conceal what he's really feeling.

I'm fine, I promise, I say. *Tell me about you first.*

It was an ambush. A whole lot of Angelica's faeries. I was so stupid to trust her. So, so stupid. As I fought them, they steered me toward the final whirlpool. When I arrived back at the surface, Angelica was there with dozens of guardians and a morioraith. I ran, but the smoke caught up to me. It paralyzed me, giving the guardians a chance to pin me down and get the chains around me. Angelica was there to control the creature. She let it scratch me, just once, just enough to keep me weak with hallucinations of the past.

I feel a ripple of the horror he's remembering. *I'm sorry. I'm so, so sorry. I should have got to you sooner—*

I'm glad you didn't. They might have taken you too.

Where are you now?

Turns out the Seelie Palace conceals a world of darkness beneath its polished marble floors. There are prison cells and torture chambers down here that I never knew existed, not even when I thought I had control of this place.

So you're at the Seelie Court? A place impossible to find unless you're shown the way by someone who knows where it is?

That's the one. Most well-hidden place in the entire fae world.

And now I understand his dejection. How will we ever find him if he's concealed in a place that barely anyone knows how to get to? He truly is beyond our reach. My fingers dig into the mattress as my hope begins to slip away. *What do they plan to do with you?*

I don't know. For now I'm chained in a cell with no access to my magic. They haven't come too close to me, which is why I still have the ring.

I draw my knees up and press my forehead against them. There are so many important things I could say or ask, but the words that swim to the surface are, *I miss you so much already.* I don't try to hide the thought. There are no secrets left between us now.

Nowhere near as much as I miss you.

My aching heart reaches out for his. I wonder if he can feel it, my longing for him. I suck in a deep breath and tell myself not to cry. I've done enough of that already. And I've had enough of the hopelessness, defeat and darkness. *Bright colors*, I say, telling myself as much as I'm telling him. *We're painting with bright colors now, not dark ones. We can fix this. We can find a way.*

I don't know if it's me or him or both of us, but I sense a change. A lift in the mood. I curl up beneath the covers and lie awake for another few hours, speaking with him—thinking, planning, plotting—until I fall asleep with the sound of his voice in my mind.

When I wake in the morning, I'm tired but energized. I'm focused. I have purpose. It's later than I thought it was, so I dress quickly and hurry to Gaius's study. He isn't there. A quick look in the greenhouse tells me he isn't there either. I run down the stairs, and then down again, below the entrance hall, to the door Chase opened by holding his hand against it. I hesitate. Gaius said he would add my handprint to the door's access enchantment just before we left for the Wishbone Rivers, but I haven't tried it yet. I haven't wanted to come down here since then.

I raise my hand and place it against the door. *Click*, and the door vanishes. A tiny thrill runs through me. I really do belong here now. After more stairs, I turn into the wide corridor and head for the meeting room with the oval table. I wasn't sure anyone would be there, but I hear voices coming from the open door. As I reach it, Gaius comes out of the room next door with a scroll in his hand. He greets me and nods for me to walk in ahead of him.

Lumethon, Kobe and Darius are sitting around a diagram of a building. "So we're still going ahead with this?" Darius asks.

"Of course," Lumethon tells him. "We can't abandon all operations simply because Chase isn't here."

"I'm not saying abandon *everything*, but this one was his. It's complex. He's the only one who's been there before."

Gaius steps around me and hands the scroll to Lumethon. "For the Seers."

"Thanks," she says.

Ana walks in then, with flushed cheeks and a towel around her neck. "Did I miss anything?" she asks. "Anyone figure out where Chase is yet?"

"Yes," I say, moving to stand at the head of the table as everyone looks up in surprise. "And I have our next mission. It's close to impossible, but Chase tells me that's usually the best kind." I twist the telepathy ring around my finger and smile at my team. "We're breaking into the Seelie Court."

CALLA'S STORY IS TOLD IN
A FAERIE'S SECRET,
A FAERIE'S REVENGE,
& A FAERIE'S CURSE

FIND MORE CREEPY HOLLOW
CONTENT ONLINE
www.creepyhollowbooks.com

Acknowledgements

Thank you, thank you, thank you …

To God, for stirring up stories in my imagination and helping me get to the end of another book.

To Cherie Reich, for being my editing eyes, and for talking me down from near panic as my deadlines soared past me!

To Dani Snell from Refracted Light Reviews, who organized the fantastic review team for *A Faerie's Revenge*.

To the early readers, who take the time to hang out in Creepy Hollow with all my characters and then write reviews about them.

To all the Creepy Hollow fans, for loving Calla just as much as you loved Violet, and for being desperate to know what would happen after that final (shocking) word of *A Faerie's Secret*.

And to Kyle, for putting up with the many, many hours I spent shut away in my study getting this book finished.

© Gavin van Haght

Rachel Morgan spent a good deal of her childhood living in a
fantasy land of her own making, crafting endless stories of make-
believe and occasionally writing some of them down. After
completing a degree in genetics and discovering she still wasn't
grown-up enough for a 'real' job, she decided to return to those story
worlds still spinning around her imagination. These days she spends
much of her time immersed in fantasy land once more, writing
fiction for young adults and those young at heart.

Rachel lives in Cape Town with her husband and three
miniature dachshunds. She is the author of the
bestselling Creepy Hollow series and the sweet
contemporary romance Trouble series.

www.rachel-morgan.com

Made in the USA
Columbia, SC
01 May 2020